The Adventures of the Great Neblinski

Book Two

THE *UMPIRE* STRIKES BACK

J R R Tokin

Edited by JK Rolling

Sage's Tower Publishing

Written by JRR Tokin

Edited by JK Rolling

2022 Sage's Tower Publishing

Copyright © 2022 by Mark E G Dorey

Cover Design © 2022 Mark E G Dorey

All rights reserved.

Published in the United States by Sage's Tower Publishing.

Sage's Tower Publishing is a registered trademark.

Hardback 978-1-63706-032-2

Softcover 978-1-63706-033-9

EPUB 978-1-63706-034-6

Printed in the United States of America

www.sagestowerpublishing.com

TABLE OF CONTENTS

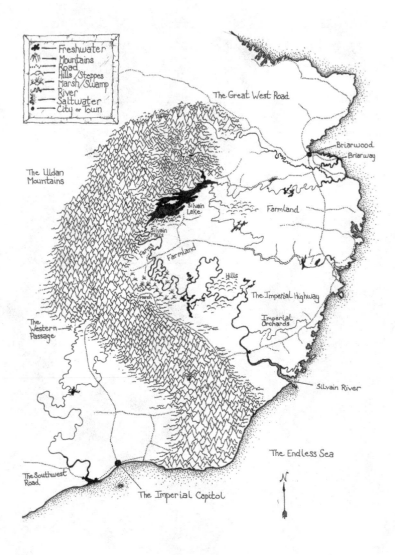

OPERATING INSTRUCTIONS

In this novel there are things to consider so that you, the reader, get the full experience of "listening" to our heroes and other characters. Much of the dialogue in this book is written in phonetics in order to give certain characters a familiar accent so that you, the reader, will have an easier time "hearing" their voices as you read. From the stereotypical New York City cab driver to the Russian soldier, the Yiddish Rabbi and even the Jamaican Rastafarian, any humor directed at any individual or group is absolutely intentional and done so with the deepest and most gracious appreciation to those who, in reality, actually *are* part of these groups and/or individuals, and *enrich* our society/s as such. I thank you in advance and ask that you forgive any offense this story might cause you. It is certainly not intended.

Indeed these are stereotypes and should be taken with more than a grain of salt.

Common accents were given to the characters so that the reader can feel more familiar with the heroes and relate to them better. Most of the individuals represented in these pages are not human, and it helps us to become involved in their story if a human persona is attached to them.

Likewise, at least one of the characters in this story has a physical handicap that is made fun of. To all of you who may suffer the same disability, NO offense intended. I also do not wish to label anyone or any group as bad, evil or malicious...well, all except the banks.

There are also many cases of ethnic stereotyping and just plain making fun of people. If you are offended by this book I strongly suggest you get some help or smoke a *joint* or do something that will mellow you out enough to realize that we all have to get along and making each other laugh is better than making each other cry.

I, the writer of the story, love all people as individuals and ask that we all have a good laugh at each others' expense. Color, gender, and so on are all irrelevant in the long run. It is who we are inside that really counts. I, the writer, *am* a member of a racial minority group.

So...mellow out and love each other. Don't stress about the small stuff that doesn't hurt anyone. There are little babies starving to death in this world so stop worrying about a joke or two already.

An original story written by:
JRR Tokin
Edited by: JK Rolling
Assistant Editor: Lise Boire
Cover Design concept and illustration: Mark E. G. Dorey
Inspired by and written for: Max (god), Peter (Beornag),
Steve (Grarr), Ian (Durik), and Roger (Raz)

INTRODUCTION

Hi again, kids! Glad you're all still with me. You are probably already aware that I ended up having to tell this story in three books.

I know, I know...but hey, listen... if I had done this in one book it would have cost you a fortune to read my story. This way it's better for everyone. Trust me.

Anyway...where was I?

Oh yeah...

In book one you learned that there was an evil sorcerer looking to conquer the free lands and rule them with an iron gauntlet. His name was Calabac (Gawd, I hate that guy), and he had an army that consisted of undead, giant rat things, lesser sorcerers, evil humans from the ice lands far to the south, Trolls, Goblins, and great machines of war just to mention a few.

Oy!

Musky and I had been captured by the sinister Calabac and his evil minions. The terrible villain was about to interrogate the both of us and there were no means of escape in sight.

Double Oy!

Durik had been magically hootspa'd up and into the great glass monument I named *The Bong*. Why? Even I still did not know.... why it happened, that is. I know why I called it The Bong. It made a *'bongy'* sound.

The Bong, in turn, was inside of a pocket dimension, accessible only through a magical door that I had hootspa'd to be only one-tenth its normal size. This door I had placed in a magical para-dimensional pocket of reality inside my magical pouch.

You following me?

Really?

Good, I'm impressed.

Inside the pocket dimension was a group of Gnomes that Musky and I (well... mostly Musky) were already in the process of *trying* to rescue.

Durik, Shiddumbuzzin's mighty paladin, and my personal protector, was now trapped inside *The Bong*, and unable to once again come to my rescue. All seemed hopeless.

Grarr, our mighty leader and tactical genius, had fallen in battle against an army of hundreds accompanied by a cloud of shadowy hatred which held magical power over the horde. This shadowy power gave each enemy within its midst mighty powers beyond human norms.

Still, he managed to lure them away while the Troll rescued an entire caravan of Gnome slaves.

Grarr had even cut the enemy down in numbers by at least a third before they had taken him completely.

A magical crossbow bolt that was designed to kill specifically *him* had pierced his lung and, in the end, had taken too much of a toll on him. He fell in battle, a hero.

Raz had taken his mighty steed Eekadinosaur eastward toward Briarwood, in search of enemies that would scout ahead of the terrible army.

The plan was for him to locate and dispatch all enemies he encountered on his way home. Once back at the city he would alert the guard and the city could make ready its defenses. He had not been heard from since he left Beornag and Grarr's company.

Thankfully, Beornag had fared better. After rescuing a caravan of Gnome prisoners who were about to be impaled, he parted ways with Grarr - who, by distracting the enemy, gave the Troll the means to make a clean getaway and save the civilians.

Then, after leaving the rescued Gnomes in a safe place in the forest, Beornag returned to where he left Grarr only to find him missing in action.

Not finding his friend, he decided to enter the fortress. Using the power of his faith he not only infiltrated the enemy's headquarters, he also managed to dispatch a number of them within a few short minutes. Using his arsenal of "secret weapons" he cleared the entire main entrance to the fortress, sending most of the gate's defence forces running away, dragging their incapacitated comrades behind them, or simply fleeing in fear and nauseated disgust, traumatized forever by the bio-toxic nightmare he had created.

Yours truly, with the indispensable assistance of my newest friend and companion, Musky Ratlove, had learned that, eons ago, the forces of evil had tried, but failed to destroy the G'nomish empire completely.

Some of my ancestors survived (obviously), yet, even though the evil could not totally eradicate the G'nomes, the damage was done and the entire civilization was sent spiraling downward into a dark age that lasted countless eons and was still in effect ... apparently.

Only the power of the one true G'nome god, Holy Shiddumbuzzin, kept the G'nome civilization from completely degenerating. His last gift (before he was due in court), to the little people he had created and loved so dearly: The gift of their ancestors' culture, an intuition and need to keep existing, to remain *"G'nomish"*.

These gifts of culture that would endure for many millennia and maintain a people's civility and unity, through the one hundred eon-long "dark age", were the only things that kept the G'nomes from extinction during those times.

My ancestors would remain in a safe place until the great deity could return.

That place was Sensimilia, the fantastical clockwork machine city near the core of the world. Our home and the great Mellow One's ark. A place that was designed by the old G'nomes to care for the species and cultivate it. To preserve it for all time.

During the absence of Shiddumbuzzin and Krawchich, while the two immortal godlings were battling it out in the court of the gods, an even more sinister evil stepped in and took advantage of the situation. While the lord of evil was being distracted by the legal events that threatened to strip him of his power, he was tricked into revealing his name to a mortal, ultimately becoming the servant of his own creation... Calabac, the evil sorcerer.

Now, kids, let me take you once again on a journey of *"high"* adventure.

...

Sorry... If you didn't read the first book you might wanna grab a copy and read it first.

Go ahead, I'll wait...

...

You're back! Nice to see you again. Did you like it?

That's *great*.

You're gonna *love* this...

Chapter - 1

"Lost and Found"

The Injoke had taken a few moments to look around the empty shit-covered market he was solely responsible for creating. He had an almost insatiable curiosity for objects, especially large piles of objects thrown around chaotically. There was no box or bag he could resist opening, just to see what was inside.

Of course this often posed issues in public restrooms, my shower, and dead people's coffins, that sort of thing. Piles of items in vast disorder were like a game for hill Trolls.

This place was like a toy store for this particular one. He rummaged through piles of armor and weapons that were not coated with feces and/or puke, and found enough equipment to arm a battalion, all of which he tossed in his bottomless backpack.

Then, as though placed there by divine intervention, he saw it… a rectangular opening in the wall opposite the shit and puke-covered stairs.

This is when the injoke began to notice a subtle aroma mingled with the titanic stench that permeated the market. It was a wonderful aroma that was vaguely familiar at first, and made his stomach begin to grumble. He began to visually search for the source of this unexpected good fortune. How he had missed this when he had first entered the place he could not fathom.

The opening was a service counter for a kitchen beyond. It was twenty feet wide, four feet tall, and was five feet from the floor. This market was also the cafeteria/mess hall for the entire evil army.

From where he was he could see through the opening in the wall. Beyond were stacks of dishes and stone mugs on counters and piles of pots and pans in sinks that were over-flowing with water, the taps still running. This was a huge kitchen. Large enough to service an army of thousands.

As he approached the window, he was careful not to step on any of the bodies, or in any of the puke or shit that was all over the place. "Someone really outta clean up 'round he'uh. Geesh, whatta sewa!" He chuckled as he bent down and looked inside.

Beyond the canteen window the cavernous kitchen looked like it was evacuated in a hurry. Many pots still boiled and bubbled on the stoves, smoke was leaking from a few oven doors, several grills were working and a few spits had meat on them, sizzling and slowly rotating around a series of trays over hot coals.

He peeked over the edge to see an assortment of bowls filled with vegetables and other things in sauces, trays of different meat loaves and jars with tantalizing pastes and jellies in them, a large pile of those *weird bread-like circular animal hides*, as the Troll described them (or, as you may know them, flat bread)-sat on a table just within his range of vision. Among it all was a bowl filled to the brim with those wonderful balls of yumminess...falafels.

"*Feel awfuls*! Ize *looooves* feel aaawfuls!" <u>h</u>e almost cried. "Oh and is dat what Ize tink it is? Is dat...Oh! Yes it *iiiis*; *ho geese*!" He was elated as he noticed the long loaves of bread sliced in two, lengthwise, next to several bottles of sauces, and everything else needed to make "ho geese".

Wait for it.

He dropped to one knee and gave thanks to Ulm. He also gave thanks to all of the "prostitute waterfowl" who perished in the creation of the delicious meat loaves for the three dozen ho geese he was gonna make as soon as he found the entrance to the kitchen.

I know. I know. Don't ask.

The window was far too small for anything more than his head or arm to fit through, and although he could have easily reached much of the food, he was on a mission to save his friends- *annnnd* wouldn't it be *great* to have some nice ho geese and feel-awfuls all ready for them (and still warm) when all that happened?

Coincidentally enough, at that very moment I had been talking to William in his lab, only three hundred feet below the Troll, and it was at that exact same moment that I was feeling hungry for no reason. I had left the exact area he was presently in only fifteen or so minutes before he started tossing bags of feces all over the place.

Kinda cool... Right?

Anyway, where was I?

Oh yeah...

He soon realized that the kitchen was accessed from a different part of the fortress.

He took a moment to elate in what he had created in the name of Ulm and laughed as he looked around at the biohazard he had created.

Beornag later swore, when asked, that the *feel awfuls* really didn't make you feel awful unless you ate too many. It's all about knowing your limit. His was one hundred eighty-three.

His friends were hungry. This was fact. How it was fact remains a mystery, but as the Troll has *also* said many times: "*It's all about believin.*"

He searched the market with keen eyes, looking for the right exit. There he stood trying to choose between two *large* exits that led to where he had not explored yet, the one he came in from and four smaller ones he would have been forced to crawl through.

The one he came in from was at the top of a non-navigable shit-covered staircase with too many pools of vomit to count, so he decided to pass on that one. Instead he threw a whole bunch of things toward the top for people to trip on, because otherwise it would be a sacrilegious waste of all that wonderful crap and barf, of course.

Oy.

His stomach began to rumble after that as his hind-brain kicked in and delivered the memory of the kitchen aromas a second time.

He could hear the sound of guards coming from the upper level beyond the stairs and he decided to take the middle of the other two exits.

He half-wanted to stay and watch them all trip and fall over each other down the shit- and puke-covered stairs, but, as previously stated, he was on a mission.

After scratching his head for a moment and trying to decide which one was the middle, he opted for the right one because it would then be the *right* decision.

In fact they both clearly led to the same courtyard. But he wanted to be sure he did everything *right*. He was down to his last bag of crap and it was almost one hundred percent Eek poop. He was saving that one for a special occasion.

He wandered through the courtyard and eventually exited through a tall arched tunnel. The same tunnel I had earlier traveled through, following the Talotian, when I was disguised as Musky's cousin, Vermin...remember? In that other book?

Really?

Well, o*kay* then...

He lumbered down the huge corridor in his great ape-like fashion, with his *Maul of the Mountain* in his left hand.

He passed by several small portals that he could not fit through before he came to what appeared to be a set of huge loading doors.

Outside were several large barrels and crates. He lifted the lids and inside was wet garbage of all descriptions. He deduced that this was the waste dump for the kitchen, more because he wanted it to be than because he had actual evidence.

It's all about believin'....

After digging in the dumpsters for a good ten minutes and having several appetizers from the bountiful harvest he had discovered (to him this stuff was all gently aged, seasoned to perfection so to speak – once you pick the pieces of napkin out of it, that is. Hey. It's just packaging), he took a long look at the huge loading doors.

He then realized that he not only was *not* qualified to form an opinion about the skill with which they were created, but that he *was* supposed to be trying to figure out how they *opened*.

After another few minutes of careful study he concluded that he had no idea what he was looking for and, as such, pulled the doors off their hinges.

Inside was a large storage facility where crates and boxes of all sorts were stacked in rows. Sacks and barrels were everywhere and filled with...you guessed it...stuff! So . . . much. . . stuff!

He entered the warehouse and shoved the doors back into the portal behind him, forcefully jamming them into place by adding a chair and table that he found next to the entrance. Then he lit a lantern that he had found sitting on a crate.

This took him well over 20 minutes to achieve, despite having a flint and steel. Hill Trolls are not very tech savvy, I am afraid. Yet he *was* successful, and soon had an aura of light surrounding him so as to allow a better look around the place. His friend, Grarr, had taught him that skill. "Grarr," he whispered under his breath as he smiled.

He held the lantern up to just above his eye level, around fifteen feet, while he took a look around.

This was a massive warehouse filled with crates and barrels and a menagerie of other containers.

Huge groups of antique furniture were placed together here and there, covered in dusty drapes.

Stacks of crates, too many to count, were everywhere. Some of the crates were piled twenty feet high and were filled with everything you can imagine.

After several seconds of just standing in silence, struck stupid so to speak by what he had uncovered, he pulled his own finger and lifted his left leg slightly. This was his silent prayer of gratitude to his deity, Ulm.

Then he commenced rummaging and looting through the seemingly endless supply of stuff in *boxes* and *crates* and *things*! *Oh my*!!

He was so excited! He frolicked and danced among the aisles and aisles of shipping containers, elating in the beautiful mystery of each unopened package of instant gratification.

After another thirty minutes of searching around, opening everything he could open to snoop inside (and singing a song about navel lint), he remembered he had forgotten something again and stopped in his tracks.

He was a mighty *hero*!

Nah, that wasn't it...

Scratching his head, he stood there for a few minutes, and as he did so he allowed the quiet of the place to surround him.

…

'Perfect silence,' he thought, *'except f' da gentle sobbin' in da distance.'*

…there it was again!

"Please…" a small voice from somewhere among the many crates he had not yet opened, whimpered.

"Hey!" he thought out loud. "Whooz is doing all da cryin' and why don't dey shut up already? Ize is tryin' ta tink here." He was quite annoyed.

He sat down in the middle of a four-way intersection, admiring his work- boxes and crates to all sides, most opened with stuffing and packing materials scattered all over the floor.

Urns, towels, plates, soap and a vast menagerie of mundane items placed carefully in bizarre feats of balance and abstract art, all in the way of anyone trying to move in the room.

There, he sat for several moments as he tried to gather his thoughts and remember what he was supposed to be doing.

Despite all the whimpering and crying in the distance he was still able to form *most* of a thought over the next few minutes, but in the end the noise was just too much for him and he lost concentration again.

Frustrated, he moved to another area where he sat down on a priceless, one-of-a-kind divan (destroying it in the process) and thought some more, scratching his head to get the "Brain Juices" flowing.

He was, just then, starting to remember something about a kitchen and … *FEEL AWFULS!!*

However, looking around, he was once again almost instantly distracted by all of the crates and boxes still to be opened.

This only sent him on another tour of the warehouse looking for clues about what he had forgotten.

He had uncovered a collection of antiquities that were each priceless beyond compare. Paintings, antique furniture, rare and valuable clothing made from exotic materials, silver and porcelain wares of the finest craftsmanship, obviously the fruition of countless centuries of stealing and banditry.

Many times he was tempted to go and see who was crying and bawling and sobbing in the distant shadows like a little elf girl and give them a piece of his mind for being so inconsiderate. *'Geesh! People was tryin' ta tink. Have some common coytesy!'*

Then it hit him: the kitchen! Ho geese! Feel awfuls! It was time for some real thinking now.

'If Ize came frum dat way... and Ize went dat way... and den dat way ...' The sobbing distracted him once again and he lost his train of thought.

"Will yooz *please* keep it down ova dere!? Ize is trying ta figya out how ta find da kitchen, and den rescue my pals frum da evil wizid an 'is rat...tings...*creatures*, tank *yooz* very much!" He was getting quite frustrated at that point.

"Please help me," came a whimpering voice from the shadows. It was female and spoke those few words with careful eloquence. The language was humanese, so the Injoke was able to understand. "I am in the dark. Please ... I am alone."

The voice was magical. Musical to *his* ears. He was unable to *not* be interested in it.

Yet...

Beornag suddenly came to his senses; he could make *feel awful- ho geese*! What an *EPIPHANY*!!

...And he could follow the sound of this well- spoken feminine voice to its source and help the poor woman. '*Ize should probly do dat first,*' he thought. '*But man … feel awful ho geese. Now dat's genesis!*'

"Hello? Is anyone there?" the voice came again.

He stopped in his tracks, placed his cupped hand sideways next to his ear (so his voice would carry) and whispered loudly: "Yes, O damsel in desperate despair. Ize is Beornag, Injoke of Ulm da Freakin Hilarious. Ize is looking for da kitchen. Do yooz knowz where it is?" He then cupped his mouth so as to hear better.

"I am sorry. I do not," came the reply. "I am a prisoner here. Please help me. Will you please help me?"

"Okay. No prob. Yooz want a feel awful, or maybe a ho geese sandwich? He asked his hand over his ear. "As soon as Ize find da kitchen Ize is gonna make up a bunch. Ize could make ya a few and drop back dis way or maybe…"

"I need to be *rescued.* I am trapped in darkness," she interrupted.

"Okay, okay. Ize is *tryin',*" he lamented. "It's not like Ize got Grarr here ta tell Ize what ta do 'en stuff. How can *Ize* find *yooz?*"

"Follow my voice," she replied.

"What's it look like?" he asked.

"Hunh?" she replied.

"Ooooh…ya voice…ahahah…yeah…I knew dat. Follow ya voice…ha-ha yeah," he said.

She sang a beautiful elfish song about two sisters and their heroic father who had fallen victim to malice. Her voice was very low in volume, but high-pitched and sweet to hear.

She sang this way for several minutes and then the song ended. "Did that help, sir?" she called.

"Brought my spirits up. Tanks. Ize truly appreciated dat." The Troll had forgotten to follow the sound and took the moment to relax and clean his toenails. "Keep singin', Ize is sure Ize is close now."

He got up and she sang the song again. This time he *did* follow the sound to a large group of containers. There he discovered a massive wooden shipping crate at the bottom of a great stack of smaller crates of all different sizes.

Starting with the smallest boxes, about eight inches across, he began opening the containers—and, when there was no woman inside he simply tossed them away, regardless of the contents..

"You must be close. I can hear you, I think," she said hopefully. Her voice was magical; there were powers at work that the Injoke was not aware of. She was casting a spell on him.

He continued searching the containers, working his way toward the largest at the bottom. "Are yooz sure yooz don't know da way ta da kitchen?" *Still*, the aroma of 'feel awfuls' lingered in his remarkable sinuses.

"I do not know where I am now," she replied.

"Well dat makes two 'a us ... Right? Ain't it always dat way? Yooz knowz? When ... No, wait." He counted using his fingers, and then double-checked his math. Then he looked around to see if anyone else was lost. "Yup, just two of us. See? It's just like what Ize was sayin..."

It was a good twenty minutes before he finally reached the last box. "Wow, lady. Yooz must be huge! Dis is da biggest box in da pile. I am guessin' yooz is in here."

He slowly pried open the crate, which was in fact a ten-foot-long shipping container. As the side came loose, the creaking of the old nails against dry wood echoed throughout the warehouse. Then he took a peek inside.

What he saw within was a pleasant surprise. "Lillia? How'd yooz get in here?" he asked in disbelief as he finished ripping open the side of the crate.

Chapter - 2

"An Elf is an Elf is an Elf"

The following wildlife vignette is brought to you by;

Murray's Cat Dairy and Boot Factory

"The fine dairy products you can expect to be packaged in boots good enough to eat out of. From our feet, to your kitchen. It's Murray's"

"Try the new Athlete's Paté with ginseng and wild leek"

Elves come in three varieties and are all among the longest-lived and the oldest of the sentient species in the empire. They have many gods whom, it is said, care little about them.

The elves, in turn, care little for their gods.

Elfish gods are not and never have been elfish. These strange and mysterious entities only associate with their own kind, and created the elves countless eons ago as a whimsical experiment. After which- satisfied with their results – they turned their backs on the elves and walked away, so to speak, leaving the elves with no gods to oversee their development.

By the time the D.O.O.B.I.E.S., *(the central council of Deities, Oracles, Omnipotent Beings, and Inter-dimensional Enchanted Societies)* had issued the proper fines to these "creator beings" for polluting a public domain (namely reality) with their "trash" (the elves), the elves themselves had established several successful civilizations and cultures. They had *earned* the *right* to exist.

The D.O.O.B.I.E.S. awarded them with full recognised self-awareness and special consideration.

Because of their innate inborn wisdom, and their ability to resist temptation, the elves were given knowledge that no other race or species possesses to this day. In light of their godless place in the multiverse, their near-immortality, and their superior physical and mental traits, they were given the honor of becoming keepers of mortal secrets while they, as a species, agreed to keep those secrets forever from mortal beings.

Little else is known about them as a culture, though many elves live among other races in the empire's many towns, villages and cities. Those elves do not usually speak about their homeland and many even try to fit into human society, adopting their customs and traditions and languages.

The three separate races of elf are...

The Sylvain: known to be the tallest of their kind, with light tan complexions with green or blue tints. They have blondish to white hair. Lillia and Alaeth are Sylvain elves.

Sylvain elves are considered by most races to be the most beautiful people in the world. This is due in part to a natural defence mechanism that surrounds each elf with an invisible bio-chemical/pheromonal cloud that cannot be consciously detected by others of differing species. This cloud has a subtle psychological effect on other sentient humanoid species making them less aggressive toward elves. It has even been used actively by elfish folks as a defensive measure. This is the reason that the Sylvain have so few real enemies.

Sylvain elves live all over the empire, but they also have their own lands and country. Far to the west, just before the endless plains, the great forests of Sylvain can be found. There the elves *grow* structures in which to live and do commerce and to practise government and to educate. Here too are the many Sylvain biolabs where they grow fantastical things from wood and other natural components.

The Sylvain culture has honored the world with many gifts of socio-political sciences, philosophies, music and art as well as applied sciences and a detailed remembrance of history. They are the empire's most valued allies.

Sylvains are lithe and spindly for the most part as a species. Males and females are both of the same average height and weight. They commonly stand between 5 and 5.5 feet tall, weighing between 80 and 125 lbs.

Their dietary needs are more specific than most sentient species in the world, consisting of 90% vegetable matter, 10% fish, and rarely meat - if nothing else is available. They are taught as young children the importance of maintaining this strict culinary regiment.

Sylvain elves are also quite magically adept and most are born with many wondrous abilities both physical and eldritch.

The Doc Alfar are the underworld dwellers, also known as dark elves because they live in the dark. These beings have shiny, almost metallic black skin and stark white eyes and hair. They are on average smaller and lighter in weight than their surface-dwelling cousins. They seldom associate with surface-dwelling peoples and are known for their cruelty.

Doc Alfar live in a very secret and isolationist society. These people live deep underground hundreds of miles beneath the world's surface. Their culture frowns upon interspecies contact and cooperation and they are thought to be extreme racists/specists.

Still, Dark Elves have been known to venture from their subterranean homelands from time to time to secretly steal away the children of other races from their beds at night.

What the elves do with these children is unknown, but those who have witnessed the kidnapping, and even a small few who escaped the Alfarian raiders, tell of a cruel and sadistic people.

Little more is known about the Doc Alfar as they prefer their isolationist lifestyle and will defend it swiftly with merciless violence.

Lastly, the **Santas Elves,** who are perhaps the most mysterious of all elves. They are creatures thought only to be legendary, and most other elves are loath to speak on the subject to any degree at all. As a result very little is known about them.

Seldom repeated legends, almost completely forgotten, speak of the Santas Elves' limitation of only being able to see the colors red and green and white. This is thought to be caused by their choice of dwellings, usually on or near the North Pole. The lack of sunlight and over-abundance of it from one half of the year to the next causes unusual optical mutations to occur in them and evolution is said to have done its work on an extreme scale.

These stories also sometimes speak of the Santas Elves' ability to be tinkerers and crafters. Some stories hint at the Santas Elves' ability to craft happiness itself, but only on one day each year, and only for the young at heart.

Santas Elves are thought to be very small, with estimates guessing at 12 to 18 inches tall. Recent findings by a Sylvain ethnologist and her Hill Troll assistant have unearthed some other clues about the Santas Elves, but no conclusions have yet to be drawn. It would seem that more study is needed on the subject.

All elves are essentially immortal as they do not die of old age. Every elf who has ever died did so from unnatural means. A total number is kept in a vault in the Sylvain homeland and guarded by a coven of eldritch masters. They refuse to explain why.

For more information about elves or for a copy of this wildlife vignette contact: The G'nomish Film Board Society, Sixty Six-Packs Street, Allthewater, Sensimillia, 420420420.

Chapter - 3

"Small Things in Big Packages"

She sat in a corner at the back of the crate, beaten and bruised, her face streaked with tears. Her right ankle was shackled to a short chain that was secured to the inside of the crate. Her nightgown was torn and dirty and her skin was stained with mud and filth.

"I am not Lillia," she explained, tears streaking down her dust-covered cheeks.

"Yooz looks just like her. Exactly like her, in factualization ... well, maybe a little dirtier, but hey! Holy double vision a loveliness…. Waaaait a second here. Is yooz *I'll-Lay-It*, da sista a da lovely and delicate Lillia whose last name Ize forgot on account a me havin' trouble pronouncin' it?" He was getting so excited he almost forgot about the feel awful and ho geese sandwiches.

"Yes! Thanks be to the gods, I am. Are you my rescuer? Did Lillia send you?" She was crying again, but this time they were tears of hope and she was almost smiling.

"Crap. Ize gotta go ta da batroom. Ize shoulda gone when Ize was dere earlia," he said as he scratched his behind and looked around the warehouse. He then sniffed his fingers and spoke again. "Ize should be okay Ize guess for at least unudda half owa, howeva long dat is. A bit longa. How's dat? Dat should give yooz an idea of how…"

"Sir?" Alaeth spoke.

"Yeah?" he replied.

She pointed to her shackle. "Hel-*lo*?"

"Oh yeah!" He took the metal ring between the index fingers and thumbs of both hands and pulled the cheap cuff apart, snapping the locking pin with ease.

When she was free he offered her a cool drink of wine from a silver decanter he produced from a large rucksack.

He then said a prayer under his breath so low she was not able to make out the words. 'Dumbass says what."

"What?" she asked.

He chuckled as her wounds faded and she became strong again.

"Oh my. What just happened?" She stood and teetered on once weak legs.

He chuckled again and gently picked her up in one huge hand. "Wow. Ize just pictured a dinasewa tryin' ta grab yooz frum Ize's hand as Ize fought it off wit only my…"

"Sir?" she interrupted.

"Yeah?" he asked.

"Shouldn't we be trying to escape, or find the kitchen or a bathroom for you?" she offered.

He chuckled again. "Yeah, hahaha." He stared at her sweet eyes. They reminded him so much of Lillia. He reminisced about the wonderful meals she had made for him and how clean and tidy everything was. How she folded his shorts and put them in his dresser for him. How she…

"Sir?" she interrupted again.

"Kitchen! That's where weez is goin'." He put her on his shoulder, instructed her to hold the collar of his chain armour and tried to gain his bearings.

"Okay…so….Ize came in dere and went dere…den Ize was *dere* and turned ta *dat* way…and den…A*ha*!" He pointed toward the only other exit out of the room, the one *not* broken and *not* jammed into place. "It must be dat way."

He moved toward the opposite end of the warehouse and the door out. On his way he noticed a particular crate that had printed on its side a familiar symbol. It was the logo for Warped Speed Wineries.

"Hey! Dats us!" he pointed at the crate as he continued on toward the exit.

He reached the door and paused before opening it. "Na…Ize can't allow dat." He then turned around and went back to the crate of Warped Speed Wine.

He took the crate and put it in his backpack along with another crate that he liked the color of. *It* actually contained many other smaller boxes of assorted chocolates. No kidding! But no tea.

But imagine if it had tea too? Wow! Right? That would be something.

Anyway, where was I?

Oh yeah…

He then returned to the door and examined it for a moment. "Oh-hoho, no*ooo*. Yooz ain't foolin' Ize again, self," he said to himself. "Ize don't know nut'n about locks and doors so Ize ain't wastin' Ize's time anymore."

He kicked the unlocked door off its hinges, sending it flying across the room beyond, striking an Ogre cook who had returned to reclaim his kitchen, after the shit storm outside his serving window had subsided.

The Ogre swatted the door aside and only suffered a minor scratch.

"Yooz not be allowed in *kitchen*!" he grunted. His multi-stained white apron was tied around his filthy, sweaty bare gut and he was scratching his crotch with his free hand.

CHAPTER - 4

"HEEE - HAAW!"

The following wildlife vignette is brought to you by;

Mosha's Pickled Cabbages

"Great heads from great heads."

"Packed to the rim in Troll-proof cans that seem to last forever!"

Ogres: The common Ogre, not to be confused with the common mother-in-law, is a relatively new species on the evolutionary stage.

The predecessors of Ogres were actually a community of hostile, misled humans who shunned society and change and took all their worldly possessions to live in a tight-knit secret civilization in the mountains far to the south of the empire.

Those dwelling in these secret mountain villages survived there for many generations, but eventually sickness and other natural disasters whittled away their population to such a degree that their gene pool became too small to support them as a people.

It was at this point in history that all of the men among the mountain people perished from a great internal war they fought over resources and medicine.

It was also, coincidentally enough, a time when a small band of Goblins wandered into the village. Normally, Goblins would rape and pillage such a defenceless gathering of humans, but they too were few in numbers and had just lost a war far to the south against the icemen of Talot. They needed to repopulate their ranks and human females were as good a mammal as any in the eyes of the horny Goblins. (See: It's Not Easy Being Green. chapter 19)

The Goblins managed to convince the human women to have sex with them. Understand that these women were the results of many generations of inbreeding and rampant debauchery and were all over the idea anyway, so there was actually no raping involved if you don't count the role-playing that took place.

Soon the first young Goblins were being born to human mothers.

These were different, though. No human woman had ever before given birth to a Goblin child. These *human* hybrids were no *kendawls* (See: It's Not Easy Being Green. chapter 19). These children were much different than any Goblin child that had ever been born before.

These children were big. *Very* big. They were born almost as big as their fathers. Many of their mothers perished in labor. Those who survived went on to copulate with many, many other Goblins in a breeding frenzy that lasted for years.

The children that were produced during those years grew at an astonishing rate and in only one week they were larger than their mothers. This was how the Ogre people came to be.

These beasts were born with three insatiable drives.

1/ They love the taste of humanoid flesh and the sound of human suffering. Ogres will track a human *male* for weeks to taste the man's flesh, cooked over open flames.

2/ They are surprisingly good at the culinary arts. Ogres have experience and practice using the flesh of many creatures in their summertime cooking events and to great success. Though their personal favorite is human flesh, they are often hired as cooks where they prepare and serve culinary extravagancies using non-human meats. These menu items are always expertly prepared and beautifully presented despite the Ogres' disgusting outward presence.

And lastly:

3/ They are known to own human slave women with whom they procreate their species.

Human females are always kept as slaves for sex and reproduction. Once an Ogre's female becomes too old to have children he will butcher her and cook her in much the same way as he cooks human men. Then he will kidnap another woman and continue the cycle.

Ogres usually have many females that they have kidnapped, usually from hunter/gatherer tribes or settlements with little access to military protection.

They are truly horrific.

Adult Ogres stand between eight and eleven feet tall, with a very few reaching twelve feet. Ogres are stocky and wide in the mid-section. They have long arms and big feet. Ogres have huge guts that they present in displays of territorial aggression (especially at pig roasts and monster cart rallies). Some Ogres oil their guts so as to create even more glare and to intimidate any would-be land grabbers.

Ogres are always a pasty off-white in color and always sweaty. They have straight hair on their heads that can be any color from blond to jet-black and even (more common among *them* than among humans) red.

These red-haired Ogres are always covered in pink and reddish-brown speckles which give them their more common name: the *Speckled Red Neck*. Males usually lose much of this hair by the time they reach middle age. This is when their hair migrates from their heads to their shoulders, arms, and ears.

Male Ogres, however, are also known for having thick coats of curly hair on their backs that eventually mix with bodily fluids and filth over years of not bathing. This filth mats up on their impressively wide backs and can act as a kind of natural armour plating that the Ogres utilize in their territorial disputes.

Most Ogres are quite stupid by human standards and can be compared to a really dumb eight-year-old with a master's degree in the culinary arts.

Ogres are strange creatures, prone to burning religious symbols, *eating* things that they also burn on purpose (mostly pigs and ears of corn and something called chili) and waving tiki-torches at frightened onlookers as they proclaim their own greatness and right to exist.

Ogres are wholly awful creatures who revel in the suffering of others and love it even more if they are the ones causing the suffering. Their stupidity makes them perfect henchmen for evil-doers (especially as cooks, vice presidents, and judges), while (ironically) their inbred nature, small brains, and thick skulls make them almost impossible to kill.

One can knock an Ogre out and believe the creature to be dead beyond a doubt and then walk away. Weeks and even months later the monster wakes up from its regenerative slumber, hungry and looking for trouble. As it lay there on the ground regenerating, nothing will eat it because even flies are repulsed by the disgusting creature. Anything coming within twenty feet of it starts to gag and turn away. It takes a brave nose that has already been desensitized by years of exposure to horrific smells to get anywhere near an Ogre without at least gagging.

Ogre *females...*

These are monsters among their *species.* They are horrific to look upon, as tall as the males, with massive backsides, and breasts weighing sometimes over seven hundred pounds each.

Female Ogres (Ogresses) have long blonde or red hair always. No female has ever been recorded with anything but red or blonde hair. No one knows why or even seems to care.

Ogresses also have oily, pasty white skin covered with oozing acne sores which they display proudly to potential male partners during mating rituals. Their hair is almost always braided in two braids, one to each side of their massive head. They braid their armpit hair as well, and decorate these long thin braids with colorfully painted skulls, bones, and feathers of small animals and birds.

No Ogresses have ever been known to congregate for any length of time before one starts a gossip chain that eventually leads to all-out violence and a parting of ways. It is usually right after one of these coven break-ups that a female will seek a suitable male with which to copulate.

Ogresses emit an horrifically noxious odor that reeks of sour milk, burning hair, and rancid fish oil. It is a funk so intense that one can actually see it as it causes a mirage effect over the monster's exposed skin. This rank odor is used to trick male Ogres, and *those* equally horrific monsters elate in their lust for the stench of an Ogress's backside.

Ogre females are quite aware of their power over males and use their epic stink to lure them into their lairs like a sort of date-rape drug. Once he is trapped there, in the confines of her chosen abode, the Ogress rapes the unsuspecting idiot for weeks before she murders and eats him.

For the record, no female Ogre has ever given birth. If it were not for their *super-pheromonal-stink* (that same reek that drives the bull Ogres into a sexually driven stupor-frenzy) they would never have sex at all. Female Ogres would be forever alone as no other creature can bear to look upon them or get any closer than twenty feet downwind of them, let alone listen to them complain non-stop.

This is why the males continue the tradition of keeping female sex slaves of other races/species in order to procreate with. Otherwise the species would go extinct...which would probably be a good thing in all actuality.

On a side note: It is said that one female Ogre *did* manage to give birth to a child. The father was an old human alchemist who had lost his sense of smell and sight in a chemical accident. He required her to do something for him so that he could create a serum with which to cure his lost senses.

In return he bedded her and gave her a child. They say the child is female and is nothing special to look upon, even as an Ogress. Yet she lives among other peoples in a town in the northlands.

I know. I know. Weird, right? But hey...weirder things have happened.

For more information about Ogres or for a copy of this wildlife vignette contact: The G'nomish Film Board Society, Sixty Six-Packs Street, Allthewater, Sensimillia, 420420420.

"CROCK... I MEAN *JACKPOT!*"

"Sez who?" Beornag asked.

"Sez…ummmm…uh…*Me!*" The Ogre replied. "Yeah! Me sez so. Me no like hairy yeti round foods. Gits out or I stomps ya good." The Ogre slobbered as he spoke. He was as tall as the Troll. His nose had a nasty yellow and brown booger in it just beyond the nostril opening and his face was riddled with massive whiteheads. Long curly hairs grew from his wax-encrusted ears like the frayed ends of a broken rope. His pasty white skin was sweaty and oily and the few hairs on his head were tied back in a damaged hair net. His dirty hands and arms had burn marks all over them and his fingernails were filthy beyond imagination. "Me not afraid of yooz! Yooz no scare me! Yooz nut'n but a big monkey. Yooz not even a ree'ow Troe. *Hmmmnphd!*" The booger shot across three tables, ricocheted off a pot on a ceiling rack, bounced off a ball of dough and struck Beornag square in the left eye.

The Injoke didn't flinch, didn't even close his eye. He gently placed Alaeth on the floor. "Yooz betta take cova. Dis is gonna get ugly. Ize would try not ta watch if Ize was yooz. Maybe hide in a cupboard or sump'n," he said as he stood up to his full height.

Now I know I said he was like seventeen feet or something like that in the past, but that was only how tall he *seemed*. In all actuality, the Injoke could only reach the moderate height of fourteen feet, seven and a half inches. Still…this was quite impressive to see. Especially when the ceiling was only eighteen feet and he could actually brace his forearms against it if he wanted to.

At that height the Injoke's hands still came to only four feet from the ground. His arms were like tree trunks and just as strong.

He picked the Ogre booger from his eye. "Yooz tinks a booga is gonna rattle Ize, bub?" He stuck it in his mouth and chewed it up. Then he swallowed and spoke again. "Ize has tasted betta boogas from da nose on a dead cow. Yooz gut no game, pal."

The Ogre was furious! He stomped his right foot and grunted so hard his face turned red in a show of dominance.

Alaeth ran for a nearby cupboard which she crawled into. She knew who this Ogre was. She closed the door and squeezed as far to the back as she could. This Ogre was to be her mate. It is why Calabac had locked her in the crate next to the kitchen. Once Calabac had realized that she was only playing him, stalling for a chance to escape, and that she could not serve his purpose anyway, he promised her as a concubine to this filthy monstrosity.

The beast would have raped her to death and then probably sautéed her in a nice white wine before serving her on a bed of crispy greens with charbroiled chanterelle mushrooms in a smoked gruyere sauce. The horror!

The Ogre then spoke again. "I be Phuktbutt! I be…"

Beornag began to hoot and laugh so loud the Ogre was interrupted.

"*Whaaat*? What so funny? Why you laugh?" he asked, confused and annoyed.

"Yooz's name is, hahahaha … hahahaha … Ph … aaaahahahaha … Phukt … ahahahaha … Phukt Butt? Aaaah hahahahahahah! Yooz's name is … Aaaahahaha!" Beornag was now on one knee, holding his side and laughing uncontrollably, tears rolling down his cheeks. "Ize tought Terdbreff was bad! Aaaaa hahahahahaha! Where does yooz guys get deez names frum? Aaahahahaha!"

The Ogre was so mad at this point he looked around for a weapon. "Ooooo! I be soooo mad now! I is gonna look for a weapon!"

"Well, Phuktbutt … What's gotten inta ya? Aaaahahahahahaha." Beornag was in tears.

Inside the cupboard, Alaeth too was now laughing uncontrollably. Tears were streaking down her face, but this time they were tears of joy. She had no idea that she possessed such a daring sense of humor. Beornag's laughter was so contagious-,she could hardly breathe. She yelled from inside the cupboard, "I can't breathe! Ahahahaha! What's gotten into him! Aaahahahaha!"

"Dat my name!" the Ogre roared. "I be Phuktbutt! I be big Phuktbutt!" He stomped his feet and yelled at the Troll. Then, reaching up, he grabbed a massive salami from a shelf and roared, shaking it at the Injoke. It was two huge four-foot-long links of the finest spiced salami money could buy. Both links were attached by the ends and both were enclosed in a strong waxed cloth casing. The things resembled a sort of giant edible exotic flail as Phuktbutt swung it over his head roaring in frustration.

Beornag staggered and crawled over to the cupboard where Alaeth was hiding. He opened the door and looked inside. She was in a fetal position, gasping for breath as she laughed uncontrollably.

"Look at 'im! Aaaahahahaha! He's Phuktbutt! Aaahahahahaha! He's gonna kill me wit dat salami! Aaaaahahahaha!"

The Ogre was now swinging his giant salami in his right hand while in his left hand he had picked up a pot of boiling water. He raged with frustration, stomping and growling and snorting loudly.

The Injoke then quickly closed the door, still laughing hard, and dove for cover behind one of the huge work islands.

The pot of boiling water struck the cupboard where Alaeth was hiding but she yelled to the Injoke between hoots of laughter that she was okay.

Our hero then stood up and hocked a giant wad of snot at the Ogre, striking him on the chin. At the same time he threw a garbage can, forcing Phuktbutt to block it, sending garbage flying in all directions. As the trash fell to the floor Beornag was already within reach. Only one stone work table was between the two behemoths.

Phuktbutt swung his salami at the Troll and the Injoke deflected the blow with an uncooked plucked turkey he was now wearing on his left hand. He had placed his maul on a table as he rushed by, shoving his hand up the dead bird's rear end (it was a 48-lb turkey, a real big one), to wear it like a puppet...Much funnier than a maul... but was it a weapon?

In his right hand he now wielded a large sack of lard. He swung the lard by the sack handle over the table full of ingredients, even as he was momentarily distracted by the feel-awful assembly station.

The bag hit with a resounding *smuk,* knocking Phuktbutt back against the wall next to the only other way out of the kitchen. He was covered in greasy, yellowy rendered animal fat and was now slipping and rolling in it, yelling his lungs out at the Troll. "Phuktbutt only greasy! Phuktbutt not open up on Tro yet! Phuktbutt gonna…"

"Aaaah hahahaha! Aaaaahahaaahaaahah! Phuktbutt's gonna open up on Ize. Didja hear dat?" Beornag had now picked up a random can and was trying to crack its lid open as he laughed at the Ogre. "Ize greased da *Phukt-butt*! Aaaahaha! And … *aaahahaha* … and now it's gonna …. aaaha hahaha … it's gonna ….. ahaaahahaha … open up on Ize! Aaaaahaaahaahaahahaaaa!"

From inside the cupboard Alaeth now sounded like she was crying for mercy. "Make it stop! Aaaa hahahaha! Please! Aaaahahahaha!"

"Hey Phuktbutt! Don't be such a stuck-up asshole! Aaaahahahaha!" The Injoke was on a roll now. "Loosen up, Phuktbutt! Aaah hahahaha!

"Aaaahahahaha!" from the cupboard.

"Yeeaaaaagh!" from the Ogre.

"Aaaaahahaha! Do yooz even know what dat means? Aaaaahahahaaha!" Beornag asked as Phuktbutt finally got to his feet.

His entire body was coated in pig fat now. "It Ogre talk. It mean: Last to Come! It be great honor to be ... *Hey!*"

The Troll was now on both knees and one hand. Laughing hysterically, reaching out with his free hand, he begged the Ogre to stop. "Yooz gotta ... y ... yooz gotta ... yooz gotta stop ... Ize surrenders! Aaaahahahahaa!"

"Dat dooz it! Phuktbutt gonna tear your head off!" He gingerly stepped forward, trying not to slip in the lard. "When I gitz my hand on your pretty litto elfgirl, Phuktbutt gonna squeeze her so hard she will ..."

"Careful I'll-Lay-It! Phuktbutts can still squeeze apparently! Aaaahaaaahhaaahahahh!" The Troll then stood up on one knee, picking up the three-gallon can of pickled cabbage he had been trying to open, and threw it at Phuktbutt.

"Phuktbutt gonna squeeze you till you pop, litto lady. Hmmmuahaha..."

The can of pickled cabbages hit the Ogre square between the eyes but he didn't seem to notice it at all. He just kept yelling.

"...I is gonna suck out your..." He paused, his eyes then crossed and he fell forward to the floor.

Beornag hopped over to make sure Phuktbutt was down and out, for at least a while. When he was satisfied that hitting the Ogre with the can another twelve times in the head was sufficient to keep the beast unconscious, he returned to the cupboard where Alaeth was hiding.

"Yooz okay, little lady?" he asked, reaching in and gently picking her up.

As he drew her from her hiding place she was still giggling.

"Aaa hehe. Yooz like dat one?" he chuckled as he sat her down and moved toward the *feel awful* and *ho gees* preparation station.

He immediately started making falafels, I mean *feel awfuls*.

Alaeth tried to help but was rather useless in the kitchen. So he sat her on the counter next to him and continued.

"You are freakin' hilarious," Alaeth suddenly said as he was sniffing the garlic paste on his fingers. "Do you smell something awful?" she asked.

The canteen window was only twenty or so feet from where she was sitting and the rank of shit and puke was really starting to permeate the areas surrounding the market mess hall.

"Naaa. Dats Ulm. Ulm is da Freakin' Hilarious. Not sump'n dat smells awful. Or maybe he does. Ize ain't neva met him personally. Ize is just really funny. Not hilarious like da great pranksta."

Then as the market began to fill with scave, he grinned. "Hey look. It's a bunch a doze rat tings and deys is all trippin' in da … maybe weez should go." He grabbed her and placed her on the floor. He then tossed all the feel awfuls and ho geese ingredients in his backpack. He didn't want her to see the mess he had made...in the mess hall. He wanted to save that for later.

He picked her up as he was watching a small battalion of scave in leather armour move across the market and toward the exit he had left the cafeteria from. The same one that led to the dumpsters and eventually to where he was now. They hadn't noticed him in the kitchen as they passed by the window, and he took advantage of this by leaving the place altogether.

He moved to the open portal where the Ogre had slipped in the lard and proceeded down a long wide and very tall hallway.

Again he put Alaeth on his shoulder and waited for her to grasp the collar of his chain cuirass. Once she was secured he loped at an impressive, steady pace, passing several human-sized tunnels and doors until the hall opened into a great round pit.

Here he was standing on a round balcony looking down into a circular shaft. At random intervals along the walls of the shaft below he could see a gush of filthy water and refuse stream out and disappear into the darkness below. He now also noticed that there was another huge opening to the left of the one he entered.

He peeked over the edge of the shaft again and found no way to descend the seemingly endless pit. The surface was too sheer, so he spat and waited to hear if it hit bottom. It didn't.

"Wait here," he said, gently putting Alaeth down on the cold stone floor. "If yooz hears anybody comin', yooz run afta me. Ize'll be in da kitchen gittin some stuff weez is gonna need."

"Right-o," she replied with a smile as she took cover behind the safety wall that surrounded the shaft. "This place reeks," she added, waving her hand in front of her face.

"Yeah. Ain't it great?" He then turned and ran back to the kitchen.

When he returned to the kitchen door he could hear movement from beyond in the market. Not wanting to alert anyone further, he snuck through to the storage closets. There he grabbed a large stack of thick paper bags designed to hold large amounts of grains and other dry products.

He also looked around on his hands and knees and found a set of measuring scoops and a large pot with a long handle. He took the largest measuring scoop and the pot, and on his way out of the room he grabbed the forty-eight-lb uncooked turkey, the salami Phuktbutt had attacked him with, and the three-liter can of pickled cabbages he had assaulted the Ogre with. All of this went into his backpack.

He once told me that he wouldn't dare to put a friend in the pack because it would not be safe, reason being he had once, as an experiment, farted in the backpack and when he attempted to retrieve it, the gaseous deposit was as fresh as the day it went in – four weeks *previous*! From that point on, Beornag would spend hours on rainy days farting in his bottomless sack for later use. You know where this is going, don't you?

After drawing a big penis on Phuktbutt's cheek and hitting him in the head a few more times with varying items he decided to return to Alaeth. Back at the pit he soon located her and lifted her back onto his shoulders.

"What is that horrible smell?" she asked as he made his way to the only other exit.

He sniffed his armpits, then one of his feet, then he sniffed the air. "Da cesspool. Ize tinks weez is right above it," he replied with an excited smile.

"I never thought I would ever smell anything so terrible in my life." She gagged.

"Yooz ain't been ta da market lately," he replied as he peeked around the corner to see what was there.

This was a hall much like the other except it was only fifty or so feet long. At the end it turned into a stairway that stopped every thirty feet and turned ninety degrees right. At each interval there was a door on the left large enough for him to get through on all fours. He bypassed these and kept descending the staircases.

Thirteen times he passed right by doors of this type until he reached the bottom where there was a different type of door. This door was iron and had a large metal wheel in the middle. It was a hatch. Here Alaeth warned him to listen first in case they were underwater. They weren't but he did compliment her on her wits. "Good ting yooz spoke up. If Ize had opened dat unda wata all da air woulda leaked outta *here*."

He turned the wheel and opened the hatch. A warm mirage of methane vapors immediately escaped, and the stench was even *worse* than the market.

Alaeth gagged and put the sleeve of her robe over her mouth as Beornag struggled to position his bottomless pouch in order to capture a few liters of the stinking gas.

Beyond the hatch was a vast network of catwalks and stairways that led to all sorts of boilers and piping systems. They wandered around in the place for almost an hour trying to ascertain what the purpose of such a room could be, all the while doing a lot of gagging.

Alaeth, having a talent for business and numbers, also had a passion for physics and engineering. She couldn't hope to understand *G'nomish* engineering, mind you, but in her primitive way she was quite adept. "I believe this huge room is where waste from the fortress is sent." She pointed to a group of vats. "That is a holding area, probably where non-biological waste is separated from the biological." She saw he was confused. "Where the poop and pee are separated from the paper and other junk people toss in the toilet."

She then pointed at a piping network and followed it along its course to another great vat. This one was different. It was far stronger than the others and had some sort of machinery hooked up to it. "This is amazing!" She was actually *admiring* the whole place now. "The architects must have been geniuses!"

"Yeah. Geniuses," the Injoke agreed as he gazed in wonder at the absolute confusion and "*above-his-headness*" of the whole place. "Can yooz find da place where da poop comes in here?" he asked.

"That's easy," she replied. "It's over here." She skipped down the space between two great vats and hopped up a forty-foot stair that was wrapped around the outside of one of the huge containers.

He followed her up the side of the huge vat to a catwalk that crossed the top like a bridge.

This was the first stage in a refining process and she was beginning to understand what was happening in this chamber.

They stepped out, onto the catwalk, and almost passed out from the hot, humid reek that assaulted their senses.

"Oh…Oh… Oh mercy. Ize's eyes is burnin'." The Troll was smiling, tears running down his cheeks. "It's … it's beauteeful."

Alaeth covered her mouth and nose and gagged a few more times. Only two or three feet underneath the catwalk was a churning brown mass of semi-liquid ultra-stench.

"This would be the first stage in whatever process is going on here," she explained. "Then it all goes, there … and then there, and there." She gagged again as she pointed out the different destinations for the sewage.

Keep in mind that thousands of humans, rats, rat-things, Ogres, Cave-Trolls, and the odd other nastiness, not to mention a dragon, was dumping their waste, eventually to this very destination. The reek was beyond description. It made the market look like a rose garden. Oy!

The Troll gagged. "In da name a Ulm… hoolgh … dis is da mudda load a' all … hoooolgh … shit-storm amunishun depots. All Ize needs ta know is … hooolgh … where da worse smellin' stuff is bein' held."

She pointed to the far side of the giant room where the smallest vat was located. An assortment of pipes with random stages of machinery led to what appeared to be a control station built into the side of the vat. There was even a chair there for a human-sized operator.

They descended from the vat they were on and proceeded to the far side of the great hall from where they entered.

Catwalks and iron stairways crisscrossed overhead as they passed vat after vat full of raw, ever-enhanced sewage. Piping of all sizes seemed to be everywhere.

"Ize wunda what deys was makin'," the Injoke said as he gazed around in confusion and wonder.

"This is a refining laboratory of some sort," Alaeth offered. "I can tell you that sheep manure, when mixed with a couple of other substances, will create a compound that becomes very dangerous and will explode with the slightest spark. Perhaps they are making explosive devices to attack the city with."

"Wow! Yooz knows a lot about crap," Beornag complimented her- in his own way. They approached the station where she studied the controls. There were mostly gauges and valve dials. But there were also three other interesting controls.

One was the release switch. "This would hypothetically dump all the waste in the vat … somewhere else". She was unable to ascertain where the concentrated shit would go, and apologized for this to the Troll.

"Oh, dats okay." He scratched his head. "Is dere any udda ways ta get da crap outta dis ting?" he asked as he started to lose interest and look around at all of the confusing things in the massive chamber.

"This looks like it, here." She pointed to a lever on the vat itself. Beside it was a small table with sample jars stacked on it. The lids were also there as well as a small white booklet.

She picked up the booklet and gasped after reading what was on it. "Are we inside of a volcano?"

"Yeah. Why yooz aksin'?" he replied.

"Because, if I am correct, the asshole who kidnapped me plans to blow up Briarwood with a giant weapon that's powered with ... *shit*!" she responded. "This is an explosives manufacturing laboratory, or at least something of the sort. I am not sure what it used to be, but right now it's an alchemist's lab for working with highly volatile and extremely explosive liquids and gasses for building weapons and maybe bombs too."

"Really? Yooz can do dat wit crap!? The Injoke looked defeated. "An Ize has been chuckin' it *raw* at people fuh years. Ta tink ... Ize coulda been cooking the stuff in da kitchen back home and makin' stuff outta it, like bawms." Then he scratched his head. "What's a bawm, again?"

She smiled. "A bomb is a device that will explode. Some are small, some are big. I think that the creep who brought me here is planning to use a device like that to blow apart the city ... I think. It actually says so in this book ... or, more accurately, it says that this vat contains the fuel for something called the *Endometer*. "Thousands of people are going to die if we cannot stop him. What are we going to do?" She looked at him with desperation in her eyes.

The Injoke would not have this lovely young lady face defeat. Her dependence on his heroics had inspired him and as such he had somehow formulated a plan.

No ... really. He actually did. "Weez is gonna steal Callous-Back's bawm, or whatever it's called and weez is gonna chuck it at *him*."

He ran to the sample station and pulled a huge, thick paper sack from his bottomless pouch. "Yooz trow da leva when Ize sez." He was smiling from cheek to cheek.

"O gods of my father, you are not thinking of ..." She couldn't believe what he was proposing.

He winked at her as he gripped the opening of the huge sack around the sample pipe. The mouth of the pipe was about three inches wide and just under it the metal of the table's surface was starting to corrode. "C'mon. It'll be fun." He smiled and winked again. "It'll work. Trust Ize. It's all about believin'."

She sighed. "What the heck." She threw the switch and in seconds she was forced to step away as the smell was so thick she was beginning to taste it in every breath.

It came out in a sort of slightly thin paste. It was sort-of like melted peanut butter. Not enough to be liquid, but still highly capable of splattering over a large area, especially eighty pounds of it hitting like a stampeding buffalo.

As the Injoke filled the sack Alaeth searched for something to make into a mask. She finally found a white lab coat and tied it around her face like a makeshift filter. Then she returned and shut the valve off.

The Troll *himself* was choking as he reached down and began tying up the huge bag of manure. "*Hooolgh!*" he gagged. " ... It's like por … *hooolgh* … like porridge … *hoooooolgh* … yooz knows? *Hooooolgh* … when it … *hooooolgh* … *hoooolgh* … when it gets cold … *hoooolgh*, and yooz hasta put more … *hoooooolgh* … more warm beer in it? Yooz knows? Ain't it awsome?"

They continued like this for another hour, filling up massive paper bags with the biocontaminant nightmare.

Alaeth commented how great her abs were going to look after being starved for a week and then going through all the laughing and heaving while hanging out with the Troll. She was unexpectedly different from her twin sister – opposite even. By the fifth bag she actually was able to stand by the controls without running off, gagging from the reek.

In all they filled seventy-one eighty-lb bags with the vilest, most horrid, rankest-smelling shit the world had ever seen.

"Weez … *hoooooolgh* … hit da … *hoooooolgh* … jackpot … *hoooooolgh*!"

Chapter - 5

"Where's There A Bathroom When You Need One?!"

Calabac's throne room was now occupied by at least twenty guards. All of which were the giant armoured scave variety. They made a half-circle around Musky and myself, facing away from their master.

The room itself was huge. The ceiling was lost in darkness.

A mighty, armoured Cave-Troll sat quietly on the floor behind the throne, his breathing shallow but still audible, speaking of his sheer immensity.

The Stealer, or who I assumed was the Stealer, stood at the foot of the dais, his hands held behind his back, mouth closed but in an emotionless wax-like smile.

My Ratstafarian comrade's still form lay beside me, his nose bleeding and his breathing all but ceased. I was still gagged and unable to speak so I threw a few choice (if not coherent) insults at the evil sorcerer.

"What?" His voice was nasally and high-pitched. It did not fit his admittedly intimidating outward appearance at all.

I was unable to respond to his demand being gagged, and this made him even more agitated. He stood again and tapped his foot. Click, click, click went the sound of his long painted toenails against the cold, hard stone.

He looked first to the guards, and then to the Stealer, and then back to the guards again. "Am I thuwounded by imbithews? Wiw thomeone pweez take hith gag off?"

The Stealer moved immediately. His smile never changed, he never even blinked, as he kneeled in front of me and reached behind my head to untie my gag. I almost thought he was going to kiss me and wished he had untied my hands too, so I could slap him for not first buying me dinner at least.

The gag was gently removed. Then the Stealer stepped backward, still smiling, his face like a pale white mask.

"Now ... thpeak, pwithonew. Thpeak or I wiw..." He was interrupted by my response.

"Yes. I am," I replied.

"You owe what?" he asked, somewhat taken by surprise.

"I am that same G'nome," I confessed.

"Ah. I thee." He strolled back to his throne again and sat. "Whayo ith the Weh'wick?"

"Th ... the what?" I replied.

"The Weh'wick you thtoopid wittow G'nome. Owe you deaf?" He was furious. His fingernails dug deep into the armrest of his throne of bones.

"Weh'wick?" I asked. "I know nothing of a weh'wick. I don't even know what that is." I tried to stall for time. I needed to think of a plan of escape fast and I had to do so with Musky in tow. '*If only he would regain consciousness,*' I thought.

I looked around the chamber some more; this time my eyes were adjusted to the lighting enough for me to see small rectangular openings in the base of the walls to either side of the room. These were just over a foot tall and looked to be ventilation shafts of some sort. Even from this distance I could tell these had not been cleaned in many years. The dust and cobwebs were inches thick.

"If you do not wevee'ew the wocathion of the weh'wick, I wiw have the gowdth taow thith petht'th wimbth fwum hith body. I have no mowa need fow him. Theya 'ith pwenty mowe whewe he came fwom." He gestured to Musky, as small points of white light appeared in his eyes like single stars in a night sky.

I looked to Musky. The poor kid was blowing bubbles with his nose in his own blood.

Suddenly – this time it was a good suddenly – suddenly his eye opened and closed twice. He was winking at me.

I had a plan as soon as I realized that he was not unconscious. "The case is in my magic bag, but you cannot get it out. Only I can access it," I explained. "Untie my hands and I will get it for you."

"Do you think I am thtoopid?" Calabac asked. "You wiw weach into that bag and poo-ow out thum thoewt of devithe that wiw no doubt athitht you to ethcape. I wiw not be tho eethewy detheived wittow twick'thter." He grinned with satisfaction.

"What can I do? Eh? I am barely under a foot tall, I have arthritis, a stone in my left shoe and I need to poop so bad I am barely holding it in. Unless there is a bathroom nearby I can run to, I think your army of rat things and your buddy over there behind the big chair can handle me if I get out of line. But you need to promise me something ... on your word as a magus." The ruse was underway ... I hoped.

He thought about this for a moment and then pointed to one of the guards. "You! Point thomething dangewouth at him. If hith handth go anywhewe othew than in hith pouch, thubdue him ... painfoowy"

One of the scave readied a big steel mace, winding up to whack me outta next week. The Stealer then walked around to my back to untie me.

I put my hands in the air and spoke. "There ... you see? No tricks. I am gonna reach into my bag now and take out the shrunken case with the relic in it. Don't hit me with that thing, okay?" I said to the scave guard.

I reached into my pouch and began to search for my dart gun, just in case my plan failed. "I need you to promise to let my friend here go. Do that and I will assist you without resistance," I lied. I was gonna do something that I was not sure would even work, but it was our only option aside from cooperating with Calabac.

In fact I had no idea what a *Sav'ma'ass* hootspa did at that time but I shall explain for you now as the next part of the tale might otherwise seem confusing: The *Sav'ma'ass* hootspa is what is referred to as a *one-off*. It is a power that manifests into an effect that is most needed at the time of casting, and its level of effect is governed by the amount of change one causes in the multiverse as compared to one's own relative power status. I was not very powerful, yet I was chosen by a god to work his will in the material world. I figured that was a pretty big job for such a small guy and as such – the hootspa should be really impressive.

So in two blinks of an eye, a sort of request went out to the council of D.O.O.B.I.E.S., *the Council of Deities, Oracles, Omnipotent Beings and Inter-dimensional Enchanted Societies - or* the powers that govern all hootspa in the multiverse for a *Sav'ma'ass* hootspa. I later learned also that the word *Sav'ma'ass* actually meant: *'I'm very drunk, help me home so I don't get arrested."* This was very old G'nomish from long ago, before the chaos invasion of the G'nomish empire had taken place and from a time when the great herb forests that now stood hundreds of feet tall were mere saplings.

"Well," I began. "I can't seem to find it. That just makes me mad. Lemme try again, maybe it's…" I held out my left hand and the bracelet/ring of levitation flashed as I released the *Sav'ma'ass* hootspa.

I quickly drew my right hand from the pouch and pointed my dart pistol at the guard with the mace. I fired and it hit the creature in the throat just under its chin.

It was at this moment that I also had a sudden…oy…sudden unnaturally strong urge to get out of that throne room.

I noticed that everyone in the room was frozen in place. This included the Stealer and Calabac. I wanted to load up a venomous dart right there. One that would *kill*. I wanted to shoot Calabac in the eye with it, but the urge to leave right then was too strong to resist. The hootspa was working and it was driving my actions to save my life.

Aside from no bathrooms anywhere to be seen since the one I found Vermin in, the Mellow One was surely watching over me. Still, another bathroom would have been nice. Just sayin'.

I used the last of my pre-prepared hootspas from my ring and shrunk Musky small enough to fit in my pouch. Then, after stealing Calabac's wallet, I ran for the nearest ventilation shaft.

I was not more than twenty or thirty feet deep into the dark, dusty duct-work when suddenly I could hear Calabac yelling commands and insults at his minions. I could hear the *TH*s and *W*s flying from every direction, so I am sure he was giving everyone in that room royal hell.

If I had stayed long enough to kill him I could have missed; in any case they would have caught me. The hootspa was not as strong as I had thought it would be. Yet I could feel this tingly feeling all over me and thought perhaps the hootspa was still working in some way I didn't understand.

I ran as fast as I could into the duct-work of the fortress. The only thing Calabac had that could catch me in those tight quarters was the thousands-strong plague of rats under his command and they would already be in the process of being instructed to do just that.

Although the duct-work was small enough for a G'nome, several rats would still fit side by side, and more than two or three at a time would be too much for me to handle. I would be overwhelmed by sheer numbers.

Then it hit me; Musky could run on all fours like the scave. In fact the scave were carbon copies *of* him, minus the dreadlocks and gold tooth and nice demeanor! He could move down here and I could use his help. Besides, I hadn't had Sabbath for awhile. I ran out of matches earlier and needed a light.

I pulled his tiny form from the bag and canceled the hootspa. He turned into his natural size and winked at me.

Then, gesturing for me to follow, he moved quickly, deeper into the shafts.

For a moment I stood there disappointed, loaded pipe and no fire to be found. Then I gave in and ran after him as fast as I was able.

I followed his tracks in the dust, noticing that these ducts had no moving air at all. They were not functioning; perhaps unfinished by the Gnomes who were still building the massive structure?

I continued along for almost an hour, following Musky deeper into the duct-work. There was no way he could know where he was. There were only tracks from one passerby, and that was him. He could not have been here ever before in his lifetime. I wondered how he could know where he was going.

I came to a six-way intersection with two of the shafts going down on a forty-five degree angle. Musky was waiting for me there.

I also noticed that there were no signs pointing out the direction to the washrooms. I still had to poop real bad. It almost made me wish Calabac had tossed me into a prison cell so I could have used the toilet.

"Mun," he whispered. "we be needin' ta be real quiet like for da next bit irey?" He looked worried.

"Why? What is it?" I asked.

"Dis be da lower level a dis 'ere place. Dere be a small army a Goblins, an dere be a dragon too. So we be needin' ta be real quiet. You pickin' up what I be layin' down, mun?" He looked so serious. More so than I had ever seen him.

"Of course, my friend. Lead on," I said, placing my hand on his shoulder to reassure him.

"I be tankin' ya too; fer bringin' I along when ya escaped Calabac. My friend, ya are." He smiled and then slinked away without a sound.

"Shut up Gladys. Nobody's hearin' nothing." I spoke the hootspa incantation softly and was engulfed in a globe of utter silence. No one would hear me even if I screamed. I then continued on following the tracks Musky left in the dust.

I estimated I was now four hundred feet beneath the main level of the fortress. We had descended many ramps and short vertical drops and had arrived at a section that I assumed was for drawing the warm air from the volcano's bowels to the many sections of the great subterranean structure.

I eventually came to an area where the shaft tapered out to be three feet wide and two feet tall. In this area the rats could overwhelm us easily with no exits in sight, so I moved as fast as

I could for almost a mile while the passage continued without an end in sight.

Even though the hall was getting larger, for me it was becoming sort of claustrophobic. The whole place was a death trap if those rats came. The fear was real. The threat was real.

Finally I came to a circular chamber eight feet tall and twenty feet wide. It took a moment to find Musky's tracks but I managed to spot them after a close investigation.

There were sixteen exits from this chamber, two of which went straight up and down via a wrought iron spiral staircase in the center of the room. None of which were bathrooms.

Oy.

Musky located a large tile in the floor that was actually a door in disguise. He lifted the tile and beneath it was a vertical shaft with a ladder descending into darkness far below.

And here I was hoping it was a secret toilet.

Oy.

To my right, somewhere down one of the many passages, I could hear the rasping, shallow breathing of something extremely big, while to my left I heard what sounded like revelry and music.

I descended the ladder, closing the trap door behind me. Once the door was secured I followed Musky down the seemingly endless ladder and finally came to a stop three hundred more feet beneath the surface.

Just then the music was getting louder and there was yelling. I deduced that a group of ruffians of some sort had been coming toward us as we descended the ladder. They were now entering the same room above that we had just exited. I moved to be closer to the wall and hid myself in the shadows there.

I could hear Goblin voices far above me in the other chamber. These were the squeaky lesser Goblins of the west mountains, those who lived in the tunnels and caverns of the near surface. They were arguing something about the "boss" not wanting to anger the "baron" and so they were going to renege on a contract, or something like that. They were, as expected for Goblins, quite drunk and rowdy.

At this moment I also took note of the fact that the ladder I had just descended was Gnome-sized.

The room I was in far below was a small, round chamber with only one other exit. Musky's trail led off into the dark hall beyond. I exited the room and followed the tracks down a long dark corridor that was five feet tall and three feet wide.

Here there were sconces in the walls only thirteen inches from the floor, and these were not the regular torch-holding variety. These were very much like the ones back home, used to hold fire stones in the greenhouses. The similarities were remarkable.

After almost 30 minutes I stopped for a short break. I was tired and out of breath.

There I indulged in a short snack of potato wedges and cheese dip. After a brief respite I began to use my schmauz to figure out where we were in relation to the volcano, and where Lillia's sister was being held (at least I thought she was in there, and with good reason).

We were literally more than a mile away from the mountain fortress and at least a thousand feet beneath it, and still no bathroom in sight. Oy.

Ahead, the hall began to curve to the northeast, and by the time I had caught up to Musky waiting at the top of a set of stairs that descended into a large room, we had traveled another two hours from the bottom of the Gnome-sized ladder.

"Musky, how do you even know where you are going?" I asked. "No one has been here for centuries." We had passed through places with multiple exits both up and down, not to mention the hundreds of side corridors we had passed by. We had made many turns and even ascended and descended a few times.

"Doze unda-tings told I, and gave I dis." He produced a small piece of paper with a map drawn on it. "Dem done told Musky ta bring ya'll da way down 'ere so dat ya cun know what ya' are s'posed ta be doin', mun. Dem says ta Musky dat you cun stop all dis evil if I be bringing ya ta where ya s'posed ta be.

"Now ya see dat big round door dere, mun?" He gestured down the stairs. "Musky c'not open dat dere one. Doze unda-tings say dat only you cun do dat. So ya might be getting ta work 'ere and doing what ya s'posed ta so we cun all go 'ome." He pointed to where the hall began to get larger and turn into a set of stairs that descended into a chamber.

"There doesn't happen to be a bathroom on that map of yours, is there?" I was starting to get weak in the old "O" ring. I knew that soon I would just have to squat and get it over with if we didn't find a toilet somewhere. Oy.

I then moved to the top of the stairs to see that they descended into a big, round room about thirty feet down, and ended right in the center.

I looked down the stairs at a large, round door on the wall opposite the entrance. To my astonishment I saw *G'nomish* writing over the arch of the portal. The door itself had no handle or lock to speak of, and was made from precious metals and stones. A marvel of design and aesthetic appeal as only a G'nomish craftsman could achieve. It must have been worth a fortune!

"Crap," I said.

"What be wrong, mun?" Musky asked.

"I just pooped my pants."

CHAPTER - 6

"OUT THROUGH THE IN DOOR"

The chamber had decorative frescoes and many ceiling murals that I didn't notice at first. I was mesmerized ... excuse me - *Klezmerized* by the door itself.

I moved slowly down the stairs and toward the door, Musky right behind me. As I reached the bottom of the stairs I could see the murals on the walls and ceiling clearer. In fact it was all one great painting.

I was so shocked by what I saw. I sat on the bottom step and gazed around me with wonder. I was speechless and somewhat afraid from the painting and what the story before me depicted.

Then I remembered my pants were full of crap. I cleaned up behind the stairs while Musky kept watch and soon I was back to normal. I moved closer to the murals at that point, to study them further, and I was taken aback by what I discovered.

This was a painting of *me*.

I'm not kidding you! I was depicted standing at the door with all sorts of nastiness behind me and I was placing my hand on the center of a great strap of platinum that lay across the middle of the portal.

I looked at Musky and said, "Okay, so if I touch the door those monsters there will appear and kill us, or those monsters are trying to kill us so I should open the door ... which one?" I then remembered the writings above the door and took a closer examination of those.

"Well ya betta be doin' sumtin', mun, and in a 'urry too. We be needen to git back ta dat dere prison level so we cun put da rest a doze dere unda-tings in dat magic bag and get us out a dis place." He stood up now as this area was ten or so feet high, and three times that wide. "Whutchya be looking at dere, mun?"

"These, my friend, are words in ancient G'nomish. It is a dialect of G'nomish that is mostly no longer used. In case you hadn't noticed, those pictures on the walls are of *me*." I gestured to a scene depicting me conducting Sabbath at the very same spot where we were now standing. "That guy standing next to me with the long tail, beady eyes, whiskers, and the big colorful hat? I'm guessin that must be you."

"Well now I done and gone seen everatin', mun! Look at dat dere! Dats I diamond en gold toot, mun, look!" He pointed at the detail in the painting and it was just like he said.

Just then he gestured for me to be quiet and cupped an ear. "Dem Goblins be on da move agin. Dey're not s'posed ta be down as far as dem is, mun- an' not dis far away from dere posts. I not be knowing what dey is up to but I 'ear dem movin' around. Sounds like dey is 'avin a party, mun."

"You can hear them from this depth and distance?" I asked, and as he nodded, "Well then ... here goes." I placed my hand on the spot depicted in the painting and read the words written above the arch:

"You told me once; get outta my store. You told me twice; get outta my store. Three is a charm; get outta my store. Now I'm back again, so open the door!"

The door began to shimmer and on the surface, the platinum strapping melted and morphed into the shape of a platinum herb leaf. The fronds were perfect and full and almost dangled off the stock-wood door.

I dropped to one knee and pulled out my fire crystal pipe. I filled it with a nice sticky mixture I had prepared back at the winery and began to conduct Sabbath.

Musky also knelt and partook in the blessed ritual.

Once we were finished, having eaten of the fried potato wedges and cheese dip, and had drunk the wine of warped speed, I again turned to the door; this time I was *thoroughly* inebriated.

I placed my hand on the door again, in the center of the holy leaf, and read the last phrase: "*I brought monnnnneeey.*"

The door began to shimmer again; this time the platinum leaf morphed into a key that somehow ended up in my hand. In its place in the center of the door was a keyhole.

"Keep goin, mun. I be *screamin'* ta be knowin' what gonna 'appen next." Musky smiled, his *diamond* sparkling in the dim light.

I inserted the key and turned it as the light became slightly brighter with each fraction of movement.

The door split from top to bottom and opened inward as a double door. Even as it did so sacred herb leaves were growing from its surface and vines wrapped and wound across every inch.

Within seconds great sticky buds were growing from the door as the area beyond seemed to vomit sacred herb plants. It was as though they had been bound in there forever and only now did they have the chance to grow out of their cage. They had become so full of growth that they were actually animated with it.

The plants and vines writhed around Musky and me, yet they never blocked our passage. Again, as though these sacred herb plants were animated...

"Wait a second." I suddenly realized what was happening. "I pocket-dialed."

"What?" Musky asked.

"I had my hand in my pocket and activated my ring by mistake. I cast a hootspa for animating plants. Sorry," I explained. Once I canceled the hootspa the plant life stopped moving so much; however, it was still pretty amazing how it grew all around us so fast ... and ya can't knock the timing of it. Right?

We stepped through the open doors entering a gigantic cavern and stood at the top of an impressively large set of G'nome-sized stairs where great herb roots grew from the stone walls of the chamber. The trunks of the massive plants had been manipulated during growth to act as the banisters for the great staircase and even held sconces for firestones. This is where the mass of foliage and buds had come from. Again, what timing, though! Don't you think?

I noticed that there was a firestone in each one of the sconces but they did not shine. I was tempted to remove one to try and discern why this was so, but decided to wait.

The chamber was more of a subterranean mega- vault than a room or hall. This was far beneath any of the rest of the fortress' areas and quite some distance away as well. It was quite likely that Calabac didn't even know about this place. However, the same architecture was used here as in the upper levels; it just seemed older and more historic-feeling – if you can imagine such a thing. It was also more advanced- refined somehow. Like an evolved version of the styles used in the construction of the volcano fortress.

"Dere be no mushrooms in dat dere Sabbat smoke we done 'ad, right, mun?" He looked around amazed at the walls and ceiling of the giant vault.

It was many hundreds of feet wide and thousands of feet long. It stretched away into the darkness so far the ends were out of range for even *my* dark vision.

The stairs tapered outward to both sides, and became ever wider as we descended toward a perfectly level plane that had been cut out of the very roots of the mountain chain far above us.

These floors had not been tread upon in thousands of years, perhaps tens of thousands. Maybe even more.

Musky stopped me at the bottom. "Pops, I be tinkin dat you be needin' ta be da one 'oose steppin' down dere first and maybe I shoulda been stayin up dere." He gestured to the top of the steps.

"No, my friend, you are a vital part of what has been happening here and you cannot be excluded from these events. I plan to write you into the great holy book of Shiddumbuzzin and G'nomish children will read about you for thousands of years to come. You are going to help me teach my people to have no fear. Your lessons are very important, Musky, whether you know it or not. Please come." I gestured for him to join me.

The guards had taken his dagger and my umbrella, but they hadn't the brain cells to take my pouch and backpack. I removed my dart gun and ammo and gave them to him. "We cannot be sure of what we will find down here. We must keep our senses and be on guard … I'm eating some more mushrooms. You want some too?"

"Ya, mun! Give I some a doze. We be tripping already, what's a few 'allucinations gonna 'urt?" We waited for five minutes or several hours and then noticed the mushrooms start to take effect (or had been affecting us all along, I can't say which), and at last we *did* finally stand up and prepare to step down onto the floor of the ancient place.

"One small step for G'nome … one really small step for anyone else other than G'nome-kind," I said as I officially entered the great cavernous chamber.

…

"Nuttin's 'appenin', mun," Musky finally broke the silence.

"I noticed. Are you coming or what?" I began to walk forward into the vast mega-vault.

"I is, mun. Lead on." He was right by my side, lighting one of his sacred leaf twists. We walked along the middle of the massive cavern for thirty minutes, give or take. The floors never changed and remained level and smooth, cut perfectly from the beautiful green granite that made up this entire area.

False seams were cut on exact right angles to create the illusion of tiles and also for the practical use of directing water to the walls for drainage. The floor was more of a road than anything else.

It was too wide to be just a path and was cut so that it wound its way through a multitude of subterranean wonders consisting of phosphorescent minerals, fungi and flora.

We finally came to an area where massive pillars, forty feet wide and hundreds of feet tall, stood between floor and ceiling. These pillars were cut from the same green and black speckled granite the rest of the chamber was made from. The entire megalithic cavern was chiseled from one giant granite deposit.

Here the road became straight, and sloped downward slightly on a ten-degree gradient. The pillars seemed endless in number as they disappeared from site into the phosphorescent haze of the underworld atmosphere.

These mighty pillars were meticulously carved to resemble the trunks of the great sacred forests from home, with hundreds of G'nomes moving up and down a spiral ramp system wrapped around the massive columns, caring for the great tree, just like many of them did at home. The artistic achievements in the ancient place were monumental to say the least. Each one must have taken centuries of G'nome hours to create.

We moved along between the pillars which were, each and every one, a unique sculpture depicting different G'nomes doing different jobs among the limbs and fronds of the towering granite herb forest.

After several hours we came to an area where the distance between the pillars started to expand to either side of us, and the ceiling rose dramatically.

Here the road had become a plaza of sorts. The pillars then lined up in opposite directions around a great depression in the beautiful green stone floor ahead of us. This giant bowl-shaped depression was a vast reservoir of fresh water that dripped steadily from the ceiling miles above.

There among the menagerie of glowing colors and contrasting shadows, filling the peak of the subterranean ceiling, was ice.

Daylight, so diffused by hundreds of feet of frozen water that it at first appeared to be a separate grouping of green glowing lichens.

The sun, defiant against such obstacles, cast its rays through the ice disc above sending beams of chartreuse and golden greens over the subterranean environment adding to the mystical ambiance of the place.

At that point I had guessed that this was the inside of a mountain. A virtually endless source of fresh water melting in a slow steady stream far above gave life to the place.

I deduced that it was once a volcano. Hundreds of millions of years ago, it had died, and over the thousands of centuries it had stood, it had gathered layer upon layer of frost and moisture, creating its own frozen cone as a peak, and we were now standing in its belly, a place teeming with subterranean life.

Phosphorous mushrooms and other subterranean flora carpeted areas of the mega-chamber, in what appeared to be very purposefully positioned groups, so as to light the sidewalks to either side of the lake. Some of the glowing minerals were mounted on tall, decorative posts overlooking beginnings of foot paths leading off into the vast array of endless gardens and forests to either side of the artificial lake. There were actual herb trees here and where they grew there were also firestones, yet they were dead, and did not glow at all.

I looked out across the elliptical lake. It was an artificial crater in the floor of the hollow mountain that had filled a third of the way with the run-off from the melting peak.

The shoreline consisted of a series of steps that followed the contour of the giant reservoir and descended fifty or more feet to the water surface, also lit with a multicolored array of phosphorescent vegetation and crystals.

The water itself was sky blue and murky from the mineral run-off that came from the slowly melting glacier above.

Of course, everything here was placed by G'nomish hand, except the ice and mountain. Of this I had little doubt, but how long ago and why had no one back home ever known about this?

I was considered to be very well-educated, and in the field of ancient history and languages I am considered to be somewhat of an expert among my kind. So why did I know nothing of any of this? Where were all the G'nomes? What had happened to them all? It would have taken many generations of G'nomes to do this kind of work. Where did they all go?

I was beginning to notice G'nome-sized benches and small gazebos around the lake and along the sidewalk. There were small statues of animals I did not recognize, as well as what I deduced to be water fountains for drinking, now dry and acting as flower pots for wayward flora.

I then recalled the visions I received from Vermin's mind, the memories of the great siege and massacre of my ancestors and realized that this, *this* was the place the army of chaos had made war upon. Not the Sensimilia I knew at all. The question was: what was *this* place?

Here and there sitting precariously on the edge of steps or hanging at the end of their tethers were small pleasure craft, rowboats, and skiffs. At one point the water level had been up to the top of the shore.

The herb trees in this place were growing feral and out of control, but with only the light from the glowing plants and minerals and what little was offered by the sun's defused rays. How this was possible was another question I was unable to answer. They were even blossoming with small buds. Nothing impressive to look at, mind you, but flowering without firestones and caretakers? It made no sense at all. No herb plant can grow without firestones. This was common knowledge ... or so I thought.

"Musky, my friend." I pointed across the lake to a tall stone arch where it appeared the roads met and became one again to carry on deeper into the mega-vault. "Meet me there by that arch. I will go this way, you that way." I directed him to the left side, or west side of the lake. "Make a mental note of anything strange."

"You be kiddin I, right? Cuz I is sayin, what 'ere ain't *not* strange, mun?" he replied.

"Okay, okay. Strange-*err* than the rest ... and be careful. We still don't know if we are alone down here ... *schmoots*." I spoke the magic word and was transparent once again.

Musky immediately took off and began to move along the outside edge of the sidewalk among the overgrown fronds of the mighty herb bushes that had been reaching out over the stone plaza.

Black stains were all over the sidewalks from the oozing love juices of the female plants. I almost slipped in it several times.

The chamber itself was masterfully crafted. Even more fantastically detailed than the fortress above (and to the south-west) of us. I then deduced, using my superior G'nomish subterranean senses, that we had traveled underground through a series of tunnels and stairs right under the empire's mountain pass and into a mountain on the other side of the imperial highway.

This mountain and the one the fortress of Calabac was cut into, the volcano, were facing each other across the road to

Al'Lankamire...more or less. By the look of the architecture here I also deduced that this place was made by craftsmen far more skilled than those who were constructing the volcano fortress.

I was unable to fathom how someone could hollow out an entire mountain, yet here I was, standing in one, and it appeared to have been done by my very own people sometime in our *very* distant past.

I could see in the distance, against the walls of the cavern, titanic beams of metal that seemed to be attached in strange ways with way too many joints to make them of any use as a structural support system. Looking around I could make out that they all touched the ice disc in the peak of the mountain. It was like standing under an umbrella! I could also see at different intervals what appeared to be machinery and gadgetry much like that which my own dad worked with back home.

The whole arrangement was attached to the inside of the mountain. The mountain was supporting the machinery, not the other way around. I wondered: what was it all for?

Along the sides of the lake, and off into the overgrown gardens, were positioned huge, round mirrors on swivels that were in turn attached to platforms. The center of each platform had a huge firestone mounted in it. What these were for I could not guess at the time, but they were only fifty, or so, feet apart from each other and they surrounded the entire lake.

It took me almost thirty minutes to finally reach the great stone arch. I took note that I hadn't detected any fauna since we entered through the magically sealed doors in the mural room. This was comforting, at least, as the underworld has its share of wild and dangerous animals.

The arch stood far taller than I had previously estimated. In fact most everything did here. There was a haze in the air that sort of diffused and distorted distances. The further away you got from something the closer you really were, if that makes any sense. Or maybe it was just the mushrooms. Either way...

Where was I?

Oh, yeah, the great arch...

It towered seventy feet in the air and was at least fifty feet wide on the inside. Its pillars were carved into the semblance of two military officers or police officers or something of that nature. I could not recognize the uniforms at all. They faced each other from either side of the roadway, holding up a great curved black stone placard.

The massive stone billboard itself was at least twenty feet tall and fifty feet across. The whole divided roadway ran under it.

Across the wide stone surface of the placard were a multitude of firestones, all set only a fraction of an inch apart from each other. There had to be at least a few thousand of them. Their purpose eluded me as I approached the arch.

From where I was, directly under the arch, I was able to see that the road continued on, but was now degrading to a thirty-five degree slope downward. It also got wider, and I was able to see gardens of phosphorescent plant life all along the center of the roadway. Obviously to separate traffic going to and from ... *wherever* it was going to or coming from.

"Yo, Pops!" Musky hollered from near the lake shore, where he was now standing next to a small structure. "You be needin' ta see dis 'ere, mun!"

I made my way along the sidewalk towards him and was able to see, in the distance, the road and great pillars that we had passed through to reach this place.

Truly this was a thoroughfare for a lot of traffic, and even more. It was a vast garden and place of solace.

I could imagine families of folk from all different walks of life enjoying this place in peace. It was possibly the most beautiful place I had ever been in my life. What was also evident was the difference in sizes of the garden furnishings, benches and seats of all sorts. These were designed for a multitude of different-sized peoples. Most of these, however, were of G'nome-sized proportions.

But what were those megalithic struts and machinery in the distance for? They were *so* out of place there.

I reached Musky in good time, and canceled the invisibility hootspa with a tear of appreciation, for the beauty of the rest of the place, still in my eye. Here he pointed at a dusty glass case atop a stone pedestal.

I approached the case and could see that he had brushed away some of the dust to reveal a plaque and a small metal hammer.

The plaque read in old G'nomish: *In case of catastrophe, shatter glass window and activate lever.*

Under the dusty and lichen-covered glass panel I could see a chrome handle. A sort of lever or switch attached to what appeared to be a porcelain mount of some sort. Written in small type beside the hammer I read: "*Authorized Personnel Only.*"

I took a breath and decided this was not a catastrophe ... at least not yet. I then turned back to Musky and handed him some more mushrooms whilst having a few more myself. "Well done, my friend. I am sure this will come in handy at some point. Let's move along and see where this goes."

We downed the mushrooms and he followed me once again. Through the arch and onto the great highway of green and black granite we walked, looking like two tiny bugs on a rock.

This cavernous tunnel was more than a thousand feet high and at least one hundred feet across with a long stone barrier down the center. This barrier, resembling a long, low stone wall, was filled with plant life. I deduced it had been gardened at one point. Water dripped here and there from the shadowy ceiling above, but only in a straight line to fall among the mosses and fungi of the roadway median. In its present state the flora were overgrown and even small cracks in the stonework were now evident, testament to the power of the impressive roots of the plant life growing there. This median in turn had a break in it every two hundred feet, so one could theoretically use it to turn around without going against traffic. This would mean there would have to have been an impressive amount of movement along this road to justify such a stupendous undertaking. I dared not guess what we would find ahead of us.

CHAPTER - 7

"SENSIMILIA"

The G'nomish empire consisted of one city, Sensimilia, and many outlying villages. The city was older than we were and we had always thought that it really didn't matter who made it because we owned it now and no one was complaining.

I was now beginning to think that all of that was wrong. Our history had been changed, or written incorrectly, for this place, where I stood now with my friend Musky, was certainly G'nomish and certainly older than Sensimilia was thought to be.

The city of Sensimilia was a pretty impressive thing to behold. It was for all intents and purposes a great timepiece, designed to assist the residents in becoming as efficient as they could and still be stoned on herb.

Here's how it worked on any typical day: I would get up when my alarm went off; the city's gears and workings made it go off at a specific time, a time I had set previously and could adjust, as needed, by simply sending a message to the engineers of timekeeping in the city works departments. After awakening for a new day, I'd make my way to a shower (exactly fifteen minutes of water allocated by the city works daily. Credit given for less water used).

Everything moved every moment in the great city. It was, however, never clanking and rumbling like one might imagine. It was carefully lubricated and polished by the works departments and core of engineers that maintained the great jewel of the empire.

In the home, appliances changed to facilitate the cooking of different meals, furniture would change for different uses, from lounge chairs, to beds, then breakfast tables and so on. The whole city was part of the wondrous mechanical ballet that made living in it so convenient and ... well...wondrous at the same time.

Streets, sidewalks and other transit ways moved as well as some of the buildings, like the works department buildings, that always seemed to be across the street whenever you needed them. Gotta love those Works people. Thanks, folks, if you're reading.

Anyway, where was I?...

...Oh yeah.

In order for the city to function properly, however, each G'nome living there was allowed to use only his or her share of the city's water supply and other resources all provided by the city. These were, thankfully, generous and of good quality if not decadent and so it wasn't so bad at all.

The heating and steamworks of the grand metropolis were provided by a spectacular set of giant sixty-foot-thick tungsten rods that theorists guessed were attached to the planet's core somehow. This was beyond all G'nomish skill and technology and so the actual "way" the city *functions* remains a mystery.

We know that we get heat from the rods and that through an ingeniously designed webwork of heat-conductive wires, pipes, ducts, and an assortment of other devices and materials, we get the energy needed to move things. We also get pressure from steam, and *that* moves things too. All of these conduits change position constantly to facilitate the various needs of the city, and to transfer their energy to whatever function is needed at any given time. From cooking to moving a piano up to a third floor window, all things were driven by the VAPE Department, and the VAPE itself.

The VAPE is the great machine that requires no maintenance at all. It is the device that actually turns the subterranean ice into steam and other, hotter vapors. The VAPE department is the crews who maintain all the machinery attached directly to the VAPE.

VAPE stands for Vapor Aeration, Pressure, and Energies.

If one needed to heat a bowl of soup, one would pull a lever to turn on the stove. Then one would fill a pot and heat the soup. After that the stove would become a sink with hot water dispensing to wash the dishes with. Quite a mechanical wonder. You really cannot appreciate it until you actually see it working.

The city proper housed exactly four hundred and twenty thousand G'nomes. Each family had a maximum four hundred and twenty members, and there were enough open residences to house four hundred and twenty visitors.

Do you really have to ask?

In the suburbs and surrounding countryside there was an additional population that floated around the six hundred thousand mark. These were farmers, miners, manufacturers and craftsmen who were the backbone of the great city. In turn, for supplying the city with food and other supplies, Sensimilia would supply its rural citizens with hospitals, entertainment, education and culture in general, as well as a standing police service and emergency response centers across the subterranean countryside. The technologies these services used came from the laboratories and technician centers in the great city.

These people and those of the city together make the empire's population around one million one hundred and seventy-six thousand, eight hundred and twenty G'nomes. This is a constant, give or take. It has always been this way as far as I could recall, or learned about.

The place where I now explored with my Ratstafarian comrade would have required about the same number of G'nomes to create...or perhaps even more. The mysteries kept piling up.

We traveled another hour along the spirally descending highway, deeper beneath the mountain's roots. There were vast distances where to either side there were open areas where the flora was growing wild. Here in these places no development had ever taken place other than to cut the road through. In other areas along the road side we found tiny abandoned villages. I deduced that these were sort of stop-overs for weary travelers where there would be places to shop, eat, and rest. These gave substance to the legends of my ancestors being powerful merchants.

Here and there were track systems and vast cable systems, but for what purpose I still did not know. Perhaps for moving supplies and commodities up and down the descending highway? I could only guess.

It was many hours before we came to the end of the spiraling highway. We had traveled for several miles along the great descending road until we finally came upon another massive cavern.

Suddenly the tunnel got larger and opened up like a great funnel. The road, too, became much wider and after some distance began to split and go off in different directions.

Here, still, the area was filled with phosphorescent fungi and other glowing plant life.

We exited the highway tunnel into the vast chamber and could now see that we had found some sort of abandoned city.

Where we stood was an area where a sort of bridge spanned over many roads and pathways below to facilitate moving caravans and visitors on their journeys to varying areas of the massive cavernous underground vault.

Here and there we encountered exits off the main road that descended into the streets below. All the while we too were descending, but we stayed on the main road as it was straight and easy to navigate.

Exotic and colorful flora hung in great heaps over the sides of the bridge, glowing and offering us a means to avoid the many roots and fallen debris that riddled the roadways.

Finally our path leveled out and entered the mighty chasm, miles across, its edges so far away I could not see the walls. The city was all around us and it looked like it was made for people my size ... for the most part.

Here, where we now stood, the roads curved in a circle to either side and away from us while the road we were on maintained its perfectly straight direction.

This cavern was even larger than the last one...*much* larger, and after a few hours we arrived at a four-way junction where the road curved out of sight to the left and right around a mass of structures. Straight ahead the road continued into a haze of phosphorescent light and subterranean dust.

From where we were standing there would be nothing but mountains above us on the surface world.

This place was very much like the way the city of Sensimilia was designed, with many roads circling a central point. These roads, in turn, were intersected with straight roads all leading to the center from the outside ring. Much like a spider's web.

This chamber was at least ten miles across. Even bigger than my home town.

I knew I was now almost *four* miles beneath the surface of the world as well as being almost six miles toward Briarwood from where we first entered the divided highway, and another four miles north. My schmauz was working perfectly.

Here we discovered an assortment of buildings cut straight out of the black basalt. The green stuff was higher up. The black stone was patched here and there with colorful glowing lichens, mosses and fungi of all sorts. Great stalactites and stalagmites jutted from ceiling and floor and were actually incorporated into the architecture. Some had been hollowed out and made into huge many-roomed buildings.

The ones that hung from the subterranean ceiling had grand stairs and elevation devices hanging from them to allow access to the megalithic super-structures.

Above and to the east, there would be a great marshland and river that led out and across the countryside for many miles to finally find the ocean. We, however, were traveling away from that. We were making our way along and under the eastern edge of the mountains steadily north and slightly east.

We crossed curving streets where, in the intersections, there were great and wonderful works of sculpture in fountains and other decorative structures. To each side these roads curved out of view while abandoned buildings were lined up to either side like motionless sentinels.

It was soon obvious that these buildings in the immediate area were designed for use by many different races, much like Briarwood was. The difference was that the architecture here was far more advanced.

It was a lot like the garden and lake area far above us. It was G'nomish built and it was old beyond belief, yet of a far more advanced society.

The gardens on the upper level and the great green pillars, along with the lake and arch, were constructed for the aesthetic, (as well as a purpose still not evident).

A sort of park for the residents of this city and for visitors traveling from the surface, perhaps? Or at least this is what I was beginning to believe. I wondered again about the machines and the ice cap. It was all too confusing and new, so I decided to just carry on and hope to find some answers.

We traveled along, what appeared to be the main thoroughfare through the vast metropolis, for several miles, and after a few more hours we finally came to a hub of sorts where the road we were on ended perpendicular to a curved road where the other streets all met in the same way. The curved road went around a large circular lot filled with wild flora. This was the exact center of the city.

Here we pretty much collapsed as we had not slept in more than a day, and food was something we had almost forgotten about. Eating, however, was not in the plan, it would seem, for both Musky and I passed out from sheer exhaustion.

It was several hours before I was awakened by my furry friend. "Hey, mun. Musky be looking around a bit and I be tinkin dat dere be no enemies 'ere, so we be okay ta look around s'more." He smiled.

I sat up, and suddenly the reality of what was happening all came back to me.

It was incredible, amazing even. A vast ancient civilization built this megatropolis, and the more I looked around the more it all felt sort of familiar.

The clearing we had been sleeping in seemed to be more alive than it was before we rested. The glowing was more evident, and the light seemed to actually warm us.

I could imagine that once there was a beautiful garden of glowing lichens and mosses in this place. Even after the eons that had passed since anyone had lived here, it was evident that someone took care of these gardens at one time. Now the plants seemed to have grown out of control, but not overly so. *'Curious,'* I thought. Yet now that we had more light we were both able to make out more of the details in our surroundings.

In the center of the garden stood a large gazebo-like building. The roof was a massive dome that was easily three hundred feet across. The 8 pillars that held up the roof were nothing less than actual living herb trees, one hundred feet tall. Their branches wove in and out of a thousand openings in the roof structure. Obviously, the dome was constructed so as to be lifted slowly ever higher as the great trees continued to grow.

We approached the building, my stomach full of butterflies, my nerves on edge, my hopes and dreams being realized. Even as we ascended the only staircase to the grand entrance of the structure I was daring to hope. I looked up in wonder to see great buds the size of watermelons hanging from the branches high above my head!

It looked as though I stumbled upon some secret and lost civilization of the G'nomes. Can you imagine such a thing happening to *you*? I was so happy I changed my shorts back by the entrance to these caverns, 'cuz right then I had to again.

After I did so we stood for a moment looking into the structure in amazement. It was empty.

No, really. I expected to see benches and statues and all sorts of stuff there. I thought we had found an actual *temple* to Shiddumbuzzin. Instead all there was before us was a flat dusty floor, hundreds of feet across.

"Look, mun!" Musky pointed to the center of the floor where he was now standing. I could see something written into the stonework there.

I approached the area and helped him brush away the dust that had been accumulating over the countless eons the place had been abandoned.

My hand came across a small depression in the floor- a hole really – and it appeared to have been made to have something inserted into it. A key perhaps? Who knew?

The writing was in old G'nomish, as opposed to ancient G'nomish or modern G'nomish. Ancient G'nomish had a lot of '*hithers*' and '*sooths*' and weird words no one uses any more. Modern G'nomish was easier and not so formal. Like saying *Hi* as opposed to *Hello*. Old G'nomish was like all those words your grandparents use, but you do not. Such as *Jovial, Lavatory* and *Assistive urinating devices* – that sort of thing.

Anyway...where was I?

Oh yeah...

The words inscribed into the stone floor were old G'nomish. They had been written so the reader would have to walk around the tiny hole in order to read them without being upside-down. I walked around the little hole and removed my firestone pipe from my pouch. I filled it with sticky heaven and lit it up. As the flame touched the herb, creating a small ember of light within the light of the pipe itself, something occurred to me.

Read!

I remembered I was supposed to be reading so I put on my spectacles and began.

Insert Firestone Here.

"Aha!" I remembered the handful of firestones I bought from Azh Stellark's place when I got my umbrella...I loved that umbrella. Man, that put a stain on my white leisure suit to know that I would never see it again. Gimme a break. I liked it a lot and have never seen one again that was so stylish and yet functional at once. What a loss.

Anyway...where was I?

Oh yeah...

Looking around further I realized something. "Hmmm ... I wonder?" I thought out loud.

"What you be tinkin' a, mun?" Musky asked as he followed me around the chamber.

"I need a broom," I said.

"Why you be needin'..." he began, but I cut him off as I remembered who I was and hootspa'd the room.

"*Fenkli, fenkli, fenkli. Woospa woospa woopsi doo!*" A great vortex of wind was created and it took up all the dust and refuse that was in the structure and even out in the garden and on part of the sidewalk and street too! As the dust was drawn up to the ceiling it was compressed into a ball that got smaller and smaller until it vanished altogether. I was then able to see a design cut into the stone work of the floor.

It was a giant herb leaf. The hole in the floor was directly in the middle of the leaf and as I studied the mosaic further, I could see that each frond ended at the tip with a similar hole; in fact, each hole was exactly the same.

I deduced that each one required a firestone. All six were empty. I retrieved the handful of glowing amber crystals from my pouch and was not even a little surprised to find that there were exactly six.

"Providence?" I asked Musky.

He had been following me in more ways than just walking along. He had been watching me and figuring it all out on his own. Musky was far smarter than his use of humanese made him appear. "I be tinkin' dat be quite da coincidence dat you be 'avin doze wichya when ya be needin dem most." He winked.

We then placed a firestone in each hole and to my astonishment they fit perfectly. Just like the way my underwear used to fit when I was younger. You know? Not falling down every five minutes. I hate that!

At last I returned to the center of the structure. From that position I could now discern that the stem of the great leaf petroglyph actually faded into part of the stairway up to the gazebo platform- like a sacred path. This gave me a feeling of growth and ascension when I climbed them.

"My friend," I began, taking Musky's hand and drawing him closer to my side, "this is a monumental occasion for the G'nomes and Gnomes alike. I am happy that you are here to share it with me. Perhaps in the days to come we will all come together and know of..."

"Ya, ya, mun. I too. Get on wit it. Da suspense be killin' I!" he interrupted with a huge grin on his face. "I not ever be part a sumtin' like dis b'fore. I be avin skill and all, but, mun! Dis be like freakin 'istory en such, en I be part of it all along!" He was really enjoying all of this now. I was glad.

Forgetting what I was saying and opting to continue anyway, I gently dropped the last firestone into the hole and it fit perfectly as suspected. Light began to move outward along the floor, following the outline of the sacred leaf. It was like the golden amber glow was actually liquid and was leaking out of the gem and slowly flowing through the cut lines. I had never seen firestones do this before.

Moments later the light followed other lines in the floor and out into the garden, then into the street and ultimately out into the entire city.

We walked out to the top of the stairs and looked across the place in awe as the entire mile-high chamber began to light up. Huge veins of firestone riddled the ceiling and mingled with the countless phosphorescent mosses and fungi. These veins lit up like the light of day in some places and the whole city seemed to come alive with its own life force.

For a moment I was forced to cover my eyes, the light was so bright and intense, but soon I dared to look again, and I was amazed at what I was seeing.

The gazebo itself had been rising in the air, so gently and slowly that we hardly noticed, and soon we had risen almost thirty more feet above the street. Its roof would ultimately rise to over two hundred feet tall.

We could see much of the surrounding area now as the garden, too, was rising. In the end what I discerned to be the Temple of Shiddumbuzzin would stand on top of a gentle hill covered with gardens that lay seventy feet above the rest of the city.

We both turned around at the same time and returned to the center of the temple. That's when I immediately noticed something else miraculous happening, and held Musky back.

There before our eyes, materializing out of thin air and covering the entirety of the gazebo interior, was another garden. This one had a fountain in the middle and was full of Gnomes (the garden, not the fountain). In the center of the fountain stood the Bong.

"Look there, Musky!" I pointed out what was happening.

"We be needin' more mushrooms, mun!" he said. "'Ow 'bout it?"

I distributed some mushrooms to him and then took a few myself. We then prepared for Sabbath, as I thought it would be appropriate given the circumstances.

The scene before us was solidifying. At first I thought it was only an illusion, perhaps to show me something I was forgetting, like letting Durik and the Gnomes out of the magic Bong box, but I could see, after a bit, that it actually *was* them, and that *place too*.

Of course when I was there *with* the Bong I was able to discern that there was some sort of edge to the pocket dimension, like a wall or barrier, but what I had no way of knowing was that it was a piece of dimension that I could insert into this world and all I needed was a spot that was exactly the same size that had an etherealistic connection on a quantum-spiritual level, thus fabricating an extra/intra-dimensional portal and diffusing the fabric of reality long enough to convince the materializing components into believing they are, in fact, on an inverted dimensional-realitizing level, real and only a part of the whole which is the area it is manifesting into. It's kind of like the way a spirit materializes into our dimension...

...

I lost ya, didn't I?

I told the big guy you wouldn't understand all this interdimensional hooha. I am sorry. *Gaw-awdd* insisted I explain it in detail. He likes technical stuff.

Now...where was I?

Oh yeah...

That whole place and everything in it, that was inside the magic box where the Bong was, continued to materialize before our eyes. How did I know this? Because I am smart *and* a hootspologist. Don't ask silly questions.

That's when it hit me. Look at all this empty prime real estate! I'm gonna make a fortune selling vacation condos!

Chapter - 8

"Speak of The Devil"

Well...all this talk about poop has inspired me to take a short break. I leave you all now in the capable hands of Sergeant Beelzebub Hornid, a patrolman out of Briarwood, whose beat, so to speak, was the west road to Al'Lankamire, the imperial capital. For those of you who have not been paying attention, that is the same road the boys ambushed the Talotian assassins on and the very same road that goes between the volcano where Calabac (gawd, I hate that guy) built his fortress and the hollow mountain where my ancestors built that lovely garden with the reservoir and the nice arch. Remember? With the statues and stuff?

Anyway...where was I?

Oh yeah...

The good Sgt. was witness to an incredible event a few days' ride west of Briarwood on that same imperial highway. It sounded exciting and I actually couldn't find anyone else who was qualified to write the next part, while I used the can, so I am letting him give it a go. I heard he was looking for a break (sort of a foot-in-the-door) into the writing biz. I thought I'd give him a hand.

He's coming up right after this next wildlife vignette.

Help the kid out. He's supposed to be pretty good.

Chapter - 9

"Aaaaah! Aaaaaaah! Aaaaaaaaaaaaaaaaa!"

The following wildlife vignette is brought to you by;

Sensimilia Foot Inspection Agency

"Keeping toe-jam out of your cheese since the dawning of time."

"A service from your elected officials"

<u>Dragons:</u> There are two basic types of dragon in the world of Oona: the classic fire-breathing six limbed *Draconai* and the *Wurms*.

Draconai are what could be referred to as common dragons. Their colour varies according to their chosen habitat. Those living in the high mountains are grey and stark white, where those living in the deep sea are black beyond description, while those in the desert are tanned brown and reddish in hew. Some are green, some are blue, and there have even been a few violet dragons as well... even a *rainbow* dragon. But that is another story altogether.

When one refers to a dragon in Oona it is almost always the Draconai that one refers to. They have four limbs for terrestrial travel, and two for aerial (or in some cases aquatic), called wings. The wings are, simply speaking, extremely strong elongated arms that end with very long webbed fingers - much like a bat's wing.

Draconai have long necks with relatively small heads. They have long snouts and an overly elasticized pouch under their lower jaws and throat. This pouch can be filled with a flammable gas from their stomachs and ignited with a scraping of their tongue over a special tooth containing a natural abundance of a mineral that creates a spark when rubbed, thus creating combustion of the aforementioned gasses. A flaming burp if you will.

Draconai have several pairs of horns on their heads, as well as barbs on their tails.

Young Draconai can spit a flaming jelly-like substance which they ignite using the same technique as the gas ignition.

Old adults are able to process calcium from their diets and mix this with crushed stone in their gullets. This they are able to use like the jelly and gas weapons, but this substance consists of burning mineral waste- or magma.

The largest Draconai ever recorded was sixty feet long with an eighty-foot wing-span. She was a "Bearer of Species," which is a name given to the largest of her kind and to those who have birthed more than one hundred offspring. These are few and far between for shortly before they reach this age they begin to go mad.

It is at this *mad* stage that the Draconai sometimes lose the use of their wings. Their other appendages also begin to mutate so dramatically fast it causes them extreme agony. At these times the Draconai will either die or find a place to go into hibernation for many years. Few of these ever awaken again. Those that do are much larger and different-looking than when they began their long slumbers. Those few who do awaken find themselves with no memories and a real bad attitude. Those few are known as Wurms.

The Wurm is a monster beyond belief. Thought to be the only living thing capable of challenging a mountain Troll, these are the oldest of their species.

So old are Wurms, that they have personally evolved over the eons and no longer resemble their previous selves at all. Or each other.

Due to the monster's immense weight and size they eventually lose the remains of their wings to atrophy. This makes them angry and irritable, and even violent to anyone trying to interact with them in any way.

Wurms are so huge and territorial that only one or two at most exist at any one time. As soon as a new one comes onto the stage there is a fight and only one survives ... always.

They are *cataclysmic*.

Wurms cannot communicate in language as they have forgotten their lives as dragons, from before they became Wurms. Trying to speak with one is pure folly as they always attack and can lay an entire city to waste in minutes.

Wurms appear to be massive nine-hundred-foot-long (or more) lizards. They can have spines, horns, extra tails, and all sorts of mutations, but they always have four or more legs. One was more than a mile long but died of old age before he was able to cross a huge river. His skeleton is stretched across that river to this day and travelers have used it for centuries as a bridge that now spans a canyon where the river once was.

There has not been a reported case of a Wurm inside the Empire's domain in recent history, yet the Emperor and his predecessors have always kept a brigade of "Dragon Slayers" trained and ready should one ever come to be.

A Wurm could lay waste to many cities and even entire nations if it were not dealt with in a timely fashion. They are the ultimate natural catastrophe.

For more information about Dragons or for a copy of this wildlife vignette contact: The G'nomish Film Board Society, Sixty Six-Packs Street, Allthewater, Sensimillia, 420420420.

Chapter - 10

"Enter the Dragons"

by Bealzebub Hornid

The west road was quiet that day. I remember seeing only two merchant wagons coming in from nearby farms for the early harvest festival back in Briarwood.

It seemed strange that the road was so clear of travelers, but even stranger was the smell in the air that morning, like every hearth in the countryside was burning wet wood. Strange, because there hadn't been rain in that area for a week.

I had been traveling along my route for half a day when I spotted it the first time. It was just a speck in the clouds moving erratically at first but as I followed, it took on a more sinister profile.

I crested a hill overlooking a valley, and there I was able to see the thing clearer just 2 miles away.

The creature's great bat-like wings clawed at the sky as though trying to tear it open. Even from that distance I could see it was huge. I followed it for another four hours before losing it over some tall trees on another high hillock.

Twenty minutes later I reined in my steed and hid her in the forest, then continued on toward the hill crest on foot.

I began to see smoke rise up over the trees and blow toward the east. As I came closer to the crest of the hill I began to hear screaming and the sounds of explosions.

I crawled on my stomach the last ten feet and looked out over the edge of a small plateau and onto another valley below. There was a farm there: several barns and outbuildings, as well as a big house. The kind of house a large family would live in. The kind that would have been in a family for countless generations. It was now nothing more than a group of giant torches. The buildings burned the way a heavily oiled fire burns.

I can remember wondering, 'What kind of creature could cause such destruction in so little time?' I then saw the people. Impaled upon long spears and burning like torches. One of them struggled momentarily, but then finally, mercifully, they slouched over dead.

There was so much smoke I could not see the thing that caused this mayhem as it flew from the scene. But I knew which way it was going. The nearest farm was only three miles away.

I ran through the forest and returned to my mount; sturdy and reliable, she bolted toward my next destination.

After a few minutes I was approaching the next farm. As I got closer I realized with horror that I was too late. The same was happening here as at the last farm, even as I approached. By the time I arrived I could only see the dark *shadow* of a great winged beast flying away. I also noticed that the creature appeared to have a rider. A very big *humanoid* rider.

I tried to follow it but it was too fast. By the time I reached an area clear of smoke and flame they were too far away to see clearly. Another two hours and it would be nightfall.

I was torn between making for Briarwood to warn them of the marauding creature, or following and trying to save as many as I could.

I decided on the latter. There was only one thing in Briarwood's arsenal that could challenge such a beast and it was mounted on her walls. It could not be brought to bear upon this mobile enemy.

I kicked my trusted steed into action and directed her toward the heart of the greenbelt. That area where the richest farmland exists. It would mean not stopping or even slowing down if I were to overtake the flying menace, but it was the only way to warn people in that area. I was duty-bound.

I rode on through the rest of the evening and into the early morning, trying to overtake the creature and pass it. Passing several other farms where I knew my assistance would be late, I moved toward a well-known valley on my patrol.

Through thickets and bramble I rode hard, trying to head the monster off and warn the farmers and their families.

Finally I came across the valley, and a series of meadows and crop land. I spurred my mount to jump the fence and we emerged from the treeline.

At that very moment, a vile and noxious wind came from the east behind me. Even as my steed carried me quickly across the first meadow toward an access road that would lead me through the crops and to the nearest farmstead, a black shadow passed overhead.

Just fifty or so feet above the treetops the creature flew by, silently approaching the farm. It coasted on its own heat, just feet above the land, hugging the contour of the terrain.

Emanating from under its wings was a trail of billowing black smoke. It sank to the ground behind the beast like a massive and ever-swelling blanket of soot draping across the meadows. I tried desperately to follow it but by that time it was well past me and heading for a light far in the distance.

Another farmhouse!

I now could see the rider atop his mount. He wielded a long pike with a small banner at its tip that fluttered in the wind. That was all I could see. The monster lay behind it, a blanket of soot and blackest smog that blocked my vision.

I tried to move my mount to greater speeds, but she was almost spent. The acrid fumes were becoming more than she could endure. After several more minutes of hard riding, she finally slowed to a stop and gave out underneath me.

Thinking of the innocent people dying on that farm, I did the only thing I could do. I drew my sword and continued on foot.

As I approached a small orchard surrounding the house I could hear people ahead begging for mercy. I also heard laughter of a sort that made my blood curdle. It was not human, nor was it anything other than diabolic.

I pushed forward, down the road and past the orchards, through a vineyard toward what I had hoped was the source of the screaming.

I came to a short fence at the edge of the vineyard where not far ahead of me was a corral and a horse. I moved to the fence as stealthily as I could and almost tripped over the eviscerated corpse of a woman lying in my path. I climbed over the fence as the smoke began to clear slightly and worked my way across the corral. I only made it a few steps before something unexpected happened.

I was knocked over by a powerful wind created by something new. Great clouds of dust and debris were being tossed about as I rolled over and over toward the area where the sounds of torture were coming from. I slammed against the fence on the other side of the corral and heard the horse scream in terror as it broke through the enclosure and galloped off into the orchards.

I looked out under the bottom rail of the corral and caught a quick glimpse of a man in black and red armour jumping atop what appeared to be a Draconai ... a soot-black dragon that vomited liquid firestorms from its gullet.

They took to the sky then, as I realized that it was not them at all who caused the great wind that had taken my balance from me, tossing me around like a doll. It had been something else. I did not know his name then, so I will tell you what I witnessed and speak of him as such.

At first I thought I was seeing a new dragon...a new *type* of dragon and a new threat, but after looking right at me, the new rider, (he was a giant creature), only a silhouette through the smoke and swirling clouds of ash and embers, saluted me and then urged his steed forward in pursuit of the black dragon and its human controller.

I remember thinking how much more terrifying this new monster and his steed looked than the original threat.

This was no human rider. Where the man in black controlled his steed from a saddle located on the nape of the beast's neck, just behind the creature's ears, the new rider was sitting on his reptilian mount like a man on a horse. This new rider was larger than two adult human males and was not hominid at all.

I regained my composure and balance and jumped the fence running in the direction where the new creature had gone.

Already, the barns had been set on fire, and I could hear people screaming in the smoke. I heard children calling for help and fought the urge to go after the dragon, its rider and the other monster as well.

After searching and following the sounds of their voices I finally found the remains of the family who were living there. Only the children survived. Six, from the ages of two to sixteen. The oldest was a girl and she was trying to gather her siblings. When she saw my uniform she screamed out to me.

I gathered the children together and took them to my horse. I was glad to see she was still breathing. I remember hoping she would survive so I could retire her in comfort for her loyalty and diligence and nominate her for a decoration from the brass.

I told the children to stay with her and then I returned to my hunt for the monsters and the mysterious riders.

I made my way in the direction I had seen them going last. I ran as best I could considering the state of the air at the time.

After about an hour I came upon a river and a low bridge where a caravan had been hastily attacked by what they described as a *"Black Dragon."*

I next passed through a farm that was burning but the people there were rushing to extinguish the fires and they urged me forward toward two *"flying beasts."* I was getting closer once again.

Later I passed by another where the farmer and his family were untouched and they cheered when they saw my uniform. They quickly ushered me onward in the direction they had witnessed *"two dragons"* fly by. They also reported that one of them had started a diving attack on the farm when the other appeared.

Once the second of them roared loudly, the attack was aborted and both of them fled southward, toward the Sylvain river valley.

The farmer's wife added that the black dragon was spewing black soot and smoke from its wings and that the second was as blue as the sky on a clear winter day.

I asked if they could provide me with a mount and they quickly complied and sent me on my way with a canteen of fresh water and wedge of jerked beef.

The new mount was lighter than my trusty mare who I had left behind with the children, but this gelding was faster and more spirited. Just what I needed to catch my quarry.

For the rest of that day, through the night and near daybreak I rode, determined to catch the invaders and their pursuers, until my horse came to a sudden halt in the forest, almost catapulting me from the saddle.

Only feet ahead of us the trees stopped and after a short strip of bushes and grass, there was a fourteen- hundred-foot drop to the great Sylvain river valley below. Here I was forced to stop. There was no way for me to get down to the valley, and bypassing it would take another three days on horseback, at least.

The sun had just risen and it was early morning when I dismounted and witnessed what I shall *now* describe.

If there was another witness, I know not of who they are, for beneath the sheer cliffs where I stood was a vast wilderness expanse where only wolves and other creatures of the wild are said to dwell. I myself was forced to use my telescope to watch from that distance (and that object is a rare thing indeed; I doubt anyone else was there with one).

In the area to my left, the cliff had given way to erosion in the last few years, and had caused the trees to stick out somewhat and obscure my line of sight toward the southeastern sky. As I moved to gain a better vantage point a giant shadow exploded into my view.

The monstrous black dragon suddenly filled my vision, appearing over the treetops behind me and passing overhead, obscuring the very sky.

Its great shadow passed over me as it flew toward the valley. In its wake it left a cloud of gaseous filth and chemical poison, its billowing blanket of pitch black smoke and ash. It choked me and caused me to fall to my knees vomiting the foul stuff from my lungs.

I then heard the foul beast roar as it moved further away, gaining altitude. I watched as it suddenly turned to face my direction. Streams of carbon dust and smoldering ashes fell from the monster's enormous wings toward the valley below.

The fang-filled maw of the beast was half-open, in preparation to belch out a stream of liquid fire. It hovered there waiting.

I had thought that it had detected *my* presence and was actually facing *me*, but it was looking at something else.

Something as powerful as *it* was.

A flying creature, the likes of a Titan, then appeared, high above the cliff's edge.

This creature was as large if not larger than what the dragon appeared to be. Certainly its wingspan was almost twice the width. Its head was more narrow than the dragon's, but longer and bonier. Its tooth-filled *beak* was balanced by a long, bony protrusion that jutted out from the back of its skull.

Its neck was much shorter than the dragon's, but the body of this monster was thicker, stronger-looking, and it was wearing armour as well.

It had a short flat tail that assisted with flight control, yet the beast as a whole was *still* as long as the dragon it was now pursuing. Like a wyvern, it had only four limbs; its front legs were its wings, but the rear legs ended with giant claws, and powerful-looking talons, each as long as a man's leg.

I had seen this monster before, once, when I was in Briarwood for my exams to become a sergeant of the east wardens.

I was told, then, that the creature was licensed, and that the owners volunteered its services for city defence if ever needed. This beast was an ally.

As it passed overhead, the wind from the blue monster's wings cleared the toxic soot and fumes from the area, facilitating my escape to an old tree. There, I took up position in the ancient oak's branches and watched.

It screeched a challenge at the massive creature even as it flew by my hiding place and approached its enemy's position high in the air.

It used its wings like great clawed hands, that sort of grasped the air while it climbed through the sky, gaining altitude quickly.

The black beast above then vomited a massive eruption of what appeared to be lava from its now-gaping maw. Great clods of smoldering, flaming mucus-like material fell toward the still-climbing pursuer. It expanded and burned with a fury, spreading across the sky.

Through the smoke and burning mayhem I caught a glimpse of the dragon's rider, clad in black chain armour, hurling his pike at the newcomer.

The blue dragon maneuvered between the falling molten rocks that were being spewed at it but the pike found its target, impaling the blue dragon's giant rider.

This, however, didn't seem to bother *him* at all, and he rallied his great bluish mount forward, the pike still sticking from his body.

The black monster seemed to realize the real peril it was in so it leveled out and continued to lay down a trail of burning obstacles in its path.

Meanwhile, the blue creature was forced to maneuver around the flying brimstone meteor shower, still continuing its climb, determined to taste dragon flesh.

But the black dragon rolled over and upside down; its rider, the man in black and red, was now drawing a longbow and notching an arrow.

I looked back at the blue creature- it had already manoeuvered in such a way that I was now able to see clearly that the pike impaling its rider had actually *missed* him- he had caught it!

I was also able to see what he was- a great beast of fiery orange and black. A Gillian warrior! I had seen him, as well, before in Briarwood. A mighty reptilian titan.

The Gillian croaked (a sort of laughter, I suspect); he had caught the pike in mid-air. Now he turned the weapon around and threw it back at the diving black dragon.

The weapon flew through the air and struck its mark. It tore a small hole in the right wing of the draconai and managed to force the monster to alter course. This put its back to the blue while the Gillian was now arming himself with a vicious-looking barbed lance that had its own banner. That banner had an emblem on it as well. It was the image of a dragon impaled on a lance.

This time it was the Gillian who released his war cry. A sound as terrible as the black dragon he was now chasing. The amplitude was enough that I heard it clearly, even from almost a half a mile away.

He lay close now to his blue-winged destrier as the black dragon fell into a diving escape maneuver.

The human fired his bow, arrow after arrow. The blue was in her prime and she must have been allowed to fly every day; she was in peak physical shape for battle. She easily avoided three arrows shot by the enemy ahead.

Everything was happening so fast I can barely explain it all.

The Gillian was clinging closely to his mount's back; the two were as one falling harpoon determined to strike the target; dropping at unthinkable speeds as the diving azure *sauraptoid* rapidly covered the distance to her victim.

Without warning, the black dragon suddenly faked a left and then a right and then turned completely, shifting even further left. The pursuing blue was able to thwart the first maneuver but was caught off-guard on the double left.

This is when the black almost came to a sudden stop, allowing the blue to fly past close enough for the black's rider to fire an arrow at point-blank range.

He shot the blue in the flank. Luckily the arrow hit the saddle the blue was wearing and she passed by the enemy without harm.

The black then fell into pursuit and prepared another volley of burning lava. Her rider had been impaled by the Gillian's lance during the near-collision, yet this human was still shooting arrows at his attackers.

The blue spiraled downward apparently aware of the imminent danger its enemy's breath weapon posed. Arrows flew past her and her rider as he reached for *his* next weapon. Still, it almost seemed like the blue was teasing its enemy into chasing it- it was enjoying this exchange.

The black's rider then switched to firing arrows that were glowing with a green energy- enchanted missiles, no doubt.

An arrow finally hit the blue and it flinched as the three-and-a-half-foot-long shaft pierced its side. This one hit at the base of the creature's throat where the great saddle did not cover.

I watched the blue then lose control of her flight path, descending, and disappearing into a low-lying cloud, screeching in pain.

I no sooner thought the creature dead than she emerged from the bottom of the cloud, and banked to one side shooting off toward the sunrise.

Soon after, the black monster appeared from the cloud in hot pursuit, and seemed momentarily confused as it could not see its prey.

It then slowed in its descent, scanning the area for its enemies.

This is when I caught sight of the Gillian warrior. He was on the *back* of the black dragon now and was climbing along the creature's spine toward the enemy rider.

In the Gillian's left hand I could see several lengths of chain that ended in vicious hooks. Its rider didn't notice his enemy's approach from behind. The black dragon was so distracted by her search for the blue behemoth that she too was oblivious to his approach.

Our Gillian was poised to strike.

I deduced that the blue had made an immediate turnaround when exiting the cover of the clouds. Bending backward, it actually flew right back *into* the clouds as the black dragon and its rider were emerging. That must have been the moment when the Gillian moved to the enemy steed.

Our Gillian warrior continued to make his way closer to the black dragon's rider, but a brief moment before he came to within reach of his enemy, the murderer turned to face him.

Clenching the dragon's hide with his clawed feet, the Gillian quickly swung his hooked chains and caught one of the dragon's wings.

Quickly, the black dragon's wing was being crippled by the many hooks now catching the webbing more and more with each struggling movement the beast made.

As I watched the chaotic mass of monsters fall from the sky, hopeful that the fiend was defeated at last, I witnessed something strange indeed.

The other rider, the *human*, began to change his shape even as he reached out toward the Gillian- now struggling to immobilize the black dragon! I watched while the black and red chain mail the enemy had been wearing started to lose its red trim and his arms grew longer.

Wings began sprouting where there was a cape and the fiendish villain began to grow in size. It was transforming, changing shape and becoming another black dragon!

Our Gillian defender pulled violently on the chain snagged in the original black dragon's wing, tangling in the webbing even more and causing it to fold inward.

I remember thinking: *How strong must one be, to be able to force a* **dragon** *to fold its wing?*

It spiraled in its descent and as it did so the many feet of hooked and barbed chain wrapped around its now injured wing, tangled into its other limbs – worsening the bondage and causing it to fall faster and faster toward the valley below. Even as it fell toward the river valley, far below, its rider was transforming into its mirror image.

During the attack, the Gillian had released his grip on the chains and had leaped off of the black dragon's back and into the air. He roared in mid-flight and a moment later the blue dragon returned from the clouds to catch him on *its* back.

I continued watching; the excitement of it all was too invigorating not to. Our Gillian climbed back into the saddle of his mount while the prehistoric creature ascended to a higher elevation.

Then, once again, they dove at an unimaginable speed, falling after their foe.

As they descended upon the retreating and falling enemy, the shapeshifter had already abandoned the dragon to its fate; the vicious-looking barbed chains now fully entangled in its wings and legs, it spiraled out of control toward the deep river mouth at the lake of Sylvain far below.

There was a mighty roar as the transforming rider began to spread its wings. It was now the size of a large wagon and its wings were almost thirty feet across, and it was *still* growing!

This is when the Gillian took up his wicked-looking trident and leaped from his saddle as his mount passed the shapeshifting dragon. He fell on top of the beast, standing on the trident's curved forks, adding his titanic weight to his strike. He fell on the monster like some kind of living missile of destruction.

I could almost hear the snapping of bone as the shape-shifter folded and began to fall, its dragon-back broken in half.

Then the unthinkable happened. As the blue dragon continued to follow the original dragon on its forced descent, the transforming creature, who I had thought mortally wounded, changed into a cloud of blackness. It enveloped the Gillian, and that was the last I saw of him. The two of them disappeared into the rapid icy waters of the Sylvain river.

There, in that area the river is mighty and powerful with impassable rapids and waterfalls at every curve in its fast and deadly waters. There is little hope that even those mighty behemoths could have survived.

I lost track of the flying blue steed and the smoke-vomiting dragon it was chasing when they vanished in the mists above lake Sylvain.

Soon enough the black smoke seemed to dissipate as I waited for something, anything to happen, but a stillness had fallen over the land then.

After an hour the birds began to return, and I knew that the whole event was over.

I then made my way back to where my horse had fallen. I gathered the children, who had still been waiting for my return even after all this time, and made sure they were safe and not seriously injured.

After seating the weaker ones onto the horses, I took them to the nearest farm. There I found some survivors whom I allowed to join us. I took these people and the children to the farm where I had taken loan of the second horse. I left them and the horse, with the folk who live there.

I mounted my trusty steed and promised her I would be easy on her from that day forward. I then began the journey back to Briarwood to report what I had seen.

Just before I left, an elder of the village told me he saw a great birdlike monster flying south eastward at high noon the day before.

Having spent two days gathering survivors, I suspected that the Gillian and his steed might have escaped after all ... or his enemy did.

I know nothing more that would shed light on this tale and I believe I just heard a toilet flush anyway.

CHAPTER - 11

"THE SHIT, ALMOST, FINALLY HITS THE *'FAN'*"

Okay, I'm back. I hope you had a...What? What's so funny? What are you laughing at? Do I have toilet paper hanging from the back of my shoe like some idiot? Did that last guy say something funny?

Well, whatever.

...Now where was I?

Oh yeah.

First off...I know you all loved Grarr, but please do not expect him to come back to life. I want to clarify that point: **Grarr does NOT come back from the dead in this story**. I am sorry but that is the way it was.

I loved him too. He was awesome. Wasn't he? I know.

But right now we have to get back to the Troll and Alaeth, Lilia's sister ...

Beornag and Alaeth had just finished tying up the last giant bag of concentrated liquid shit and were chuckling, between gagging reflexes, about how awesome it was going to be watching Beornag hurl them at bad guys from the walls of Briarwood.

Once the Troll had put all the sacks into his bottomless backpack, he lifted her onto his shoulder and looked around the general area one more time.

"Ize was hopin' weez wooda found anudda way outta heeya," he said, squinting to try and make out an exit among all the panels and pipes that seemed to be everywhere.

He had left a trail of absolute mayhem in his path and by now there would definitely be bad guys searching for them. He was not about to walk right into them by backtracking. He needed an escape route. He found himself wishing his "foreskin" was as strong as his hind brain. That way he could think ahead of what he thought of and know what to think of when he needed to know what he was supposed to be...rememberin'...and stuff.

"Look there." She was pointing to the top of one of the huge secondary holding tanks that were situated in the middle of the vast production facility. "That looks like a set of stairs coming from the top of that tank. They lead up to some sort of small building suspended from the ceiling. Let's try that way," she suggested. "I think that it might be some sort of control office or something like that. In any event we can at least get a better look around from up there and maybe spot a quicker way out."

Wow, this dame was pretty smart. He decided she was a lot like Grarr, but not so pointy; and growly; and violent; and tall; and tattooed; and scary-looking; and military-like; and ... he decided she was nothing at all like Grarr, but liked her anyway, and then moved forward.

He swaggered over to the massive container in only a few strides, and climbed the side of the tank using the many pipes and attachments that riddled the surface.

Halfway up he suddenly stopped and descended to the floor again.

"What are you doing?" she asked, obviously annoyed. "Shouldn't we be escaping?"

They were heading straight back to the vat from where they had stolen all the liquid reek.

He stopped next to the massive crap-tank and pulled a piece of white chalk from his bottomless backpack. He then drew a picture on the side of the vat large enough for *anyone* to notice, of a hand giving the "bird."

"Dats Ulm's mark. Dese fiendish villanaytuhs is gonna remembuh dat Ulm was heeya." He then placed her back on his shoulder, and returned to climbing.

This time he stopped in mid-climb and took her in one hand, holding on with the other. "Wouldn't it be cool right now if dere was a bunch o' little flyin' machines flyin' all around weez as Ize tried ta valiantly rescue yooz from whateva weez was facin' below. And as weez was climbing Ize was desperately tryin ta swat dem from da air as deyz tried ta stop our accent? Huh? Wouldn't it, dough?"

"Wh... what?!" she questioned. "Injoke. We need to get up *there*. I have no idea what you are talking about." She sighed. Then she saw that he was really excited to hear her opinion and she decided to try not to hurt his feelings. "Okay. Yes, that would be dramatic and we can maybe write a book about that when we get home, but right now we probably don't have time to talk about it. I think we *should* be escaping."

"Can Ize say Ize was valiant? Hunh? Can Ize? Pleeeeze? In da book?" he begged as he ascended the structure with relative ease. "When weez *writes* da book, I mean?"

"Of *course*. You *were* valiant and *still* are. I just think you need to be concentrating on getting us out of this place before we start planning on selling the rights to our story to some *Gnome*, or druid casino owner so they can make..."

The Troll's right eyebrow raised as he half-opened his mouth and held up a finger for a second, then as she was continuing along with her *'non-stop gabbing'* he gave up and continued up the last few feet.

"...a fortune selling copies in book form. I wish the stories were true about those little guys. You know they say that Gnomes used to be the accountants of the world? At least that's what they say. It would make my life easier. That's for sure. I wouldn't have to keep our accounts balanced any longer. Lillia is terrible with finances and money."

Once atop the structure, Alaeth's predictions were correct- the stairs thereclimbed another forty feet up and attached to the side of the suspended building.

He continued his ascent, all while making sure Alaeth was secure and in no danger of falling off or being harassed by imaginary tiny flying machines.

This building had a large barred window that they were able to peek into. Inside were pipes and cables and all sorts of confusing contraptionry.

Here there was a large platform made of a metal screen strong enough to support the Troll. After walking around the building they found a huge set of steel bay doors on the opposite side.

A series of long metal cables came out of this building, each as thick as a human's arm and stretched out into the factory to eventually meet junctions where they veered off in different directions.

At those junctions they saw other buildings much like the one they were now standing next to. The cables went into these suspended buildings through separate openings just over the doors.

"This looks like some sort of device for moving things around." She scratched her head and continued, "The cables are like tracks for carts that hang from them, and this building next to us is where the machines are that make it all move." She pointed out several suspended carts moving on cables in the distance. Once in a while one would stop over a vat and tip to pour out its contents into the tank.

She then turned and moved toward the huge doors. "Injoke, do you think you can open these without bending them or tearing them off the hinges?"

"Ize can try," he replied, stepping closer to the large double doors. "Ooo! Ooo! Ooo! Is dere a prize if Ize can do it?"

"Ummmmm ... a prize?" she asked, perplexed as he pranced in place on his toes (quite gracefully, I might add). "I guess the prize would be – we will be closer to escaping?"

"Well *dat's* good. Ain't it?" he replied, perplexed that she would judge such a wondrous prize as freedom so nonchalantly.

"Absolutely, it is!" she said with a warm smile. "Can you do it?"

He looked at the doors and could see that these were not merely loading bay doors, nor were they even fortress doors. These were thick steel doors and when he tried to get a finger hold to pry them open he was unable to. The seam between the two metallic panels was almost nonexistent. "Ize is sorry!" he *fake*-wept and bawled. "Ize can't get a grip at all."

Suddenly, just as she was about to chuckle, there came a strange screeching sound like fingernails on a chalkboard, only accompanied with wet farting noises and the spewing of mucus and other nastiness, echoing from far across the factory.

This horrific cacophony was coming from the direction of the big hatch they had originally entered the facility through.

A moment later that hatch filled with a shadow.

A cloud of black smoke moved into the vast facility like a droplet of ink within a glass of water. It moved with a terrible, intelligent purpose and it was not alone.

CHAPTER - 12

"NOW THAT'S JUST GROSS!"

The following wildlife vignette is brought to you by;

Fran's Cans

"Made to order custom machined metal packaging trusted by Semsimilia's finest boot cheese Affineurs and Picklers."

"Our pungency-trapping technology cannot be beat"

Anaga are not creatures indigenous to Oona, but were brought to the world through vile and fiendish methods.

An Anaga is, simply speaking, a denizen of a dimension of suffering and cruelty.

Anaga exist because people in the material world can be evil. It really is that simple.

When a person is so evil as to disgust their deity in such a way that would make said deity actually turn away and not even *"see"* the person any longer, that person becomes subject to the Anagas' attention.

Once that person's mortality runs out, their immortal life begins and so does their suffering at the hands of the Anaga. They are swept away to the Anagas' plane of existence where horrific things happen to them.

Very few of these beings last long enough to become a *new* Anaga. They begin as a smaller and more piteous-looking version of the person they once were.

However... (and most unfortunately for them) ... Soon after, another evil person dies, and the most disgusting and vile parts of that person's body and personality grow out of the first villain's body and persona. These people become melded in a grotesque bond of suffering and debauchery.

Soon enough, more evildoers are sent to the new Anaga and they, too, meld with the monster, ever growing and morphing themselves into something mind-numbingly horrific.

This horrific process continues forever and some Anaga are so full of suffering beings they become elders among demonic forces-virtual gods of suffering and infection.

Those Anaga who are older and more evolved, actually feed from the energy created by the suffering of the lesser demons. They use each others' sufferings and hateful memories like seeds to grow their sustenance.

On the material plane of existence, greater Anaga are giant demonic monsters capable of challenging the likes of dragons and even lesser gods.

Anagas prefer to live in pools of filth and feces, vomit and puss. A facsimile of their natural environment.

This grotesque substance heals them and keeps them from burning should they be exposed to other dimensions for too long.

It is known that the *fabrics* of most realities are toxic to them and so they wear the bodily excretions of all of the evil people they have absorbed. These excretions are kept safe in pools close to where the Anaga come and go in the material plane, and they are quick to gather it all up and take it with them should they decide to leave.

This disgusting coating can last hours, giving the Anaga time to conduct their evil among mortal people in the material plane. Their time is limited before they have to return to their pools of mucus and filth to rejuvenate.

It is not possible to summon an Anaga, but one can enlist their services if enough suffering is offered as payment- and if one knows a being known as *"The Postman."*

It is almost impossible to purposely contact the Anagas unless one chooses to suffer an entire lifetime of pain and humiliation while also causing it to others. Only *then* will an Anaga take a mortal seriously.

Elder Anaga resemble great maggots almost indescribable in their grotesqueness. Some are 50 feet or more in length and have the bodies and faces, souls and personas of thousands of despicable people from cannibals to rapists, and all forms of debauchery and malice between, all of them integrated into the monster's form, their own bodies and personalities infused into its being.

Lesser beings are said to have gone mad just at the sight of one of these horrific monstrosities or at the sound of the cacophony of gibbering and lamenting voices that come from the hundreds of faces that line the beast's diseased and festering underbelly.

Great and *elder* Anaga have a mane-like strip that runs from the base of their long, crooked necks to the end of their feces-caked tails.

This mane is actually many hundreds of arms that used to belong to those wretched souls now cursed to be part of the Anaga's belly where their faces scream in torment and insanity forever. These arms are never near the faces that own them and as such are constantly slapping and poking at the other faces, blindly reaching down toward the gut of the beast, increasing the overall suffering that the creature produces.

The Anaga's head, its primary visage, emerges from a *foreskin-like* mass at the end of its long *phallus-like neck*. This *main* face looks like an ancient old human man except that its features are twisted and grotesque. Its teeth are yellow and stained with bile and filth, and seem far too long- and there are way too many of them. They are always smiling a perverted, menacing smile.

An Anaga's nose appears to be a huge, diseased scrotum which pulses and oozes snot and puss always.

It has a long, pasty yellow and purple, prehensile tongue which it uses to lick the filth from its infected nose constantly.

An Anaga's ears seem shrunken and deformed in various ways-never symmetrical, and always oozing infectious fluids that cake up in the wiry hairs that grow there.

The Anaga's eyes, sunken and full of malice, are tiny points of cold light that seem to float in the middle of pitch-black pits.

Anaga are mad beyond description by human standards, and can be prone to violent arguments among their many personalities controlling the many arms and faces that cover their bodies.

These *fights*, where the suffering actually cause suffering upon the other souls, *also* suffering among its maddeningly multiple personalities, keep the Anaga powerful as they feed off of the prejudices, fears, hates, and other negative emotions that ooze from the souls of the damned.

Anaga speak a gibberish that only *they* fully understand, though they are also able to speak the languages of all of those who suffer their curse- and it is even said that they are able to speak across time and dimension, which is how they are able to spread distrust, disloyalty, suffering, and despair across the multiverse, forever.

An Anaga's body has two very long arms which are kept close to the body much like a praying mantis. At the end of these arms are hands with as many as eight fingers and three thumbs each, all of which have too many joints and end with filthy and infectious nails.

The monsters' feet are even filthier- large, awkward and covered with sores, they stick out at the ends of long, gangly, almost human legs.

Anaga defecate and urinate almost constantly when aroused and as such they walk through and even dance in the filth that they excrete, giving them a crusty sort of pad on the soles of their oversized feet. As with the hands and fingers of the Anaga, their feet also have too many toes, and all of them are infected with varying fungi and bacteria.

For more information about the Anaga, or for a copy of this wildlife vignette contact: The G'nomish Film Board Society, Sixty Six-Packs Street, Allthewater, Sensimillia, 420420420.

CHAPTER - 13

"CAN YA SMELL IT? IT'S GETTIN' CLOSE!"

Within the fluidic black tendrils of smoke and darkness were two creatures so vile and foul that Beornag could *feel* the *un*holiness emanating from them even at such a distance.

They appeared to be twenty- or thirty-foot-long maggots, their bellies covered in human faces, all expressing agony and suffering, hatred and perversion. Each monster possessed a larger head and face that would appear and then vanish in the folds of their foreskin-like necks. These larger faces were humanoid-*like*, very old and gaunt human males. Their yellow-and brown-stained teeth were freakishly long and their diseased and puss-oozing tongues were constantly licking the mucus and sticky blisters that wept filth from their infected and swollen, scrotum-like noses.

Leaking scabs and open sores covered their wrinkled and bluish lips.

Here and there along the monsters' underside a face would spew a stream of yellow and brown bodily fluid. They would then sob and wail in their own tormented voices, exhausted by their endless suffering. The sound of it all was nauseating and maddening at once.

These sickening fiends also possessed two legs that were remotely human-like, but very long and emaciated. Their abdomens hung between those sickly-looking legs like great oily, bile-covered, bloated and lumpy tumors.

Each monster possessed several such bulges that were in actuality separate, rancid, fat deposits in their guts that periodically burst, spewing a yellowish liquid and milky white mucus. This covered the surface of the floor in front of the beasts and as they defecated into this diseased mass, the many faces hanging from their obscene underbellies were licking it all up again, screaming and crying out their torment and misery.

Both creatures were draped in loose, jiggling, pasty whitish-gray and bluish-brown skin that was covered in sweat and bodily filth of all descriptions. Closer to the rear ends of the monstrosities' tapering and obscene bodies, the faces were stained with their own urine and encrusted in their own feces, forever suffering, their voices only chaotic notes in the cacophony that was the voice of each horrific demon.

These creatures also possessed many arms, most seeming to reach out in search of mercy, clawing impotently at the air like a sort of mane of insanity that ran the length of their maggoty spines.

These were human arms, devoid of hair and glistening with cold, oily sweat. These arms would sometimes jerk into action, reaching down to the underbelly and violently slapping a nearby face, thus adding to the condemned soul's torment. Two of the monsters' arms were much longer than the rest. They were folded (praying mantis-style) next to the undulating, obese bodies. Their elbows nearly touched the floor; sagging, loose skin dragged along behind, leaving trails of puss and infected blood from weeping sores.

Their wrists ended with hands that each had eight fingers and three thumbs, all tipped with foot-long claws that were filthy beyond description.

As they entered the massive production facility, the black smoke reached out in several directions and the Troll could see plain enough that the tendrils of ink-like gas were searching for something or someone.

"Ize tinks weez been found out," Beornag whispered with a worried look on his face. "Ize ain't neva seent anyting like doze tings b'fore. Ize is tinkin' doze is sump'n frum anudda dimenshin or sump'n like dat. Deyz is fartin' enuff evil fer me ta smell 'em frum all da way ova heeya," he offered, apologetically. "Vampiyas is one ting, but Ize ain't neva faced deemins."

"And how are we ever going to get past that smoke ... thing?" she added. "I feel so lost. Injoke, if ever there was a time to pray, I think now would be it. I just hope your Ulm is listening."

He scratched his head and strained to think of what to say. After a brief moment he faced the door and spoke quietly.

"Knock, knock ..." He then turned to Alaeth with an expectant look on his face.

"What? ... Oh ... *Oh!* Knock, *knock!*" she responded. "Okay, I'm game ... Who's there?"

"Awe crap," he replied.

"Awe crap who?" she asked.

"No ... no. Ize *meant* awe crap. Ize ain't neva been too good at knock-knock prayuhs. Not really sure what ta say afta dat." It was true. He had no prayer for opening doors. It is precisely why he usually kicked them off the hinges or ripped them open.

Peeking over the edge of the platform, they could now see more enemies entering the facility. These consisted of a dozen or so *Tallow Shins*, a handful of Cave-Trolls and another Ogre who looked a lot like Phuktbutt the cook, but with a lot of pickled-cabbage-can-shaped dents on his head and face.

They watched as the *Tallow Shins* and one of the giant maggot demons approached the vat they had climbed to get to the stairs that led to their platform hiding place.

Several of the armoured humans, the *Tallow Shins*, began to scale the side of the giant container as the horrific demon barked orders at them in many languages and voices at once.

Meanwhile the black smoke was also converging on their position. In only a minute or so they would be found.

Beornag pulled his great maul from his bottomless backpack and prepared himself for battle. He somehow knew he would not win against the demon, especially when he would be so occupied by the *Tallow Shins* (no matter how waxy their leg bones might be).

He, right then and there, decided this was his fate and he would try and hold them off of Alaeth as long as he could, before he would be forced to use his maul as a demolition device and bring the ceiling of the massive factory down on top of them all. At least the enemies here would be stopped and shit production would be halted as well. *'Dats one way ta bring da house down,'* he thought.

Just as he was about to stand up and roar, the doors behind him began to open, accompanied with the sound of machinery moving their great combined weight.

Almost as soon as they started to open Beornag heard a familiar voice.

"Pehvis *Grizzly*? Dat be *yooz*? Why *yooz* in poop basement?" It was Terdbreff, the Cave-Troll who had seen Beornag perform at the Gruel and Grog many months previous and had become the Troll's number one fan. The *very same* Troll who had received an autograph from *Pelvis Grizzly* (Beornag) in the main entrance to the mountain fortress, earlier that day!

"Terdbreff? Is dat *yooz*?" Beornag asked.

Terdbreff gasped with elation and opened the mask of his helmet. "Yooz 'members Terdbreff's *name*? Terdbreff be so honored now." He blushed. "Terbreff is Pehvis' biggest fan. Terdbreff want to…"

"Yea, yea, dat's great buddy," Beornag interrupted. "Weez is gonna get ta dat real soon, but foist weez needs ta be goin' dat way sos yooz kin take us back ta da mess hall for da big performance." At this he saw Terdbreff's look of excitement and anticipation of seeing his favorite performer in action. "Hey, yooz wanna help us do da show, dere, Terdbreff?"

Terdbreff's jaw dropped almost to the floor. "Me? Terdbreff? Do show wiff *Pehvis*?" A tear began to swell in his eye and his bottom lip quivered ever so slightly as he was about to continue.

Once again Beornag interrupted him before he could finish. "Course, yooz. C'mon, let's get goin b'fore da fans start gettin' antsy." He winked at, and picked up, Alaeth while ushering Terbreff back inside the building. "Let's get deez doors closed up before dat reek gets in here too much too- Peeeeeee-yoooo!! Right?"

"Firs me need to do job. Only take second." Terdbreff then stepped back out through the doors and moved toward some panels on the outside of the building. The *Tallow Shins* and the animated darkness would be arriving on the platform any second.

Beornag was trying to formulate a plan of action while he looked around the room beyond the great doors. It made him want to smear earwax on one of the windows ... so he did—in the form of a rudimentary happy face ... which somehow seemed to help.

Alaeth was amazed at how easily Beornag dealt with the stress of the situation. She began to make mental notes on his behavior, and was realizing how actually effective he was at simply *'lucking out.'*

Inside, the structure was a one-room building that had several giant spools of cable attached to some winches and gears, loaded onto large axles.

Here, there were cogs and spindles, gauges and all sorts of the things the Troll would usually get himself into trouble with, (but right then he was on a mission, and he needed to make a getaway, and fast).

Soon he heard the *Tallow Shins* climbing the stairs as Terdbreff was turning a wheel to adjust some feature of the cable system. "Weez betta get goin', bud. Ize heeyas da fans comin' up dose dere steps and dayz is gonna mob us fer autographs and den weez will be late for da show!"

"No way!" Terdbreff said defiantly, as he jumped into action. "Me gitz yooz dere, Pehvis. Not yooz worry. Fans not slow show." He hopped back inside and approached a control panel where he pulled a lever, causing the doors to close again.

At the last moment Beornag thought that he had spotted the first *Tallow Shin* while the fiend stepped onto the platform. Then, thankfully, the doors were closed. He sat back, sure that the enemy did not notice the trio through the small opening in the door for that split second. They had escaped ... sort of.

"Where to?" the Injoke asked.

"Terdbreff know fast way. We use kay-bow car."

"What's a crowbar cow?" the Injoke asked.

"*Kay-bo ... car*. It be way we travo to upside of fort. Den we not have to see fans," he offered, quite proud of himself.

"Terdbreff, yooz is a *genesis*," Beornag praised his new buddy.

"*Genius*," Alaeth corrected him with a whisper in his ear.

"Yeah, dat too. Gee-nee-yuss. Dat's my numba one fan Terdbreff." He gestured for his new *stage manager* to lead the way.

Terdbreff then guided the two to a door that led to a tunnel with another iron staircase. This led out of the structure and into a circular shaft. From there they entered an area where there were a dozen or so ways out.

Here they moved along a particularly large hallway, wide and tall enough for two Trolls, until they eventually reached a ramp system.

They then ascended several landings to finally arrive at a large chamber filled with a series of rods and strange metal beams that seemed to vibrate and hum. Terdbreff warned them not to touch the metal struts and pipeworks; "Yooz be fried fast," he said.

On the other side of this strange chamber they found an exit large enough for them to pass through where they arrived on a large round platform that overlooked another factory-like area, this one smaller and more mundane. The pipes and ducts *here* were of a more archaic feel. These were for transferring water and fresh air throughout the fortress, (or at least so Alaeth surmised).

In this part of the citadel's inner workings they traversed many catwalks and staircases, through a maze of maintenance shafts and air duct workings, to finally make their way to a massive circular stairwell that climbed along the inside of another, even greater shaft. They proceeded upward into a tangle of cables, pipes, and ductwork that they surely would have gotten lost in if it were not for their new guide.

After ascending a couple hundred feet they reached another large platform; this one was round and had a group of storage lockers to one side and what appeared to be several large cages on the other. These cages, each, had several huge cables that stretched into the darkness above and below. These came from the tops of the cages and from the confusion of machinery mounted on their roofs.

Here Terdbreff suggested they stop for a short rest while he summoned a cable car.

After fiddling with some machinery near the cages, (that seemed to start a chain reaction of clanking and thrumming and the slow movement of some of the cables), he went to a storage locker, located at the other end of the platform, where there were even more strange machine-like devices stored.

Here he removed a large metal suitcase. He then placed the case on a large desk and opened it.

His desk looked worn and in disrepair. Its top was covered with papers and doodles in colorful wax pencil, as well as a small plaque with his name and title on it: *Terdbreff: Maintenance Supervisor.*

Inside the case was a velvet cloth which he unfolded to reveal the contents while explaining. "Dis be Terdbreff *speshow* stuff." He removed, from the suitcase, 3 of 6 goblets, a bottle of VERY old Elfish wine, a small leather pouch, and a cheesecloth package. "Terdbreff keep speshow snacks here."

He offered them a goblet of the wine and some of the very best aged cheese and venison jerky Alaeth had ever had. She commented on this and Terbreff explained. "Terdbreff smarter den most Tros- not Pehvis Grizzly doe. Him be smartest Trow of all. But me be smart and master say Terdbreff bring *all* him family to great army of Trow freedom. So Terdbreff is chief of all family den and make many golds. Terdbreff think of future and girlfriend, Grizzly Fate frum *Grool an Grog* who watch dishes say Terdbreff invest his golds. Her be Terdbreff's girlfriend." He blushed. "Grizzly Fate...So Terdbreff buy lots old booze, cheese, season meat, and stuff like dat. Want truffle?"

"Wow, Terdbreff, you are quite industrious," Alaeth praised him.

"Yes, Terdbreff think someday he sell all for more den him make here ever. Den Terbreff buy land frum humans and be owner. Den Terdbreff family not be hunted *no* more."

"WHAT!!?" Alaeth gasped. "Who *hunts* you?" she asked, climbing from Beornag's shoulder and making her way to Terdbreff's side.

"Cave Tros live in caves. Human wants *speshow* rocks frum caves and come and take frum Tros. Tros say no. Humans take still. Tros be angry and fight. Humans fight back. Others help. Tros lose. Must live here now in fort of master." His head hung low; he sounded ashamed.

He continued, "All Terdbreff's fault. He bring people here to save us all in big army of Trow freedom. Now we all be dead in war to come anyway. Too late for Terdbreff leave and family follow. Bigger Trow serve master and he take chief stick from Terdbreff. He be Groynchies. Many family love Groynchies. He be big cave Trow chief now. Much muscles and bigger dan Terdbreff. Groynchies say all Tros be his. He *own* us all. He smash any not say so. Terdbreff too small to fight Groynchies, so family follow *him*. Now Terdbreff just follow along."

"Awwww. Dats a bummuh, Terdy. Can Ize call ya Terdy? Ooo, how's about just Terd?" Beornag asked.

Terd nodded his approval.

Beornag continued "So yooz is sayin' all da Trolls in dis here mastuh's awmy is servin Groynchies cuz he is bigga, and badduh den anyone else?"

"Terd say yes. Dat be how is now. But Pehvis Grizzly is big hero for Terd. Terd be sad and sobby and terd go to Grool and Grog in human water town and see Pehvis sing and be funny wiff different name. Terd so laughing he go back and sees show again. Terd laugh more and be happy when Terd be most sad of all life time." He smiled at Beornag with glossy eyes.

"Injoke, are you hearing this?" Alaeth asked.

"Ize is!" he replied, his lower lip quivering, a single tear escaping from his tiny, glossy-black eye. "Ize gutz fans datz loves Ize so much deyz is..."

"What?! N... no! Not that!" she interrupted. "His people were coerced into all of this. They are being threatened by a bully who controls them through fear. Calabac probably put the humans up to attacking the Trolls in the first place. Ooooo, I hate that guy!" She clenched her fists. "Gods of my fathers, I swear *my* people would not have attacked if they were not somehow threatened ... I am sure of that," she explained. "Terdy, sweetie, can you get Pelvis and me out of this fortress?"

"Umm, Terd say yes. Why pixie ask this?" he replied. "Terd tinks she was venticulous dummy 'til now."

"I am an elf, Terdy. Now listen to me. I am Beor ... I mean Pelvis Grizzly's friend and adviser. Aren't I, Pelvis?" The last was directed at the Injoke with a wink.

"Yup," the Injoke answered. "An she's real good at baggin' crap too," he added, flashing her a wink of approval.

"Terdy, your people have been lied to by the master," she began. "As have all of the other peoples that serve the master ... at least that's what I am guessing." She took his hand (index finger), as he shed a tear of self-pity. "This ..." she gestured towards Beornag. "... is the Injoke of Ulm. *Ulm*, Terdbreff. *God* of Trolls." She moved to face him directly, *he* sitting cross-legged on the platform, *her* standing as tall as she could on her tiptoes to see into his glossy eyes.

She reached into his colander-like helmet to wipe the tear from his face and continued. "I see you love your people, Terdbreff. I see you are sickened by having to stoop so low as to allow an impostor to sit in your place as your family's head. Groynchies is bigger and stronger, but Groynchies doesn't have *friends*."

A second tear escaped his other eye, then a third. He looked to Beornag and spoke with a trembling lower lip. "Really? Dis pixie be real elf? Terd never see elf before ... and *know*. Many at Grool and Grog, but me not know til now I see. Me tinks she is dummy for show and Pelvis make her voice. Now Terd see she now no dummy after all."

"Ize personally knows several personages of da elvish p'suasion," Beornag explained, "... and deyz is like anybody else. Dere's a rectal wart in every crowd, but for da most pawt- Ize likes elvish personages. Deyz likes naychuh an' tings dat belongs dere. Like Ize ... and yeah; I'll-Lay-It, here is an elf-a-fised personage- official 'en all."

"Terdy ... sweetie, listen..." Alaeth added as he turned to her with a confused half-smile on his face. "*You* should be the leader of your people. I am 97 years old and *I* know this is fact. I studied Sylvainian peninsula fauna and flora and majored in hill dwelling cultures of the northern realms when I earned my third degree from the University of Briarwood.

"Always, the Trolls have been led by a cave-dweller, because *your* people are *usually* the smartest of your multi-racial species. The hill Trolls are wisest and rarest, and have always acted as advisers and teachers.

"The mountain dwellers are your prophets and oracles and the forest dwellers are the keepers of the wilds- and there are many more of your peoples who are all part of what may have once been a pretty impressive network of Trollish alliances. You were once a proud and noble species of many cultures with your own leaders, languages, and traditions. This is a documented fact that cannot be denied. This is what bad people like the master have taken from *your* peoples, Terdy." She gently touched his cheek with her relatively tiny hand, the gentle benevolence of which he was suddenly enthralled by.

Alaeth was an elf—a species of self-described protectors of life and the natural world, as well as having almost uncontrollable powers to befriend. He did not want to resist her. She *was* his friend.

Terdbreff was silent with a blank look on his face while she descended from his lap and paced the floor. She was on a mission now and was going to make things right. "Terdy ... how many of your *actual* family are here in the fortress?"

"Oh dat easy." He counted on his fingers and was actually doing multiplication. "Fourteen cave Tros here. Plus Terdbreff. All dem be Terdbreff brothers frum same mother." He then counted again. "Lots others too, all Cave-Trolls here ... Many like oranges on many trees- plus four forest Tros, but dem is juss janitors. Den dere be one mountain Tro. Him sleep lots. Him is big as him peoples gets and lots miles to north layin' in valley- him sleep. Den all dem swamp peoples an doze harleys, oh, an dere be Pehvis. Him like family too now, too."

Beornag smiled warmly.

"How many *total*, of your people and the other Trolls, serve the master?" Alaeth asked.

"Ummm ... me not can count dat big. Many, like herd of cows. Big herd. No, not good. Like apples on tree? ... No, still not big enough ... Like ants in hill. Dat how many. Mountain Tro be biggest of *all* kind. Him got family of Goblins living in him belly button me tinks. Dat how big him be. Terdbreff see him many months past. He like many mountains tall, and big. Master say him wake up mountain Tro when him get to water town of hummies. Den him be all confused and master tell him dat hummies try and kill all Tros. Groynchies be sayin' dis too an big mountain Tro be knowin' is truths, cuz us Tros all say so, and him make water place hummie town flat. Mountain Tro as big... as big many mountains ... almost ... or maybe bigger. Terdbreff not can count that big."

Beornag, who had totally lost track of what was happening at that moment, was confused and bored stiff, so he began to daydream and wander around the general area, looking for stuff. Alaeth seemed to know more about what was going on than he *ever* did. In fact right at that moment he had no *idea* what was going on. He was planning a new strategy to get rich and was falling deep into thought as he stood up and began to walk in circles, his hands behind his back.

He tried to look like he was listening and contemplating (so as not to be rude) but he was actually daydreaming about ways to make wine from freshly squeezed rocks. *Cuz rocks were plentiful and were easy to grow and keep alive.* Beornag had already started a rock farm in the winery's sub-sub-*sub*-basement (aka the sewers), and although they were growing slowly, he was positive more bat guano and carrot peelings would quicken up the process. His main issue was the way the bottles kept breaking when he poured the buckets full of rocks into them. This was gonna take some deep thinking.

Moments later, Alaeth was calling his name. "Hunh? Oh ... Yeah. Ha hehe. What was dat?"

"Are you listening?" She seemed a bit peeved.

"Yeah, sure. Why?" Beornag fibbed... then, "Okay, no. Sorry. Ize was not listenin'. Ize ain't heard nuttin', after you said cheese burguh."

"Wh ... Wha ... What are you ... cheeseburger? I never said ..." She seemed a bit frustrated.

"Wasn't dat yooz? Well whataya know. It mustuh been dem fat people dat came troo heeya a minute ago," he explained.

She gave him a perplexed look.

"No?" he asked. "No fat peoples? How about doze clowns wit dat ... No? No clowns too?" He grinned sheepishly. "Sorry, Ize was attendin' a whole uduh, *imaginary* conversation. Ize gits dis way when Ize is hungry."

"What about show?" Terdbreff interrupted.

"Show? *Show!?*" She pleaded. "Are the *two* of you even *trying* to see what is happening here and how we can all help each other?"

"Ooool! Ize do! Ize do!" The Injoke was now dancing on his toes again with his arm waving in the air.

"Terdbreff not know." The other Troll confessed. "Pick him. Me *want* know now." They thought she was playing a guessing game. "Terdbreff curious."

Alaeth took a deep breath ... well, more of a sigh of frustration really, and then explained, "The two of you ..." she gestured to them both, then sighed again, "... are *exactly* what your peoples need (*I can't believe I just said that*). You see all Trolls are related, just as all elves are. Long ago your peoples were corrupted by an evil force that controlled you through manipulation and displays of powerful magic, a weapon your people never possessed and as such were impressed and frightened by.

"They also laid waste to your spiritual beliefs by using ridicule, and murdering all of your leaders and spiritual guides. Your entire culture was destroyed and you as a people were scattered and divided. Having no leadership, your peoples ended up as rogue wanderers- ever in search of seclusion from the evils that threatened your kind- all the while being forced to steal and pillage from weaker people just to survive, or as slaves to those who possessed the power to manipulate you through the threat of powerful magic, and use you to further their own selfish endeavors." She then took another sip of her wine. "This really is exceptional."

The Trolls seemed to be enthralled with what she was saying. "Beornag, where did you learn what you know about Ulm?" she asked. Ulm was a name she did not recognize and she was used to recognizing the names of deities, even those who were not widely *recognizable*. Alaeth was very well educated and possessed a couple of impressive degrees from the U of B.

"Well ... Ize ... ummm ... It was in dis 'ere book. Ize got it from a temple 'uh nice peoples when Ize was younguh- afta Ize was a slave in da mine." He removed a chain from around his neck and produced a small book that was attached with the use of strong baling wire. He handed it to her. "It's writtin' in hill Trollish. Dats Ize's language by da way." He winked.

She accepted the tiny book, which in her own hands was actually an impressive tome. She also knew there was no such thing as hill Trollish. It was written in common humanese.

She removed it from its protective, make-shift silk wrapping. At least the Injoke used expensive silk to preserve his treasure.

The faded leather surface had the symbol of what appeared to be a hand, painted in faded colors, and was so worn that it appeared to be giving the "flip-off-finger." The title was unreadable except for three letters from the common alphabet: U, L, and M.

She dared to open it to a random page, half-expecting the wrath of the Trollish god to come down upon her, but instead she was slightly startled when the very action of opening the book unfolded other pieces of paper and cards from between the pages; an ingenious design that popped up to form a sort of three-dimensional picture.

Each time she turned a page a new diorama would form from the unfolding card and paper between the pages. There were no words written within, but it appeared to show a story about an ancient (and hairy) old Troll who flew through the sky in a huge cart suspended in the air by a lumpy balloon and pulled by stags.

This Troll, dressed in red and white, was wearing a great black girdle and tall, black boots. He was throwing things at people below as he flew overhead. He seemed to be howling in each and every one of the pop-up three-dimensional pictures. Much of the color was faded and even a few parts were missing, but it was evident from the expensive silk that the book was wrapped in, and the delicacy with which the baling wire had been wound around it, that this book was precious beyond imagination to the Troll.

Of course she recognized a child's popup book, if not the specific legend within, when she saw one. She also decided not to comment on her own findings about the book.

"Where did you find this, Beornag?" she asked, warmth in her voice. She gently and reverently turned the pages with the utmost respect and caution so as not to damage the already worn and faded *relic*. "I mean ... who *were* these people who gave you such a treasure, and under what circumstances?"

"Dat is a long and sad story. Ize would raduh not tawk about it in da evil fortriss, if dats okay wit yooz two," he replied, his head hung low. It obviously made him uncomfortable, so she felt it wise not to pry.

She suspected that Ulm did not actually exist and that the Injoke was actually referring to an imaginary friend from his childhood, and that the book was all he had from a collection of blurry memories. Perhaps Ulm was Beornag's way to "fit in" with society.

She found herself wishing she had studied his people more, but being a southern species of Troll, his kind never used to frequent the warmer regions of the empire, and the surrounding nations, and as a result Alaeth's knowledge about hill Trolls was limited to being able to recognize one on sight, but little else. Her specialties lay in the histories and cultures of those in the warmer, Sylvanian peninsula.

Even so, most species of Troll, indigenous to the area, were either endangered or extinct. These two were the first she had ever actually, *formally* met.

For that matter, Beornag was the first Troll she had *ever* actually met. Of course she knew of his existence. She shopped in Briarwood and liked to keep up with current events. She had even seen him once, walking through the streets in the market district when she had been visiting the port city on a re-supply trip. She actually stalked him for a few minutes to make note of his mannerisms until he made contact with a terrifying creature- green-skinned, and armoured- an Urk. It was then that she felt it wise to leave them both alone.

Terdbreff and his people, however, were another story altogether. Alaeth practically specialized in Cave-Troll history, biology and culture. All she had told him was fact. Up until now, however, she never really recognized the tragedy of what was Troll history and, like so many others, accepted it as just the way things had always been.

Trolls had never really complained about their place in society, as far as she knew. Now she was beginning to realize that this was only because those who *would* complain were usually silenced. Even in the Empire, where all races were said to be welcome, there still existed prejudice and bigotry.

The irony was that among the rest of the imperial citizenry the Trolls' unfortunate history was common knowledge, but the Trolls themselves were kept in the dark about it all, to keep them as a working class of quasi (and in some cases *actual*) slaves. It occurred to her that she never really considered talking to a Troll before, because she never expected to learn anything from one. She realized that she, in all her years studying them, had never really thought to get to *know* any Trolls.

Suddenly she felt ashamed to call herself educated or civilized ... or open-minded. Her own racism ... *speciesism* began to haunt her thoughts. She quickly dismissed them and decided to change her views about Trolls, as comfortable as they used to make her feel.

The Injoke was a fascinating creature. Although he appeared for all intents and purposes to be a complete idiot, he was, in fact, in possession of a sort of natural talent for being wise out of sheer luck. Since she had been with him she had witnessed several occasions where they should have been killed, or at least discovered by the enemy, but instead something happened that forced them onto a new path that saved them from the last. He simply stumbled upon the next best thing to do, or path to take. It was almost *supernatural.*

She suspected, however, that *his* people met a similar fate as Terdbreff's, for they were even fewer in numbers than other Troll races. His were almost the rarest of them all; many believed them to be mythical creatures. In fact, in most of the world they were considered to be legendary.

CHAPTER - 14

"A TROLL BY ANY OTHER NAME..."

The following wildlife vignette is brought to you by;

Coverghoul Cosmetics

*"Un*clean Makeup ... *Co-*ver*ghoul."*

In all there are six Troll races in the world:

Mountain Trolls:

Who can grow as tall as a mountain and live for many thousands of years, (mostly sleeping). These gargantuan beings are in a state of constant mental exhaustion because their brains are, on a monumental scale, too small for their bodies and, as such, they constantly have to shut down some of their bodily functions in order to utilize others.

It is written in an ancient dwarfish text that there was once a mountain Troll so wise, and yet so huge, that he was able to make his home on top of a mountain peak where he would answer the questions of weary pilgrims, asking only for food in return. People would come from all around to scale the mountain and speak to the great Trollish oracle. Eventually almost one hundred percent of his brain was evolved to be dedicated to thought, memory, logic, philosophy and the physical upkeep of his giant head, which continually grew because there was a demand for more knowledge, and thus more brain matter, with every new visitor/wisdom-seeker, so much so, that the rest of his body shrank to be smaller than an elf, while his head was said to be hundreds of feet wide.

He was later joined by three others of his kind, who all suffered the same inevitable fate. They all grew so old they petrified, right there on that mountain.

Today those four are a tourist attraction that many humans claim to be sculpted by their own ancestors. Each year more and more rush to see the great spectacle that are the four founding fathers of their civilization.

(As a footnote: most complain that they were not allowed close enough to the megalith and that they could not see it very well. Of course, this is because at a closer inspection the masses would easily discover the ruse and realize the four faces were actually those of petrified Trolls, and not those of their own revered ancestors immortalized forever in stone).

Other mountain Trolls can spend hundreds of years sleeping, waking up only to take a stroll to a lake for a drink, or to some secluded place to relieve themselves before a quick snack of anything they could pick up that didn't scream, eventually returning to their eons-long slumbers against a mountain or under a pile of avalanche debris.

These, the greatest of the mountain Trolls, are the largest of all Troll-kind. They can grow to be over a thousand feet tall (it is believed there is no limit to their size) and are capable of causing catastrophic damage to anything that might be in their path. They seldom notice *anything* because their brains, as stated, are working overtime just to make them move.

On rare occasions, a mountain Troll (and other Troll species) will become what is known as Limbah. When in Limbah (also known among Trolls as Rushing), the Troll becomes extremely pale and bloated. It is also prone to fits of vocalizations where the repulsive creature can spend its waking hours yelling nonsensical and offensive things across the countryside, all the while stuffing itself with animal fat and bovine excrement. These are the most feared of all, as they seem to live forever and make everyone else's lives miserable.

The only way to quiet a Rushing Limbah Troll is to kill it with liberalism. Even other Trolls will readily volunteer to euthanize a Rushing Limbah Troll with detailed social planning or by supporting the arts, especially before his sickness spreads. Luckily these fits of verbal idiocy only last thirty to sixty minutes at a time and they do pause now and then for a couple minutes to catch their breath.

Hill Trolls

...also called Skunk Apes, Sasquatches, Yeti and a multitude of other misnomers. These creatures have an uncanny aura of good luck even during periods of bad luck. For example, a Troll who was sent to prison could likely find himself getting the best cell because the guy who had it died unexpectedly just as the Troll was entering the facility.

Or a Troll who was swindled out of his money for a handful of *"magic"* seeds throws them outside after realizing he has been tricked, then later, by accident, ends up growing a garden of beautiful prize-winning watermelons from those same seeds, winning first prize at the fair and getting his lunch too.

Although seemingly adolescent in intellect, and sometimes straight-up stupid by human standards, hill Trolls have remarkable wisdom/luck where their own well-being is concerned. They are known to make decisions on a whim and without thought, usually leading them into severe trouble or even apparent ruin, only to somehow, inexplicably and even miraculously (at a not so later date), come out *ahead* of the game.

Hill Trolls are usually reclusive creatures who live in very small family groups, or are seen alone, if seen at all.

Although possessing very little understanding of numbers, alphabets, and written tongues other than pictographs, these remarkable creatures have an adaptive natural ability for learning and communicating vocally (albeit sometimes clumsily) in any number of languages. (It should be noted that they also almost always speak with an accent so thick that they are still not understood by those who they are trying to communicate with in the first place).

Many people believe hill Trolls to be a missing link between human beings and apes.

The hill Trolls themselves just want everyone to make up their minds as to *what* they are so *they* can start blaming their relatives for all the crap that they've put them through.

Cave-Trolls

These are scaly, warty, spiny, callous- covered, gray or olive-green hulks of muscle and ... ahem ... intellect, who can range from a mere four feet in height (known as the Djeaupeshee people) to twenty-foot titanic monsters (known as resslers).

Djeaupeshees, the smaller of these, are cunning and thoughtful and sometimes even eloquently spoken creatures who are the smartest of their kinds (and partial to pinkie finger decorations).

They sometimes develop overly extended pinkie fingers due to the sheer weight of all the gold and other precious metals and gems they add to the collection over many years.

The oldest of this variety can be recognized by the huge assortment of items attached to their proudly worn pinkie rings. Some even utilize their rings, covered in metals and stones, as weapons. These smaller examples of the Cave-Troll subspecies are also the shortest-tempered, and it is advisable to approach them with caution. Though they can sometimes be friendly and welcoming, one must pay very close attention so as not to offend the Djeaupeshee Troll. These relatively small powerhouses can erupt in fits of rage-filled vengeance against those who would offend them.

Their favorite weapon is the simple writing pen, which they always carry as they have a fetish for writing things on the insides of bathroom stalls (particularly) or any place they can. The Djeaupeshee's pen is usually used as a stabbing weapon and with deadly effect. Among the Djeaupeshee Trolls there is a secret society, or at least *was*, which followed ancient martial art studies that evolved around the simple writing pen. No one knows why. This martial art was known as *"Mi Frenz Pen"*

The larger resslers are fearless warriors, and some are quite naturally adept at operating machinery and other simple inventions.

Resslers can also, sometimes, be seen ranting and raving about belts (a clothing accessory they seem to be obsessed with) while partaking in shows of dominance among the males and even (rarely) females. These displays are often joined by medium-sized Trolls known as Ma'ne'jurs.

These Ma'ne'jurs often gather about them many of the larger Trolls with promises of falafels and hoagies, as well as the odd jug of sour milk. Ma'ne'jurs are Trolls too small to be effective as warrior Trolls, like resslers, and not as smart as their smaller cousins the Djeaupeshees, but are known to be sneaky and sometimes downright cunning. These are the ones who usually end up as group leaders and even chieftains.

Some of these larger Cave-Trolls can also be exceptionally intelligent for their kind and even learn to read and write. Their true talent, however, lies in their ability to pick up on and adapt to the technology of others. Even if they cannot understand a device they will somehow still be able to operate it like an expert with little practice.

Tredbreff is a rare Ressler/Ma'ne'jur combination whose kind have only been recorded a handful of times throughout history. A mutant, if you will–massive, yet smarter than most Ma'ne'jurs

<u>Swamp-Trolls</u>

These are the only Trolls to ever learn to domesticate animals, namely the hard- and soft-tailed harleys and the giant Zorkobian crotch lobster.

They are remarkable creatures that only communicate in a bastardized version of common humanese, and only with sentences that include suggestions of either acts of senseless violence or celebration or both.

For example: A Swamp-Troll wants his friend to accompany him to his knitting class, so he says, *"Yo, man! Let's go kick the shit out of a pair of socks with a couple of spikes! It'll be awesome fun!"*

Swamp-Trolls stand on average around eight feet tall. They have varying colors of skin similar to human beings. They also grow facial hair much like human beings. In fact they appear to be fearsome, massive, human brigand-like people, for all intents and purposes- just much bigger.

They are *not*. Do *not* be fooled. They are monsters. Some are downright evil. Most are at least extremely dangerous when provoked.

For the better part, Swamp-Trolls remain in their dark mysterious abodes for many months deep among the cypress and mangroves where their females elate in exotic courting rituals that include dancing with tall golden poles.

Boisterous and sometimes brutish creatures, they (luckily for everyone else) only venture from their steamy abodes once in a while to interact with each other in rowdy celebrations, where they drink their horrible alcoholic invention known as bykr.

These *bykr parties* always involve competitions where the Trolls partake in the trick-riding of some of the peninsula's rarest creatures, hard-tailed harleys- and where they serve freshly steamed crotch lobsters straight from an Ogre's underwear and into a bubbling pot. These *bykr parties* are becoming harder and harder to locate as the species is, unfortunately, fading from the world, their traditional songs and dances all but forgotten as their younger generations are drawn into the cities and towns with the promises of sparkly lights and falafel stands.

Forest-Trolls

These are beautiful creatures resembling twenty-foot-tall, pudgy, animated piles of stone, with large, glossy, black obsidian eyes. They are exceedingly rare and even mythical in most parts of the empire. They are solitary, peaceful caretakers of the world's oldest and rarest flora and fungi- the protectors of plant and animal species that can only be found in very few places. Places where no other peoples ever walk.

Forest-Trolls are rumbling and rolling groups of living stones and pebbles that form the creatures' bodies. They procreate only once in their impossibly long lifespans and produce very few offspring that gestate within a dead tree for almost a hundred years before being born as a small worm-like creature that will later metamorphose three times, as a liquid, a mist, and finally a mineral- or, more accurately, a group of many different minerals.

Although it would seem they are more elemental than biological, and certainly not Trolls, they are in fact *self*-identified as Trolls and have always associated themselves and their purposes with Trolls and Trollish interests. No Troll, especially Forest-Trolls, would ever knowingly disrespect or endanger nature and the natural way of things for no good reason. Thus all Trolls are considered to be kin to Forest-Trolls.

The oldest of them are known to develop varieties of moss and lichen on their skins that actually, eventually, evolve separately as unique species of flora, indigenous to each specific Forest-Troll.

These creatures are believed to be peaceful and prefer to be left alone. They are also known for their unique ability to grow veins of precious gems and metals in their skins and "tissues."

Sadly, before the empire had formed, and *actually* begun to enforce laws to protect the almost extinct species, these poor creatures were nearly hunted into absolute oblivion for their hides as well as their organs, which were, quite naturally, massive single gemstones that could be measured in the thousands of carats each.

Th'rdkyend- aka: Alley and Inn Trolls

Who are so elusive that whole generations of humans are known to pass before a single one is even (authentically) spotted.

Even then, as the event is so rare and unheard-of, every time one *is* spotted the unfortunate person telling the tale is joined by hundreds of spotter wannabes (who only want attention) while the poor schmuck who *did* see one is called a liar and a fake, and is grouped in amongst the attention-seekers. In fact, some of these authentic Troll spotters eventually become ridiculed into hiding and the life of a hermit, far away from the heckling mobs.

Only the Elfish scholars have *always* known of the existence of the Th'rdkyend, while most other races see them as myths or have no knowledge of them at all. These creatures are said to suddenly appear, usually in alleys or roadside inns, often in the alleys between roadside inns (a sub- species known as Alleyinns).

They arrive in groups, accompanied by bright lanterns and strange sounds.

They are said to be quite short and gray-skinned, with disproportionately large heads and big black eyes. When spotted it is usually just before or just after a rare sighting of a hill Troll, sometimes strangely in sync with a sighting of another rare (and just as mythical) creature: the honest politician, (Although there is absolutely no evidence of the latter actually *ever* existing). It is as though seeing one would somehow trigger a sighting of the other. Many non-Trolls believed this to be a sort of conspiracy to cover up the assassination of an important inventor, (possibly of *quality* men's hosiery and undergarments), just saying.

Most Trolls were eventually manipulated into servitude and oppression so long ago no one even remembers the actual truth, and instead quite often tells a hyped-up or watered down version that always ends with the Trolls losing because *they* were the bad guys or at fault.

G'nomish ancient history shows that Trolls are much older than most races. Even as old as Elves, especially the Forest-Trolls, but not quite as old as G'nomes. However, it does not explain how they became the slaves of humans so long ago and why the human species eventually took control of any Troll who was not part of an undiscovered primitive tribe living in the wilderness regions of the world.

The Trolls have never tried to be a sovereign people as they are always kept separated from working with other Trollish races. They, in simple terms, are quietly kept from communicating with each other as a people.

Thus they have been, and are still, subject to whoever is paying for their next meal or tricking (or forcing) them into their next crime.

Either that or they are chased into exile and seclusion where they are sometimes forced to raid farms and small towns for food just to survive. This, of course, only strengthens the contempt that humans and most other *civilized* people feel for most types of Trolls.

That was the way it had always been, or so it seemed to the Cave, Swamp, and Hill Trolls.

To most humans, Trolls are like barely tolerated stray dogs one might feed scraps to from the back door- generally *not* given any sort of respect as unique peoples and distinct cultures, and mostly treated with no attempt to understand them as such.

Trolls have been unwittingly absorbed into most societies as either useful, brutish working-class dummies, or as the stuff of nightmares to be hunted down and destroyed.

Those who find themselves in the favor of their smaller masters usually speak that master's language and worship that master's gods, if the Troll is permitted to worship anything at all.

Some imperial citizens even accuse Trolls of *stealing* imperial culture, and will openly complain that the Trolls don't simply go back where they came from.

Of course, most of the Trolls in question are *exactly* where they had come from and have *been* coming from for hundreds of thousands of years before humans had even existed as anything other than omnivorous monkeys.

The Empire, however, is as close to a haven as can be found for Trolls. Trolls are actually better off living near Briarwood and the surrounding areas than any other place in the known world.

Farmers (for example), in the Empire, often hire local Trolls to pull plows at a much greater speed and depth than any oxen could hope to achieve.

Trolls are actually welcomed in rural areas where groups of farmers will erect a *Troll house* to attract a Troll who will soon learn that it is prosperous to help the farmers. Some Trolls even walk "pa-Trolls" to keep herds safe from predators.

Then there are those Trolls, like Terdbreff and the Injoke, who venture into urban areas on a regular basis and are seen as exotic and even iconic parts of those communities' local color and culture.

Truly at least one Troll, our very own Beornag, is somewhat of a celebrity in his home of Briarwood, and his face is even on the travel brochure where he is referred to as Briarwood's own *stand-up Sasquatch.*

In fact, pretty much everyone in Briarwood, until corrected, assumes he is something—*anything*—other than a hill Troll, as *they* are "only legends."

He, and others of his kind who have been equally lucky in their travels, are even used as a way to *describe* a specific village or town. Like a landmark pub or the stray dog everyone feeds. *"You know? ... that place with the Troll who farts smoke rings?"* – or *"What was the name of that village we were in where that Troll sang with that philharmonic orchestra?"*

The rest of the world, unfortunately, is not as hospitable for the slow-thinking Trolls (though *they* have no idea for the most part that this is so).

More often than not, normally good, law-abiding Trolls are subjected to being outsmarted into acts of crime, or downright lynched for their measly possessions or land holdings by liars, swindlers and social parasites–(also known as Corporate Financial Institutions), even though the Trolls themselves are actually protected under the Endangered Species Act.

Theirs is a sad story. The ever-present plight of Troll-kind was something that even I, up until the time I started getting to know Beornag, accepted as "just the way it was."

For more information about Trolls or for a copy of this wildlife vignette contact: The G'nomish Film Board Society, Sixty Six-Packs S treet, Allthewater, Sensimillia, 420420420.

CHAPTER - 15

"OKAY, OKAY, *NOW* THE SHIT *FINALLY* HITS THE FAN."

Now back to Alaeth and the boys...

She then spoke up. "Listen, guys ... Calabac, the, pfft, '*Master*' here, is planning to destroy everything and turn it all into *garbage* and *rot*." She seemed agitated about whatever she was going on about so the two listened slightly longer, before returning to their equally short daydreams, which seemed to always get interrupted by newer and better daydreams. "He has tricked most of his army into serving him and bribed the others with lies to gain enough power to summon whatever he is going to summon."

She *absolutely* knew more than Beornag did ... or remembered. "Ize just gotta ax; how does yooz *knows* all a dis?" he inquired. "Ize is only axin cuz Ize just came here for yooz, sos Ize can get a reward and buy a new cat. Ize trew mine at da guys upstairs. *Oh*, an cuz Ize likes ya sista and wanted ta help *her* out- dat too a'course.

Oh *yeah* an ta rescue my buddies." He smiled. "Oh! An cuz now Ize likes yooz too." He smiled warmly.

"Calabac needed a virgin to sacrifice, or something ..." She immediately looked at Beornag and added, "... Shut ... up!" (He had looked like he was about to say something). "...in order to entice the demon god to come here from its *own* world. Only with her blood, or something, will the demon come and possess whoever Calabac chooses to carry its power and will. At least that is what I got from listening to him go on about how great he was. Beornag, he thought *I* was that virgin." Then, "I said shut up!" She shook a threatening finger at him as he once again was about to interrupt. "... and Calabac spoke a *lot* around me."

"He loves to show off and has an enormous ego. It was easy to trick him into spilling the beans. He actually said he was in love with me at one point and I almost convinced him to pack it all in and become a gentleman farmer with me as his wife. Can you believe that? Oh god, just gag me."

"Wow. Ize bet William woulduh *not* liked dat at all," Beornag said, scratching his brow.

She was impressed that he knew about William, but decided to just accept that he did. "Poor William. I believe Calabac had him murdered and replaced with a doppelganger, After he found out that William and I..." She fell silent for a moment, then: "Terdbreff, do you think you can get your family to follow Beornag instead of Groynchies?"

"Not sure. Who be Boarsbag?" he asked, confused.

"Yeah, who's Boarsbag, en whutsa dingleplunga?" Beornag added.

She looked at the Injoke ... then at Terdbreff ... and then back at Beornag again, and all was silent for a moment.

Then another moment later...

... and then finally ...

"Oh! Ah haha ha-yeah. Dat's Ize, brudduh," the Injoke said to Terdbreff. "Ize's *stage* name is Pelvis, Ize's real name is Boarsbag, Injoke of Ulm."

"Beornag," she corrected.

"What?" he responded.

"Beornag - that's your name, not Boarsbag," she explained.

"Den whose dis Boarsbag guy?" he asked.

"There's no Boarsbag, Beornag," she tried to explain. "That's just how Terdy says your name."

He turned to Terdbref. "Maybe yooz should call me by da name everybody calls Ize in Briarwood: Pelvis. 'Cuz dats Ize's name when Ize is bein famuss an' stuff."

"He knows that, Injoke," Alaeth interrupted.

"'Course he does, silly. Ize just told him. Look who ain't payin' attenchin' now, *aaah*?"

"Boarsbag gotta fight Groynchies. Only if Boarsbag win, family will follow," Terdbreff lamented hopelessly. Obviously thinking that the Injoke was not up to the challenge.

"Hmmm ..." Beornag began to scratch his impressively wide if not deep brow. Then he moved his attention to scratching his crotch as he stared off into some memory or daydream. "...Da last time Ize had groin cheese, da docta told ize ta rub it wit..."

"Beornag?" It was Alaeth. "Honey, you have to stop for a moment." She took a deep breath, and then exhaled. "Terdbreff is talking about *Groynchies* the usurper of Terdy's throne, not that nastiness *you* were referring to just now. You are going to have to fight a giant Cave-Troll who is bigger than even *you*, sweetie. You understand now? Huh?" She rubbed his upper arm to comfort him. "But nice try. Now listen to Terdy and let him finish, okay?" She then gestured for Terdbreff to continue.

"Groynchies gots magic. Him gots suit dat protecs him." Terdbreff looked worried. "Nuffin' break Groynchies' suit. No sword, no mace, no axe or hammer. Master make it. Terdbreff know."

"Dat's funny cuz Ize got dis 'ere weapon dats also's s'posed ta be indescribable an Ize is itchin' ta see what happens when Ize whacks dat big bully wit it." He proudly presented his maul. "Suit or no suit, weez cannot allow dat traita ta continuize his bastardly mechanicalizations."

"Dastardly machinations," Alaeth corrected him.

"Yes! Not havin' a dad who can fix a lever or wedge ain't no excuse for bein' a jerk," he agreed.

He then looked to Terdbreff again, all decked out in heavy iron-plated, spiked armour with a terrible-looking, jagged-edged battleaxe on his back. His helmet was like an upside-down colander made of blackened steel and riddled with spikes like a giant sea urchin. In the front there was a sort of hatch that was presently wide open, exposing Terdbreff's wide, smiling face.

The Injoke took several steps toward him and shoved a large cigar into Terdbreff's mouth, lighting it for him and speaking as dramatically and as eloquently as (Alaeth could imagine) he was capable of, while the twisted roll of herb began to sparkle and shoot little embers of multicolored light and smoke from the burning tip.

Alaeth was so lost as to what these two were about to do next she was ready to scream. It was like babysitting dinosaurs. The worse thing was that she was almost ready to resign herself to believing she would never actually escape, but at the same time anticipating the relief of what a sure and sudden death would bring by not having to try and follow the mind-boggling logic of those two behemoths any longer, all the while secretly enjoying every minute.

"Terdbreff, Ize's friend an road mannijuh f' dese last long an meeninful minutes gone by just now ..." Beornag stood next to the shorter, stockier Cave-Troll and placed his arm around the great green monster. "Fan club president an loyal supplia a fine cheeses, wines, an quality jerked meaty treats. Yooz, whooz is possibly da most intelectualized (but less attractive, tall, talented and wisdomized as Ize is) of all Trollish populisms, Ize is axin yooz, brave son a da mustiest caves nort a anywhere ... operatuh a claustrophobic, yet surprisinly drafty transportationalizin contraptionisms ...

"... Will yooz come wit Ize? Will yooz follow Ize, Beornag Injoke of Ulm the Freakin Hilarious, t' do battle wit dis upslurpa a' Trollish freedomisms?

"Yooz can't de-feet him alone, Ize's girthy compatreeit, but weez can bote take a foot each an *co*-opratize ... allowin' us ta *de*-feet owa mutual enema togethuh, once and fer all ... or in mutualizationing ferevuhness ... or ... which evuh makes more sense, cuz Ize lost track a what Ize was talking about." He scratched the top of his flat head and noticed he had LOST HIS PROPELLER BEANIE! "Just a sec," he said with a shocked look on his face.

Then he loped over to the stairs they had just ascended and disappeared over the edge of the platform.

A moment later he returned with his beanie once again atop his neanderthalic brow. He smiled and looked around, nodding periodically at his two friends to show his continuing involvement in the discussion, mainly because he had forgotten what was said last, and who had said it, and didn't want to look like he had lost track of what was going on.

He looked behind to see who everyone was looking at. There was no one there. He then looked back at his new friends smiling as Alaeth gently tapped her foot with her little arms folded in front of her and her cute little nose all...

"Aha!" he suddenly remembered. "Weez is gonna pound da crap outta Groynchies and unificationalize Trolls everywhere. Yooz will lead em, buddy," he elated, putting his arm around Terdbreff's shoulder once again, guiding him in a purposeful and dramatic tour of the round platform, using his massive other hand to trace a frame in the air for an imaginary picture in front of the two behemoths. "Imiginize ...yooz on da Trone a da kingdum. Weez can live in da forest and call it ... *Trollywood*. Yooz, the fearless and justificationalized emperor penguine a da whole freakin' genetal tick's pool. "Yooz, my compatree'it, is a good head soze deyz is gonna be in good hands. Ize on da udda hand will use Ize's great healin' hands and as such should get good head ... Ize tinks ... *AND* ... Ize will educationalize our populisms all about weez's holy creator, Ulm The Freakin' Hilarious."

"Groynchies gone now," Terdbreff reported.

"Dats *great*!" the Injoke elated. "Did yooz use dat special yelluh cream dat da docta gives ya when yooz been sleepin wit ..."

"No, Beornag." Alaeth corrected him. "He is talking about the *bad* Troll who is bullying all the *other* Trolls into serving Calabac,"

"Well den ... um ... maybe somebody should give *him* some a dat yellow stuff dat ..." he tried again.

"No, listen. His *name* is Groynchies, and he is a *bad* Troll and he has left the fortress, but *you* have to fight him and win the adoration of the other Trolls so you and Terdy can unite your peoples," Alaeth pleaded, desperately trying to clarify things for the Injoke again.

"Where'd he go den?" Beornag asked. "An how do yooz propose weez find da willin' damsels to give me ...?"

"Wine!" Alaeth interrupted. "Such wonderful wine. Where is Groynchies, Terd?" *Did I just say that?* she added to herself

"Him lead Trolls wiff awmy of master to water town pace to make all burn. Dey leave long time ago. Two or fifty hours I tink," he answered.

"Did you *hear* dat, *I'll-Lay-it*? Two or fifty *hours* even. Dat's a long time! Weez betta get a move on if weez is gonna catch dat awmy before suppa and in time ta do whateva it was dat weez was plannin' ta do." He sighed. "Ize is wishin Grarr was here right now. He can rememba stuff like whut weez was disgusting."

"Discussing," Alaeth corrected him.

"Na, not really. Grarr's akshally pretty clean, an polite. He wears dis really nice cologne too. Ize don't read all dat good but da picture on da label is of a guy wit a pretty dame givin 'em phala..."

She suddenly interrupted him. "Beornag, you mentioned before about your friends that you needed to rescue, remember?" she inquired, thankfully changing the subject.

For the record and in Grarr's defense (as he is unable to represent himself here at this time), the girl in the picture is giving the guy a flirtatious look ... not a "phalatatious look," as the Troll was about to say.

"Grarr ... Durik ... da little old guy..." He was counting on both hands now. "... an' f' da life a Ize, Ize can't rememba who dat last guy was. It'll come ta Ize dough. Ize knows it." He smiled.

"Where are they being held?" she asked.

"Oooo! Terd knows dis one!" Terdbreff held his hand up, waving it back and forth in hopes of being picked.

"Ize ain't got a clue," the Injoke thought out loud. "Hey! Ize taught out loud! Ize really done it! Yooz heard it, right?!" he added proudly.

She sighed again. This time it was sheer mental exhaustion. "Okay, Terdy. Where are they?" she pleaded.

He stood straight and as tall as he could. His eyes focused on some imaginary point and he began to verbally present his answer as if in a spelling bee. "Da blue fightin' guy, who smash all dem snow humies on road, is in basement of master's magic house part of footriss."

He smiled and took a breath. "Little old big-nose Goblin, in black pajamas who smell like 'spensive cheese be free wit rat man, sum pace in footriss."

Again he smiled. "Green Grarrrrrr guy be chased off, an' darkness monster take army an kill dat one."

Okay...let's take a real short break so you can take a headache pill, or whatever it is you need to do in order to absorb any more of what these guys are saying ... just be glad you don't live with them. Oy.

...

...

Ready? Okay then...

...!!!...!!!

What now?!!!...!!!

It's my agent, kids. I have to take this. One second, please. Sing a song or something, I'll be back in a jiffy- LOVE my G'nomeys.

Okay, what!?I'm tellin a story here! These kids are reading, for crying out loud!

Well, okay ... who is it?

Who?!

Peter Jac ... wh ...who? He's got Taika Wai-who with him?

Well tell him I'll call him back, I'm busy telling a story about someone telling me a part of a story I am telling, because I wasn't there for the part I am telling the story about! It's quite involved and I can't be disturbed.

Wha ...? A what!? A ... A movie?! What the heck is a movie?! Just tell him I'll call him back.

Jeesh. Amateurs. You write a couple books, make a couple people laugh, grow some really good herb – and everybody suddenly wants to be your friend.

Anyway ... where was I?

Oh yeah..

"Hunh!?" Beornag exclaimed as he froze in place.

Just then a cage descended from the darkness above on the cables and slipped perfectly into one of the cages that were already on the platform.

Then two gates, one on the outside and one on the inside of the cage, rolled open on a set of well-oiled tracks simultaneously. Terdbreff approached and stepped into the huge freight car, gesturing for them to follow.

"Terd, did yooz just say dat Grarr is dead?" the Troll asked.

"Maybe yes and probly cuz darkness monster take lots humies and rat guys an even dead humies too. Only one Grarr an he gitz sticked wiff Tro' bote frum stickshoota. So I sezin' yes probly," he reported quite officially as he boarded the huge cage/cable car. "Demz be gone chasin' Grarr, eighteen hours and three and seventeen quarters of minutes and a half week ago."

"Holy crap dat sounds like a long time! I didn't know Grarr was dat old ... and ta tink ...weez only just got here an already all dat time has passed. *Ize* ain't even dat old! Or at least Ize wasn't dat old when Ize first got here! "Do yooz tinks we could be time sharin', or travlin', or whateva makes betta sense? Maybe Ize is yooz's uncle, Terdbreff! Or even maybe yooz's grand- fadda's grandson, or ya mudduh's uncle's third cousin-in- law! Ize means ..." The injoke followed Terdbreff onto the massive freight elevator continuing his analysis of current events *and* their *most probable* effects on the space-time continuum.

It was possibly better that the Injoke completely forgot about Grarr's death right then. If he had digested the information completely he might have lost it right there and decided to fight the entire army of evil single-handed, in hopes of a quick death and relief from the misery of losing his best friend- his ... *family.*

Alaeth followed, mentally exhausted, and almost reluctantly she took a place in the back of the huge cage-like cable-car. The gates magically closed behind her as she spoke to Terdbreff, gnawing on a stick of venison jerky. "Take us to where the blue fighter is, Terdy." She held onto a rail that was actually for that exact purpose, as Terbreff made adjustments to the machinery that controlled the functions of the elevator. "This meat is soooo freakin' good. Have you had any of this, Injoke? I mean it's absolutely decadent."

"Terdbreff! Is weez gonna time travel?" Beornag asked, with a gasp of amazement. "Cuz den Ize could actually taste dat exact piece a meat dat *she* is eatin' now, but Ize could do it layta! Or before. Den yooz could have a go at it, and den weez could do it all over again. Dat one piece a jerky could feed da entiya planet! Oooo! Ooo! Maybe even da *world*!"

Terdbreff put his arm around the Injoke's shoulder, and did his best to mimic Beornag's theatrical and animated physical embellishments with the other, free arm. "Graytess of funny Tros, Boarsbag Insocks, Terdbreff's loyow fren and helper into Tro king big chair hopefoowy sumday maker guy." The instinctive Trollish penchant for the dramatic seemed to be surfacing in Terdbreff now.

"Yes, O newly appointed leada a da Troll-vilized woyald an' beyond. What can Ize, Beornag Injoke do ta ..."

Alaeth could take no more. They were spending more time talking about things and honoring each other than they were trying to escape. She interrupted them. "Will you *please ... just ... get us ...* to the *blue fighter* before Beornag's *next* birthday, *for the love of gods*?!"

"Ooo! Dats in only less den a week, on Chooseday- only sixty-tree days from two and a half months ago yesterday! Ise's gonna be five," Beornag reported proudly. "Dat is if dis time distortion don't wreak havoc wit my age."

"Terd!" She was beginning to grind her teeth.

"Sure. It be dis button." Terdbreff pushed the last button needed to make the cage ascend, finally, into the darkness above.

Beornag then started a theatrical commentary of their current events as the car rattled its way along the cables that guided it on its vertical path. "An so da stall-wart-infected, adventagerous traveluhs an deir diminuitive, yet classy, elfish broad refugee wit da nice rack, ass-end up and front-end too, dependin' on which way weez might be facin' at any given moment ... on a parrotless journey into ..." He was interrupted again.

"Please ... just ...stop talking for a moment!" she screamed.

From here, the cable car/elevator ascended (silently) hundreds of feet through a vertical shaft lined with a chaotic menagerie of pipes and cables, shafts and ducts.

When they finally slowed it was to approach a structure that housed a hub of cables. The mechanical sounds that accompanied every function of the cable car system echoed throughout the vast shaft and duct workings of the fortress interior. Alaeth wondered why such a system of machines was not being put to more use.

Theirs was the only car they had seen since leaving the *poopfuric ass'id* factory now many hundreds of feet below them.

Yes, that is what the Troll decided to name the stuff ... Poopfuric Ass-id.

Many shafts branched out in several directions and at different angles, each with its own series of cables and tracks sized to facilitate several different sizes of cable cars.

Their own car swung gently on its support lines as it followed a new track of cable into the hub building and finally to a gentle stop.

"Ooo, look!" Terdbreff was pointing to an Ogre who had set up his *feel awful* stand on the boarding platform their car was presently docked at.

"Nooo waaaayyy!" Beornag roared as he forced the doors of the cable car open, leaped from the giant iron cage onto the platform and proceeded toward the ethnic food vendor, Terdbreff following closely behind.

Alaeth, at first, was about to protest, but then finally decided to surrender to the whim of sheer stupidity and two of the biggest idiots she had ever encountered in her entire life. Lovable idiots, for sure. But *this* was something, she had decided, that should be bottled and used as a weapon.

Stupidity Under Pressure.

Then the cable car began to move again.

The Trolls then gathered up their *feel awfuls,* after paying an Ogre named Nozpikr, and raced across the platform to catch their car.

Alaeth had to admit, she was not the least bit frightened at that point. This alone should have been enough to convince her she had completely lost all grasp of reality.

What happens at the evil fortress, stays at the evil fortress, she thought. *I'm never getting out of here anyway. I might as well just go along with them and die laughing.*

(on a footnote: In another dimension, at the very moment she spoke those words, a little-known god of an oppressed, yet somehow happy people had just become substantially more powerful than he was, and he laughed out loud).

She had just accepted a mysterious (if not outright questionable) beanball sandwich type-thing, from a monster in an evil fortress, whose name described a disgusting habit involving bodily excreta, and was now (hopefully) continuing her escape from said fortress with her companions (yet even *more* monsters), while enjoying the aforementioned legume-like mystery and washing it all down with a glass of wine that could easily be worth a fortune in platinum ingots.

Yet here she was and she was alive and out of that wooden box the *'lord of the lisp'* had her locked up in. She had to admit the Injoke *had* managed to keep her relatively safe so far (and with a few good laughs to boot) AND he did somehow manage to heal her wounds when he found her. (Though she expected it might have been more a reaction to the *magical water* he had offered her. Perhaps it had been enchanted and he was using the liquid to strengthen his claims to be a true leader of a faith.)

Although he was sad and a bit pathetic, she had decided that he meant no harm and his fantasies were just his way of getting people to like him. He was either a very sweet and well-meaning charlatan or ... well ... a sweet and well-meaning idiot. She decided it didn't matter anymore; this was the most fun she had ever had. Getting kidnapped was totally worth it and if she was to do it again she wouldn't change a single thing ... well ... not so far ... sort of.

She might be *kind* of having fun, but she was doing so with two Trolls ... she wasn't stupid. She was well aware of the kind of hooliganism two bull Trolls could get into. In fact, she was in the *middle* of that very same variety of mayhem and the unbelievably stupid and random occurrences that were the moments that make up a day in the lives of a couple of bull Trolls.

In a very ironic way she was actually living the dream, so to speak. Think about it: she went to university to learn about trolls and earned an impressive degree in that exact discipline. This was a dream field study for any xenologist specializing in Trolls.

The Two behemoths had made it back to their car just as it finished a track change and was beginning to leave the hub. It exited through one of several gates smaller than the one they had entered. As they *enthusiastically* ate their *feel awful* sandwiches and priceless hundred-year-old Aldarian eldar nectar (expensive wine from Terdbreff's private stash), they began a slow but short descent to a junction where the car once again switched cables.

Terdbreff was quite adept at operating the vehicle and he soon had them underway and headed toward a large iron gate at the end of a long, dark shaft.

The three enjoyed the last of their *feel awfuls* and washed them down with another bottle of exceptionally good wine. This bottle was from a human vineyard and a favorite of Terdbreff's called Ernie and Joolly's Gallows.

As they approached the end of the shaft the gate opened ahead, flooding the tunnel with a soft, eerie green light.

Soon after, to her dismay, Alaeth could hear the sound of hundreds, if not thousands, of iron-shod boots on flagstone, great wheels grinding, and horns sounding out in the not so distant distance.

They passed through another short tunnel, and as the eerie green light grew in intensity, another big iron gate opened where they emerged into a massive, sloping and curving hallway filled with the sounds of marching soldiers, and the steady, rhythmic chinking of a million links of chain and scale armour, worn by a force that moved as one single entity.

Through the cable car's iron gridwork decking they could see below a terrible army of the walking dead, mobilized and marching through the great corridor beneath them in the same direction their car was traveling. The air itself seemed to glow with a sickly green haze.

As their car found a linking cable to the main thoroughfare, it began to follow the curve of the vast corridor along a main track system, located in the very peak of the vaulted ceiling.

Like a river of shuffling and rotting death, the terrible force made its way forward along the grand entryway and toward an ascending ramp leading outside to the southeastern slopes of the volcano fortress.

All along the inside wall of the subterranean superhighway there were breaks in the surface where mirage-like waves of heat sometimes escaped the volcano's core to drift among the passing troops and their terrible war machines.

Colossal skeletons of mighty and ancient pachyderms, and other titanic animals now long extinct, towed machines of war so otherworldly in design and material that Alaeth was not able to even fathom their possible uses.

For Beornag this was a place he was able to actually recognize. It was the main entrance! Where he had first laid siege (and a generous layer of mixed feces and vomit) on the fortress (and several of its residents)!

"Hey, Terdbreff! Weez is almost at da mess hall!" Beornag yelled over the sound of marching far below.

"Oooo! Terd 'members now!" he exclaimed and adjusted the controls before Alaeth could protest.

Instead of docking only thirty feet from a clearly marked and unguarded exit on their left that led quickly and efficiently out of the fortress, the car made a sudden right turn into and far above what was once the main trade floor and marketplace for the fortress' denizens.

The air here, even this far from the shit- and vomit-covered surfaces far below, was thick with the actual taste of the horrific mixture of bodily expulsions that was now fermenting in small lakes below. "For fuck's sakes, please get us out of this stench!" Alaeth yelled.

She gazed in a confused state of repulsed horror and real disappointment for not being present when the whole shitstorm happened.

She required no descriptions of what took place there. She had been in Beornag's company for less than a day and she already recognized his handiwork. She gagged several times and reveled in what must have been a horrifically traumatizing experience for her captors. "Up yours!" she yelled at them, laughing, gagging, and shaking her fist.

As she gazed upon the mayhem below and imagined what had transpired not long past, she wondered what might have gone through the minds of those unfortunate souls who had undoubtedly been bathed in excrement and vomit.

She was disappointed that her sister, the artist, hadn't the courage to live a little, and that she was not present to witness all of this. *Surely, this was enough to provoke a creative response,* she thought, barely holding back her laughter.

She looked over at Beornag who was now gazing out over the battlefield/marketplace, his eyes all glossy with a kind of homecoming look; like an artist scrutinizing his greatest masterpiece. She decided right then that he was magnificent. Her best friend ever.

Below them were several creatures *each* almost twenty feet tall. These were the Forest-Troll/night janitors, cleaning up the indescribable bio-catastrophe the Injoke had left in his wake after his initial ... ahem ... *purge* of the fort's defenses.

These were creatures who were once the wardens of the moss-covered stones and clear streams of ancient forests and glades all over the empire and its wildest frontiers. Now they had been lowered to slave status.

She could barely hold back her tears.

Their once multi-layered lichen and moss coverings of vibrant greens and almost shining silvers were now reduced to dull grays and lifeless arid browns. Their stone-pebbled skin, once sparkling with rare minerals and even precious gems and metals, was now scarred and chipped away-at.

Alaeth knew these creatures only from books. She never dreamed she would ever see one, let alone the last ten of them all in one spot!

Here, she actually wept for them. She knew what they were and how infinitely special they were. Reduced to cleaning up for the very same powers that stripped them of their freedom and stole their rightful homes in the deep forests of the world. "It's so sad, Beornag. Look at them." She gripped his lower arm and he gave her a gentle hug.

"Weeze is gonna save doze guys, don'choo worry *Ill-Lay-It*. Weez will. Ize promisez." He, too, wept, and growled.

As the cable car passed over them, the forest trolls looked up and pointed, alerting each other to the intruders overhead. Being the Forest variety of Troll, they were biologically incapable of making any sound louder than a slight whisper, thereby making them great, so-called *invisible servants*, like busboys, bellhops, or in this case the night janitors. This, however, also, made them terrible guards and as such no one was alerted to the trio's presence as they made their way across the high ceiling of the still worse-than-sewer-like marketplace.

As much as the Forest-Trolls tried to call out to the Cave-Trolls and *Tallow Shins* within sight, their already whispering voices were completely drowned out by the great army, now exiting the volcano fortress through the very gates Beornag had originally arrived through.

Then, suddenly, the car came to a stop.

"Terdy?" Alaeth's voice was trembling with confusion, sorrow for the Trolls, and fear.

Their car had crossed the marketplace and had paused before entering a great hallway. "No worries. Terdy know whut I is doin'. Stage not far and maybe we see Terdbreff bruvers from same muver."

The car squealed slightly and jumped suddenly as it switched from a flexible cable support to a rigid system mounted to the wall of the corridor ahead.

Eventually the car slowly descended to level out only a few feet from the floor, as it made its way closer to what appeared to be a boarding ramp for a major hub of cable cars, now abandoned; theirs was still the only functioning car within sight.

Here the car followed the tracks through a mechanical frame that transferred the unit to another track system that ran along the floor.

It moved along the outside of a curved corridor (as large as the one that the undead army was, at that very moment, exiting the fortress through).

This one also had war machines lined up along the opposite wall from where they were now descending, but these were of a kind that Alaeth was able to recognize as being of this world: catapults, ballista and other siege engines of wood and metal.

As they looked back at the open gate to the market, the Forest-Trolls had given up on warning their masters of the intruders and their Cave-Troll prisoner and returned to their duties of cleaning the market.

Soon the cable car once again slowed, then came to an abrupt stop at a disembarking platform. Beornag and Alaeth both turned to see Terdbreff casually pulling levers and turning dials and switches.

The cable car doors then opened with the sounds of hydraulics and moving gears, and there on the embarkation platform stood a small army of *Tallow Shins* and armoured Cave-Trolls.

Before any one of them could speak, Terdbreff was stepping out onto the loading ramp making his musical presentation to the troops.

"*Naaa na-na-na, na naa naaaaaaah.*" He dropped to one knee while he moved to the side, gesturing with his long arms for the confused assault force to applaud the arrival of the superstar standing inside the cable car ⁻(who was at that very moment desperately trying to pull a large bag of shit from his backpack).

As Terdbreff turned to see Pelvis Grizzly's grand entrance, a massive, eighty-lb bag of ultra-condensed liquid feces flew past him, striking the Talotian ... eh, excuse me, the *Tallow Shin* commander, who was standing in front of his troops waiting for an explanation.

The officer was actually forced to back up a few feet from the sheer impact of the massive excre-missile (as the Troll *later* decided to name his invention) while fecal soup, that was *not* saturating *his* entire body, was splattered all over several troops standing behind him and to his sides.

A single, tiny droplet of *poopfuric ass'id* (again as the Troll liked to call *that* particular stuff) managed to backfire and hit Terdbreff's left pectoral armour plate. It slowly ran down the pitch-black, generously worn and scarred surface of the armour component, actually stripping the paint and leaving a narrow, shining trail of freshly exposed alloy.

A single tear formed in Terbreff's right eye. "Me never wash dat piece again."

Chapter - 16

"The Taming of the Shrooms"

It took me about ten minutes to find a source of water nearby in the form of what must have been a public drinking fountain, and another five minutes to clean up. It had not been a big poop and I was happy to have had a change of clothes in my bottomless backpack.

Hey! Gimme a break- I'm gettin' old.

By that time events in the great domed enclosure were coming to full fruition. It was evident that those within the almost fully materialized scene filling the great gazebo were now realizing that an entire underground city was now materializing before *their* eyes.

What had been black walls to them were now becoming transparent, as their hiding place within the garden of The Bong (and what I was understanding to be a temple of the Mellow One) merged together as one.

Musky and I, once again, crossed the gardened court and climbed the stair to the temple's entrance (but not before I hung my wet clothes on a nearby park bench to dry).

As I ascended the last step the image solidified completely and all the Gnomes that had been inside the Bong box, which itself was inside my magic backpack, now stood and moved toward me.

I stepped into the garden, which was already attracting small flying insects to its pungent and sweet aromas, and as I did so the great Bong, which stood in the middle, began to bubble and glow.

Huge plumes of thick, heavy, white smoke poured from the large opening in the top as the bowl-shaped bottom glowed ever so brightly and began to emit noticeable warmth.

I took control of the moment and gestured for them all to look upon the Bong as it reacted to my movement. The closer I was, the brighter the lights became.

"Behold!" I exclaimed as I pointed toward events which I was sure were about to unfold. "Lost tribe of Sensimilia! You, who stand before me, who were the unda-tings! You, who were once, and are now once again, Gnomes! Look and see a miracle from our creator and lord of mellowness."

I walked forward as the assembly of Gnomes once again fell to their knees in reverence and moved aside, making way, as I approached the Bong. The closer I came to it the warmer the air around it became and an image within became clearer and clearer.

Durik ... again I felt like a parent must feel. It was like he really was something special. Like ... he was my own son.

The Gnomes reached out to touch my clothing as I passed among them, and I was relieved to have had the foresight to have changed my last pair after my accident.

Oy.

I continued ever closer to the great glass cauldron with anticipation and hope that Durik would finally emerge from its mystical depths.

Inside the bulbous lower body of the Bong, his shape was materializing clearer and clearer, spread-eagled and floating in a bubbling cauldron of smoky tendrils and sparkling lights. I could hear a voice then...

Yup, you guessed it.

"*Szvirrrrf,*" he said.

"Whattaya think *so* far? Not bad, eh?" I was feeling preeeetty good about my progress to date at that point.

"*Your path is clearer than anticipated. Others are near — though far away,*" he said.

"That's good, I'm guessing. Right? That's good?" I was beginning to wonder what he was getting at ... and thought it a good time to ask for a pay hike.

"*Though distance in time is great, time is short in distance,*" he said as I almost had an aneurysm trying to figure out what he was getting at.

"What the heck does that mean?!" I asked as tentacles of herb vines grew about my ankles and wisps of sacred pollen danced in the air about my wide-brimmed hat.

By this point the whole massive dais that was the floor of Shiddumbuzzin's gazebo/temple had transformed into soil and flowering herb plants. The garden of The Bong, with all of its phosphorescent stones and fungi; its bushy bud-laden herb trees that circled the great device in rings of flowering sticky wonder; its lovely garden furniture (which I actually hadn't noticed before- sorry:) was in its full glory.

Durik's form was now fully visible within the massive bowl-shaped reliquary that was the belly of The Bong. He floated within, spread-eagled and facing us all, his eyes closed as though he was dead- though I knew he was not.

However, I did not see the strange-looking sword that had been in there before and wondered for a moment where it might have gone.

That weapon of gold and silvery serrations that took control of me and gave me courage like I had never experienced. It had left something behind in me. Even then it was tangible to me.

The Gnomes had all gathered around me at this point and were *ooing* and *awing* and quite entertained by it all.

"What shall become of our paladin, oh mellow one!?" I suddenly exclaimed. My voice carried throughout the temple, as everyone unexpectedly fell silent.

Then "Mellowwww onnnnne," the Gnomes added in unison.

"Why is he trapped within the mystical confines of the Bong!?" It felt like my voice was carrying into and throughout the entire city. I gotta tell ya, between the pheromone-erupting elf women, sex teleporter-thing at the volcano fortress, and *this*, my libido was in full function.

I thought of Schnipsy just then. She was...

Never mind. Where was I?

Oh yeah.

...Again I must remind you that it seemed at the time that the great mellow one was becoming more and more lucid (if not stoned) as I became more dramatic in my communications with him. The more I worshiped him, the greater Shiddumbuzzin was becoming! Or so it seemed.

The Gnomes were absolutely astounded by all that was happening around them as together in sync they added: "Booonnnnng."

The garden was now coming to life fully (as opposed to mostly) and the sacred trees were beginning to reach for the ceiling of the massive dome, their trunks full and thick as a Troll's waist. The firestones in the rotunda's roof glowed ever brighter the closer the buds reached and all around us humming birds and small flying insects of all colors and sizes were arriving.

These beautiful creatures came from down the main street and quite obviously from some unknown opening to the surface world, perhaps in the main reservoir chamber miles back and above us. Summoned by the holy events that were taking place, it was as though they had flown all that way just for a whiff of the sacred herb in full flower—which was spicy, skunky, citrusy, and magical.

The whole city continued to light up as it became ever more evident that firestones were actually running like veins all throughout the great metropolis and surfacing from the green and black granite in the forms of useful lighting, tools and appliances. Each lamp post had a vein running up its center to surface precisely at the top, flooding the immediate area in dim amber light. All the firestones I had seen since I entered the reservoir far above and *thought* had been placed there by mortal hand were actually part of a single enormous firestone deposit made up of interconnected veins that must have resembled a mass of crystal spider webs within its protective shell of hard, ancient stone. In the very womb of the mountain high above.

Here the basalt and granite of the cavern had been carved into the lampposts, buildings, and even the public furnishings. The entire city was one massive sculpture, while the firestones themselves had been grown or cultivated *within* the structures to somehow form the city's network of lighting and heating, and for the conducting of hootspa energy.

It was as though the precious crystal had grown *into* the other stonework, like fungus bores into the fabric of old rotting wood. Yet I could see no geological evidence that could explain how it had come to be so perfectly arranged, so as to actually be part of every inch of the great city, nor could I explain how such a massive deposit could exist in one spot.

The streets were pulsing with flickering lamps that had lain dormant for eons, and only now were being coaxed back to functioning with the energy of the Mellow-one's new life force.

The sounds of water could be heard underfoot, being pumped through complex plumbing systems. Fountains that had sat dry and silent for so many eons were now coming to life. Their many figures, monsters, and characters of some forgotten

G'nomish legends spewed and sprayed water in decorative and creative ways.

Small gardens were suddenly animating here and there as they were fed life-giving water from automatic systems all over the city. Plants and trees that had sustained themselves for countless millennia on very little, now gorged on the new source of nourishment.

Great rivers of firestone pulsed and thrummed overhead, lighting the entire city in waves of amber radiance. Among these rivers, and suspended from the ceiling, were great mechanical systems for carrying elaborately decorated rail and cable cars. These I would later learn were used to transport people and goods all over the great metropolis.

Even as the *Holy One* began to answer me, we could hear the workings of titanic machines coming to life in the very far distance. Some of the Gnomes were actually startled by the cacophony of screeching and groaning, as megalithic metal components began to grind into operation after ages of slumber. So loud was the sound that it was able to travel from miles above, and away, to finally reach us, miles below. Even the very ground beneath our feet shook ever so slightly when the sound first arrived. We thought it was a seismic event...and indeed it was, manifested as the city itself shrugging off the many eons of dust and calcification like a falling fog in its gridwork of streets.

"Our guardian is in dangerrrrr," the Great One spoke. Waves of amber light and warmth fell over the gathered congregation

with every word the Mellow One spoke. "*The evil that is Calabac means to summon my most hated foooooe. A creature that will devour what is left of your people and my creationnnnns.*" His voice was full of despair and worry. I felt it as if it was my own. It resonated throughout the garden and all of us felt it thrum in our bones, as much as our ears.

His voice was not, however, loud or discomforting; instead it was soft and soothing, but filled with the sorrow of great loss. As he continued to speak his voice crept through the ancient city like a thousand tendrils of tranquil music, remaining mellow and soothing to such a degree that the congregation of Gnomes surrounding me were calm and in a state of divine joy. They all seemed to begin humming together, like a mantra of some sort. I would later learn that they did this when one of them was missing, hurt, or in danger. My own people of "new" Sensimilia, deep in the world, never did anything like this, and I also later learned it was developed out of desperation by the Gnomes for the purpose of summoning the mercy of whatever gods might *bother* to listen to their lamentations, in the absence of their own *unknown* deity.

It was absolutely amazing! To think, for thousands of generations, these poor people had had their culture and religion erased from their memories through *education* and *progress* and were turned into disposable workers, then suddenly finding out that they actually *have* a culture and a creator of their *own*! For them it was a dream come true.

At that moment I decided it was my solemn duty to Gnomes, not to a god but to those poor people, to lead them from the darkness of ignorance into the light of salvation and liberation.

Go figure.

But first I had to understand what the heck *Gaaaw*-aaawd was trying to tell me. Honestly, sometimes it's like babysitting. Oy!

"I am not sure I understand, Great Mellow One, please explain why our guardian must be protected?" You gotta admit that part would be confusing, if you think about it. "Isn't it *his* job to protect *me* ... O Mellow One?"

"*Our guardian is ... was ... the servant of evil ... once upon a time.*"

Wha'!?

"*He was the vessel that carried a force within his flesh so utterly vile as to be the favorite of the very god of cruelty and evil manifested. This was the most hate-filled, insufferable beast the multiverse had ever vomited into existence ...*"
There was no way these Gnomes were following any of this. Heck, I was so lost I decided to sit down and fill my pipe with a pinch off one of the many sacred flowering herb trees.

"*...Now, Calabac, has created the horror anew in the form of our guardian. Our guardian, Durik, is only a kind reincarnation of a very terrible half-demon military genius named Thukoooooooov. Thukov perished herrrrrre, on this plane of existence many, many thousands of years ago and now has returned through foul hootspologyyyyyy.*

"*Calabac planned to put the soul of a god of evil into Duriiiiiik, so I stole away the flesh and gave it a new awarrrrreness. It is our guardian now. He is* **our** *Durik, but the entity who laid claim to that flesh is powerfulllllll* *still and can destroy the eternal spirit of Durik, our guardian. Durik is an infant soulllll and has little power in the spirit world between plannnnnes. It is there that the evil will attack frommmmmmm.*

"Durik is only **one** *young soul and the thing that is Krawchich,* was Thukov, *is manyyyyyy. Too many to counnnnnnt. We must therefore keep the guardian safe from Calabac's evil magics until Thukov, the demon, is inevitably summonnnnned into some other form that our enemy is no doubt already in the process of creating.*

"Then and only then can Durik do battle with the beast for possession of his bodyyyyy. It first needs to possess another mortal beinnnng."

Then a somewhat familiar sound. *"Tshhhhhht ... tshhhhhht ... One sec ... ahhhh, only then can Durik slay the fiend, once and for alllllllll ... cough ... ahem ..."* There was a short pause and then ... *"The people of this great city are all gone nowwwwww. Only their children survived the massacre that took place here at the hands of Thukov and his army of evilllllll. Many of those children were cast into slavery and forced to create the Fortress of Firrrrrrrrre. For thousands of centuries they have labored to create what Calabac has forced them to maaaaaake."*

I stood up in response to these last words. "Who were these people, Great Intoxicated One? Share with us, your faithful minions of laid- backness."

"These were the G'nommmmmmes."

I was speechless.

"A few escaped into the caves and after many eons, some were able to create your home, Szvirrrrffffff," he continued. *"The blood of countless generations of other G'nomes is in the stone and machineworks of Calabac's fortressssss. I was powerless to help themmmmmmmm"*

Wow, right? "Oy. Okay then, where are they now, O inebriated lord?" Remember what I said about babysitting?

"*They are herrrrrre, among you, Szvirrrrffffff. You have founnnnnnnd themmmmmmm.*" I could tell he was planning to fade out, so I had to talk fast.

"The Gnomes here are the descendants of the G'nomes who once inhabited this place?" I started with that, but then added, "How do I get Durik out of the Bong? Is there anything else I should know at this point, because I am starting to feel a bit lost as to what to do next, and why can't I find a quality men's hosiery that won't fall down without underwear suspenders, or ride up my butt crack when I sit down or bend over?" I figured that should cover it. "What I wouldn't give for a decent pair of shorts! Oy!"

"*Yes, Szvirrrrrrffffff. These are but a fewwww of those who are still imprisonnnnnned. They have the power to save the worrrrrld.*"

There was a short pause and then the sound of coughing again, followed by drinking and swallowing sounds and then finally... "*Where was I? Oh yeahhhhhh. Durik is the key to Calabac's plannnnn. If the foulness of Krawchich the evil one is summonnnnned, and Durik has not been prepared to receive the monster's tormented soulllls, it will spread to find another host, or host of hooooosts. It wants to be Thukov againnnnn but will not stop simply because it cannot finnnnnd the Thukov hooooooooost ... Durrrrrrik* **is** *that host.*

"*Calabac needs him. But we do as well; his greatness it yet to be revealed.*"

In case you don't remember, Krawchich was mentioned before in this story, way back near the start when the Holy One was telling you all about us G'nomes.

Remember that?

No?

Go back and read it. I'll wait...

You're back?

Well done.

Now where was I?

Oh yeah...

Krawchich was the entity that almost decimated G'nomish culture- the evil deity who wanted to play a prank on our own Holy and most Mellow of Creators. *He* is the same guy who *possessed* a half-demon military genius named Thukov and used him to rally and lead a host of evil in an attempt to completely wipe the G'nomish civilization from history.

This demon in question was not a demon at all. It was the manifestation of one of the gods of chaos and suffering!

"It is a creature of many evil and corrupted soulllls. Entities that in their own times and worlds were the foulest of allll that caaaame before and after themmm. "They are the vilest of things, who can onnnnly exist as a legionnnn of criminal, and predatorial minnnnnd.

"Krawchich uses that combinnnned power to exist out of sheer will and stubbornesssssss. Otherwise, the evil could not exist at all." I could feel his presence begin to fade again- like he was tired ... distant. As though he was fading in and out.

"What about anything else?" I yelled. "I asked, before, about anything else that might help! And I still don't know how to get

Durik outta that Bong! And my underwear keeps creeping down when I bend over or sit down repeatedly! For god's sake, can someone make me a decent pair of underwear already? Oy!"

A moment of awkward silence.

He was gone. No answers. Wouldn't you know it? I just get the answers I was *looking* for and working so hard to find, when he dumps a whole *new* load of questions in my lap ... Oy.

I looked to Musky, who was smiling cheek to cheek and then to the gathered Gnomes. Then I looked back to Musky again and then to The Bong.

I pulled up my shorts, tucked my undershirt into them and concluded that no one was gonna just give me an answer right then and there; (or a decent pair of briefs).

All in attendance were either more intoxicated than I was, simply from being caged up in a small enclosed area with a few thousand heavily pollinating herb plants of the god-like potency variety for the last eighteen hours, *or* they were simply too confused and uninformed to be able to offer a valid opinion on the matter.

I therefore decided to conduct Sabbath right there in the temple of Shiddumbuzzin. It seemed like a good plan all around.

Almost everyone partook...

(*children*- I'll explain later).

It was monumental ... and worth remembering even. I stood at the base of the Bong, and gazed in wonder at it all. Durik was floating inside of the thing in a catatonic state.

I couldn't believe what had happened to me over the last few months- or the last few days for that matter.

I walked to the front of the altar and sat down on the second step from the top, to give me something to lean back on.

The people ... my people, were awaiting my words patiently. I STILL cannot imagine what was going through their hearts and minds. Many of them wept in obvious joy and reverence. God himself had just spoken, and he loved them all.

Warm firestone light pulsed in gentle waves throughout the temple, and as tendrils of pollen danced and twirled among the congregation, the Gnomes hummed a musical mantra: bonnnng, bonnng, bonnng...". Some of them tapped out rhythms using the buttons on their worn and humble attire. Others clicked with their tongues, some hummed very low and made dramatic baritone pops and bmms–or lack of a better description.

The ladies among them sang in voices so heavenly and spiritually uplifting that I was compelled to weep with joy.

The children danced in the aisles and rejoiced. It was unbelievably uplifting. They better make a musical scene in a ... what did those guys call it ... a movie? Whatever that is- or I'm calling my lawyer..

Anyway, where was I?

Oh yeah ...

Even William and Musky assisted me by handing out samples of the sacred herb, potato sticks, and cheese dip I produced from my bottomless backpack. They were also much better dancers, so I went back to the altar area, slightly humbled.

But, only slightly. I was doing pretty good, at that point, and as the whole dramatic and impressive event seemed to crescendo to an obvious spot where I should say something, I addressed them again.

...

Wait... did I already address them once, or was this the first time? I forgot.

Oh yeah, I did. Didn't I?

Anyway...

"I speak to you all today not as a Redeye ... not as a hootspologist ... not even as a guy with a handful of impressive degrees from an exclusive university. No ... I speak to you as a G'nome.

"As *you* are G'nomes, so am I. As I am a G'nome, so are you. *We* are G'nomes." I needed some better material. I was instantly starting to lose them.

"Listen to me, O G'nomes who were once unda-tings! These are the potato sticks of liberation!" Free food. The last resort. "This is the cheese dip of salvation and this ... *this* is the herb of re*lax*ation, *in*spiration, and the *Gnomish* nation. Partake and join me in praise of he who gave us herb and a racially adept ability to smoke it." I continued, "It is *he* ... Shiddumbuzzin ... who sent *me*, the Cloud Walker, to *you*. *This* great metropolis *belongs* to us. Go forth into this great city and find your place among the many abodes provided, for it was your *own* people who created this place for *all* of us."

I went on a bit about back home, made some mention of my journey to find them all, gave my uncle Jonah's carpet emporium a plug and repeated the Mellow One's name often enough that after a bit, every time I said his name, the entire congregation would repeat it reverently.

Nice, right? I wish you kids were there. It was really nice.

Now, where was I?

Oh yeah...

The constant supply of cheese dip, from my personal stash in my bottomless pack, and the use of a minor prayer to create more potato sticks, gave me the extra edge I needed to keep them all paying attention long enough to give them the basic gist of what was happening.

I decided to write a description of the past day's events in the Book of Shiddumbuzzin while the pipe was being passed around. Opening the divine book I saw an entry I had penned when I stated to Durik that *a book could not be judged by its cover*. I wasn't sure if he ever actually understood what that meant, or how much it actually applied to *him*.

I glanced toward the bong. Why was I so worried? I returned my attention to those who required it most just then. These were wonderful, resourceful folk, whose very faith in a god whose name they had long forgotten had saved them from disappearing forever as a people.

Again, I wept with joy- pure, divine joy.

Just a sec, kids. I need a second.

Okay, I'm good, just a little misty. Ya had to be there.

Now...where was I?

Oh yeah...

After updating the holy book I took a young adult Gnome under wing, so to speak, and taught him the basics of loading up a smoking pipe and keeping it lit. I then sent him around the crowd offering it to any who wanted to sample the sacred herb.

The stress they had all suffered before was now beginning to subside. This was visually evident in their smiles and the way they hugged one another, and moved about, exploring the temple and then the gardens.

Still there was music among them. Beautiful music. Sorrowful, hopeful, prophetic lyrics, and soul-wrenching harmonies. I had never experienced anything like that back home. I too was joyous, and wept with joy many times that evening.

As the very young were still developing and their tiny lungs were not accustomed to the sacred herb (remember I said I'd explain later?)- and also because their tiny brains were already facing the daunting challenge of rediscovering and reclaiming their lost civilization (as well as also developing at a delicate yet extremely fast pace)—I decided that a Gnome or any other persons who would *choose* to partake in Sabbath should also be of an adult age in order to be permitted to do so, and that they should at least be physically developed enough to withstand the power of the sacred herb, and that no one should ever feel coerced into sampling it ... ever.

Children, who were naturally innocent and therefore holy in the extreme, did not require Sabbath like us soiled and jaded adults- *from the book of Shiddumbuzzin and the Latter Day Gnomes.*

This I *wrote* in the holy book and explained to all present. They, of course, were happy to comply with such a logical and sensible precaution; these were their children. If they required the medicine, they would receive it, but if not, allow them their childhood.

Once I was satisfied that I had documented the past twenty-four hours (or so) accurately (or at least as I remembered it happening- remember the mushrooms), I decided to take a census of all the Gnomes present as well as their skills and trades. Of the one hundred and seventeen present, there were many craftspersons among them. Mostly engineers, machinists and masons.

They explained that when Musky had initially rescued them all from the jails, most of the men and stronger, younger women had all been on duty, continuing the construction of Calabac's fortress. Their shifts were later—when they were expected to inspect the progress of the previous shift, and prepare the work schedules for the following day.

Those Gnomes who were present were some of the elders and children of the adults still being forced to work for that villain, Calabac. (Oooo, I hate that guy).

These old people had been assigned to train the young and prepare them for a life of servitude, while those younger adults and stronger and larger children kept up the steady pace of construction that Calabac demanded. To slow production meant having to sacrifice lives to the Anaga demons.

I did manage to find four Gnomes who had secretly been training each other to use the miner's pick as a weapon. They had been planning an eventual escape for over a year before I came along.

These "warriors" I armed with a few of Durik's weapons (one actually was a type of cruel-looking pick) I had previously stashed in my bottomless backpack when I was in William's laboratory. I instructed these three-foot-tall warriors to stay together and begin a search of the city for useful information and items that would assist their ... *our* people in the struggle to once again become a civilization.

I also instructed them to report to the temple and inform the eldest Gnome of their findings as soon as they finished their sweep of the city.

The four set out, but they also took two engineers and a healer with them as well as William for his proficiency with machinery and his alchemistry skills. He had eagerly agreed as he had become (understandably) fascinated with the city and its ever-growing life force.

The Gnomes' lack of linguistic expertise belied their hidden intelligence and creative minds. Once they had been set to task, they were of one singular force. They worked together almost symbiotically, as a team and without argument. Just like back home.

This was a force *evolved* to work as one for the greater good.

I was surprised when, after I had explained what had happened to them and why they looked different from me (the whole invasion of evil and destruction of the empire thing), they remained calm. They took it all in with surprising ease and agreed that I should continue on my quest to stop Calabac.

They had been telling a story of deliverance to each other for eons and believed it with a passion. *This* was all expected to happen, to some degree, by every Gnome alive during that time.

One rather elderly Gnome, named Phuc (no kidding, and don't make fun of the poor old guy, 'cuz he's really nice), drew me a map of some of the lesser-used corridors, tunnels and ductwork inside the volcano fortress.

He showed me a place on the map, where he said Calabac found and kept machines of war that were *not* being used by his armies. He said that no one in Calabac's armies could even figure out *how* to use them.

419 Gnomes died, hiding the fact that they could understand the controls that they were shown. Each was taken to the machines where they were told to operate the mighty hulks. Only 2 of those Gnomes returned to tell of what had happened to the others.

Phuc was lucky enough to be the next in line when the master finally gave up and accepted that the Gnomes simply did not know.

Phuc, however, knew *exactly* how to use them. As did at least two other Gnomes- both of whom were still in Calabac's Volcano Fortress.

He suggested that Musky and I make our way back into the volcano and steal away with one of those machines. He described how to make them work and how to control some of their more useful functions, then suggested I use one to rescue more than ten thousand Gnomish slaves who were being held in Calabac's fortress.

Oy!

From his description I deduced that Phuc was either completely off his rocker or he had given us what may have ended up as our ace in the hole. Either way, I sensed he was special among his group, if not ... *our* species, and I would later be proven correct.

His information was accurate and his concern for our people was sincere. He expected me to deliver on a promise made to his ancestors the day they became slaves to their conquerors and began to tell the story of the *Cloud Walker and the Titans of Freedom*. It became my responsibility to *deliver* the moment I accepted that role and gave them hope.

I appointed Phuc as Vice Redeye, and temporary leader of the Gnomes and gave him the title of *Holy*. Then I left him with the responsibility of making sure that all those present had shelter and were taken care of while I was gone.

I created some simple foodstuffs, again with a basic prayer, gave them a short sermon on patience and its virtues, and a quick lesson on how to harvest and prepare a bud for burning. Then I located Musky and began readying myself for battle.

I was, at that moment, not thinking about the dangers I was about to face.

Instead, the idea that some evil force had tried to wipe my entire species from the world, and was *still* trying to do so, had my shorts up in a bundle- let me tell *you*.

I had faced Calabac once and was still around to tell about it. I had infiltrated his heavily guarded fortress of evil cruelty and debauchery, made my way past demons and guards and monsters of all sorts and I was *still* around to tell about it.

In your face, Bernie.

I was determined that I was gonna get that machine, and those Gnomes, and I was gonna make Calabac pay for trying to bring back the worst nightmare my species had ever faced.

"Musky, my friend. I have here a detailed map of the Fortress of Fire." I showed him the particular areas I needed to go to as I unrolled and flattened the drawing on the steps of the temple.

"Yeah, mun. I be knowin' some a' dat dere," he commented as he recognized parts of the map.

Then, "Yo, mun." He half-hugged me, squeezing my right shoulder and smiling. "Musky be honored to see all a' dis. Ya know?" His eyes were glazed. "Musky be like some 'ero and shit, ya? Like a 'ero in a great story 'an shit, ya? Wit yer peoples and shit- yeah?" His voice quivered with emotion.

"Not like *shit*. Not *some* kind of hero. Yes, you are already a hero, as true as a hero can be in my books. You are my friend."

He gave me a hug, then- we *were* friends. I could feel it.

Remember, kids. Hug your friends- it feels really nice ... forever.

Where was I?

Oh yeah...

"We need to return to *this* place." I pointed to the area where the waterworks ran through the prisons for the slaves. "The Gnome who drew this map for me said there are almost eleven thousand Gnomes in those prisons- give or take a few. We must go and free those people. That is my mission."

Honestly, a week earlier I would have said: *"Have fun going to war, fellas. I'm moving south where my allergies will hopefully clear up."* But there I was, planning to re-enter the one place I had so desperately been trying to escape from.

All I really wanted in the beginning was to rescue Lillia's sister ... *next* it was Durik ... *then* my entire *species* ... *AND* the entire Al'Lankamirian *Empire* ... and now the *WORLD* even?!! I was starting to get a stress-belly from it all.

Oy!

I loosened my belt a notch. "First we are having Sabbath and I'm picking a few of those buds in that temple for the trip," I said, defiantly, as I led the way back into the temple. "Nobody better complain about it either. I am almost out of herb and I think I deserve a bit for the road."

"You be 'avin any more a doze shrooms, mun?" Musky asked as he followed close behind.

I thought for a moment, then: "You mean the hallucinogenic ones from the glow in the dark cave that we might *still* be in?"

"Yeah, mun. Dem ones. You be 'avin more a doze?" he asked again as we reached the first ring of herb trees.

I began to look for an appropriate bud to harvest as I replied. "We picked all of them, right?" I asked.

"Yeah, mun. But we be eatin' em like dey be *candy* so I is tinking you ain't got many left, an I gonna be needin' em if I is going back to dat dere volcano a tird time, mun," he said as he twisted an herb leaf into a tube and lit it with a match.

"We picked about twenty pounds, Musky. I haven't eaten *that* many ... have I? I mean ... I *hope* I haven't ... although it would *explain* an awful lot."

The thing about hallucinogenic mushrooms is that you can get so baked from them you don't realize you *are* that baked and ... so ... you might take some more – *Then* you're so baked you cannot remember if you ever *did* take more – so you take some *more* and get even **more** baked. This goes on until you run out of mushrooms and finally realize how many you *actually* ate. It is a circular process of ever-increasing measures of complete mellowness that only the most experienced of *"shroomnivors"* should ever attempt to experience.

Luckily *I* was such a shroomnivor so my worries soon faded. I searched my bottomless backpack and eventually pulled forth nineteen pounds of extremely potent psychedelic mushrooms and realized I had probably eaten half a pound and Musky had eaten the other half. *Holy crap!* I thought.

I then paused for several minutes to interrogate Musky with a barrage of questions about what had happened in the last twenty-four hours, so as to insure that I was not, in fact, *still* hallucinating on those very same mushrooms and *still* in that cave where I found them.

Once I was satisfied that I was in fact experiencing *real* crazy, unbelievable stuff (as opposed to what? I mean ... in *that* atmosphere? Was there *other* stuff that *wasn't* crazy?) I picked a beautiful eleven-ounce bud from a lower branch. (See? Eleven-ounce bud! That's pretty *crazy*!)

I held the huge flower cluster in a beam of light that pierced its way through the still-developing canopy of massive herb trees, its sparkling purple tendrils of sticky wonder seemed to dance and sing like a chorus line of tiny herb pixies- or something ... Damn, it was beautiful.

Sorry. I digressed, didn't I? I'll try not to do that again. I was moved- you had to see them.

Oy! Just *talking* about those buds is enough to make me forget what I was saying ...

Now ... what was I saying?

Oh yeah ...

I took a moment to clear my mind and put everything together in a nice package; Krawchich, a god of evil and chaos, felt it would be amusing to attack and destroy all of G'nomish creation, driving The Mellow One into theocratic bankruptcy. He did so by possessing a mortal human-demon mix called a cambion, named Thuckov.

He chose this specific being for the creature's seemingly instinctual understanding of war, tactics, strategy, and his ability to command. Krawchich was also vain, and the mortal, Thuckov, was beautiful ... from where he came. So this creature was perfect for the god's amusement.

Meanwhile, Krawchich's own follower, *Calabac*, turned coat and discovered, over many millennia, a way to trap the god in a mortal form, but only if the god could be reincarnated *in* that form.

You see: Krawchich had *already* possessed Thuckov once, in the great descending- when Sensimilia was destroyed–and thus had lived as a mortal.

Thuckov's mortal form perished, eventually, of whatever means, but the spirit of the god of evil passed into the spirit *world*, where it, Krawchich, was forced to go to court for his crimes.

From what I could tell, *Durik* was a reasonable facsimile of Thuckov enough that Calabac could use him as a vessel with which to carry the demon-god's power and command it for his own purposes.

This is why I now needed to protect Durik from whatever Calabac had planned.

You following me now? I know, I know. It's a lot to digest. He's a good kid, though, so please, stay with me.

I pocketed the bud and bagged the fungus, then I gestured for Musky to follow as I exited the temple. "Phuuuuc!" I yelled from atop the stairs.

Several Gnomes turned suddenly and looked in our direction, then went about their business.

"What be wrong witchya now, mun?" Musky asked.

"I need to find that guy who I am putting in charge here while I'm gone," I replied. "PHUUUUUC!!" I yelled again, this time louder. "I gave him a special title- he's like a special servant of the temple. I like him. Maybe if I bless him he will be*come* holy. PHUUUC!!!" This time even louder.

"Well, ya don't be needin' ta curse all loud at 'im 'en shit, mun. No wunda why 'e not be wantin' ta come."

"Wha ... what?" I asked as Phuc came running up to me from around a corner.

"Yes be to Cloud Walker. What's him be wantin'?" He stood almost two feet tall and was twice my weight but was thin and gangly from his hardships as a slave.

I hugged him. He seemed to like that. I kinda did too.

See? Hug your friends.

Then I continued, "Holy Phuc, I want you to make sure the people find shelter and stay hidden. Then I want you to return here to the temple and wait for the fighters to come back.

" Phuc, ya hafta make sure that when *they* return, *they* are to keep you safe until I return with the rest of our people. These are my orders, Holy Phuc, do you understand?"

"Phuc yeah!" he replied with vigor. I then blessed him: "Be safe, be silent, be stoned" and recruited him as the first acolyte of the faith; the Vice Redeye, the *"Holy* Phuc."

He ran off barking out directions to the other Gnomes, who all obeyed him without question.

"Come, Musky. We are going to steal back a war machine," I said as I led him out of the gardens.

CHAPTER - 17

"IN THROUGH THE OUT DOOR"

We made our way up the main drag, toward the exit from the city. The streets were laid out exactly like *New* Sensimilia (my home), except they were static and made from the earth itself, or, more accurately, the granite, basalt, and firestone deposits.

Here the buildings never moved. Not like back home. They did, however, possess a certain style or feel to the architecture that, if one *knew* both places and took a moment to consider it, one could logically hypothesize that the two cities were created by the same people but at different times in their history as a civilization.

We passed by fountains where masterful works of art were carved into stones that were not indigenous to the area but must have been imported for aesthetics. Giant megalithic boulders of alabaster, limestone, turquoise and jade, to name just a few. Many of these were statuary depicting different G'nomish heroes, all of whom I did not recognize.

These figures, along with those of other beings, immortalized in the acts of worshiping, assisting, or hindering the G'nomes, were carved in extremely fine detail. All, or at least most, of these figures were spitting water, pouring water, or in some way adding to the overall effect of using the water as part of the art piece. The people who made this city did so over an extremely long period of time and spent millions of G'nome hours just to make the fountains that occurred at every intersection.

We passed through several rings of the city where the curved streets intersected with the straight one we were traveling on. Each time we did so, we viewed a new historical or mythical event (that I was not familiar with), represented in statue form as part of yet another fountain.

Gardens were in abundance as well. Although they were overgrown and unkempt for the most part, they were beautiful all the same. Many plants bore fruit, as did the fungi. This gave me assurance that the Gnomes would not starve in my absence.

There was also phosphorescent plant life of all sorts, from fungi to simple subterranean grasses- along with glowing minerals which created mosaics of color that were breathtaking to say the least. Anyone living anywhere in the city could look outside and see beauty.

We traveled along this path for an hour, until we finally reached the foothills that sloped up toward the south along the elevated highways.

We moved along those thoroughfares, back toward the great divided highway we had arrived on initially.

This great ramp was paved with colorful tiles in a mosaic that depicted a massive gold herb leaf on a black field. We reached the top, and even at that distance, I could smell the sweet, skunky aroma of the sacred herb in full blossom erupting from the center of the city.

Almost five miles away in the distance I could see the giant forests of herb stretching to envelope the canopy of the Temple of Shiddumbuzzin. Tendrils of sacred pollen reached out in all directions across the city, sparkling in the subterranean lights.

I paused momentarily and looked back upon the miracle that was *Old* Sensimilia.

Her windows were, even then, still lighting up here and there as the great metropolis awakened from its ancient slumber.

The colors of the phosphorescent gardens were laid out like glittering quilts along the city streets, while her waterworks continued to animate her fountains with their heroes and villainous adversaries.

Some of the larger fountains had parts that would actually move with the flow of water, like animatronic golems anchored in place, and even from that distance I was able to discern their motions.

It was beautiful beyond belief. It was, *I-wish-my-mom-could-live-there* beautiful. You know what I mean? It was really comforting, and welcoming.

From where we stood looking down into the city, nestled in her subterranean valley, I could imagine the streets bustling with a million G'nomes. Trade and mercantilism alive in the markets, children moving in groups among the grand gardens, learning the many trades that their culture and traditions demanded them to master, and grand theaters where shows of hootspa, or dramatic performances, were offered to the public.

I saw what truly must have been the great halls of education and training, where the greatest minds of the empire once taught all who might ask, where knowledge was for all to own.

From our new vantage point, high atop the exit ramp/overpass, I could see the old city as a whole. Here, I could clearly discern that it was in some ways kind of like the Sensimilia I grew up in ... apart from the aforementioned differences in materials and technology.

The pollen in the air combined with the multi-coloured waves of phosphorescent light that pulsed through the countless gardens gave the whole place the illusion of being alive and moving. It occurred to me that those who escaped the horror those eons ago must have been trying to emulate this city when they created *New* Sensimilia–*my* home ... If they were the ones who created it at all.

There was so much I still didn't know. Like why/how did we forget all of this? Who were those G'nomes who escaped? Where did they learn to build such technological wonders and why didn't they leave their descendants with a clear design for a better pair of shorts?

I sighed. Old Sensimilia, her streets decorated with mosaics of green and black, her ceiling lit up with sparkling, throbbing waves of firestone light.

A center of culture and art, she must have been beautiful enough to marvel even the most well-traveled adventurer and large enough to accommodate at least ten times the population of *New*

Sensimilia. Where one was a work of efficient mechanical genius, the other was a work of artistic vision and beauty.

As we continued we passed a boarding dock for the cable car systems that I had not noticed when we had initially entered the city, and there were several of the vehicles docked there.

These were quite decorative, constructed from fine metals and gilded with precious ones. The decorative gilding depicted great insects and clouds, and these covered the surface of the cars wherever windows were absent.

Upon closer inspection we discovered the outer surface beneath the gilding to be coated with deep blue enamel.

Their interiors, though having not been opened in many hundreds of centuries, perhaps even thousands, were well-preserved. The floors were carpeted in rich, deep purple and there were many rows of earthy-colored, wooden seats.

Each side had several long windows that allowed for a slightly downward-angled view. This was no doubt provided for the passengers, specifically for appreciating their beautiful city below.

What was obviously the operator's station was *also* quite decorative. Even the wheel with which the pilot would stabilize the vehicle was carved in the form of a serpent biting its tail. It seemed every inch of the city was carved or cut into an artistic relief.

'What had happened to us?' I thought. *'What happened to our artists and our visionaries? The G'nomes who made this place?'*

I didn't want to leave. But we were on a mission. Musky seemed to understand without me saying a word. We traveled for about an hour in silence.

Another hour and we had made our way to the ancient city's exit- a colossal hole in the wall of the vast underground cavern.

Beyond, it curved upward, into a divided, two-way, megalithic road to the surface.

As we journeyed up the long divided highway, we could hear, ahead of us, the sounds of the colossal machines working in the distance much clearer and getting louder the further (higher) we traveled.

Again we were forced to stop and rest on occasion. This time a couple more rest periods were required as we were now traveling uphill. We did so at the provided areas; places where it was *evident* there had once been trading markets, eateries and inns. These were small villages with homes and one even possessed what must have been a temple to The Mellow One.

These spots were there to also allow travelers a chance to adjust to changing air pressures, as they ascended to the surface or descended into the deep earth.

I tried to imagine these people ... *peoples*, sharing this resting place in peace. I wondered if humans and elves might have shared this place with Dwarves and Trolls ... and, of course, Gnomes.

Here, too, the firestones of the sacred temple were sending their life's force. It happened, even as we ascended the great spiraling highway to the surface.

The windows of the structures were soon aglow with warm and welcoming amber light. Our rest periods were relaxed, and our conversations were all about the wonders we had witnessed so far. And Musky's homeland, far to the northeast.

This was our connection, he and I. We were both so far from home we felt we might never return. We knew what that felt like. I *really* liked him then, at our last stop. I knew he was always going to be my friend- that I was always going to be his.

We remained on schedule, however, and reached the reservoir in time to witness the great, many-jointed machines of the hollow mountain in the act of breaking through the corrosion that had accumulated on their gears and joints over countless eons.

The titanic engines came to life before our very eyes, as though planned to do so, and proceeded to their designated duties. As small as we were, we felt a *million* times smaller beneath those colossal machines.

The massive, multi-jointed columns that hugged the curved inner walls of the hollow mountain were now detaching for the most part and were reaching out from the inner edges of the mountain wall at its base. It reminded me of a spider on its back reaching inward to clean its belly.

As this took place we were forced, on several occasions, to take cover and avoid being hit by calcium and limestone buildup falling from the joints and bearing cases of the ancient constructs. It rained down like hail in some places, as it fell from the colossal metal appendages hundreds, and even thousands, of feet above.

These arms, for lack of better words, groaned and screeched against the ages of mineral buildup. Small birds, and even several bat colonies, were disturbed by the new activity and the cacophony of noises. At first, they flew about in confusion for a while, but later their numbers thinned and I concluded that there was an exit somewhere from this chamber to the outside world.

The bats also reminded me of Nikodemius, my *familiar* pet bat. My mental connection with him was severed the moment I began to climb the Mountain Fortress of Calabac. Now that I was outside the effects of Calabac's magic shell surrounding his volcano, I expected to *feel* Nikodemius's mind, but he was still silent. I feared the worst—he was with Raz when I saw him last. If he was nowhere to be found, what had become of Raz?

My thoughts were interrupted by a series of particularly loud screeches that came when a very long mechanical arm carried a block of ice, several tons in weight, over our heads.

This, it placed gently into the receded waters of the artificial lake. I took special notice of how the machines avoided us, as though they could *sense* us and were trying to work *around* us.

These were not support beams as I at first suspected. They were, in fact, giant, individual, mechanical multi-jointed automatons.

They had lifted themselves from their resting places, like great caterpillars against the walls of the hollow mountain, and had begun harvesting ice from the ice cap more than a mile above us.

Together they worked to perform this task, while other, similar mechanical arms began tending the surrounding gardens, doing maintenance on other machinery, and all descriptions of megalithic endeavors.

A mighty ring of metal plates and gears encircled the top of the mountain's conical peak, like some sort of animated window frame, its center glowing softly from the sunlight being diffused through the ice within the frame, a great greenish glowing moon in the twilight of the mountain's belly.

From there a hundred arms, with a hundred joints, worked their many hands and fingers to maintain the ice, and simultaneously harvest it. Even as ice was being removed, water was being pumped from somewhere and sprayed against other areas of the ice cap. Places where the light was brighter received more sprayed mists than the thicker ice, which was being harvested.

The thinner areas were becoming thicker in turn. What purpose freezing the water, then melting the ice only to freeze it again was serving was beyond me. It seemed to me to be redundant at that time.

All along the walls of the hollow mountain were other mechanized systems all coming to life and returning to their long-absent tasks. What appeared to be colossal legs were unfolding and stepping out into the forests and among the trees.

Attached, against the inner walls of the mountain, halfway up, was what resembled long mechanical tentacles, with machinery of all descriptions attached all along their lengths. Hundreds of compartments then opened in the sides of the machinery attachments, and smaller arms unfolded from within, stretching out and into the flora. These worked the trees and bushes like thousand-legged centipedes tending their gardens, yet still attached to the main limb.

The machines that surrounded the lake were coming to life as well. Smaller arms with utility tools on the ends, worked their way along many ingeniously hidden tracks to reach points where their cleaning and maintenance skills were needed.

One particular machine, that we did not see at first, was independent of the main system and, once filled with the glowing energy of the firestone hootspa, it released its umbilical cord from a windowless structure, and moved like a huge box of appendages along the shore of the lake.

This behemoth began tending to and cleaning the other components of the reservoir with its seemingly endless supply of utility arms. It would later make its way around the whole facility, cleaning and maintaining all of the machinery and synthetic surfaces, while vapor pumped out of an orifice in its back to the sounds of wheels and cogs and all sorts of contraptionry working from beneath its metal skin.

We were, at one point, startled into taking cover when the ear-splitting sound of titanic, mechanized gears being forced into functioning against centuries of corrosion and the elements blasted out from above us.

We watched as a giant set of doors, several hundred feet tall, began to open high up in the side of the mountain.

Once free of their eons-long mineral buildup, the titanic doors slowly glided apart, allowing sunlight to leap into the dimly lit mega-structure and fill the forests with a whole new vigor that was almost *immediately* visible.

Flocks of birds and swarms of insects flew through the many beams and rays of light now flooding in through the ever-widening crack in the mountainside. The dust of countless eons fell from the colossal machinery and only added to the overall effect of the light being broken into beams and rays.

Great wads of vegetation fell to the floor from a thousand feet up as it was ripped away from its centuries-old roots anchored deeply into the very stone and metal of the colossal doors.

The giant mirrors that encircled the reservoir proper all began shifting and turning to catch the sunlight and redirect it toward specific areas in the great hollow mountain and back toward the divided highway. These, too, screeched and groaned so loudly that we were forced to cover our ears and take cover more than once.

A more thorough inspection revealed that the destinations for these redirected beams of sunlight were gardens, situated all around the inner edge of the mega-vault's walls. Many smaller mirrors were also situated all over the walls to catch the beams of life-giving light and redirect them over specific areas of foliage.

As we returned to the great artificial lake to continue along the road, we were again amazed to see an amber glow emanating from the depths of the waters. It was a tiny, yet extremely bright firestone deposit deep under the milky blue waters. So bright was it that I was able to make it out clearly, even through the thick mineral saturation of the lake's depths.

It had to be three hundred or more feet beneath the surface and must have been radiating light as bright as the sun.

The hootspa from it was so powerful that it animated the machines and maintained the entire place. It was, to me, tangible.

I could almost taste it. I had not even noticed the condensed jewel cluster when we first passed it, as it had not been glowing, and was not visible then- *unactivated*, I thought.

Now it was alive with thrumming and pulsing with a light that seemed to almost leap from the milky teal waters of the lake.

In retrospect *nothing* had been glowing when we first arrived, despite being saturated with firestones. Aside from some phosphorescent minerals, lichens and fungi, Musky and I had made our exploration in virtual darkness.

It was as though all the firestones had been in a sort of mineralogical slumber until the Bong was merged with the temple of Shiddumbuzzin (and in fact that was exactly what had happened). Well, almost. Close enough for you to get the general picture, anyway.

I *now* deduced that this place was once a great agricultural chamber. A sort of hothouse for growing herb and other agricultural products perhaps. I was only guessing at that point. It turned out that I was right, though.

Anyway, where was I?

Oh, Yeah...

You heard me mention how the G'nomes were as old as the Trolls, and *they* were older than the elves? Well, let's just say that we had a long time to figure things out.

The hollow mountain was actually something my ancestors had created to both connect them *to*, and protect them *from*, the surface world back in the days when my people lived much closer to the surface.

Sensimilia, my home, came later, after those who survived the great descent found each other and rebuilt ... as I understand it. A whole other story. Maybe I'll write a book.

Anyway...

Where was I?

Oh yeah...

Those were the days when real hootspologists were common among G'nomekind, before they were all wiped out by Krawchich and his evil horde.

If I had *only* had more time I might have explored this part of Old Sensimilia more thoroughly. But at that moment there was work that needed to be done that could not be delayed any longer. So we moved onward.

I knew what machines were. My people worked and designed machines as a matter of common practice, but this place was something more. This was a technology both older *and* newer than the craftsmanship that was used to build *New* Sensimilia. This mega-metropolis was many times larger than my home as well.

We continued on our way even as the massive doors were still opening. Across hundreds of feet they parted, allowing the sun to enter the confines of the mountain's belly, flooding the forests and gardens with natural sunlight. I retrieved my shaded spectacles from my belt-pouch and put them over my eyes as I allowed the warm light to flood over my face.

After several more hours of searching, we relocated the stairs that took us to the green granite megalithic roadway with the fancy pillars. Remember those? The ones that had all the nice carvings in them? Yeah, those.

Well, *that* long vaulted underground roadway eventually led us back to the entrance where we had found the murals, that depicted us finding the murals, that depicted us finding the murals ... you remember those murals, right? The ones that showed me and Musky together, yet were older than the skidmark in an Ogre's underwear? Remember? I crapped in my pants there.

No?

Obviously you haven't smoked enough herb. Go ahead, I'll wait.

Better now?

Great.

Now where was I?

Oh yeah ...

... We passed through the chamber of prophetic paintings and re-entered the long tunnel that would lead us to the underbelly of the volcano.

Many hours we walked down the tunnel until we finally arrived at the small chamber with the ladder that ascended to the secret door to the fortress.

It was here that we paused and I produced the map from my pack to study it some more. "We will need to go here first, Musky. Holy Phuc said there were old machines of war there and that if we are gonna have a chance at rescuing the prisoners, we will need those machines to do so."

He nodded his agreement and looked closely at the drawing. "Well, mun. Da way I be seein' it, I be tinkin we got two ways ta choose frum." He drew an imaginary line with his finger on the map, as he showed me a route that stopped in a room halfway to our destination. "Dis way be fast and most a da way we not be needin' ta worry 'bout a ting. But when we be gittin 'ere, mun? Well ... dat be where dat black dragon be livin' and im not be too 'appy to be seein' anyone a us tings any'ow. But, if we be gittin' past 'im it be clear sailing straight ta da prisons." His finger slid across the map to the spot marked as the waterworks.

"I have never even seen a dragon before, Musky." I was worried. "The closest I have come is a giant flying dinosaur. Are dragons big? As dangerous as I have been led to believe? What's that other choice we have?" I was unsure if I had it in me to face a creature of such legendary power as dragons were rumored to possess.

"Ya, mun. Dem are da werss tings ta be fightin' wit fer sher, an dey is real big too," he replied as he started to draw another route that was substantially longer than the first." Now dis 'ere be safer but more fightin' I'm tinkin'. See 'ere?" He pointed to several spots on the map that were directly in the path we needed to take. "Doze be guard postins where dere be Tallotian soldiers, maybe some a dem dere Goblins and even maybe a Troll, but at least dere be no dragons, mun." He smiled, his fake diamond sparkling in the light of the glow-in-the-dark mushroom he had earlier inserted into his puffy rainbow-colored hat.

This was an easy choice. "Well, if I had to choose I would have to pick Goblins and Trolls over a dragon, I guess."

"Dat be good tinkin', mun," he replied with a wily smile. "Asides, dem Goblins be partyin' up a storm up dere when we was 'ere last, so dey won't be noticin' us sneak by. Dey be trippin' n' shit."

With that, I prepared an assortment of combat hootspas as Musky loaded the spring pistol with lethal darts and twisted a few of his herb leaf cigarettes he called *spliffs*.

Once the preparations were finished Musky led the way up the ladder. I hadn't noticed before how deep the ladder had gone, as I was probably in too much of a panic from all the terrible things that had been happening, or perhaps it was a flashback from the psychedelic mushrooms; either way it was a lot longer than it seemed going down.

At least three hundred feet later (I'm not even exaggerating), Musky paused at the hatch to listen. (It took us, like, an hour to get up that ladder, oy).

After a few moments to catch our breath, he looked down in my direction and reported the coast was clear.

Then he pushed open the secret hatch and we ascended into the place where we found tunnels branching out in all directions.

Again, we had been here before. This was a crossroads for several hallways, plus a multitude of vents and ducts.

The architecture, once again, was that of the fortress.

I felt a bit strange again too. Almost as though the floor was moving under my feet. Everything was eerily silent. I had felt this before while in the Fortress of Fire, but now it was more intense.

Taking care not to travel in the direction where I had previously heard something large having a power nap, we instead moved slightly upward and to the east as our map directed us to do.

Soon the stench of stale beer, cold pizza and cheap cigars could be detected drifting down the tunnel toward us. After about two hundred feet more we reached a staircase that led up to a large chamber with flickering lights and a smoky atmosphere.

The steps themselves were slightly larger than G'nome-sized and were cut from a dark gray basalt, not the green granite we had left behind beneath the secret tile door. Here I was able to feel the mountain again. The funny thing is I could no longer feel the rest of the world. My *schmauz* was silent.

Suddenly, I realized that this was the strange feeling I had experienced earlier, once again creeping me out to no end.

I had a strong impression of powerful hootspas at work, perhaps *dark* hootspas. What was I thinking? Of *course* it was dark hootspa. It certainly was not good hootspa ...

... And furthermore ...

Why is it when things are bad humans always say it is dark, or *black* even? I grew up in the dark, and many of my relatives, like myself, love the color black and wear it whenever we can. You know they say it's slimming? That's what they say. No kidding.

So, let's not say *dark* hootspa, and let's *instead* call it *evil*, or simply *bad*. If you want you can call it *capitalism* or *monopoly*, that's okay with me, but I am just gonna call it *evil*. I know. Same difference.

Any self-identified *evil* people who might be reading this and are offended, should stick it in yer asses.

Now ... where was I?

Oh yeah...

No sounds of partying could now be heard from the place ahead, yet it was surely the same corridor we had earlier heard the Goblins celebrating from.

"Let I go ahead a bit now, mun. I be looking ta see if it be safe up dere. Okay?" Musky asked.

"A prudent suggestion, my friend. I shall wait here. Be careful," I replied as something just then came to mind. I remembered that I had Musky's cousin Vermin locked up in my bottomless pouch. Boy was I mad at him. The nerve of that guy, getting himself all possessed by an ancient demon, and trying to recreate the destruction of my species. At some point we were gonna have to figure out how to get that demon out of him and then he and I were gonna have words, let me tell you. But that would have to wait, as Musky had already disappeared in a flash up the stairs and out of sight.

I then took a moment to try and remember if I had tossed anyone else in my backpack/bottomless pouch in the last few days, but couldn't think of anyone.

I did, however, remember that I had Durik's arsenal in my bottomless pack and decided to take out one of his boot knives to use as a short ... okay, okay, *long* sword.

I was ready for anything.

CHAPTER - 18

"THE THINGS YOU FIND IN THE SUBWAY"

Moments later Musky returned with news that the coast was clear, and I was exhausted from holding up that dagger. Honestly I don't know how you guys do it! Those things are heavy! I put the thing back into my pack as he finished his report.

I then followed him up the stairs and into what amounted to … a giant subterranean nightclub. It was abandoned recently, too, I might add.

"Doze dere Goblins left in a 'urry, mun, look." He guided me into the huge chamber and was pointing to the surfaces of tables where half-finished drinks were left behind- and half-smoked spliffs and cigar-sized herb twists were sitting in ashtrays.

Here and there, half-eaten unrecognizable things that I don't have enough pages to try and describe to you were still in wrappers, or slung across the floor, as though someone had dropped them while running.

Suspended from the ceiling above us was a great ball decorated with hundreds of small mirrors. A lantern high up on a far wall was lit and hooded to make a beam of light that bounced off the many tiny mirrors on the ball's surface, creating hundreds of little spots of light that swirled around in a circle covering the entire room.

Good gawd, it was tacky!

I found myself feeling glad I had taken so many psychedelic mushrooms, though, as I watched those little lights dancing around like a cloud of fireflies doing synchronized swimming.

In other spots there were lanterns with colored shades, and in the middle of the room the floor appeared to be a great glass disc with many colored lights flickering and dancing under the surface.

There was a stage and on it were instruments that had been dropped in a real hurry. Behind a set of drums was a banner showing in Goblinese the name of the band: P'sole 'n Nudtz.

Here and there were padded railings, for leaning against presumably. These had narrow shelves on them, obviously for holding beverages. They were all Goblin-sized.

All along the walls were comfortable-looking benches and tables, some separated by small dividers. Scattered across the glass floor was an assortment of small yet very tall tables with tall stools that actually had steps leading to the seats.

A kiosk was located against a far wall with what seemed to be a limited kitchen arrangement.

Against another wall were several stalls where there were three goats, seven cows, a donkey and eleven sheep. All of them seemed to be smiling. Don't ask.

I deduced that the circle in the middle was a dance floor, the kiosk in the middle of the far wall was a bar, and this place was a sort of Goblin private nightclub. The livestock was something I (at the time) had no idea about. Maybe it'll come up in a vignette or something.

I know what you're thinking: a Goblin nightclub? But is that really so hard to fathom? Why are human beings always so shocked when monsters try and have a bit of fun too? Huh? Why? I ask.

Anyway ... where was I?

Oh yeah ...

Musky was correct in believing the place had been evacuated in a hurry, but there was no evidence as to why.

Again, my superior deductive reasoning skills surfaced and I concluded the Goblins were either out looking for Musky and me, or they were called away for some *other* official reason that amounted to no good.

I then took notice that many of the booths and chairs had jackets, handbags and other personal effects that had been neglectfully left behind.

One of these effects was a small pouch, buttoned closed in three places, and when opened revealed about a pound of Goblin brain cheese!

Holy you-know-what, right?!

Knowing Grarrr would be pretty happy to get that later, I pocketed it in my pouch. (Remember I was still under the assumption that Grarrr was alive and well.

I know. I'm sad too. But we have to get back to the story. Burn something. I'll join ya.)

Ready?

Where was I?

Oh, yeah ...

After I pocketed the brain cheese and returned to the search, Musky kept watch on the only other exit, a barred exit that led to a big tunnel full of water. It was not a sewer as there was no stench.

This was clean water.

During my own search I uncovered a scroll that had been tossed, or dropped on the floor. It was written in humanese, which I happen to read and write relatively well. At first I struggled with the faded words and broken style of the handwriting, but then noticed something about the illustration. This was a wanted ad.

Wanted: Dead or Alive – The Blood Baron!

The weird thing was the illustration, which, unlike the type, was quite well done. The artist had a real good eye and managed to capture Grarr in full color.

It was *definitely* Grarr in the picture, monocle and all. At closer inspection I read that "The Scave were offering a bounty on Grarr's head" and it was being offered to the Talotian people specifically. The reward promised was immortality, no less, and one thousand imperial platinum ingots. Someone wanted Grarr dead in a really big way.

My question was: what was a Goblin doing with a wanted poster for Grarrr? It was my understanding he was some sort of minor celebrity among them. They loved him.

Keep in mind, I at that point had no knowledge of where Grarr had come from or what his past was. I did figure out that Goblins knew him and that he is widely respected among them (thus regular deliveries of brain cheese), but the poster called him the *Blood Baron?*

Chapter - 19

"It's Not Easy Being Green"

The following wildlife vignette is brought to you by:

Morti and Selma's Pickle Emporium

146 south and 58th on Feldstein Avenue. Tell 'em you heard it here, in this book, and get a free "Super Dilly" in wax paper (with any purchase over G30.00).

(Only available in New Sensimilia. Void where prohibited. Limit one per customer. Offer expires next Friday. Briarwood residents add 17% shipping and handling.)

<u>Goblins</u>

(There are two basic types of Goblins in the world: true Goblins and Urks).

Goblins are rowdy two- to four-foot-tall troublemaking nuisances to the rest of the world.

In small groups they are what amounts to a mob of pre-teen hooligans, but in numbers they can be like a plague of angry baboons.

The *real* peculiarity of these creatures is that they have no females in their species. Instead they are able to procreate with any mammalian creature of the female persuasion and they are known to do so ... a *lot*.

Goblin mothers- whatever the species—give birth to several ten-inch-tall Goblin babies, known as *kendawls,* within thirty days of conception, which is usually via gangbang.

These relatively thin and disproportionate kendawls then nurse from their mother, or eat whatever meat she can provide in order to save her own life.

Finally, within a week of being born, they mature enough to be taught (by their fathers, for the most part) to drink, smoke, fornicate, vandalize and use weapons ... their *culture*, if you will.

Goblins are the ultimate socialists. They have an almost hive-like society and a racial ability to work as one, somewhat like G'nomes and Gnomes. They are frighteningly efficient.

True Goblins are also the only creatures who treat each other with absolute equality. There are no Goblins who are more valuable than any other within their numbers. They are as individuals almost incapable of selfishness.

This, in itself, is strange considering their IQs range from that of a mentally challenged lower primate to that of a scholarly human being. The smartest of them treat their almost animal-like brethren with absolute respect and brotherly love.

I'm not even kidding you. It's kinda beautiful, to be honest.

The latter treat their sometimes genius brethren like loved and honored trainers and caregivers. Those that are unable to make decisions for themselves always follow suit with whatever the nearest Goblin might be doing.

This is mother nature's way of also keeping the population in check.

At some point a Goblin horde gets so enormous that one Goblin eventually strikes another, which starts a chain reaction where every single Goblin in that particular Goblin horde ends up striking the next one, and ever so harder as it gets passed around and around, over and over through the Goblin masses- each round weeding out the less hardy until only one remains. That last Goblin then sets out to find a mate and the cycle then starts again.

True Goblins are also easily impressed. If you are strong and can pound the crap out of anything they might be afraid of, they most likely will let you tell them what to do.

Urks

The mighty Urk, more commonly known as the Great Goblin, is not truly a natural creature, indigenous to anywhere, but is in fact a type of construct or golem-like creature that can only come into existence as a result of a most heinous act. (Like politicians and bankers getting away with crime or—to them—showing up for work).

In fact, the greater the crime against society, the sicker the actions taken to enact the crime and the greater the loss of innocent life, the more powerful the Urk created.

See? *Just* like them.

Urks are fierce, antisocial monsters, who love the taste of human, elf and many other hominid races' and species' flesh. They are horrors driven to first destroy their creators (ie: Those who committed the heinous act/s that brought said Urk into existence) and then make war on their creator's people in any way they are able.

Rarely do Urks succeed in doing much damage past that which they inflict upon their creators before being lynched by a mob, and as such they are rare creatures. (This we all can be thankful for). They are designed for genocide. They are perfect for it.

Urks will attack anything they might see that they might fancy to attack and destroy for no apparent reason at all. They are always deadly and never merciful.

Urks have no understanding of law, order, or civilization and think on a very different level than other humanoid beings.

Urks are incapable of remorse, guilt, or compassion and are born with a sense of superiority that drives them to be among the vilest of all creatures to ever have existed. (Again, just like bankers and politicians.)

Urks are always male. Solid black to black-green-skinned, they stand on average six to six and a half feet- They are terrifying ... always.

In rare cases Urks can reach as tall as seven feet, but reports of them reaching almost eight feet tall are exaggerated at best.

Nod, nod. Wink, wink.

Urks possess forty-eight razor-sharp fangs. Their bite is scissor-like. The power in their jaws is enough to easily bite through bone as thick as 2 inches.

They have claws strong enough to tear flesh and even bone into splinters and shreds.

They are *monsters*.

Urks immediately speak and understand the first few languages they are exposed to. They have heat-sensing vision as well as powerful senses of smell and hearing.

Urks also seem to possess a racial ability to command Goblin-kind at will and force them to do their bidding. No one knows why.

This is achieved through the use of natural hypnosis that the Urks are "born" with but which only affects Goblins.

It is believed that this is caused by a pheromone release which is activated by the presence of Goblins.

Again, no one knows why, or how *exactly*, but the pheromones are said to act like a sort of drug that causes the Goblins to bow to the Urk's slightest whim, which usually translates to war against its creator's people.

It should be noted that this effect was something extra that the creator of the Urk Curse* was not expecting.

*The Urk Curse refers to a powerful spell initiated eons ago by an evil sorcerer bent on destroying the world, but who was instead destroyed by his own creations, the Urks. The spell that creates an Urk was cast upon the planet and not any specific person or place and therefore is impossible, so far, to counter. As a result Urks continue to come into existence and will continue to do so as long as the requisite evil exists, however rarer, and rarer the case might be. Truly it can be said that the level of evil and corruption, among people in any given area, can be measured by the Urk population it supports and not the opposite.

That said, a single Urk could easily stir up a horde of Goblins, every one bent on serving that particular Urk's whim, until he was replaced or destroyed.

An army of Urks could (in theory) start with a small number of Goblins each and within only a few months breed an invasion force of Goblins numbering in the millions. The prospects are truly terrifying.

Luckily, no Urk has ever had a high enough IQ to manage the logistics of commanding such an army and the Goblins always end up killing each other before they get to be more than ten thousand or so. (That and Urks just do not like each other all that much and refuse to cooperate with anyone on any level).

However, if you are an Urk, you need not try to impress a Goblin horde at all. Goblins have always served Urks. They do so in the same way that loyal dogs serve their generous and merciful masters—eagerly.

It is advised to always avoid an encounter with an Urk, as they are always territorial and aggressive.

Urks come into the world created from the decayed remains of innocent murder victims and precisely one full lunar year from the deceased's time of death.

They emerge from the earth beneath the bodies of the dead as fully developed adult specimens. They are the result of one sorcerer's insane imagination and need to make the world suffer.

Unofficially, it has been rumored that there once was an Urk that for some strange reason was able to function as a member of a civilized society. However, this is unlikely and only hearsay. No actual evidence has ever been put forth to support such a claim ... Nod, nod. Wink, wink.

So the civilized Urk remains sibling to other tales of fantasy like Yetis, Vampires, and G'nomes.

("...Urks are true monsters. These creatures are created through terrible events that include the murder of innocents. Yes, good reader, Grarr, our very own Grarrzy was created from the aftermath of a terrible ceremony.

I did not know these things about Urks back then, or it might have biased my view of who Grarr was as a person.

As it stands, it is no one's fault; the circumstances of their creation...")

From the Book of Shiddumbuzzin and the Latter Day Gnomes.

Urks are unable to procreate, but like elves they are nearly immortal in their long lifespans.

Urks are rarer every time one of their ever-depleting numbers fall to death's early embrace. Their *kind* appears to have a finite number that is ever depleting, while their only means of generating new members into their *race* is, more and more being avoided, *they* are becoming rarer and rarer.

For more information about the Urk and Goblin, or for a copy of this wildlife vignette contact: The G'nomish Film Board Society: Sixty Six-Packs Street, Allthewater, Sensimillia, 420420420.

CHAPTER - 20

"MORE THINGS YOU FIND IN THE SUBWAY"

I pocketed the wanted poster and finished my search.

It was behind the bar that I was eventually forced to call Musky to my side for assistance with a magical lock that my hootspa was unable to override.

I had located a heavy iron safety box built right into the wall and had to push a chair over next to it in order to be able to reach an elaborate-looking keyhole.

I then climbed up onto the chair and took a long look at the sophisticated locking mechanism.

It was a lock more than complex and was protected with magical runes beyond my power to counter.

Musky cracked his knuckles and deftly manipulated a plethora of picks and other thin instruments he took from his satchel. "Pffft. Musky not worried, brah. We be into dis 'ere in a sec."

In only moments he had the lock picked and the safe opened. Inside was a strong steel key. We examined it for writing, or identifying marks that might tell us where it was supposed to be inserted, but there were none. (...and, no- it didn't go into the hole that opened the safe ... we checked).

Musky, however, after some silent thought and no small amount of talking under his breath to himself (along with some very impressive athletic manoeuvres while searching the entire lounge), managed to come up with a secret door where the key actually *did* belong.

I joined him at the door where he inserted the key and turned it. Several tumblers fell audibly within the (once again) impressively advanced locking mechanism, and the door popped open a crack.

These locks were advanced by even *my* standards- and Musky's *too*, I might add. It was curious to me how and why Goblins would have such things. What could they have that could be so...

As Musky slowly opened the door a sweet, spicy, familiar aroma escaped into the lounge.

Teeheeheehee.

Inside were several shelves of *Goblin brain cheese!*

I know, right?

We're talking a hundred and forty pounds of the stuff. Just sitting there!

Woohooo!

As I entered the vault the fragrance was almost overwhelming. I shed a tear of joy... and then several more, as I looked at the floor, imagining some omnipotent being watching us find this sacred gift. "Holy Shiddumbuzzin."

Insert sigh of spiritual comfort here.

We then, quickly, emptied the safe and broke the cheese into smaller chunks that would fit into my bottomless pouch.

The task was made all the easier when Musky suggested I use a shrinking hootspa on the stuff.

...

That pause was on purpose.

This in turn gave me a reason to make a mental note: Research a more effective enlargement hootspa. (right?) I decided I was going to surprise Grarr later with a big birthday gift. Maybe the following Tuesday. (remember, kids, I still was unaware of Grarr's defeat).

We then made our way to the exit – a set of very strong steel bars from floor to ceiling that at first appeared to be a huge portcullis.

In the center there was a locked gate, but on closer inspection we saw that the lock was actually not set, and the mechanism was completely open. (Again evidence that these Goblins left in a real hurry... recklessly even).

Normally this would not be unusual for Goblins- but leaving behind their booze and food, dirty magazines (sorry, did I not mention those? I must have forgotten.) ... and *brain cheese*? That was strange indeed.

Beyond the barred gate was a massive tunnel full of water. To each side against the walls were catwalks that were wide enough for an average human to fit.

From holes in the walls and ceiling, here and there, water would periodically flow into the great underground river below.

We followed the catwalk cautiously, Musky always moving ahead and returning to report.

In this way we travelled for another full hour until we finally came upon a tunnel that Musky explained was our next obstacle.

Here the air was cool and comforting. It smelled clean, like untouched stone, deep in the heart of the world, like home – almost. This was all pure and clean water that we were passing by. I breathed deeply.

We sat down there at the entrance to the next leg of our journey. It was then that we both agreed we had not eaten anything substantial since before we both entered the fortress; Musky, almost nothing for three days before as he was captured and in the prison caravan. (Plus, we had the munchies like you would NOT believe). Musky had also been extremely thoughtful and had allowed all the Gnomish prisoners to eat the last time I hootspa'd food.

This time *he* would eat, and I would make sure he did.

I warmed our repast with a simple hootspa, and was happy to see him enjoy the food.

I really liked this guy. Holy Shiddumbuzzin, he looked like a rat, but he was my *friend*. I was somehow ... *not* afraid of him ... he *was* my *friend*.

Where was I?

Oh yeah...

Of course, we both had snacked here and there but right then we decided that a meaningful repast would do us both some good.

After we dined I conducted another Sabbath (you can never have too much Sabbath) and we continued on our way. This hallway twisted and turned every fifty feet or so, on a perfectly level plain.

We moved along this corridor for almost an hour before we finally came to the entrance of a huge chamber filled with water.

It was a sort of aquatic sepulchre and it was several hundred feet across—an immense pool of water.

Here, the ceiling was lost in darkness and distance- too far even for my dark vision to reach.

We stepped onto the catwalk (which was coated with some kind of resin or rubber), which made its way along the wall about two feet above the water's surface around the massive chamber.

In the middle, descending from hundreds of feet above us, were titanic pipes that reached down and into the dark depths of the pool.

Great machines were attached to the pipes and walls for use in pumping the water. The amount of liquid that could be pumped through such a system was unimaginable.

It was then that I remembered feeling something strange about the whole structure- the volcano-fortress, and its physical relationship with the planet.

You see, all G'nomes are attuned to the rhythms of the planet; the microscopic movements of tectonic plates, the flow of magma and lava, the harmonic thrum of the underworld that most would not even notice at all. It was this *sixth* sense that gave me the eerie feeling that I was then experiencing.

"It feels like something is wrong with the mountain above us, my friend," I explained as I paused at the chamber's entrance in a cold sweat.

Water dripped here and there from high above, and we could see small albino and phosphorescent fish swimming near the surface of the dark pool.

"I cannot detect the mountain above us at all. It is as though it is not attached to the world, like it's floating apart from the rest of the planet."

Imagine trying to explain, to a being born blind, what it was like to see. *That* is what it is like to try and explain the G'nomish sixth sense we call the *schmauz*.

Some G'nomes were more *schmauzy* than others but every G'nome is born with the schmauz. My s*chmauz* was extra-sensitive. A gift, perhaps? Divine providence, maybe? Puberty was awesome. (Schnipsy, my darling)

Anyway ... where was I?

Oh yeah ...

We entered the chamber and began to make our way along the catwalk and toward an exit, on the opposite side of the room from where we entered.

Again we noticed the many blind albino fish that were in the water below our feet, but this time there were more.

Even as we walked more and more began to break the surface and they were getting bigger too.

"Mun, I be tinking we should be movin' fasta. If doze fishes gits any bigga deyz is gonna jump up en eat us." Musky was now moving along the safety railing, three feet above the surface of the catwalk, his tail sticking up in the air so as not to tempt any of the fish into jumping up to bite it off.

"I am familiar with this species of fish, my friend." I tried to reassure him. "These are *Bolt Catfish*. As long as we do not touch them we will be safe. They cannot jump from the water as they are too heavy. These ones are even heavier than normal, which tells me someone is feeding them, but for what purpose?"

"Maybe dem is fa eatin' ratsta's, mun," he offered.

"No, they eat only algae and minerals. They are harmless if you do not touch them," I replied.

"What be 'appenin if Musky be touchin' 'em, mun?" he asked as he paused from climbing back down off the railing.

"A powerful surge of energy will shoot through your body and turn you to ash, even if you are in the water," I explained. "As long as we do not jump into the water or reach over and touch them we will be perfectly safe."

"I is tinkin' we should still be movin' fasta, mun. Just in case, ya know?" He stepped off of the guard rail and continued at a quicker pace in the lead.

Suddenly (oy, that word again) we were startled into halting our progress when the massive pipes began to shake and moan with the weight of hundreds of thousands of gallons of water being pumped from the reservoir.

The water level began to drop dramatically. So much even that we thought the cistern would empty completely.

Far below, the fish were flopping and flipping all over each other and as they did so I pointed out to Musky their special defense.

As their bodies touched each other they gave off powerful jolts of energy, much the same as *lightning*, which I had been reading about just a few days previous.

There were far too many fish to count, and they were of varying degrees of maturity.

I noticed that this particular school must have been living here for a long time. At least as long as it takes to establish a colony of such a size. What purpose they served was still a mystery.

They continued to sparkle and release bolts of energy as we carried onward.

After several moments it all ended and water was being pumped back into the cistern.

However, this time the pipes were silent and the water came from holes in the walls about fifty feet below us.

The pipes seemed to be for *taking* water from this place, while the river system we had seen earlier must have been the source for the orifices on the walls.

Or ... what do I know? What am I? A plumber?

Anyway, where was I?

...Oh yeah.

The fish soon discontinued their panic-stricken activities and continued along their daily routines, once the water levels started to return to normal. It eventually leveled off to its original depth just before we reached the exit from the room.

There we came to a stairwell that was not Gnome-sized at all. This was made for human-sized legs. I remained at the bottom of the stairs while Musky made his way ahead and scouted for danger.

As I sat in silence I witnessed the water level suddenly drop again, accompanied with the pipes moaning and groaning. I witnessed the whole room, once again, shake as this happened. Still I could not figure out the purpose of it all.

The fish far below all let off electrical reactions in a sparkling net of lightning, a visual display that was breathtaking and beautiful.

Here, I also took note of several long copper rods that were jutting out into the school of wriggling and flopping fish, just under the water level.

My superior intellect kicked in after that process repeated itself two more times, and I deduced that the fish were being used as (sort-of) *lightning-cows*, and being *milked* for their natural defence – *electricity*.

Somehow the energy they were creating was travelling down the copper rods to some other place where, perhaps, it was being stored, or even being used for something.

I was still baffled, though, despite my latest revelation. *Why?* I thought, *Why would they need such amounts of energy?*

Musky returned after twenty or so minutes, to inform me that the stairs were clear. I activated my magical ring and used it to levitate up the human-sized steps. Musky stayed in the lead, as we ascended the forty flights of stairs (oy) to finally come to a landing ten or so feet long that ended at a door.

"Behind dis door dere be a short tunnel, mun. Den we be needin' ta run across a big 'allway en 'ide in a bunch of garbage," he explained as I lit my pipe and passed it to him.

He drew from the glowing crystal device and smiled a bit. Then he exhaled and took another draw, finally returning it to me.

"Dere be a mighty lot a dem Talotians in dat dere 'allway, mun, an' we be needin' ta be real sneaky-like ta be getting past dem all, an' down ta dat duct openin'," he explained. Then he showed me a spot on the map where we would enter a vent much like the wickedly decorated one we found when we first entered the fortress. I dug through my pack for some more psychedelic mushrooms and shared them with him.

I nodded my approval of his plan and used my ring to turn invisible. Musky in turn opened the door a crack and peeked out. After a split second he gestured in my direction for me to follow.

At the end of the short tunnel, I entered the main thoroughfare of the fortress and floated, as fast as I was able, across the massive hall.

Above me I heard a strange sound of squeaking and squealing, rattling and thrumming, and so I looked to see what it was. As I did so, a low-ranking guard came running out of a bathroom and straight into my back, ruining my concentration and causing me to *first* fall two feet to the floor and *then* become visible.

Above me a huge cage was moving down the great corridor, suspended from massive cables and tracks in the vaulted ceiling more than a hundred feet up. The guard almost ran right past me as he was trying to figure out what he had collided with.

He looked down at me for a second, and then it all came to him. Just as I saw the realization of what had just happened reflected in his eyes, a tiny glass dart pierced the left side of his throat. Musky had shot the villain with my dartgun.

The guard slapped at the area, as one does with a mosquito, the action cracking open the tiny dart and releasing the toxin. A second later he was falling to the floor.

A second guard now came running from the same direction that the first had come from. This guard had seen me materialize and instead of entering the washroom (his initial plan), he moved to attack me.

"*Saaaliqa! Effall eh gan'oshmine!*" he yelled as he reached for his sword. Whatever the heck that meant. I assumed he was sounding the alarm as the guards further down the hall were beginning to react!

Musky called out to me from his hiding place while I paused, lying on my back, not knowing what to do.

I had been surprised and had just had the wind knocked out of me. The Talotian had finished drawing his sword and was preparing to impale me as the huge cage-like apparatus moved by overhead.

Guess who was in that cage? Go ahead ... take a guess. Small world.

Anyway ... Where was I?

Oh yeah ...

From out of nowhere a two-foot-tall tempest of fur and razor-sharp teeth erupted into a death whirl, or something I have no other words to describe. Man, that guy was impressive when you fed him 'shrooms.

Musky had jumped onto the guard's face and tore out his left eye with his small (but obviously sharp) claws!

As he did this he gave the man several facial piercings and bit the end of the guy's nose clean off. Even as he was tearing the hell out of the guard's face he was warning me that more guards were coming.

I tried to call out to Beornag, who I had recognized through the haze and screening of the cable car far above me, but the shouts from the guards and a terrible commotion from something else happening farther down the great hall made it impossible for my tiny voice to carry that far.

I watched for a split second as the cable car made a sudden turn further down the thoroughfare and disappeared from sight around a bend.

I then rolled to one side as the guard tried to pull Musky from his face, screaming in pain and shock at what was happening to him. Blood was now spraying from the wounds in his face and throat.

I managed to come to my feet, just then, facing more than twenty Talotian guards, all looking straight at me as they advanced, weapons drawn.

One of them pointed his sword at me and yelled out in humanese. "You! Get on the floor and surrender or we shall kill you both!"

I poised myself, preparing a special little something I had been studying of late and had recently been – shall we say – inspired to add to my arsenal of prepared combat hootspas.

The guards quickened their pace and became even more fierce as one paused to aim a crossbow at Musky.

I focused my hootspa on the powers that came from the earth, drawing upon the great electrical energies that tectonic friction can cause. "*Crackzzzzzpliztiztal!*" I yelled, as I pointed a glowing left palm at them.

The guards all came to a sudden halt as they realized I was a spellcaster, and was preparing to destroy them with my awesome hootspa skill and power.

Unfortunately only a tiny spark shot from my hand and quite literally bounced off of one of the guards' shields to land on the floor next to him and sputter out.

They all relaxed for a moment, and some even began to laugh, but soon they were re-oriented and moving toward us again.

"Dat was freakin' patetic, mun! Wha da 'eck do ya call dat now, eh?" Musky scolded me while drawing his adversary's dagger and dispatching him. The man fell to the floor, blood spewing out of a gash in his throat.

I suddenly remembered the schmauz and a realization came to me. This mountain was not attached to the rest of the world.

Bingo! It was actually floating on a microscopic membrane of water. The guards were only thirty feet away now and would be on us both in seconds.

Once again I reached out to fractures and faults, this time those of the mountain itself. I was looking for a specific source of friction energy- the *bolt catfish* in the cistern!

It took me only a split second to find them and connect my hootspa to the electricity they were transferring to the mountain each time they touched a wall or the floor of their home, the reservoir.

"*Crackzzzzzpliztiztal*" Even as I yelled out the words many of the guards began laughing again.

However, this time the glowing spark landed right in their midst. An eerie electrical light that it was emitting rapidly increased in intensity until (after only a moment) it exploded in a cloud of showering sparks and frizzling sounds.

Smoke suddenly filled the area around the Talotians. They choked as the area became noxious, filled with ozone and carbon dioxide.

The super-heated air that surrounded the group began to ignite their clothing, as crackling bolts of glowing white and blue electrical energy tore through their bodies, dancing among their ranks.

Eyes exploded and blood spewed from rips and tears in their faces, as they instantly cooked from the inside out.

Those guards who were not touching the main heap were spared the electrical damage, but were forced to retreat as their hair and clothing were burning out of control. The smell of noxious vapors and the sizzling flesh of their comrades drove them to flee in panic.

"'Oly freakin' mudda a creashun, mun!" Musky rejoiced. "You da *mun*, mun! Wooohooo!" He enjoyed a victory dance as he cleaned his *new* dagger.

I looked around quickly to gain my bearings. I had been in that place before, but I was at the other end of the hall. I remembered the doors on the outside curve of the thoroughfare.

These led to – or at least *one* did – a bathroom. I took a moment to see if I needed to go.

I didn't. Go figure.

Just around the bend further down the hall was the main entrance to the fortress. The cable car I had seen carrying the Troll was traveling in that same direction.

From down the hallway we now heard a new sound. This time something large was roaring and getting closer. It was soon evident there was more than one of whatever was coming up that hall.

It also became painfully evident that Musky and I were not going to arrive at the entrance to the vents and ducts before running into whatever was doing all that roaring.

I leaped from the floor and activated my ring, improving my speed as Musky tagged along. It was perfectly clear that he could have, at any moment, left me and made it to the vent without getting caught, but still he stayed with me as I attempted to move faster, trying to think of a solution.

"We be needin' ta 'urry betta, mun!" Musky lamented as he almost ran circles around me.

Understand, I was traveling as fast as any *human* could run; Musky was simply *far* quicker than any human *could* run.

"You go ahead. I will turn invisible and catch up. I know where it is supposed to be- the vent, I mean," I offered as I gestured to my ring/bracelet and winked.

"Go straight ta da vent, mun. I be waitin' dere fer ya. Good luck." With that he was off and soon vanishing among the massive amounts of debris that were piled in the hallway.

I drifted by piles of garbage lining either side of the hall. Here I saw some weird creatures tossing items from the huge piles over the guard rails and into the volcano core. These were the Forest-Trolls, cleaning up the mayhem that Beornag had earlier caused in the marketplace.

The heaped piles of junk consisted of some pretty weird stuff. I mean weird for just lying around. Pretty much anything you can name was in that pile, from boots to canteens to clothes to weapons to parts of structures, packaging, and a lot of other things, too many to describe. It would take another book to list it all. These all seemed to be brand new except for one strange fact...

*These things are all covered with **shit**!*' I thought as I floated past the seemingly endless bank of shit-covered garbage. The reek was unimaginable.

I then began to recognize some items. Things I had seen at the market when I passed through, with the demonically possessed human guard, while disguised as Vermin, Musky's previously demonically possessed cousin.

I know, I know. Demons, dragons, Trolls, Goblins? Who is with who and where? It's like doing algebra.

Anyway, where was I?

Oh yeah...

There was crap everywhere. There had to be hundreds of pounds of the stuff splattered all over the piles of rubbish. I was soon beginning to gag from it all as I moved further down the great hall and toward the vent.

Then, suddenly ... oy (that word again), two creatures came around the corner that scared the crap outta me. That was a tragedy in itself, seeing as I was quickly running out of clean clothes and I had even left a set on the park bench back in New Sensimilia! Oy! What a schmuk!

Anyway. Where was I?

Oh yeah...

Two great behemoth-sized rat beings came into view and I was almost *paralyzed* with fear. Each was almost as tall as the Troll and wearing full plate armour.

Both carried heavy hammers and shields and both were looking straight at me, despite the invisibility enchantment that my ring was providing.

My brow glistened with the sweat of fear while they snarled and squeaked.

Once they looked toward my location, they roared again and began to move very fast toward me. The fear in me was enough to make me faint, but somehow I managed to stay my ground and verbalize a hootspa.

God was with me. I was righteous. (I hoped).

I pointed both open palms at the oncoming beasts and yelled over the noise of what appeared to be a mobilizing army of undead coming down the other end of the hallway, leaving through the now-visible main entrance.

Oy!

I realized at that same moment Calabac was on the move and was emptying his fortress of all his armies. He was moving on Briarwood. Who else, right? It would take no longer than a couple of days to reach the port city. I could only hope that someone was warning them. Perhaps Raz.

Both my hands began to glow with what appeared to be burning embers. I spoke the words, *"Tshhhhht. Tshhhhht. Whoooooosh!"*, and from my palms a great stream of smoke erupted. The smoke was so thick that it might have even been able to hold up a small amount of weight. It was almost liquid!

I watched as the smoke engulfed the two scave *knights* and quickly manoeuvred behind a shit-covered canvas banner, still hanging from its supports. From there I could see them stumbling in the thick smoke, becoming ever-so-intoxicated and blind to their surroundings.

Quick thinking caused me to cast the same hootspa again, *two* more times until the gargantuan monsters were almost completely inebriated.

Then I conjured some giant bread sticks, using my food hootspa, and covered them with cheese dip from my backpack. It was almost sacrilege to waste the divine *paté* on these two vermin, but it was all that was coming to mind and frankly I hadn't a lot of time right then to be creative, so I sort of played it by ear and hoped for the best. Like being *Troll* by association.

I then did the unthinkable. I moved quickly *toward* the disoriented and extremely stoned scave sentinels.

"Hey!" I yelled at them.

They both turned in my direction and one tried to smile but ended up bursting out in uncontrollable laughter.

This is where I cast *another* hootspa. "May I offer you a lucrative investment opportunity?" The magical incantation echoed in their ears, a tantalizing promise of wealth and eternal happiness. My *charming* hootspa began its work on their puny minds.

I came within arm's length, just then, as I noticed Musky returning from his hiding place to assist me. I signaled him to stay his attack as I approached the closest scave.

I waved a cheese dip-covered breadstick the length of Grarrr's arm at the monster, all the while shivering in my boots and casting another charming hootspa. *"It's a good deal."* The second vocalization ringing in the creatures' ears was too much for them to resist.

They looked to me expectantly, begging almost verbally to be blessed with the cheese-covered loaf.

I floated right up to one of them and placed my hand ever so softly on its ear, cupping it so as to enhance the next phrase of the hootspa. *"Svenkle eq fl'misfaaaaaah,"* I whispered as I imagined him tearing apart his buddy and anything else that hated me. I then pulled away quickly as the carnage began.

My scave turned suddenly and leaped high into the air, at least six feet, covering the ten or more feet between it and its comrade with ease. The other scave was not ready for the assault and it was knocked to the floor, as *my* scave (Mick, let's call him Mick. I've always liked that name. Mick it is.) *Mick* landed with full force on top of him, pinning the beast to the floor.

Still disoriented and confused, the pinned scave was again unprepared as the front of his armour was ripped open, exposing the chain mail cuirass underneath. I propelled myself in the direction that Musky had gone as Mick was deeply involved with the gory task of disemboweling his comrade/adversary–who never stood a chance.

Here I felt a new courage I had never felt before. *'Wait til everybody back home hears about this!'* I thought as I came within eyeshot of the vent where Musky was waiting just inside. *'Let's see Bernie top that one!'*

As I approached the opening I looked toward the intersection where this hall, the way out and the way into the market area met. There, making a final right turn to exit the volcano fortress, was the last of the undead and their terrible machines of war, beginning the two-day journey to Briarwood.

Holy Phuc had better have been right when he described the great war machines we were searching for. Calabac was ignoring them because the overconfident asshole believed no one knew how to make them work. I was hoping he was wrong.

We were almost there now. As I entered the vent I could hear the sounds of murder fading as Mick was finishing up his gruesome duty. He was, no doubt, now gorging on a bloodied cheese-covered baguette.

Musky had his hand in the air when I arrived. "'Igh five, mun! Dat was tinking, eh?"

I slapped his hand and joined in the revelry. "This old guy still has a few tricks up his sleeve," I said as I gestured for him to lead the way. "Can we find a bathroom on the way? Do you think?" I added.

Sure enough Musky led me down a side tunnel that brought us to a vent in a bathroom on that same level.

Finally. "Aaaaaaaah," I thought, as I cleansed myself again. I used a simple hootspa to clean and dry my garments (seeing as they were all that I had left) and redressed. Once suitably relieved and washed up, I rejoined my furry friend and we continued onward toward our destination.

Traveling for about ten minutes we finally came upon another four-way junction in the ducts. "Musky gonna go ahead a bit, bruh. You be stayin 'ere while I see what we is facin' next. Ya?" he suggested with a smile and a sparkle from his zircon. I agreed and he disappeared toward the northwest.

I waited for several minutes before he finally returned. "We be 'avin ta fight agin, mun." He paused to catch his breath, and then continued on, "Dis time it ain't bein a easy one too." He gestured down the duct he had explored. "Down dere, mun is one a doze *stealers*, mun, an 'im be 'avin two monstas wit 'im. Doze is dem Rock monstas too, mun. Musky not be sure we be ready for dem tings. Doze is craaaazy creatures, mun."

"Ive never heard of rock monsters before. They sound dangerous, but we will still have to try. It is our only option now. We cannot go back, it will take too long," I lamented as I began to prepare for a big Sabbath before we walked into oblivion. " Besides, there's an army of undead now filling up that hallway." I gestured behind us.

"What about dat stealer, mun. 'Im be indestructible and everytin. Ya c'not chop, cut er slice doze tings. Dem grows back t'gedda, mun." He looked worried.

"I faced one before. You are right. They are fearsome in their powers, but I know their weaknesses, so here." I handed him my pipe full of special herb from the Garden of the Bong (which from now on we really should be referring to as the Temple of Shiddumbuzzin) and he accepted it reverently.

As Musky slowly and gently brought the contents to an ember, I spoke. "O Shiddumbuzzin, mellowest of *Mellow Ones*. Great Creator of all that is G'nomish and sacred to us. We ask that you look upon us with favor as we, in our time of need, face a great danger. We ask...." He handed me the pipe, just then, and I accepted as he exhaled, filling the air duct with smoke. "Where was I? Oh yeah. We ask that you ... wait. Did I say that already?" I asked.

"Yeah, maybe you did, mun. When you *tink* you been sayin' what you is asking now, mun?" he asked ... I think.

"Wha...?" I responded. "What the hell was I just saying?" I asked.

"You be meanin' when you was talkin 'bout da stealuh an' 'ow you be knowin 'ow ta make 'im weak?" he asked.

"Wha...?" I replied.

"*What?*" he asked.

"*What?*" I said.

"*What?* What?" he asked.

"Wait," I suggested.

"What?" he replied.

"I said, *wait*," I clarified.

"What I be *waitin'* fa, mun?" he asked. "Musky got ta be sittin' down, mun."

"I can't remember," I confessed. "Oh ... wait! I know now. I remember. Wow, that was a potent bud!" I exulted. "All I got was what was in the air from your exhalation and Holy Shiddumbuzzin! Whew!" I took a long, deep draw from the firestone pipe and handed it back to Musky.

Somehow it all came back to me. "We ask O Mighty and Mellow Protector–O Provider of light, warmth, herb and hootspa. Guide our sword and *our* hootspa to be true to their marks and help us defeat our enemies." I smeared some cheese dip on a slice of potato wedge and handed it to Musky. "This, my friend, is my cheese dip and potato wedge. Eat it and I shall be slightly envious and be forced to have one too."

The holy words were coming to me, as though I had spent my whole life preparing for that moment. I then poured a small chalice of wine and handed it to him. "This ... this is my wine of Warped Speed. Drink of my wine and be blessed with new *liquid* courage."

Musky partook in the entire ceremony and when we finished, and had cleaned up our holy picnic, and had a few more mushrooms, I followed him into the tunnel to the southeast.

Moments later we turned around and continued in the correct direction, which was northwest.

After a few minutes I could make out a light ahead, where there was a large room identical to Calabac's throne room. "Wait," I whispered. "Come closer," I said as Musky crawled over to sit right beside me. "I have some hootspa that might help us both. I will need to cast magic on your person. Is that okay?" I asked.

"Do it, mun. It be good stuff, ya?" he asked with a twinkle in his incisor.

"Very good stuff, just like before in the vaults," I replied, as I began a series of hootspas that would cause us to turn invisible to all enemies for the next hour and automatically heal the next few wounds we might suffer. I was able to make Musky as strong as a giant and I coated his dagger with sacred resin from the holy bud. For myself, I prepared something very special that I thought would be perfect for this special occasion.

Once finished and refreshed, we continued on the next thirty or so feet and stopped on the inside of a decorative vent. Peeking through, I confirmed the room was much like the throne room, except this one was almost barren of furniture and decor and was exceedingly dry and dusty.

Two great piles of stone that looked strangely out of place were at either end of the long rectangular room. These were covered with dry, dying mosses and lichens long dead. I could make out the remains of dried mushrooms and toadstools and other once-colourful fungi, now mostly desiccated and barren of life, covering the stone, and just then something made me feel quite sorrowful. Somehow this was a crime against all life.

Okay, the dead plants were kind of sad, but it's not like they reminded me of home or anything like that. I had no explanation. I did, however, also notice that it was a very overwhelming feeling. I actually wept, and so did Musky.

Other than the piles of sorrowful stones, the room was barren save a set of three chairs facing each other over a round stone table.

These were in the very center of the room. The stone piles were each at a different end, and it was our task to cross the chamber at its narrowest in the center. This *seemed* easy enough.

I floated and Musky crawled silently into the room. Once we had entered I heard a voice.

"*Sssssoooooorvisssst Ooooolnassssss.*" It reverberated through the room, a loud whisper that seemed to cling to my ears like a sickly pus clings to a wound.

It was an incantation. Definitely magic, and by the time I realized what was happening, the two piles of stone were moving toward us at incredible speed.

The spell that I had heard being invoked had been cast from the darkness high in the vaulted ceiling. I remembered seeing darkness like this before, when we had first arrived in the fortress.

It was so utterly pitch that even *my* advanced and superior vision was unable to pierce into its secrets.

The spell itself was a binding magic- foul energy used to enslave and manipulate. This was *Evil* magic.

Just the words were enough to cause me to stagger momentarily in order to keep control of my senses. My stomach began to sour and I felt like I might vomit.

Musky had disappeared from my sight as a hundred or so tons of stone rubble fell on top of me.

I instinctively held up my hands to protect myself while the rubble came pounding down over me, but seconds later as I opened my eyes, I saw that I was trapped inside a dome of stone and dying vegetation.

I looked around and noticed something that caught my attention: two eyes of obsidian—glossy and almost empty. They gazed into my heart and for a moment our thoughts were connected as if we were one creature.

I was humbled—this was the only species alive that were older than G'nomes. A Forest-Troll. Its eyes begged for mercy as it battled against the evil forces that were compelling it to destroy me. Its eternal spirit was in a lethal war against itself trying to tear away from the absolute hunger the evil instilled in it for G'nomish blood.

I helped it to surrender to the struggle somewhat by giving it *permission* to throw me at whomever was controlling it. This allowed it to avoid killing me, but afforded it a release by throwing me violently. So the evil magic was not resisted, just interpreted differently than the caster had intended. It's nice to be smart.

Half in hopes of saving me from itself, and half that it was sending me to my demise, the ancient behemoth stood tall and scooped me from the floor. In one fluid circular sweep it lifted me and tossed me toward the chairs in the center of the room.

As I flew through the air I saw Musky at the far end of the room running around while another Forest-Troll tried to capture him.

My telepathic connection to the first Forest-Troll was severed as soon as it let me fly. Yet, even as that connection was severed, I was able to still feel its sorrow and pain as clear as if they were my own. Like an echo of its hurt.

Oooooo, was I angry.

This rage had brought me to my senses in time to realize that I was traveling at breakneck speeds and rapidly approaching a collision with – *ME*!!?"

No kidding! There I was standing on the round table with a terrible-looking ... *'Hey, wait, that's Durik's dagger!'* I thought. Ooo, the thought of *me* stealing Durik's stuff from me was infuriating to say the least! *I* had been the one on that table casting evil hootspas at Musky and me, and now I was pretty mad about it.

As I hurled through the air toward *me*, I yelled out the verbal components of the *surprise* I had prepared for this yutz: "*Phlamanski-matzma-erupsha*!" From my hand a stream of glowing stones erupted and spewed out at *me* on the table. They exploded violently, sending me and *me* flying backward in opposite directions.

I (and *me*), soon, however, regained our composures as the nearest Forest-Troll behind us continued to fight against the terrible magics being cast on it by *me* on the table.

I landed on the table's edge and faced *me*, just as I heard a squeak from over the *me already on the table's* shoulder.

Are you still following me?

Good ... unbelievable, but good.

The other Troll was about to squeeze Musky to death. It had caught him and had a firm grip on him as he struggled, his eyes visibly about to pop out. Only his artificial giant's strength from the hootspa I had cast upon him kept him from being crushed immediately.

As this was happening, I cast a second hootspa. *"Coraspha magmania imprisia!"*

Me fell to the table's surface, suddenly covered in rapidly cooling lava. Small fissures in the surface cracked open, revealing the glowing hot contents from under the smoking skin of the liquid stone.

From within, steam and burning fluids spewed out and onto the table's surface across from my position, as scabs of cooled minerals fell to the floor.

The remains of the stealer that managed to spew from these fissures and cracks was so heated that it either vaporized quickly or burned with a sickly green flame. Sounds of sizzling, screaming and bubbling then escaped from the pyroclastic coffin–the monster's last words.

Just then I saw the Forest-Troll drop Musky to the floor and stagger backward. The evil *me* had been the Stealer and I had destroyed it by engulfing it in a coating of white hot lava. Having nowhere to escape to, it incinerated before it could regenerate!

Okay, okay, enough with the applause already. I was great, though, right? Thanks. I love you guys.

Now where was I?

Oh yeah...

Musky was regaining his composure, coughing and struggling to stand up. I drifted across the chamber and landed beside him. "*I'll bill ya.*" I spoke the prayer aloud as I touched his forehead.

His wounds were instantly healed *and* he got a nice little head rush for a second as a bonus. The boss is good that way. You know? Where after-effects are concerned and that sort of thing – always pleasant for the most part.

Anyway ... where was I?

Oh yeah ...

The two Trolls were now slowly approaching us, as Musky reached for his dagger.

"Wait, my friend." I placed my arm across his knees. "Stop. They are not our enemies."

"Dat pile a rubble tried ta kill I, mun! Whatchya be callin *dat,* eh?" He said, looking down at me, panic in his eyes. "I be callin' *dat* enemy."

"They were under an evil spell," I explained. "These creatures are *the* oldest living things in the whole world. They are truly the children of the earth. That is why we are still alive," I explained.

It took me about ten minutes to fully calm and explain everything to Musky, so I will try to be brief in this description for *you* reading this book.

Forest-Trolls are connected to the earth much in the way that fish are connected to water. They must have it. They need to touch it always. However, if the water is stagnant, the fish slowly die. The mountain was stagnant, because it was disconnected from the earth by the mysterious membrane of water.

Our new friends, the Forest-Trolls, were dying because the mountain was dead, stagnant so to speak. When the first Troll touched me it immediately recognized me. Not only my race, which is second only to them in age, but me personally. This creature was alive when the first G'nome crawled through the *crevasse* deep in the deepest earth. It witnessed everything the world has become and changed and evolved into. Everything we, my people, have evolved into. Everything *I* had evolved into. These creatures could see everything that happened all the time while touching the natural earth.

G'nomes are innately connected to the earth as well. We evolved to be miners and diggers long before we were civilized. As a civilization we are still expert miners and diggers, but we also evolved to have culture, technology, knowledge and such. Through all the eons of our development, however, we remained connected to the deep earth.

This was remembered and felt, as the Forest-Trolls had always felt my specific presence in the earth, along with all living things so connected.

This primal connection was beyond the meager power of any mortal magic, such as the variety that the Stealer was tossing around. It overrode his spell and was what caused the Troll to stay his hand against me, while the other continued to attack Musky. Musky, being of a very young species, by G'nome or Forest-Troll standards, was not linked with the creatures in the way a G'nome was. His people were enjoying their own spiritual renaissance that way.

The two Trolls stood over us while I explained everything to Musky. In the end it was quite the turn around. He strutted around them, most pleased with our new findings. "I is *nu*ttin' ta mess wit, bud*deeeee*." He grinned as he sang his mantra. "I be takin dese 'ome wit us, mun. I be wantin' dem ta come livin wit I on da islands, mun," he said as he patted one on the leg.

I took some time to use what limited hootspa I had prepared that could be substituted as a healing force upon the Trolls. Their anatomy was of mineral and friction energy, like my hootspa I had blasted the Talotians with earlier.

However, the Troll's electrical energy was grounded and harmless to the touch. It acted with the ore deposits on the surface of their hides to keep them from crumbling apart, charging the metallic deposits, turning them into powerful magnetic connections.

In honesty I had barely even heard of these creatures until that moment when I had made the mental connection with it. In that short time it had transferred to me more knowledge than I could have memorized in a month reading about their species.

"They are slaves, my friend," I explained. "Not animals, but old and wise beyond our understanding." It was true. "They are slaves to Calabac because he found their only real weaknesses. They need to be in physical contact with the planet.

"This fortress is just enough to keep them alive and no more. They have been starving here and in their weakened state they were susceptible to Calabac's, or more accurately, the Stealer's magic," I explained as I admired the giants standing over us.

I cast several hootspas reviving some of the flora on their skins, and other hootspas for healing the wounds they had suffered at the hands of human Troll hunters. I touched one and tried to make contact with its mind. It immediately received my attempt and thanked me.

I explained to them where I needed to go and what I needed to do, as quickly as I could, and asked if they could help. In the process it accessed my own thoughts, learned the truth, and realized the danger Calabac represented to the natural world.

Up until that moment they had thought they were fighting for the freedom of Trollkind. They had been tricked into service. Now they were pissed.

The sad part was, even if we *were* victorious, with the help of the other Trolls, people would still probably treat them the same – even if they saved the world. Greed and the desire for the wealth that could be harvested from a dead Forest-Troll were all it would take for most species to decide to cash in and kill them. What could I do to stop it? I decided that Musky was correct and that these creatures needed to be better protected. If there were forests on Musky's islands then I was gonna see to it that they got a few new residents.

Somehow it understood my feelings, and I conveyed a plan for them to flee the terrible Fortress of Fire and find sanctuary in the deep forests of the western mountains, until I called upon them again.

Figuring this was gonna be the best I was gonna get from these guys, I explained the plan to Musky and suggested he lead the way to the place where the war machines were being kept.

The Trolls pounded a massive hole in the wall where the exit had been. Even in their weakened state they were powerful adversaries. The locked doors shattered as well.

I, at that moment, decided to get my ears checked when I got home. I thought I heard a trumpet being played terribly from one of the vents exiting the room.

Musky then joined me at the vent lighting a spliff. "Dat was not as 'ard as Musky be tinking it was gonna be, mun. We be on a roll now, I be tinking. Luck be wit us, ya?" he said with a smile.

He then deftly opened the grate and we entered a new set of ductworks. Behind us the two Forest-Trolls waved goodbye and then exited the room, on their way to Briarwood.

"Did you hear that?" I asked as once again I thought I heard something in the not-so-far distance ahead. A voice yelling in fear perhaps.

"I taught it was dem mushrooms," Musky said with a sigh of relief. "I 'eard a fella yellin about some shit, mun. Is dat what you be 'earin too?" he asked.

"Not sure what it was saying but yeah, a voice yelling way up ahead," I agreed. "Maybe you should go ahead and scout again, I will be right behind you."

The hootspa that had been making us invisible to enemies was still working, as well as the one that increased Musky's strength.

As for myself, I was all out of lava, so hopefully we wouldn't run into another stealer. But I still had a friction storm and a few other tricks as well.

I floated as fast as I could down the ventilation duct after Musky's shrinking form as he moved faster ahead. The sounds were getting louder now.

There were definitely many voices ahead. Most were yelling in a language I was unfamiliar with, but every now and again I would hear a word or two yelled out that sounded vaguely humanese.

As I approached a spot where there was an opening on the left side of the duct with a screen over it, Musky returned to report.

"It be a *craaaazy* ting dat be 'app'nin down dere, mun." He was smiling from cheek to cheek. "Dem stupid Trolls," he laughed."Dey be fightin' wit each udda an makin' all kind a mess, mun."

"Is that the direction we have to travel, Musky?" I asked.

"Oh ho ho ha, yeah, mun, bad news is dat." His expression changed to worry.

Outside, through the screen, was a great hall similar to the main entrance and the outside ring of the fortress. This hall was silent and empty, all but for the sounds of combat in the distance.

Musky explained that we were fairly close to another hall, like the one I was looking at through the vent, but it was an even smaller ring- inward towards the core. He explained that the Trolls were just beyond the duct opening where we had to go in order to get to where we needed to be.

"How many Trolls do you think, Musky?" I asked.

"Maybe fifty a doze ones dat be wearin' dat metal armour and carry doze big weapons, and some a doze Djeaupeshee Trolls wit da long fingas too, mun," he reported. "Too many fer I ta be fightin' even *wit* yer 'elp, mun." He looked worried.

"They were fighting among themselves?" I asked.

"I be lookin' fast, cuz people were trowing tings all over da place an screamin' an yellin' en Musky was not ta be getting caught, mun. What I be seeing was a lot a Trolls fightin. Dat is what I be seein. Musky not be stickin' around ta be getting caught, mun," he explained.

"Alright," I said as I took a deep breath. I noticed a rank smell coming from further down the vent and the sounds of yelling had stopped. "I believe you, and I am glad you didn't get caught."

I took a moment to make sure we were not just way too high on mushrooms.

We were, but that was beside the point. We both ate a handful anyway just to be sure. "Let's have a look, shall we?" I said- in slow motion.

We continued along the duct and then made a ninety-degree turn to the left. The way he was changing color was amazing. He even turned tartan once. We continued for a few more minutes until he stopped us at a junction. He explained that the Trolls were just around the corner and that we needed to be real quiet again. His twin brothers concurred.

Once I realized my x-ray vision was non-existent and no amount of adjusting the brim of my hat was going to change that fact *and* that I did *not* possess the hootspa or knowledge to time travel, or change into a tiny spider by crossing my eyes (have *you* ever eaten a half-pound of phosphorescent psychedelic mushrooms? Well then...), I concluded that the mushrooms were *really* kicking in, so I complied and floated silently around the corner as directed.

Musky was a foot or two right in front of me as we approached an open vent. I was just about to suggest he have a shower as soon as possible, when I realized the rank smell was actually coming from the opening just ahead.

Someone was talking outside as I approached the vent. I immediately saw many pairs of giant metal-plated boot heels facing me, as I peeked out to get a better look. The area outside was a sort of deck, overlooking another wide hallway the same as the last, near the main entrance, only this was curving at a tighter angle around and under the core of the volcano. This one, however, looked mostly unused.

There were some sort of great rail tracks running along the length of the long hallway in both directions. Some climbed up along the walls and were even interconnecting with a cable system much like that which I recalled seeing the Troll riding in earlier. The one that had been suspended from the ceiling in the main upper hall.

Remember that one? Good. 'Cause I gotta tell ya, I was beginning to think it never actually happened.

Anyway, where was I?

Oh yeah...

I then took note of what the speaker was saying, just as I began to also notice all the tied-up (and beaten-up) human guards all stuffed into what might have been the same cage-like cable car I had seen the Injoke in earlier. They appeared to be covered with...

"...crap an awe sorts cool tings dat makes us laugh and be happy, Troll freedum army!" There was a massive Cave-Troll and he was addressing a large group of other Cave-Trolls. "Dat be right says me to fellow Troll k'nigits. Dis Boarsbag and him buddees be good guys on us guyses side. Right, Pehvis?"

The reek was mind-numbing and many of the normally hygienic Cave-Trolls were now in the process of wiping muck from each other's armour.

"Holy inebriated lawn ornaments! It's da Redeye!" Beornag exclaimed as he pushed his way through a crowd of about fifty armed Cave-Trolls in camouflage-suits, *Lillia* riding on his back.

He somehow managed to reach me without stepping in shit, which seemed to cover the entire area ... everywhere ... on the Trolls ... the steps ... the walls ... the human prisoners ... the cage ... everywhere. The mess was simply traumatizing.

Yes, ironically, Beornag was untouched by the bio-hazard, and as *Lillia* was riding on his shoulder, she too had been spared whatever fecal disaster had occurred in that place.

I wondered why and how she ended up here in the fortress, as the Injoke reached the vent and bent down to look past my shoulder.

Still he did so without getting any crap on him. How this occurred even to this day is inexplicable.

"Who's ya buddy dere, Redeye?" he said with a friendly smile. "C'mon out, little guy, weez ain't gonna hurt ya. Dis here is da great army a da..." He looked back over his shoulder. "Hey, Terdbreff! What's weez callin aw'selves again? Ize f'got."

"Great Trow Freedum Awmee," came the response.

Just then as I was about to speak, the Injoke looked straight at Musky and exulted, "Hey! Yooz is da udda guy Ize is s'posed ta rescue, right?"

Chapter - 21

"The Legend of Puff Puff Pass"

The next part of our story I have asked the Mellow One to tell. I was not present for the following events and as such could not do them justice. The Great One, however, was kind of the *cause* of what is written here next, so I believe he is the best one to tell it like it was (*and because he schmootsed up the prologue, remember, from book one? I want to give him another chance to be part of the writing thing. You know? He gets lonely; give him a break. We need to get him out more anyway. He spends way too much time shacked up in that paradise of his. Don't tell him I said so, though.*).

Anyway, kids. Have fun and don't get too scared. This part's about a *monster*.

There is a place in the west, deep in the foothills of the mountains there, where the setting sun casts sinister shadows over ancient forests.

In these foothills there are places that most people have never seen. Not even elves have stepped foot in these woods. Only the Goblins dare to tread those lands... and perhaps a young human boy seeking adventure, many years ago... but that is another story.

They say in this place there can be found a monster. A creature from nightmares. Silent and invisible, it haunts the deepest parts of those old woods.

A creature covered in green and gray fur that hangs from its body, like the mosses that hang from the limbs of some ancient swamp-dwelling tree. A terrifying behemoth with tiny, pitch-black eyes ringed in blue and silver that can pierce a man's soul.

This beast wanders the forests and valleys of that place, ever searching for flesh and blood, driven by an insatiable lust for carnage. It hates humans with a passion- or so they say.

A beast as tall as a castle wall, with arms like great pythons, capable of ripping trees out of the earth, roots and all.

It is said that its mouth contains a hundred massive white fangs all surrounded by swollen, blood-drenched lips and its claws are always stained crimson.

The beast is cunning too. It hides its scent from those that would detect it with the flora and fungi of its primal abode. Sweet and succulent flowering herbs and all manner of natural fragrances it uses to cover its own musk.

Those brave enough to settle on the borderlands of the creature's territory tell stories of the thing coming out of the forest and stealing cows, ewes, and other milk-producing livestock. They say the beast cooks them in their own milk. In fact there are many tales of the creature stealing all sorts of livestock and doing terrible things with them.

These farmers and settlers do not try and stop the beast, which is seldom caught in the act of taking the animals, but instead suffer their losses and are glad that the victims are not of their own kin.

This is how it has always been in *that* place.

A long time had passed since anyone had gone missing in the night. The creature of the old mountain pass had not been seen in a generation.

Yet... they knew... it was still out there.

Livestock were still disappearing, fewer than the old tales used to say, but the elderly who remember swear it is the creature from the legend.

The legend of Puff Puff Pass.

At the foot of the mountains, where two peaks meet as one and a great rock lies over it like a megalithic arch, the ancient winding road of *Goblin-kind* deteriorates from countless ages of neglect.

Here is the legendary pass where the hordes used to come from, raiding villages and stealing children and women. But that was long ago. Longer even than the last recorded case of the monster being seen in that area.

Just before the pass, through the mountains, is an overgrown and broken set of stairs that were there even before the arrival of the Goblins hundreds of years ago. At the foot of the stairs is a valley, where there is a farm surrounded by tall, straight fir trees.

Pines and spruce, along with the odd patch of birch, encircle the valley on all sides.

Here there is a path in the far southern corner of the barley field on that farm where those ancient stairs begin. At the foot of the path is a tall stone with old runes engraved in its surface. The language is long-lost and forgotten, but locals know what it means all the same. It is a warning to stay away.

The path leads off, up those ancient stairs and into the forest. It continues up the overgrown ruins of a long forgotten civilization along the hillside. Here the trees seem to bend over the path as though trying to reach those who would travel under their limbs. They are old and untouched for these days, no one is brave enough to set foot in that forest.

An ancient pathway curves and winds through raspberry patches always picked bare, between piles of boulders with strange paintings on the surfaces, massive monoliths of natural rock, glacial deposits from an ancient and uncivilized time.

At the top of the hill where the path opens onto a series of meadows, a river flows cold and rapid out of the tall mountains across the plateau and beyond to the southwest. It cuts across the far end of the fields, through a vast swamp where reeds and tall grasses are laid flat by the autumn winds.

The river is low, as the effect of the fall season creeps up the mountainsides and freezes the moisture there that would normally feed its waters. Yet, even so, it is wide and cold and still somewhat deep.

On that side of the river Sylvain, there is a marsh where people never venture. No one returns from that place. Locals say that the beast hunts there sometimes. In fact, they say more people have gone missing there than any other place in the region of Puff Puff Pass.

The ancient path through the mountain pass was deemed too unstable for merchant travel, and too narrow for any military use. Most of the pass, it was assumed, had crumbled and deteriorated. Originally thought to be built by a Goblin horde, to allow them access to what people described as their underground village, this makeshift road was usable to some extent, at one time in history. However, it was not the Goblins who built it; the workers who constructed this road were far older.

It is long forgotten, whatever became of the Goblin horde. Most say that the creature of Puff Puff Pass ate them all, for it was not long after the beast arrived on the scene, in legend and folklore, that the Goblin sightings began to run thin.

On this night the cool autumn breeze that came up the pass carried with it a sound. A sound that would prove to be something that had not been heard in those parts for a thousand years or more.

It is alone in its lair. Awaiting the return of...

Wait... there it is again! The sound of something it *must* find. It doesn't know why. The need is primal and the creature is *driven* into action.

Deep, thrumming, it feels the sound in its bones, in its loins, in its soul. A sound so beautiful to it- this sound is pure elation and it must find the source! It must have the source!

From miles away the sound rumbles out across the creature's domain, calling it, begging it to come forth and be seen. A voice that promises destiny.

A terrible monster erupts from its bed of dried leaves and grasses. It moves with the agility of something much smaller and avoids the collection of furniture and other items in its lair. It likes to collect things. It likes the things that men make.

Men.. the *enemy*.

It roars at the moon and the sound echoes throughout the mountain pass.

Moments later the residents of the farms, nearest to the old and forbidden highway, rush for the shelter of their cellars as the voice of the monster is heard raging from the crumbling walls of Puff Puff Pass.

Farmers and their families cower in their basements trembling with fear as a shadow erupts from the ancient road and passes by the windows. Its footfalls shake the very ground as jars and bottles rattle on shelves.

On this night it is not interested in the farmers, their families, or even their livestock. Tonight it is answering a call so primal and ancient it will stop at nothing to reach its quarry.

It moves through the farms leaping over fences and loping across fields of wheat and barley still being harvested. A great mass of green, grey, and brown shaggy fur, a monster from ancient nightmares, it is the quintessential *legendary* monster. It leaves little evidence of its passing, only the odd tuft of fur on a sharp branch, or a distorted print in the mud.

However, on that evening, the farmers and their families would know without a doubt that it had been among them. Behind it, the beast leaves a trail of destruction. Sheds pushed over, fences torn out of the ground, and the terrible screaming hooting roars heralding the passing of the monster, the legend of Puff Puff Pass.

Moving in a straight line toward the source of its prey, the creature rips its way through the forest, tearing a great path through the trees and shrubs, leaving behind a trail of chaos and destruction. Animals ahead run for their lives as the monster rampages through the night, never tiring, never losing track of its intended destination.

It pauses momentarily to tear up assorted grasses and wild flowers and rub them against its rough fur, disguising its pungent musk with the scent of its environment.

Then it stops at a hillock overlooking a great marsh and sniffs the air. There is a scent on the wind. A scent that cannot be ignored. It breathes the smell in deeply. The scent is near but faint. It knows this scent.

Man.

It is familiar with this scent.

It is the enemy.

This is the only thing that could take it from its intended course of action. An instinctive *hatred*.

Another greater instinct now takes hold of the beast and it follows the aroma, momentarily forgetting about the sound that was controlling its earlier actions.

Tiny black eyes, too small for such an enormous skull, pierce straight into the early evening sky.

Now the moon is already low on the horizon. Soon it will be high above and the night will be red. But something is wrong. This is the *creature's* marsh. Why are *humans* there? Why are *men* there? *Soldiers!*

Rage!!

Across the river a large group of them are moving toward the bank. The beast makes note that they have animals with them. It is angry. How dare they allow their livestock to graze in that marsh! Do they not understand the dangers involved? Do they not care?

Another scent comes from their direction, but now it is fading. Blood...blood on the wind. Not man blood. Something else.

The scent returns. It is coming from the river. The creature also detects the phero-chemicals of a primal message, hundreds of eons in the making. *This* on top of the familiar aroma, on *top* of the stench of men. This new scent is even more faint, as though fading from time spent away from the source. It is the original scent it decides to investigate. It *aches* to find the source.

Something or someone among those humans was carrying that scent. Whatever was *not* the men was *carrying* that scent!

Rage!!

The men are coming into my marsh! the creature thinks. *How dare they!!* But still it longs to find the source of the sound... and the scent, for they are connected, and the creature realizes as much.

It is smart.

The monster crawls toward the leader of the humans now less than a hundred feet away. It growls in a low voice as it prepares an ambush. It moves like a silent wind on all fours through the season's last tall grasses, bending in the evening breeze.

Almost invisible, closer and closer it moves, slithering on its belly now, almost snakelike between the low hillocks.

The moon begins to disappear behind a blacker than black cloud that moves along the ground.

Now the monster lowers itself to a prone position and awaits the coming invaders. It is cunning. It is full of hate for these creatures.

These are the same men that did cruelty to it, many years ago.

It had escaped their hateful lands and come to these places decades ago. It is now infuriated that it will have to deal with them again, so far from their own country... Where the creature was born.

It is filling with rage ... It *will* destroy them ... *all* of them!

The leader of the men crawls ever closer. He is stalking. He is low to the ground and moving slowly. How *dare* they hunt in that marsh. The stupid man-things do not even see the beast. It is fully adapted to its environment. It is the color and texture of its surroundings.

In fact, its surroundings actually grow from its thick furry hide in spots. It is perfectly camouflaged. It is silent. It is patient. It is a monster.

The smaller animals that the humans bring with them are now crowding together on top of the beast's back. It is powerful. It is strong. Stronger than these puny things. They believe they are ascending a small hill. They are dead wrong.

They roar and fight. Even the men seem to struggle for things in the night. Things that men made. They are arguing (or something), but the beast does not care. They are fighting among themselves, or so it seems. They scream and throw things at each other and when enough of them finally crawl atop the creature's impressive mass, it explodes from hiding!

Men and their animals are thrown in every direction. The humans are weak! The creature rips the spine and skull of one man completely from his still-running body and beats another human with it, until that man too dies of horrific wounds. The marsh grass is soaked with steaming blood as one after another of the humans and their animals are ripped apart.

Among the blood are streams of glowing green liquid but the beast does not stop to look at this strange substance. It doesn't know where the stuff is coming from nor does it care.

They are decapitated, disemboweled, torn limb from limb. The carnage is unimaginable. The sounds of screaming are mingled with the snapping of bones and the ripping sounds of flesh and skin being torn from living victims.

All of the small creatures that came with the men are stepped on and crushed under the great hands and feet of the beast as it rampages through the ranks of soldiers and verminous animals. The great spurs on its feet impale soldiers as it moves through their ranks like wildfire through dry autumn grasses.

Limbs and heads fly in all directions as though an *army* of creatures were fighting the men.

Only moments later a scattered few are running for their lives across the river. The vermin are all dead. The black cloud retreats up into the sky and off to the west. Blood and carnage are everywhere.

It sniffs the air. Somewhere among the blood, mangled meat of the countless corpses, torn bits of armour and weaponry, marsh gasses and autumn breeze off of the river, was the smell of something so instinctually tantalizing that the creature doesn't even pursue the retreating humans. Instead it searches for the source of the overwhelming musk.

Attached to this scent is another aroma that the monster recognizes.

One of the enemy is carrying that sweet-smelling black goo that the Goblins often have with them.

Finally it finds the source. The thing that was not a human, not one of their pets. This thing *too* was a monster once. Now it is lifeless in the beast's hands... in *her* hands.

Remorsefully, she slumps to the ground, looking out toward the southwest from where the strange sound had come.

Now it remembers the sound. But like a dream, its memory even now is fading away.

It sheds a tear.

The sound is gone.

The autumn air is still- quiet...lonely.

CHAPTER - 22

"DON'T JUDGE A MAN UNTIL YOU'VE WALKED A MILE IN HIS PEOPLE'S FECES."

"Injoke! How did you find us?" I rejoiced. "And how did you know about Musky?" I added, my heart almost exploding with the joy of seeing him alive and well.

"Weez been lookin' all ova da place f'yooz guys! Where's Durik?" he replied as he stepped back and away from the vent. "En Ize don't know either whose muck knees is, but Ize knew Ize was s'posda rescue sumbody else! Woah! Ize gots premature ignition!"

"Premonition," *Lillia* whispered in his ear.

"Oooo! Yooz too? Yooz just read my mi..." I then interrupted him before he hurt himself, or someone else.

"He's back at the temple," I said as I peeked out at the small army of armoured Trolls standing in military formation on the dock. "Long story, I'll tell ya later. Maybe in a book," I said in reaction to his confusion about the temple part. "What's with these guys? I gestured at the Trolls, and why would you even think to bring Lillia here?" I added. Of all the irresponsible things to do! Bringing an unarmed delicate flower like Lillia to a place like that!

"I am *not* 'Lillia'," *Lillia* answered.

I noticed her voice was a bit sterner than usual, slightly deeper as well.

"Please don't tell me this is Grarr or Raz," I said, thinking one of them might have been magically transformed into Lillia, or something like that. Hey... ya gotta admit. In that situation, quite literally, anything could happen. It *had* and was *still* happening. It's not like shape-shifting and morphing things hadn't al*ready* happened. *Right?*

"What da heck are yooz gettin' on about?" the Troll asked, standing up to his usual crouching-over position. "Lillia's back at da winery, Redeye. Dis is I'll-Lay-It, Lillia's sista, who I might add was rescued by yours truly." He smiled proudly. "Oooo! You wanna feel awful?"

"Alaeth?" I asked. "*Feel awful?* Why would I need to feel awful?"

"Yooz doesn't *has* ta have *two*, yooz can have just one only if yooz wants, silly," he explained. "*Du*-uh."

"Wha..?" I said.

"Never mind that," Alaeth interrupted. "You must be one of Beornag's friends. I assume by the conversation you are having, you know my sister, Lillia. My name is Alaeth. I need to thank you." She was quite graceful as she slid down the sleeve of the

Troll's chain shirt, to land gently on the floor. She walked ever-so-delicately towards me, never touching the poop smears and crap puddles that littered her path. "Thank you ever so much." She reached in through the grate to shake my hand. "I wasn't sure how much more of these two I was going to be able to take. How do you do it? My gods, it's like babysitting a couple dinosaurs who won't shut up," she whispered through the opening.

I took her hand and was about to shake it when...

"What the hell is that *terrible* stench?" Then I looked again at the assembly of Trolls. "Why are those guys all covered with liquid *shit*?" I added, as I now noticed that it wasn't camouflage they were wearing. "I'm still not hearing anything about this Troll army standing around either. Are we *prisoners* now? What's *happening*? For the love of... they're *covered* in *shit*! Why are they *covered* in *shit*?!" I was traumatized. "I am sorry but I am having a hard time keeping up with all of..."

I was interrupted again. "'Ere, mun. Smoke dis." Musky handed me a herb twist and lit it with a match. I drew deeply and moments later I was relaxed.

"Okay... First things first," I began. "Oh, and thanks, Musky," I added. "I am the Redeye, Szvirf Neblinski. A pleasure to make your acquaintance," I said to Alaeth as she held my hand through the vent opening. "My apologies for my outburst. This has been a trying series of events for me, and now *this*?" I gestured to the shit... it was everywhere. There were also two (of what looked like) massive, wet, empty paper sacks.

"I be Musky," my Ratstafarian comrade spoke up, waving at her from over my shoulder. "I is a good guy, mun. Please don't be killin' I."

Even in her disheveled state she was stunning. I had almost forgotten how beautiful Lillia was. Alaeth was no different. Her...

Then it once again occurred to me: "What's with the Trolls? I can only assume we are not prisoners ... right ... *Not* prisoners? Emphasis on the *not* part?" I asked. Holy crap, these guys were scary-looking. The *small* ones were around four feet tall and were wearing sort of casual (yet stylish) white uniforms. Some of them carried what looked like chains of jewelry dangling from their arms, at varying lengths which looked pretty dangerous if not just a bit gaudy and awkward.

Their larger compatriots were from ten to fifteen feet tall and were clothed head to toe in pitch-black chain armour with rough-hewed plates of blackened steel patches here and there. The whole effect was terrifyingly primal-looking. These monstrous creatures were armed with shields and great maces, swords, and axes. Their helmets looked to be huge, spiked colanders. Beyond the faceplates of their helmets I could tell that they were gagging, and many of them were attempting to clean the feces off of each other to no avail.

"Deze guys is wit us, Pops," Beornag said with a huge smile, once again bending even closer to the floor and peeking into the vent. "Dis is da Great Awmee a Trow Freedom." He looked back over his shoulder. "Did Ize get it right dat time?" he asked.

"Yup. Terd say good stuff, Pehviss," came a voice from far in the back of the crowd of Trolls. This one was a little larger than the rest, and had a *spikier* colander on *his* head that was of slightly better workmanship than the rest. I was glad that he was not some sort of sentient, animated turd, although at that moment he smelled like one and it was not all that far from the realm of possibilities.

"Ize rescued da king a da Trolls, Pops! Ya shoulda been dere." the Injoke said as he turned to face me again. "It was like Ize was a hero or sump'n! Ize battled all kinds a monstas and stuff too. Man, it was awesome!"

"Okay, so these guys are buddies of yours now? Is that correct?" I asked as I stepped ever so carefully and slowly out from behind the vent, taking extra precaution so as not to step in any of the mess.

O merciful Shiddumbuzzin, you kids should feel blessed for not having to smell what I smelled as I stepped onto that platform. The stench was like nothing that had ever smelled bad before in the history of creation!

I gagged as I tried to cast a cleaning hootspa. The ordeal took me almost fifteen minutes *just* to get the stench under control, and another forty minutes to use my hootspa to transport all the liquid crap from the Trolls to the platoon of humans now stuffed tightly into the cable car Beornag and his comrades had arrived on. It was priceless. You had to be there. Ahh... the memories.

We then moved away from the mess, leaving the humans to moan, gag and *enjoy* their incarceration, with a bit of a bonus added in the form of one hundred and sixty pounds of liquid shit.

In that time I took a few moments to properly introduce myself to everyone. Beornag was at first delighted that his rescue quota had been filled, but later was upset when he counted again and noticed he was still missing someone.

"Yooz, I'll-Lay-It"–which is exactly how he thought it was *supposed* to be said–"Durik, Musky ova dere and Beornag. Now dat's five, ain't it? Why does Ize keep missin' sombody when..." We allowed him his moment of deductive reasoning as I finished up.

"Ey, mun. Doze tings ya be wantin'? Ya know dem dere machines? Well, dem be not too far now, mun. If all we be needin' ta do is get doze, and den rescue dem little Gnome peoples, den let's get on wit it sos I cun get da 'ell outta dis place, irey, mun?" Musky spoke up, map in hand as he looked around at the towering resslers and the snarling Djeaupeshees with their dangerous-looking pocket pens and pinky ring weaponry.

"You are right, my friend. We have delayed long enough." I had thought of sending everyone off to Briarwood to try and warn them of the coming army of evil while Musky remained behind with me. He and I had done okay up until then, but my hootspa was drained. I was powerless without some rest. The cleaning of the poopfuric acid (he insists that I call it that) had depleted even my emergency stores of hootspa and emptied my magic ring as well. I was almost defenceless at that stage and had no choice but to ask them all to come along. "Look around. We have a small army of Trolls. Let's see something try and stop us now."

I gathered everyone around me spoke a brief prayer. Then Musky and I were anointed honorary mijitt resslers (whatever that was). They insisted on holding the ceremony right there and then. It would have taken more time to argue with them than to just go along, so we humored them.

I then explained what we needed to do in order to save Briarwood, Durik, Alaeth and her sister and perhaps the entire world.

Then I did the same thing again two more times, and finally a couple of them caught on enough to inspire the others to follow suit and listen for the fourth and fifth tries.

After that we moved along the tracks as a fighting force. The resslers surrounded Musky, the Injoke, Alaeth and myself, with Terdbreff in the lead, his terrible-looking serrated axe held firmly in armoured hands strong enough to crush a rock.

The Djeaupeshee Trolls all chattered and waved their wicked-looking writing instruments in the air. They wanted blood. They were among those Trolls who first understood my explanation of what was happening. Some even took notes. They even helped to explain it all to the others with detailed and insightful illustrations and diagrams. Which I am not so sure really helped all that much, as they were prone to offending each other by sometimes having slightly differing versions of what was being said, which all too often led to small fights and arguments that ultimately *we* would have to mediate and dissolve.

In the long run, though, we all *finally* understood what had to happen and the Trolls did their part as our new bodyguard/ entourage. (I still, at that point, couldn't believe the amount of shit they had been covered in and was very happy that I had enough hootspa left to clean it all off of them).

As we traveled along the tracks, Alaeth explained what had transpired since she had been rescued from her prison box (poor girl). She told us about the storeroom, the countless priceless works of art and mounds of gold and jewels that were there. She also gave praise to the Injoke for not taking any for himself. "He is so *honest*. I mean, anyone else would have filled their pockets, but he simply walked past it all and just took a case of wine that he said was his anyway," she said.

Of course, jewels and gold we had plenty of, so he never thought to take any. Even if he did know what they were worth, he still wouldn't know what they were *worth*, because that, to a Troll, would be worthless. Again, the Hill Trolls' ability to be completely oblivious to the value of money, and how much money any given thing is worth. As Beornag would say, *"Yooz can't make feel awfuls outta gold, so why is it wert so much?"*

We traveled this way for another hour. The hall was gigantic. Two hundred feet tall *and* wide with two sets of tracks on the floor, two on the inner wall and a set of cables on the ceiling. All of these were old and rusted. They had not been used in many decades- or centuries.

Here, I noticed, the architecture was slightly different. In this area the walls and floor were made by the same craftspeople who created the hollow mountain across the pass. These tracks were the *same* technology as the machines in the other mountain. I deduced that this part of the volcano was constructed by those who built the other mountain, but here construction had halted ... probably when chaos and evil fell upon old Sensimilia during *The Descent.*

Obviously Calabac had attempted to continue the construction with the aid of the Gnomes, the only beings he could find who were related to the original creators.

Here the architecture had cleaner lines, and the machines were sharper-edged. Here the tracks were made of steel, not iron, and the blocks of stone used to create the structures were far larger than those of the upper levels of the fortress.

I took note that the cables above were different than those back at the dock where I had found the Injoke and his army of Trollish warriors. These were larger, stronger, and there was a third one. Where the car back at the docks used only two that were about four inches across, these three were easily twice as thick as I am tall. These cables must have been used to move something massive at one point. Perhaps these were the cables that the machines used to move the great building stones of the fortress's lower levels.

Curving, this hall stretched along the lower belly of the volcano. The whole structure was a marvel to even imagine, let alone see with my own eyes. The mountain was one of the largest in the whole chain, the base being several miles across. Only twenty percent of it was actually above the surface of the world. The rest sat deep underground on a thin layer of pressurized water. The throat of the volcano was at least three miles deep and its belly was a mile in diameter and filled with superheated mud.

An entire mountain that was artificial, ancient beyond belief, and without explanation. Whatever purpose these two megalithic creations really served, or were to serve, I could only speculate. The mathematical skill alone, to be able to create flexible seams between stones, was impressive enough. But how those ancient crafters managed to *grow* crystal and ore right into the very fabric of the stonework was beyond my imagination. It could only have been through divine intervention.

Our course took us steadily along the curving hall, around and under the very gullet of the volcano, until we finally came upon a stairway that led up to another docking platform.

I estimated we had walked three quarters of the inner hall's length, steadily on a curve around the mountain's center. We had passed several small docks along the way. It was at these places where I was able to discern the changing architecture and technology.

Here the tracks converged onto one single set. There were no cars here, but it looked as though the place might be a docking area for the car system, when the cars were not in use perhaps. Again, I could only guess.

Here the stairs had three sets of footprints in a thick covering of dust and ash from the volcano's constant churning.

One set belonged to Terdbreff, as he was ordered to the task of keeping everyone out of these areas; now he was with us, very angry at Calabac, and totally curious as to why he was supposed to keep people out.

Another set, he explained, belonged to Calabac himself, as the villain had spent many hours in the place doing something he was not willing to reveal to *anyone*.

This last set of prints belonged to a stealer. The only other person allowed to enter this area.

Their prints followed the stairs up *and* down and were made at various points in time, which was evident by the amount of dust that was or was not covering them.

I asked Musky to scout ahead, while Terdbreff and the Injoke attempted to calm the Djeaupeshee Trolls who were now beginning to chatter angrily.

Moments later Musky returned to inform us that he had found evidence of recent use. He suggested that I and he be allowed to check out the platform thoroughly before the small army came up and disturbed any evidence.

I agreed and we ascended the stairs.

At the top we paused at a jetty large enough to facilitate fifteen or twenty cable cars of the largest sizes. At that time I had deduced that we had climbed up to a major hub for the cable car system, but there were too few of the cables and tracks present there. This was more like a final destination–perhaps the garage for the cars to be stored when not in use.

This last platform was massive, and I eventually came to realize that it was some sort of loading bay. There was a small crane at the edge of the jetty that looked to be for lifting large items on and off of cable cars that might dock there.

Back at the massive hall that brought us to that place, now a fair drop (for me) from the platform, the tracks ended, and there was a sort of emergency braking system for stopping any cable cars that might arrive from going further down the tunnel.

Here the tunnel continued with a sort of paved road, leading away into the darkness, curving out of sight.

We searched the general area and soon found signs of recent use. "Look, my friend," I whispered to Musky as I signaled over the edge of the platform for the Trolls to remain silent and still, "are these more footprints?"

Musky nodded as he joined me. "See 'ere, mun. Dis be were Calabac be steppin' off a somtin' and onta dis 'ere floor, 'ere," he said. "An dis be where dat big Troll wit da spikey 'ead be steppin' too, mun." He showed me some other massive prints that I had thought were discolorations in the stone.

"You mean Terdbreff?" I asked.

He smiled and was about to laugh, but then caught himself. "Ya, mun. Dat fella."

"You can tell it is him just by the *prints*, and *Calabac* too- just by looking?" It was amazing what he was sometimes able to discern where I saw nothing at all. The original prints we found on the stairs were set in thick dust and easily spotted. Here on the platform, the dust was much thinner, being exposed to the constant breeze that came up the tunnel. The prints left by Calabac and Terdbreff, to me, were only vague depressions at best.

Musky certainly had an impressive skill set; it occurred to me that I had never asked him what he did for a living before he became a prisoner.

'Tis a gift, mun." He smiled, his fake diamond sparkling in the light of his phosphorescent fungi hat-decoration.

I looked over the edge of the platform again and signaled for the Trolls to join us.

The Resslers immediately started tossing Djeaupeshees up and onto the platform where they burst into a psychotic fit, searching for enemies. Some, frustrated at not finding anything to stab at, proceeded to decorate the walls of the place with graffiti.

I would later read a bit and be pleasantly surprised to find some really nice poetry, philosophies, and even a couple short stories among strings of written music that I (as I had some small bit of training in if I don't say so myself) was impressed with. Simple lines of beautiful notes, that if played could lull a baby to sleep in seconds. Those Djeaupeshees were the most eccentric of their eccentric species – if that is even possible, considering the Injoke.

There were two main exits from the massive dock at either end of the long platform, one at the north end and one at the south.

Both massive doors were closed and locked tight. I hootspa'd the south one, but was unable to break through the magic that held it shut. Musky then took a shot at the locking mechanism and soon had the door slightly ajar. I approached cautiously, with two Djeaupeshees in tow. The Injoke and Terdbreff were busy organizing the Trolls and gathering the few (still frantically vandalizing) Djeaupeshees who refused to stop drawing beautiful nudes of varying races all over the walls. Again, I almost got an erection- they are THAT good at their art.

Knowing this was probably going to take forever, I decided the two Djeaupeshees who were curious enough about what I was doing to follow me, and Musky, would be sufficient security to explore the open portal. I was the first to look past the door, with Musky looking over my shoulder; we peeked into the chamber beyond.

The room was well-lit and filled with all sorts of experimental devices. It's ceiling held circular glass orbs that radiated light; some were hanging from long cables and actually gave off a steady warmth.

This place was made for human-sized occupants. It was fifty or so feet, side to side and about ten feet tall. Tubes, beakers, bubbling flasks of unknown liquids and gasses and an assortment of strange items and tools of science were placed on tables and shelves.

The hanging globular lights were grouped in a circular pattern in the center of the place.

Directly under the ring of lights was a round, tall, conical shelf-unit with hundreds of flasks all set in orderly fashion, kind of like a decorative artificial fir tree of sorts.

Here, I deduced, was where Calabac had placed his personal laboratories, where he had been involved in the creation of terrible creatures and the summoning of demonic monsters.

Sure enough, I found a summoning circle. The thing had been recently used and kept in working order. I was tempted to scry for its recent purpose, but decided the risk of being noticed again by a stealer from the past was too great.

I returned to the conical structure in the center of the room that held hundreds of flasks.

Each flask was a tiny phial with a piece of leather bound over the top, tied in place with another piece of leather and sealed with a glob of wax. Every phial was identical and the black wax topping on each leather stopper had the same symbol pressed into it – a seventeen-pointed star.

In these I found tiny humanoid forms, still in the developmental stages. They were all curled up in fetal positions with threads and cords coming from them, and up into the lid of each flask.

The figures within the flasks were basically human in shape, but were a faded olive-green color and too spindly to be human embryos. Their large eyes were closed, but as I studied one I noticed it open its mouth a crack, revealing a single strip of serrated bone.

These were tiny stealers!

It was at that moment I realized in horror that each and every flask contained one of the foul monsters. There were hundreds of them. Maybe thousands! An entire army of the nightmares!

By that time Terdbreff and some of the others had entered the laboratory. The larger Trolls still remained on the huge platform but a handful remained at Terdbreff's side. His honor guard.

"Guys, we need to destroy this room and its..."

Well, that's as far as I got before the djeaupeshee Trolls went berserk. They took about two minutes to break every single glass beaker, bottle, jar, and carafe in the place to tiny shards on the floor. They also set fire to the squirming little half-developed stealer demons before they could slither off.

Never underestimate the IQ of a Djeaupeshee.

I had made a mad dash for the exit once the glass started to fly. When I returned to the room it was unrecognizable. The walls were covered with poems, lyrics, love letters, advertisements and just about anything that you might find written on a wall. One Troll even wrote out the words to a ballad so quickly his pen caught fire and he was forced to dispose of it! Luckily there were a few in the lab and his weapon was replaced in good time.

"Wow, talk about the pen being mightier than the sword!" I exclaimed as I inspected the mess.

Now that everything in the room was utterly destroyed (*and* decorated with illustrations and fine penmanship, I might add), I noticed that the lab had another door that led to a stairwell. The stairs in turn led up fifty feet to another chamber where there were several workstations. Each station contained a chair and a crystal ball, as well as other administrative tools. These all faced a long window that opened into a massive, artificial cavern.

The cavern was big enough to house a large army, machines and beasts of burden included. However, nothing moved in there. Even from that distance I could see the eons of dust that were covering everything. Enormous tarps were draped over three large structures each the size of a small fortress. These *mounds* of cloth and gadgetry resembled coliseum-sized circus tents with strange contraptionry (there's that word again) sticking out from under the covers.

We searched the room we were in for some access to the greater chamber but found no way out save the way we came in- or through the open portal in the wall that overlooked the great chamber beyond. The floor below that portal was fifty feet down.

The place we were in seemed to be an office for directing operations in the cavern. (I'm kinda smart that way).

I also managed to discover a secret drawer which contained three keys. These keys were each numbered from 111 to 113. I took all three, then Musky and I returned to the now-destroyed laboratory.

We went back out onto the dock where I approached Terdbreff, the rightful king of the Trolls. I bowed in respect, and then asked about his footprints.

He explained that part of his duties included the daily inspection of the great cavern and its contents. Though Calabac was unable to learn how to use the machines, he was still determined to keep them from enemy hands. Still, he never expected to have to deal with intruders.

After explaining to him that we needed to get into the great room with the tarps, he gestured to the other huge sliding door at the other end of the ramp.

"Me say dems is not workin' tings. Sos yooz be not habbin' good uses a' times goin' by, little cheese Goblin person-guy, if yooz wants ta seez dems," he explained. "Terd seez doze many long times ago and always doze not working, an still not."

After explaining to him the importance of making them work, and that I believed I could do it if I was given a chance, he and the other Trolls decided that would be a pretty awesome thing to see and so they ripped down the... ahem... security doors and made way for me to enter the vast chamber.

Inside, it was as I expected. Two to three inches of dust everywhere. Only a few footprints were here and there. Mostly they were Terdbreff's, but there were also a few barefooted human tracks, and what appeared to be the tracks of someone wearing the boots of a courier that I deduced belonged to the Stealer who took William's identity. The freshest of these all left the room, so I deduced we were most probably alone in that place.

I passed through a sort of short hall, where there was a second set of steel doors, even mightier than the first. These were wide open and leading into the main chamber.

Beyond the open portal a vast cavern had been constructed to hold three or more of the gargantuan masses that were hidden under the enormous tarps. Its ceiling was hundreds of feet high as well. Dust, from eons gone by, hung in the air captured in Musky's phosphorescent mushroom which was illuminating the area.

Three massive tarps were each pulled tightly over three great mounds of machinery and contraptionry that, at that distance, appeared to be nothing more than strange, giant circus tents. Their towering support poles held up heavy canvas tarpaulins that draped between the tall points, like a pavilion for giants and titans.

I was in awe.

I soon asked Musky to take a look around the place while we waited, and after a few minutes he returned to report the place had been empty for many weeks since the last visitor, who was Calabac. "I be knowin' dat villain's footprint anywhere, mun. Him gots dem long sharp toenails and all dem toe rings too mun. Freaky dude him is."

As the Injoke, Musky, Alaeth, and myself entered the cavern, Terdbreff assembled his warriors on the platform. We crossed over the threshold of the entrance and into the mega-vault, but just as Terdbreff was about to follow, the other, much thicker sliding doors dropped shut behind us with a mighty bang.

I stood there helpless. These great doors proved to be too much even for the Trolls to open. The Injoke on one side, and Terdbreff on the other, and still the five-foot-thick steel door would not budge.

There was a small set of holes in one side of the doors, presumably for drainage in case of flooding (who knows?) Yelling *through* this, I instructed Terdbreff to try and find another way into the room while we explored the place. I had completely forgotten about the window in the office at the top of the stairwell, or I would have had him go that way. In the end he might not have been able to fit inside the stairs anyway. The architecture there was designed for humanoid beings, not giant monsters.

"Okay, folks, listen up," I began as I gestured for Alaeth, Musky, and Beornag to gather around me close to the entrance to the cavern, "I have to assume that these are the three machines that Holy Phuc - I'll tell you later -spoke about." I gestured towards the three colossal mounds filling the better half of the cavern. "We need to take a look at those things and somehow find a way to enter them. Holy Phuc - again, don't ask, I'll tell you later - said there will be a control station inside of these machines. Once inside, the operating instructions are supposed to be all written in ancient G'nomish. I will understand this and be able to make them work again... in theory... Oy."

"Um, scuze me," the Injoke interrupted.

"Yes?" I said.

"Do yooz tink if Ize was ta run way ova dere an fart, it would be far enough away so as not ta bodda any a yooz?" he asked. "Ize gotta awful fart dat needs storing, an sometimes a bit leaks out da sides when Ize tries ta pull da bag ova Ize's ass. Yooz know what Ize means? Yooz know, when dat happens? Ize hates it when dat happens."

CHAPTER - 23

"*THE UMPIRE STRIKES BACK*"

Alaeth spoke up, electing to be the first to venture deeper into the massive room. "Look... there. It looks like the back wall has a long seam down the center." Excited, she broke into a run toward the area she was referring to. Musky bolted forward to remain near her should she run afoul of any of Calabac's tricks or traps.

Beornag lifted me up and placed me on his shoulder. He then followed the two, just a leap and bound behind, as they made their way between two of the structures. From my own vantage point I could see now that the tarpaulins covering the heaps were only that. I instructed the Injoke to begin removing the covering from the lone machine, while we waited for our comrades to explore the rest of the cavern and the areas around the other two megalithic contraptions.

Beornag began by asking me to untie several knots, in several ropes, that were holding the tarp in place. I used the last of my simple hootspa stores to do so on all three machines.

He then pulled up the side of one of the tarps and we looked under the edge at something incredible- and I mean INCREDIBLE!

The Troll gasped in disbelief and literally fell on his rear end, a tear escaping from his left eye. "Redeye. Ize can't believe it. Look at what weez has found!" He stood up again, well as stood-up as he gets, and pulled the tarp back further so I was able to see exactly what was there. "It's da magic sleigh a Ulm. Just like in da book!"

Meanwhile, Musky and Alaeth had made their way to the end of the two–two-hundred-yard-long machines that were paired closest to the seam in the wall. Here the two brave souls searched the back wall for an alternate exit.

"I be tinkin' dat dere be a way ta open dis 'ere, elf gurl," he said as he showed her a seam along the floor, thus confirming her suspicions that the entire wall was a giant set of double doors.

"You go that way, I'll go this. Call out if you find something... Ratsta-man," she said with a wily wink. Then she turned around and ran off into the darkness.

Of course she was able to see to some extent, being an elf and having limited dark vision, but Musky insisted she take his glowing mushroom before she was able to get away. Then he, too, was gone.

He moved along the wall looking for a station where the controls might be, steadily hopping on all fours, his satchel now wrapped about his waist like a belt pouch sitting on his rump.

He explored the entire length of his side of the massive doors but found nothing that could be a control for their operation. He even took a moment to search a length of the connecting wall, but still there was no gadgetry or machinery at all that could be used.

As he moved around the hangar, the great machines towered over him like two massive sleeping dragons, silent, ancient, and almost terrifying just to look upon.

Musky had never seen such things before. He had been to the capitol many times and had even traveled abroad on several occasions, but he had never encountered anything quite like these titanic machines.

He began studying the many joints and latches, bolts and gold strapping, hoping to find some clue as to how to open the doors.

Musky was a kind of genius this way. He was relentless in his quest for understanding. Fearless as to what he might discover. His curiosity was legendary.My best friend in high school, Murray Gershwin, was that way. He also grew *really* good herb.

Love ya, Mur! If yer readin'.

;)

... That's what the kids do. It's me winkin' and smilin'. Get it? It's kinda witty, right? Ya gotta love the kids.

...

Sorry- where was I?

Oh yeah...

For Musky the world was his to know, and he made use of that philosophy whenever fate allowed. He's so awesome at dinner parties, and any celebrations for that matter- lots of stories to tell. Ya can't NOT like him.

He made his way closer to and between the hulls of the two mega-machines, moving between long, straight *spikes* that were pointing downward at varying angles.

Each spike was hollow and consisted of long, perfectly straight metal tubes. Much like long, thin telescopes. He had seen one of those before, in Al'Lankamire, the capitol.

The entire surface of the great machine, spines included, was decorated with golden filigree, in the form of insects and insect wings-or so it seemed at the time. He was so mesmerized by their beauty and technology that he was caught unaware.

Among the long spine-like protrusions that were sticking out from under the hull of the machine was a pair of eleven-fingered, three-thumbed hands, and as they unfolded and reached out to grasp him, the belly of the wretched beast swung forward and down from the tarpaulin above, to land gently on long, filthy, pasty grey-white legs.

A hundred screaming, tormented, suffering faces cried out at him from the demon's diseased belly.

He was caught in the vice-like grip of the Anaga's claws.

Remember those guys? Yeah... they suck. Wait for it.

Some of the faces spat at him, some begged him for mercy; others screamed, vomited, and convulsed uncontrollably. Some laughed maniacally while human-like arms from the creature's back reached down, slapping and abusing the faces violently.

The air was instantly squeezed from his lungs and he was unable to yell for help. His life began to flash before his eyes. He only wanted to go home. He only wanted to do the right thing.

The creature defecated constantly as puss and bile spewed from boils and pustules on its cancerous gut.

He was brought up toward the end of what looked like an uncircumcised penis, unrolling and erecting toward him, squeezing out a yellowy thick goo that dangled and stretched to the floor.

This was the creature's neck. It hung with loose skin that was covered in sores and scabs. What appeared out of the unfolding, rolling flesh was the face of a twisted, mad ancient human, its eyes sunken and ringed in darkness.

The Anaga's maw was filled with way too many elongated human teeth, all stained and rotting in varying degrees.

Its breath was like an acrid steam as it opened its mouth and brought him closer to his doom. Its nose was a swollen sack of fermented snot and the yellowy, sick fluid ran down its upper lip and into the awaiting tongue that lapped it all up with a vigor.

The sound of the thing was maddening. Hideous laughter mixed with lamentations, screams of agony and the sounds of overexerted bodily functions running amok.

The faces that covered the belly of its bloated form continued to squeal and spurt out rancid fluids and pusses that soaked into Musky's fur and began to pool on the floor beneath him. He was being devoured!

Alaeth had made her way along the wall far enough to see that there was nothing at all ahead of her, all the way to the end. She was delighted that the mushroom she was given was excellent for lighting her path once she covered the stem and some of the cap with a rag she had torn from her lab coat – the same one she used as a gas mask at the crap factory. Remember that one? Underneath the lab coat all she was wearing was her torn and filthy nightgown. The same clothes she was wearing the night she was kidnapped.

She decided to take a closer look at the great machine she was next to instead of venturing further. *Perhaps there is some clue as to how to open these doors inside the machine. In a control station, as the Redeye stated,'* she thought.

She grabbed hold of the edge of the tarp that Beornag and I had already unsecured. With a mighty heave she pulled at the edge and despite her tiny size the tarp slid off easily, threatening to bury her in its many folds.

She dodged this easily (she *is* an elf), and waited a few seconds for the massive tarp to finish falling. Then she returned to the under-belly of what appeared to be a mighty ship–of sorts.

It was only a moment later that she had discovered a hatch, or more precisely, *two* hatches – one on either side of the ship's bow. In fact that is almost exactly how it looked to her. Like the bow of some great red, green and gold ship.

It all seemed oddly familiar for some reason, and she wondered where she had seen these ships before. There is no way she would have forgotten anything like this. Yet...

Alaeth was a scientist. Her mind was wrapped around numbers and facts and the *workings* of *things*; she *could* have been a *G'nome* in another dimension. The machine she was now looking at was both frightening and fascinating, and the scientist in her kicked in.

Still she simply could not shake the eerie feeling that she had looked at one of these things before. She had up to that point not even seen the rest of the vessel - No more than the forward section, and only a small bit of that, but she was convinced she had seen it before... *somewhere*.

She's actually smarter than Lillia... who is as smart as *I* am.

Now... before I digress...

See? I caught it that time. I'm payin' attention.

...

Where was I?

Oh yeah...

She took a short look at the hatch and quickly deduced its function. Opening it was easy. She turned a wheel that moved a complex mechanism inside the door. The hatch swung open slowly and a telescopic ladder unfolded in front of her.

She took a deep breath, let it out with a sigh and climbed the ladder as best she could. She had not seen such efficiency in machines before. Her heart began to race with excitement and anticipation.

She made her way through a vertical tube, almost too small for her lithe, elfish frame, and along a ladder that was almost useless, as it *too* was so small.

Remember that I had explained about the machines being made by my ancestors?

She expected to eventually reach a spot where she would be too large to continue exploring the structure, instead, and to her pleasant surprise, she emerged from the tunnel, on an angle, into a hall large enough for even the Troll to stand in, if he was to crouch – which to him was standing anyway... sort of. He's kind of weird that way.

Here, her glowing mushroom illuminated what amounted to an empty cargo bay. She took a quick look around the area and soon located a stairway up in the center of the rear half of the chamber.

Elves have an evolutionary power much like the *Schmauz*. It keeps them from getting stuck in holes.

At the top of the stairs was a round open portal, just large enough for her to pass if she crouched.

She worked her way up the hall on a forty-five degree angle and into a room where she found several rows of lockers, like those which might be found in a barracks or a public swimming pool.

She moved along the rows of lockers until she found a stairwell that went up twenty feet.

Everything here was made from steel and gold and exotic wood trim. Every surface was a work of art depicting flying insect wings (again- or so it seemed).

She made her way up the stairs and onto the upper deck. Here, above her, she could see the remnants of the great tarpaulin stretched over a number of masts, making the thing look like a great tent with many poles.

Across the deck further toward the bow she noticed what looked like a large hut built into the ship.

It took her only a moment to reach what she suspected was the control station of the massive vessel. Elves are exceedingly fast.

A moment later and she was inside the structure and trying to figure out what did *what*.

There were so many dials, gadgets, contraptions, switches and levers she hardly knew where to start- there were butterflies in her stomach.

Just then she heard something strange.

It sounded like a baby crying in the distance. She moved toward the control house's exit, grabbing some sort of tool as she passed a workstation.

Exiting the structure she heard it again, but this time it was not alone.

She cringed, physically reviled, as the voices of a hundred insane entities screaming out gibberish and insanity joined the mind-numbing wailing of the baby's hopeless screaming.

Gods of my father! She thought as she realized from where the sounds were coming. *Musky!*

"It is so bee-au-teeee-fulllll." The Injoke sighed. "It's da bestest ting in da whole worrrellld." He actually teared up.

It was unbelievably massive! Each ship was many hundreds of feet long and at least one hundred feet across their deck at their widest.

The hull of this one (I would later learn) was made from heavy straps of metal I was unable to identify, as it was all coated in bright red enamel and bright green trim. Here and there were filigrees easily mistaken for depictions of insect wings and other insect-related artistry, in a menagerie of golden filigrees.

However- these were the leaves of sacred herb plants. '*My people made this,*' I thought.

From the bottom, sticking out along the forward belly of the great ship, was a series of long tubes that were a foot across at the hull but tapered out after twenty feet to only three inches in diameter.

There were also two, large-G'nome-sized hatches in the bottom, neither of which the Troll was going to fit into.

As he tugged on the tarpaulin, the whole massive cloth began to slide off and onto the floor of the great hangar.

After a mighty cloud of dust had settled, we witnessed the vessel *disrobe* before our very eyes.

This was a titan among ships, its many masts each draped in an assortment of cables and chains. I was again... in awe.

Two *huge* wing-like appendages extended from either side and just aft of the center of the ship. These each held separate, large and ovular pods, each with large lenses mounted to the forward ends.

Sticking out from the center of these giant, multifaceted discs were other long tubes; these were larger than the forward groupings, and they were each housed in a strange accordion-like structure.

I deduced that these were for moving the tubes, as if to aim them. '*Weapons?*' I thought.

Each hull was supported by two gargantuan *skis*, one on either side. These *skis* ran the entire length of the massive vessel's underbelly, and were aerodynamically designed.

Beornag began to climb the outside of the great ship, carrying me in one hand and yelling incoherent things at imaginary flying things.

It scared the hell outta me (to be honest), as I had no idea he was just passing the time while climbing and was playing make-believe along the way.

Oy!

We climbed up eighty feet to a safety rail which the Troll leaped over easily.

Here he stood on the forward section of the deck. We could see the entire hangar from there.

It was then that I realized exactly what these things actually were.

These were *flying* ships.

I know, *right*!?

They were even *armoured* with huge metal plates, with many areas designed to allow cover for those defending the ship... or so I guessed.

The *spines* or (more accurately) *tubes* that pin-cushioned the front and rear of the vessels were obviously something like my pixie dart gun, but on a much grander scale.

Oy!

The ship was widest just past midriff and was much the same design as most ocean going vessels except for the pylons mounted on the sides of the hull.

On the front under the very nose of the ship was a figurehead of a G'nome: an ancient face with a long beard and wise eyes. Many such faces were incorporated into the design and decor of the vessel.

Again... what I first thought to be insect-like decorations, I could now see were a filigree and gildings of sacred herb leaves, and intertwined vines of Sensimilia–my people's sacred and ...

Sorry. I got misty.

Where was I?

Oh yeah...

Beornag insisted that these faces were, in fact, images of the face of Ulm. I explained that these were G'nomish faces and he responded, "No way, pops! Ulm's a *G'nome*?! Ize nevva would'a tought. Cool dough, right? Weeze is related!"

I felt honored.

He took only a few great loping steps forward and we were standing on the edge of the wheelhouse section, still looking back over the vessel.

Here, to either side, was a G'nome-sized stairway that led down twenty feet to the open deck below.

There I saw several points where one could enter the ship, if one was not so large as the Injoke. However, here *also* was a vast, open, flat deck where many refugees could be kept while being transported. In fact, just one of these ships could carry a small army... or neighborhood of civilians.

We were now standing on the roof of the command center of the ship and boy was I feeling proud. Here the wheelhouse was just under us, with the controls for the ship, and the instructions I would need to make it function. HOOTSPA!!

The upper deck was stretched out behind us as we now faced the stern.

The Injoke took a small leap and we landed on the deck, in front of the entrance to the command house-facing the bow... Get it? Good.

So sturdy were these magnificent ships, that even after eons of neglect, they did not move or even shake when his enormous weight came down upon the deck.

He began to move forward toward a hump-like structure in the center of the great ship, when he stopped suddenly and turned to look behind us.

"Pops, wait here," he whispered, looking quite worried. Then he placed me on the deck and loped away so fast I was unable to protest.

Moments later, when I was just about to make my way toward one of the access ports, I was stopped in my tracks by a horrifying sound.

It began as a baby crying, mixed with someone screaming profanities, while suffering from throat cancer. Then a wheezing and bubbling was added to the noise, along with many other voices.

As each maniacal voice added its own to the cacophony, three, four, five more would join in and as each did so, the gibberish and lamentations became more and more frantic and maddening.

Only a hundred feet in front of me, from behind the metal dome in the center of the ship's deck, emerged... an Anaga demon!

Not again! I thought, crapping my pants.

Do I really have to describe one of these things again, kids? You pretty much know what they look like now, right? Good.

Now, where was I?

Oh yeah...

Oy...

It looked straight at me. Suddenly there was recognition in its black pit-like eye sockets. Its eyebrows raised and it screeched and cackled like a banshee in many voices at once.

"Nebli, nebli, nebli, chchch, Neblinski! Yeeeeeehahahahahah!" it laughed and screamed maniacally.

It knew my name! Good gawd, it knew my name! It continued to yell, the many faces on its maggot-like gut now joining in and working in unison, all looking at me and screaming profanities and spewing fluids in my direction.

Its countless hands were flipping me off, giving me the bird, and pointing in my general direction.

It would reach me in seconds. I had to think fast. I had no hootspa left. I had used all my power reserves cleaning crap and battling that other me. I hadn't yet taken the time to rest and re-energize. I was defenceless! Even my ring was drained! Musky had my dart gun, for crying out loud! All I had left was the dirty dozens, and I was thinking this thing was not up for a round of rock-paper-scissors either.

Suddenly it hit me. I reached around and pulled off my backpack.

The thing was getting closer by the millisecond!

I worked as fast as I could; opening the satchel, I reached inside for my last-ditch effort, my last stand so to speak, my final hope among hopes.

I pooped my pants *again* and the creature, with one great leap, was now upon me!

My diminutive size was all that saved me, as it reached out with those long, emaciated, pale arms, clasping at the air with its clusters of fingers and thumbs.

As I darted between the many human-like arms, now struggling against each other to be the first to grab me, I endeavored to draw an item from my pouch. Here... there... jump... roll!

I used every ounce of energy I had to avoid the terrible creature. Holy crap was I scared.

Still I struggled to draw the *box* from my pouch. I had to *try*. Right?

I was going to attempt to flee inside and back to the temple. I was in a state of panic—remember, kids. These things had the ability to scare Beornag and probably Grarr too!

I actually pooped again.

"*There!*" I thought as my hand grasped a small rectangular container. "That's gotta be it." I *almost* prayed.

I drew the box from the pack, relieved to see that I was successful in locating it under such stressful conditions.

The relic fell to the deck as I commanded the shrinking hootspa to cancel. Growing to full size it *thumped* against the metal of the ship's decking, the sound reverberating throughout the great hangar like an alarm.

I reached the latch and flipped it open, but just then, a blast of white-hot energy came out of nowhere and exploded against the Anaga, sending it flying across the deck. It screamed in a thousand voices as a burning hole in its side sizzled and spewed steaming, boiling, putrid fluids all over the place.

I, too, was sent sliding across the deck, but in the opposite direction.

I was able to watch as the Anaga recovered from its fall and regained its footing.

The explosion caused me to slide through the thing's fluidic mess, toward the starboard-side guard rail.

Even then I was hoping the fiend would not do what I now suspected it would do next.

Even as I approached the guard rail, bones broken and bleeding from multiple lacerations and burns, I realized what I had left within the demon's grasp.

"Relic! Rel, rel, relic-c-c-c-c! Yeeyaaahahahahah!!" it screamed as it scurried across the deck toward the box of Bong. Its entrails were spewing out behind it from a smoking hole in its side.

The last thing I remember was thinking, '*What have I done? I just gave that thing a doorway to the temple, the city, the Gnomes,* Durik!'

Then I hit the guard rail and the lights went out.

Chapter - 24

"Mizz Painless"

Again, I speak not as a witness to these next events, good reader, but tell only what I have been told, as I personally was lying prone against the inside of the guard rail, bleeding from internal injuries, with broken bones and multiple burns and lacerations. So I hope I tell all of this next stuff correctly, and I don't leave anyone out or anything.

Ready?

Oy...

The monster reached the box as I fell into a coma. That's right, kids. Good old Pappa Szvirf wasn't smokin' the filter yet. I only *looked* dead. But holy crap I was close, let *me* tell *you*.

It gibbered and laughed, celebrating its victory. I had flipped the latch for it already and it simply lifted open the lid. It ignored the fact that it had just been blasted across the deck by a ball of energy from an unknown source.

It smelled something, tasted it in the air. Tasted it on the evaporating sweat of these new *victims*.

The *relic*.

It lifted the open box, now a full ten feet long and five feet wide; the lid dangled open as it studied the container like a predatory insect deciding what part to eat first.

Its main head now emerging from a fleshy, unrolling mass of drooping skin and mucus, it chuckled audibly and looked into the door.

It almost inserted its long neck right into the box but then, it saw the garden of Shiddumbuzzin in full bloom, beyond... "Hhhhiiiiiissssssssssssss!!" It snarled.

From beyond the box's opening, the sounds of the great machines that were working in the distance of the old city crept into the massive hangar bay.

The wavering colors and little spots of light that emitted from *The Bong* were now escaping through the portal that was the box; tendrils of pollen and glistening wisps of smoke from temple braziers, where sticky buds burned, crawled through the portal.

Instantly, the smell of holy smoke began to invade the immediate area.

The foul beast stepped back for a moment, its many twisted faces scowling and grimacing as if revolted by the divine aromas.

It suddenly stopped its chattering, and lamenting, and fell silent.

Soon after, with a disgusted grunt, the demon let go of the box and let it fall to the deck with a loud, resonating thump.

Without warning, terror in its many faces, hatred in its *one* face, the fiend then rose up on its long legs, lifting its spindly-looking arms high above its main head. It laughed and screamed in joy and pain and envy and jealousy, like madness manifested.

It then brought its long, bony appendages down across the box, with enough force to break a stone bridge, its loose flesh flailing out behind its arms as the sickly white limbs descended upon the lid.

But, just before the moment of impact, another white-hot ball of energy flew from the other side of the bay over my still form and across the deck to strike the fiend with such force the monster was sent tumbling backwards.

Sparks and colorful flames spewed from the wound as it rolled over and over, first striking and then going over the *top* of the starboard rail.

Meanwhile the box had begun to shake and rattle on the floor. It soon jumped up on its own, and stood straight up on end; the lid swung open and flooded the deck with colored, sparkling lights and aromatic smoke effects.

Alaeth ran across the deck to the starboard side of the vessel *she* was on. She looked out over the hangar bay and caught sight of Beornag leaping over the guard rail of the vessel at the far and opposite end of the hangar; she *too* looked for a way down from the ship she was presently on, so she could run to Musky's aid. She was sure now, after seeing Beornag leap over the side of *his* ship and run toward the area Musky was searching, that her new Ratstafarian friend was indeed... in trouble.

"Think, Alaeth, think." She spoke aloud to herself in frustration. Then she remembered the strange tool in her hands and sighed.

'*I'm becoming a Troll,*' she thought, then desperately tried to figure out the device's use. There was no way she could reach Musky in time if it was truly an emergency. They had separated more than twenty minutes ago. She was lost for an idea when she looked down at the thing in her hands in defeat.

It took only a moment for her to deduce that it was a weapon. '*Nice,*' she thought.

Then from the corner of her eye she saw movement on the upper deck of the far vessel, the one Beornag had just disembarked. Her elf eyes engaged and she brought the image closer.

'*ANAGA!!*' she thought before looking back at the tool.

She then closed her eyes and breathed deeply. Exhaling slowly, she spoke aloud: "What is it, Alaeth?" She mimicked her father. This was the question he presented to her almost daily, challenging her wits and exercising her mind. He was so proud of his genius daughter.

She missed him so much.

There on the side of the tool was a diagram of someone using it. "Thanks," she said, looking up with a smile. There were also several symbols that looked suspiciously like warnings.

"This is a weapon," she said out loud again. Now there was screaming and chaos coming from both ends of the hangar.

There were two of them?! She held the tool like the person in the diagram printed on the device's side, flipped a button that armed the thing, pointed it across the hangar, and looked through the long tube that was mounted on top of the device. Once the button was pressed, two long firestone crystals, one on either side of the device, began to pulse with a low amber light; the instrument *then* began to thrum and buzz with a power she had not expected.

Across the hangar on the deck of the first ship a horrific creature was dancing around like a chicken with its head cut off, spewing filth all over the ancient vessel.

"Sucks to be you," she said as she squeezed the trigger of the weapon.

Instantly she was sent flying ten feet backward, her shoulder almost dislocated from the kickback the weapon produced.

She regained her footing and held her shoulder for a minute while she swallowed tears of real pain.

Then, after a short moment, "Fuck this!" She sat up and located her weapon. She picked it up and returned to her vantage point. "You and I are gonna be great friends, honey," she said to the device."I like it rough."

Smiling, she then returned the weapon to the firing position and looked through the tube again. This time the thing was examining a long rectangular box even as a hole she had just made in the fiend's side was spewing fluids and smoking violently.

The Anaga opened the lid and looked inside, but then, suddenly, it dropped the box, repulsed, as lights and smoke began to pour out of it.

Its horrific voices screamed in rage as the demon lifted its arms, preparing to destroy the container.

'Really,' she thought. "Please..." and decided that anything *it* wanted to destroy she *didn't* want destroyed.

Three of its hands were holding the still-smoldering wound in its side, while great globs of yellowy fat were melting, dripping fluids all over the deck.

She took aim at the same spot and braced for the kickback that her new best friend was about to create. Then, just as the fiend's arms were coming down upon the box she fired.

The blast struck home and sent the villain flying across the ship's deck and over the starboard side.

She looked again through the tube to see what had become of the box. There it was on the deck, standing straight up like a doorway to another dimension.

It was here that something caught her attention peripherally. Something large came flying over the other, closer vessel.

It came from the direction where she thought Musky had last been.

She fell to her knees as what she was seeing became soul-crushingly clear.

She screamed in horror as Beornag's limp form arced *over* the deck of the closest vessel, dragging behind the tarp that was covering the massive ship. He landed on the cold stone floor and slid many feet, eventually coming to a halt under the vessel she was on, leaving a streak of crimson in his path.

"Noooooooo!" she screamed as she ran for the nearest access portal.

Chapter - 25

"Stage Fright"

Beornag dropped eighty feet to the floor of the hangar, swinging from the spines that stuck out of the front of the vessel.

He no sooner reached level ground than the sounds of *evil* began to increase in volume as more and more voices of insanity were added to the macabre choir of suffering.

Such was his courage that he *still* loped across the hangar in great leaps and bounds, as fast as a slow horse can run.

(*What?* I couldn't think of a better way to describe how fast he could run. Gimme a break).

As he closed the distance between himself and the sound of the evil, the Injoke began to search his pack for a bag of crap.

Yup.

He moved along the port side of the closest ship, just under the tarpaulin's edge. From the maddening cacophony of hideous laughter that was now echoing throughout the hangar he was able to deduce that the thing was having fun, so he figured Musky was losing whatever fight the poor little guy was facing.

Solution?

Pound the bad guy, of course.

He rushed along the narrow space, between the port side of the giant ship and the hangar wall.

Finally retrieving a massive bag of liquid shit just as he turned the corner at the stern of the vessel, he faced the Anaga!

It was sticking Musky into its gaping maw, head-first. The poor little guy looked like he was almost dead.

Beornag lost his shit.

He threw the eighty pound *excre-missile* of rotten fermented *poopfuric ass-id* at the demonic monster as he yelled his prayer at it. *"Yooz's mamma is so ugly, when she goes ta da beauty pahlah it takes all day... just ta get a estimate!"* The distinctive sound of a snare and hi hat could be heard in the distance as the villainous beast dropped Musky ten feet to the floor, its skin sizzling under the power of the holy verses and the poopfuric acid.

I'm not even kidding you. *Holy shit*, right!?

It screamed, covered in the worst kind of feces *ever*, as it turned toward the Injoke, a hundred voices yelling, heckling him, booing and hissing at him.

Smoke streamed from the creature's pale, glistening hide, as the slime and sweat it was covered with evaporated under the intense heat caused by the holy words issued forth by the Injoke.

Beornag too began to emit smoke as the crowd of tormented faces continued to heckle and boo him; their material was harsh and it was among some of the finest trash-talking history has ever heard.

Ooooo, I hate those guys!

The Injoke's power was draining away from him now as the demon *countered* his attempt to banish it back to its own plane of hellish torment.

He was used to being adored back at the Gruel and Grog. He had never before imagined himself being heckled. He was the ONLY comedian in the entire empire. Briarwood loved him.

But now, he struggled with his punchline. This monster was terrifying to him. He now felt *real* fear. Like the night the humans killed his father. He was unable to become angered. He was terrified- *Paralyzed.*

They beat his father to death because the majestic being refused to be a slave any longer.

He remembered the last words Stupid, Beornag's father, spoke to him..."Hate don't fix it. Find someone ta' love, Ize's good son." Then the Talotian slavers drove a spear through *Stupid's* heart, and killed him. The slavers murdered his father while he watched.

Even after that, *somehow*, he did find love.

It was Grarr who saved him and fed him and taught him to be smart.

"Grarr's like Ize's Pops, only scary".

But now Grarr was *dead...*

...This suddenly struck him via "hind brain."

In other words, he suddenly realized this fact. *Knowing*, and realizing, can be two different things.

Grarr was dead...

Terdbreff said so.

Boom!!

This demon had found Beornag's weakness...

Son of *Stupid* and *Meat, brother of Durik and Grarr, and Raz, yes, even Raz*.. Beornag's weakness was Love. He was always, *secretly*, terrified of losing the ones he loved. He was all too familiar with that experience, and it sucked. Beornag missed his people (and/or family...always).

He was secretly miserable, yet remarkably good at fooling *most* folks into believing that he was jovial, *all* of the time- because he wanted to find joy. *That* was his quest, his very *life's* purpose.

Ask me later to write a book about this guy. He deserves one.

Now...where was I?

Oh yeah...

It was also his *duty*, as an Injoke. He *firmly* believed this. Ulm *wanted* him to make people happy.

Of *course* he loved Grarr. Grarr had saved him AND Durik from slavery.

Grarr obviously loved *him*, and Durik too. They were family.

And... *of course* Beornag loved Durik too. At first Durik was his *puppy*- then, soon, graduated "officially" to *little-brother* status.

Of course he was grateful for his fortune and chance to live free and make a real difference... he wasn't stupid... he was just not all that smart... sort of.

Yet... He longed for his Ma and his Pa- people who looked like him.

Like I did. I felt that way too, in the basement at the winery.

In *truth*, the Injoke of Ulm could not be swayed from his faith – period.

However... this was no ordinary creature tossing him a few insults. *This* was a demon of the foulest sorts. It was a beast he had never been tested against before. A power he had never faced, and as such had no idea how to defeat.

The scent of death filled the air.

Yet such was his courage and devotion to his friends... his family... what was *righteous*... that he faced the demon *anyway!*

But, now he was struggling just to maintain the monster's interest. His words, their joy and humor, were being lost to the monster's cruelty and hatred for decency.

This creature felt *no* joy. It could not really laugh, and as such was immune to the Injoke's *Reasoning*.

His words, his jokes, his divine power was deflected with bigotry, falseness and abuse coming from the audience... the Anaga's entourage of hundreds of cursed souls.

Now the demon was actually destroying Beornag's confidence in his ability to make people laugh.

He fell to one knee, as he watched the beast take up handfuls of the liquid shit and feed its many faces- momentarily forgetting about him.

The sight was maddening. He was losing his audience! He was *dying out there*!!

He tried to stand, wondering what to say next... "A Redeye, a Injoke an' a hairy dwarf in a grass skirt walk inta... a... a restaurant an ax ta be seated...." He coughed as the creature turned back toward him, its main head now emerging again from its sleeve of pasty white flesh. It smiled at him, licking the *poopfuric ass-id* from its lips.

"Ppppppp ... Ppprrrrimate ... Tasssssss ... Tassssssty ... yeeeeeeeeeeeeeeeessss." It moved faster than he imagined it was capable of.

"Aw crap!" he said as he remembered he forgot to pull out his maul with which to pound the monster.

As he regained his footing, standing up, he tried to remember the words to his prayer. "...Table fuh tree? Da head waituh axes ... ummmmm ... aaahhhh ..." He struggled with his memory, trying to recall the punchline as the creature came ever closer, jibing him, insulting him, bullying him, heckling him.

Again his endurance and strength waned and he fell, this time to *both* knees.

"Mmmmmmmm ... Issss gonnnnna have sexssssss with itsssss mouthhhhhh. Yessss I issss. Heehehehehehe!" The demon licked its lips as a long, bright-red, glistening member appeared from a fold in its sickly pale gut. "I likesssss hairrrry onesssss. Yessss I doesssssss. Yeeeeyaaaahahahahaha!" It leaped through the air like a great locust and landed on top of the Troll.

He struggled with all his strength as the beast's ever-enlarging, (diseased) phallus bent and wriggled toward the his head like some kind of prehensile tail, spewing yellowy-green fluid all over his beautiful, chestnut-colored fur coat.

It continued jibing and heckling him as its sex organ came closer to Beornag's face, actually grazing his cheek once and leaving a streak of sour, cheesy-smelling yellow puss.

Its hundreds of faces bombarded him with insult after degrading insult, as the hellish monster used its evil magic to smash away at the faith he had in himself ... his words ... *Ulm's* words.

Then as the Troll was gasping for air, trying to remember the punchline of his already forgotten prayer, no longer able to stand, the beast grabbed him by the mutton chops and pulled his head toward its puss-covered member.

As this was happening, the twisted faces on the thing's belly licked their lips and drooled, like the condemned perverts that they once were when they were alive as people.

They watched it all happening with lust and debauchery in their eyes.

This is what they were before their torment and suffering began in the hells. A thousand hands slapped, clawed and poked at each other's faces.

Then there was a flash of color as a ball of rainbow shot past his line of sight so fast he almost missed it.

The demon let go of him as its phallus fell to the floor, wriggling and spewing rancid juices all over the place.

Musky had regained consciousness and had completely severed the demon's penis with his new dagger!

This dagger he had recognized when he took it from its previous owner. It was enchanted, and had Elfish markings. (Musky is far smarter and experienced than one might expect from his use of Humanese).

He also realized that those markings were etched under moonlight with captured sun beams, as only the Elfish metalsmiths knew how to do.

See? I told ya- smart.

That in turn meant that his weapon was especially effective against things that were susceptible to the harmful effects of sun or moonlight like *demons*!

I *hate* those guys.

"Fuck *you*, muddu fuckuh!" he squealed at the demon. "You done messed wit da wrong Ratsta now!" He hopped to one side, then another, so fast the Troll could hardly follow as he, in turn, desperately tried to roll to the opposite side. He barely noticed a ball of white light shooting across the hangar toward my last known position.

The demon, who was screaming hysterically in many languages at once, retrieved the stump of its amputated sex organ and shoved it back into the folds of rancid fat that hung from its underside between the countless faces.

Some of the human-like arms took up the severed phallus and began feeding it to the many faces that were attached to the thing's gut. These tormented souls devoured it as they wept and bawled with pleasure and shame.

Adzadkast Tse' kuman'et'thtah, lord of shame was its name. It then grabbed the Troll by the left ankle, as he *desperately* tried to crawl away.

Lifting the Injoke off the hangar deck, it then slammed the troll to the stone floor several times before swinging him up into the air, like he was only a rag doll; the rigging on the mighty vessels literally rattled slightly.

Screaming hysterically, the monster then swung the Injoke around once again above its head laughing and exulting in the vulgar things it was going to do to the Troll's now-lifeless body.

Musky had been searching his pouch for a weapon that might hurt the beast.

He drew a flask of flammable oil from his satchel and threw it at the creature. The bottle hit the demon square between the eyes and smashed, spilling the contents all over the monster's upper body. This seemed to annoy it enough that it lost interest in the Troll's limp form and tossed him away like he was just a *tiny* thing.

Musky watched in horror as the Injoke's body was thrown up and over the nearest ship, more than a hundred feet into the air.

Beornag's body hooked onto the edge of the tarpaulin covering the ship, and dragged it along behind like a great streamer, until he hit the hangar deck with a wet, cracking thud.

In shock, Musky stood motionless for a moment, as the scene seemed to play out in slow motion.

'Holy fuh', mun!' he thought, paralyzed with terror.

Suddenly, before he could think further, the creature had him once again, this time by the scuff of the neck.

Musky turned one hundred and eighty degrees inside his shirt, his hands first disappearing and then reappearing from the sleeves of his rainbow-colored garment, his dagger still in hand. He swung the tiny blade in a downward arc and cut deeply into the fingers of his assailant.

Hissing in pain, the beast let go of him while the blade cut easily through its flesh and bone. Its severed fingers and thumbs fell to the floor and danced about as the hideous main head emerged again from the fleshy sleeve to gaze at its newly amputated fingers in fascination.

This gave Musky an opportunity to escape its now-loosening grip. Once free he rolled to one side and produced a match from his satchel strap, where he had a small pocket for carrying them and his herb twists.

He struck the match with his thumbnail and it ignited immediately. He then flicked it at the monster, as the fiend continued to study its own dismembered digits. The match hit its target and the monster erupted into a conflagration.

The fire didn't last, however, as the creature seemed to expel sweat and other bodily fluids through its skin, extinguishing the flames.

Without even looking at him, the villain reached out at Musky, again, faster than he was able to counter.

Its second hand squeezed him, the same way it had the first time.

Musky still managed to call for help. "I is needin' 'elp, 'ere, mun! Somebody 'elp! Musky... mun!" Then he heard his ribs cracking, as blood squirted from his nose and his tongue was pushed out of his mouth.

He began to lose consciousness as he felt the creature's long, infected fingers dexterously grasp and then tear out his gold incisor, the one with his lucky diamond. He heard it laugh in its many insane voices.

Then, he was dying.

Soon there was darkness.

CHAPTER - 26

"HACKEM"

Alaeth climbed through the hatch and slid down the ladder, her new best friend/weapon now slung over her shoulder. She looked around for Beornag and almost cried when she saw him lying lifeless in a pool of his own blood.

She rushed to his side to see that he was in fact still conscious and smiling. "Hey, dere ... (cough, cough) ... pretty lady. Ize has fallen ... (cough, cough) ... an Ize can't get up." He chuckled as blood drained from the wounds all over his broken body.

She moved her hands over him, just inches from touching his shattered frame. She didn't have the faintest idea of what to do for him. His bones were protruding from so many wounds she lost count. Many of the visible bones were badly splintered and shattered and he was bleeding out fast. Between sobs she tried to get him to instruct her on how to save his life, but he only had the strength left to smile gently.

Then she heard Musky's voice yell out in agony and this startled her into action. She kissed Beornag on the forehead and said, "Sweetie, listen, I will be right back. You stay alive," she wept, "until I return. Okay? Promise me."

He nodded slightly, even as his eyes were closing. She couldn't bear to watch as she stood and faced the direction Musky's voice had come from.

"Hey! Asshole!" she yelled. "Come big or stay home!" She cocked the weapon and engaged a system she had not noticed the first time she used it. She was still not sure what it did, but she *did* know the first setting only made these things mad, as was made clear when she saw the one she had already shot running toward her from the other end of the hangar.

'*Uh oh,*' she thought. '*Two of them? I might as well just give up now.*'

Just as she was sure it couldn't get worse, the other creature made itself visible as it came out from around the ship *it* was behind, still carrying the lifeless body of Musky in its hideous claw.

Both!? At the same time?! There was no way! But she was damned if she was going down without a fight.

Here, both monsters stopped dead in their tracks. A sound came from atop the ship where my own broken body was lying still.

Even Alaeth was distracted by the sound as the lighting in the room suddenly dimmed dramatically.

"*Bonnnnng!*" Again it reverberated throughout the hangar, like some legendary bell. "*...Bonnnnng!...Bonnnnng!*" Over and over like some beacon for ships on stormy nights.

She raised her weapon to her shoulder and looked through the tube towards the source of the ringing. At the bow of the farthest ship stood a figure, not silhouetted in the still-dimming light of the hangar, but an actual source of new illumination. It stood there for a short moment, glowing like a burning star. It had its own light show.

As she watched the being, his light growing in intensity, he suddenly leaped from the eighty-foot rise, covering half of the hangar deck, and landed gracefully.

He then made a few more leaps and bounds, finally jumping straight over the heads of the Anaga, to land between her and the demons. She could hardly look at this newcomer. Instinctively, she turned away as the fiendish monsters squirmed and slithered forward, toward him.

As the newcomer rose slowly from the crouching position he had landed in, she was able to see his features clearly. He was terrifying.

This was *another* demon... something worse, to be sure.

This one was *not* a mindless servant of twisted and excessive indulgences of the flesh, *not* a beast of suffering and disease.

This was, if anything, a *prince* of the hells!

It looked straight at her and smiled, as though reassuring her that the pain would not last long. She almost welcomed the end. She was slowly, unconsciously lowering her weapon as she was calmed by the simple gaze of this blue-skinned demon in mirrored armour.

I know! Right!?

Keep readin', it even gets *better*.

She sighed and lowered her weapon all the way as the glowing avatar began to snarl.

He was now turning away to face the oncoming Anaga who were still slithering and crawling piteously across the floor.

His light grew brighter and took on an amber-like quality. The walls of the hangar seemed to be on fire with the radiance of it.

Hundreds of sickly voices, those of the Anaga and their host of suffering, all began paying this new creature homage, as they groveled on their bellies, begging for his approval. "Greatessssst of Massssstersssssssss. Look! Look, Greatest of Masssssssterrrrs." One of the fiends gestured toward its own blood-covered hands.

Other faces screamed for the prince of hell to fornicate with them. They begged to be allowed to feast on his excrement.

They cursed his mother and offered their own as a sacrifice. He was their lord, their master and creator, and they loved him.

The demon closest to the new one sprouted a grotesque head, drooling and licking snot from its own upper lip. It lowered this head almost to the floor in submission as it displayed a gift for its master.

It smiled diabolically as it held out its clawed hand, displaying Musky's limp form proudly. "Look, masssterr..."

It was interrupted when the blue prince of hell reached behind his back and drew forth, seemingly from nowhere, a broad-bladed sword of gold.

He twisted the handle with both hands and the weapon itself began to screeeeaaaam like nothing that had ever been heard before. "*Rrrrrrrriiiinnnnnnng, dinnnnnnnnnng ding ding-ding-dingdingding!*"

He swung the mighty weapon in a single stroke while moving like a streak of sunlight across the floor. "Rrrrrinnnng-ding-dingdingding!!" A split second later and he had cut the monster completely in half.

The screaming voice of the weapon was the sound of hundreds of teeth racing around the edges of the golden double blades, tearing everything in its path to hamburger and shrapnel.

Even as its guts were pouring out over the blue, mirrored menace, and he was stepping away though the unclean monster's convulsing body halves, he exploded in a flash of light that, to the Anaga, was like a storm of fire.

Rank smoke began to fill the area as their flesh sizzled, fried, and charred. They convulsed on the floor as they screamed in thousands of tormented voices at once.

The two halves of the first demon were dissolving rapidly where the blade of the golden serrated weapon had cut through its body. Its flesh turned to sparkling gases before fading from existence altogether.

The second monster was still trying to reach out when it realized the fatal error it had made. "RELIC! YOU?! Not Massssterrrr! Mussssst kill iiit! KILLLLL IIIIT!!" It screamed as it somehow found the strength to stand to its full height. It towered over the glowing demon prince, as tall as Beornag.

Its flesh was bursting into flames as it lashed out at him. It opened its mouth to an impossible size and vomited a black sticky goo all over him.

Alaeth watched in horror and confusion, as she stumbled backward, falling to the floor. She struggled to move backward toward the ship, crawling on her back as she watched on, at the titanic clash that was taking place.

Luckily she had thought to wear the shoulder strap that was attached to her new weapon, or she would have dropped it from sheer panic and shock.

This new... thing... was beyond wondrous. His armour was seemingly untouched by the larger, lesser demons... it seemed like it was made of windows to other worlds of amber light and sparkling embers.

The Anaga's entrails and bodily fluids simply slid right off of him while wisps of smoke seemed to flow from him like a cloak billowing in the wind.

Suddenly ...

Gawd, I hate that word.

Suddenly ... the Anaga did the unthinkable. It screamed out a name. It was the name of another of its kind. A thing not as powerful as it was, but a demon all the same, and it would not arrive alone, for the name was that of many. It was the name of a legion of tens of thousands.

A swirling vortex appeared in front of the glowing sentinel and almost drew him into its depths. He stepped back momentarily and regained his footing.

"Monster! You die now! *All* of you die *now!*" he roared maniacally, his eyes glowing with a power so intense that Alaeth could see tendrils of smoke emanating from them. He opened his mouth and inside was a light brighter than a thousand suns, as though it was a gateway to the sun itself! His hands burst into raging balls of flame and glowing embers. Tendrils of sparkling vapours escaped the corners of his mouth while he roared at his opponents.

It looked to Alaeth like he was filled with the power of all the stars in the sky.

Suddenly...

Sorry.

Suddenly, thousands of hands began to claw at the edges of the vortex as it materialized into a bottomless pit.

From the dark, fiery depths of the phenomenon, lesser demons came by the hundreds every moment.

Alaeth clawed and crawled across the floor to escape the horrors she now was witnessing.

They spewed out of the pit so violently, fighting to be ahead of each other, that many arrived mortally wounded and died shortly after, dissolving into rancid pools of goop.

Meanwhile, the mirrored warrior was once again grasping his weapon in both hands as he advanced on the ever-growing force.

So many were there that Alaeth was sure this new person would be overrun by their sheer numbers. He would be completely covered by sticky Gnome-sized, diseased maggots with spindly legs and tormented human faces, all trying to have sex with him while simultaneously trying to devour him. She had to struggle mentally and emotionally just to remain sane during it all.

Thousands of teeth shattered harmlessly against his illuminated, mirrored armour while their claws slid along its glass-like finish.

As soon as they noticed their own reflections in the polished surface of his suit they exploded in fits of self-mutilation and uncontrollable gibberish while turning to cinders around his feet.

She almost fainted while the remaining, larger Anaga, *still* left standing, vaulted into the air and was headed straight for him.

This demon's titanic weight alone should have been enough to at least knock the wind out of the newcomer..

Instead, as the Anaga fell toward him, the blue menace grinned maliciously, and grasping his sword with both hands, he once again twisted the hilt in two different directions.

"Rrrrrinnnnng, dinnnnng dinnng dinng ding dingdingdingdinnnnnnnng!" The teeth of the mighty *relic* screamed as they danced around an edge of holy platinum, ripping and tearing away at whatever they touched.

In an instant the villain was cut clean in half while the weapon continued to roar with a loud, mind-numbing, buzzing doom.

A maddening mechanical sound, it cast absolute terror into the demonic horde that was still, even then, pouring into the hangar through the hole in the floor.

The Anaga's innards spilled out, dissolving into a sickly, sweet-smelling ichor as it screamed out its last curses in agony.

Sparkling, swirling tentacles of glowing amber and silvery light streamed from the enchanted weapon, as the sound of its buzzing engine and the scream of metal against metal filled the cavern.

He kicked the body parts into the hole as the smaller demons still tried to grasp his armour and pull him down into oblivion.

He swung the blade from left to right, up and down, as easily as if it had been made of paper and wood. He could not be stopped. He was merciless. He was righteous.

She was in shock momentarily as the sound of the buzzing, serrated blade screamed out even louder then, echoing throughout the cavernous hangar bay. It was a cacophony of technological mayhem mingled with the agonizing calls of his victims. Thousands of them.

Bone, flesh, and even otherworldly material were torn open and mangled by the hundreds of small shining blades that streaked around the edge of the weapon. It sawed through everything it touched like a hot knife through boot cheese. Pieces of the unholy host flew from the blade, spraying and covering the deck in his immediate vicinity.

Over and over, the mighty sword screamed as it literally chewed its way through their demonic bodies, causing panic and mayhem among their ranks.

Soon the enemy began to struggle and fight each other to be first to escape this terrible being. Many were sacrificed and pushed toward him as more of the cowardly creatures fled for their lives, back into the pit from whence they had come. Sort of like politicians.

Alaeth had turned tail and ran for the shelter of the nearest ship when the hole in the floor first opened up. She was now all the way back to the vessel's main deck. Her lithe Elfish physique made moving through the confines of the ship relatively easy. She was also in peak physical health for her species- which is impressive to say the least.

She peeked over the edge of the port side of the mighty ship, while the vortex of evil was still closing far below.

She was terrified and almost began to weep. "Pull it together, Alaeth!" She growled like an angry lynx, gripped her weapon and held it close while she forced herself to watch what was happening.

The glowing being with the screaming sword stood motionless beside the now-shrinking mouth of the pit, his sword now only growling and purring like a mechanical guard dog, as it belched smoke from the machine parts in the hilt.

His armour was shining like so many amber mirrors as though it had never been touched by the blood and filth that she had witnessed him get covered in.

Pools of rancid goo were scattered all over the floor; he had slain hundreds of the foul beings before they made their retreat back into the abyss.

He looked up at her then and startled her. His eyes were no longer smoking, although they still glowed with an eerie *green* light. He smiled, though he did not show his teeth, and he spoke:

"Vhere be Poppa Szvirf?"

Chapter - 27

"The Mushroom Flashback"

Well, kids, it looks like old Poppa Szvirf finally met his demise. The world is in a schmutzle and most of my buddies got their asses kicked royally.

Oy!

Surely Calabac would now march upon Briarwood, destroy our home, and pillage the lands, yada-yada-yada.

I REALLY hate that guy.

All seemed lost save for the mighty hero of Shiddumbuzzin.

But...

Could Durik now defeat the evil machinations of Calabac? Could he alone save the world?

Well, maybe Raz will help him. Would all of you like that? Well, maybe—you never know. It would be cool, though, right? Raz is pretty awesome. I love the guy... gal... whatever he is.

Anyway, where was I?

Oh yeah...

I know what you're all thinking, kids. Yes, even *you* ... the ginger guy in the back with the green sweater, and you too, Morty, yes, even you. I remember ya... yeah, I autographed that book for you at the bookstore, right? I love ya, buddy.

Anyway...

I know what's going through your heads right now, kids...

Why, Pappa Szvirf? Why should we look forward to the next book? You're dead now and so is the Troll and Grarr too- and God knows who else?!'

Well, kids. The story isn't over yet. That's why.

I promise that some really exciting stuff is gonna happen in the next book, too. You're really gonna like it. I promise. I totally promise. Honestly—I'm not even Orange.

There's gonna be a whole war and everything (two or three of them, in fact), plus legends coming true, more adventure, more crazy creatures, and a lot of stuff I haven't even mentioned yet.

Plus ... *You* know. Tee-heehee. Herb. Right?

So ...

Keep an eye out on the bookstore shelves, or wherever you kids buy books these days, for a copy of...

The Adventures of the Great Neblinski

Book Three

Return of the *Redeye*

ABOUT THE AUTHOR

JRR was born in 1964 and grew up in a single-parent home aboard the international space station orbiting the Moon. Early in life, his mentors recognized something in him that inspired them to push him to aspire to ever higher limits.

At age 15, after receiving his first two master's degrees, in quantum physics and medicine, he climbed Mount Everest and was responsible for rescuing 34 stranded Sherpa guides and their clients from seven yetis and a host of saber-toothed snow leopards. With only a stick of gum, a pickle, and a paper clip he managed to create a complex series of challenges for the enemy which distracted the monsters while the Sherpa guides fled in JRR's self-designed and self-constructed arctic exploration vehicle (which he assembled on site). After defeating the enemies he descended the mountain using the skins of the Yetis as a hang glider and became the first man to ever pee into a shot-glass from 2000 feet while breaking the sound barrier. (It is unknown if a woman had previously attained this prestigious title).

At age 20 JRR sailed across the Pacific Ocean on a raft made from handcrafted egg cartons, used sneakers, a tube of super glue, and seventy thousand tonnes of pressed flowers. On this perilous journey, he faced a school of thirty megalodons and fourteen giant prehistoric squids, slaying them all with his Swiss army knife and rugged good looks, thus ridding the world of their species forever and saving future egg-carton sailors from certain doom. He was presented with the international "Legendary Nautical Creature Slayer" award by the Union of International Marine Guys. It was also on this same trip that he discovered (without question) the truth that the world was indeed a sphere when he ended his Pacific crossing by landing in Halifax harbor, on Canada's east coast. After delivering the *Titanic* survivors he had rescued along the way, and confirming his astronomical findings to the authorities, he was joined by legendary musicians/composers Frank Zappa and Jimmy Hendrix. Both of them were so humbled by his greatness that they offered to teach him to play guitar if he signed their pizza boxes. He declined, saying: "Guys, you already did teach me everything you know" and signed their boxes anyway. He then went on to form a band with the aforementioned musical geniuses, winning that year's Grammy Award for Best New Album in all styles and kick-starting Frank and Jimmy's careers. He did so under several assumed names, of course.

When he was 27 JRR decided to visit England where he spent his days tutoring the physically disabled, curing polio, running an international endangered animal rescue center, and inventing

Break Dancing. His favorite student, Steven Hawking (who at first wanted to dance), would later be praised among his peers in physics for his almost legendary ability to remain completely still for hours at a time. He was able to achieve this through JRR's teaching in the art of self-defense known as Tai Huan Ahn. It was also there in England where he invented the dog breed known as the Corgi, base-jumped from the Big Ben clock tower, discovered and colonized France, and acted as the MC for the grand opening of the massive tunnel under the English channel (which he also designed). The queen of England herself awarded him with "The Royal Decree of All-Time Greatness" and purchased more than seven hundred corgis from his rescue center. She also made him heir to the throne and said he was officially the sexiest man on earth. (a title he maintains to this day)

He declined the British Throne and instead asked for Canada's independence (which he was granted - making the colony of Canada free and turning it into a democracy at last). On top of that, he was also given ownership of Scotland which he soon gave back to the Scottish people and in turn was awarded a position of lifetime nobility, making him their king for all time and leading to his starring role as William Wallace in a mega motion picture. So impressed were the Danes and Icelanders that they too voted him in as their King for life, and soon after that nineteen other countries around the world followed suit. Such was and still is his greatness.

All of these honors he politely declined, stating that he simply didn't have the time to invent the internet, discover the cure

for

The Black Plague, develop a propulsion system for interstellar exploration, win the Olympic gold medal in the triathlon, and be everyone's king all at once. After teaching these countries the art of democracy and trusting they would be okay without him, he awarded them their independence and went on to earn a Master's degree in Greatness from the University of All-Time Awesomeness.

However, all of this was not enough to quell his passion for adventure and a need to challenge his greatness. At age 30 he married the princesses of Turkmenistan and fathered three hundred and eleven children, all of whose names he remembers.

Alas, this too would not be enough for him to fill his life. When his last child was grown up and on her own being the first female Pope, he retreated from society, secluding himself in a cave on top of Mount Fuji for seventy-seven years where he astral-projected nightly into another cave on top of Mount Kilimanjaro on Canada's south coast near a minor province known affectionately as America.

It was there on those very same cave walls where he wrote his tomes of power known as *The Adventures of the Great Neblinski* (still being studied to this day by the most intelligent minds on the planet). It is said that he remains there, in those caves, protected by a thousand ninja warriors and the Royal Canadian Mounted Police, writing impossible stories that challenge the limits of human achievement. It is also said that one day he will return to his chosen homeland of Liechtenstein on the yet-undiscovered continent of Australia, where he will invent water, discover a new type of food, solve the energy crisis, and make first-contact with interdimensional intelligent societies.

ABOUT THE CREATOR OF THE AUTHOR

I grew up in a housing project. My mom was an artist and taught me how to be creative. This was her gift to me. We lived in a rough neighborhood, but I didn't know better. So it was home. In my late teens I was drawn into a criminal subculture. It was pretty rough. I didn't want to be there any longer. I didn't want to upset my mom. In my early 20s, I began to see myself going nowhere, fast. I was a good artist, a good storyteller, but nowhere to test it. I needed an escape.

Quite by accident, I stumbled onto a community of creative people who took me into their numbers. I soon found among them, a group of 5 guys who shared their cannabis with me, and invited me to play a tabletop role playing game, on a weekly basis. I had heard of RPGs in high school, but never really had a chance to experiment with them before. I was intrigued with fantasy stories and took them up on it.

Those 5 guys kept me medicated, interested and entertained for several years. They inspired me to write the Adventures of the Great Neblinski (TAOTGN). They probably saved my life, or at least kept me from jail. My epic fantasy, "The Adventures of the Great Neblinski" is based on the weekly adventures we experienced-me and my 5 friends: Shiddumbuzzin, Grarr, Beornag, Raz, Durik, and yours truly, Poppa Szvirf Neblinski.

WHO IS JRR TOKIN?

JRR Tokin is a fictitious character, created by author, Mark E. G. Dorey. Mark is a fantasy author and artist from Canada. JRR Tokin is a pen-name he created. When his story was first written, Canada had strict laws pertaining to cannabis. He was a father of two and wanted to protect his children from the stigma that was attached to cannabis. He was medicating with cannabis at the time. So, he created an alias. NOTHING about JRR Tokin is actually true. [Except the part about water. He DID invent water].